praise for rudy rucker

"Rudy Rucker should be declared a National Treasure of American Science Fiction. Someone simultaneously channeling Kurt Gödel and Lenny Bruce might start to approximate full-on Ruckerian warp-space, but without the sweet, human, splendidly goofy Rudy-ness at the core of the singularity." —William Gibson

"One of science fiction's wittiest writers. A genius . . . a cult hero among discriminating cyberpunkers." —*San Diego Union-Tribune*

"Rucker's writing is great like the Ramones are great: a genre stripped to its essence, attitude up the wazoo, and cartoon sentiments that reek of identifiable lives and issues. Wild math you can get elsewhere, but no one does the cyber version of beatnik glory quite like Rucker." —*New York Review of Science Fiction*

"What a Dickensian genius Rucker has for Californian characters, as if, say, Dickens had fused with Phil Dick and taken up surfing and jamming and topologising. He has a hotline to cosmic revelations yet he's always here and now in the groove, tossing off lines of beauty and comic wisdom. 'My heart is a dog running after every cat.' We really feel with his characters in their bizarre tragicomic quests." — Ian Watson, author of *The Embedding*

"The current crop of sf humorists are mildly risible, I suppose, but they don't seem to pack the same intellectual punch of their forebears. With one exception, that is: the astonishing Rudy Rucker. For some two decades now, since the publication of his first novel, *White Light*, Rucker has combined an easygoing, trippy style influenced by the Beats with a deep engagement with knotty (or 'gnarly,' to employ one of his favorite terms) intellectual conceits, based mainly in mathematics. In the typical Rucker novel, likably eccentric characters—who run the gamut from brilliant to near-certifiable—encounter aspects of the universe that confirm that life is weirder than we can imagine." —*The Washington Post*

"Rucker stands alone in the science fiction pantheon as some kind of trickster god of the computer science lab; where others construct minutely plausible fictional realities, he simply grabs the corners of the one we already know and twists it in directions we don't have pronounceable names for." —*SF Site*

"Reading a Rudy Rucker book is like finding Poe, Kerouac, Lewis Carroll, and Philip K. Dick parked on your driveway in a topless '57 Caddy . . . and telling you they're taking you for a RIDE. The funniest science fiction author around." —*Sci-Fi Universe*

"This is SF rigorously following crazy rules. My mind of science fiction. At the heart of it is a rage to extrapolate. Rucker is what happens when you cross a mathematician with the extrapolating jazz spirit." —Robert Sheckley

"Rucker [gives you] more ideas per chapter than most authors use in an entire novel." —*San Francisco Chronicle*

"Rudy Rucker writes like the love child of Philip K. Dick and George Carlin. Brilliant, frantic, conceptual, cosmological . . . like lucid dreaming, only funny." —*New York Times* bestselling author Walter Jon Williams

million mile road trip

by rudy rucker

million mile road trip

a novel by

RUDY RUCKER

night shade books
new york

SCI
FIC
RUD

Night Shade books may be purchased in bulk at special discounts for sales promotion, corporate gifts, fund-raising, or educational purposes. Special editions can also be created to specifications. For details, contact the Special Sales Department, Night Shade Books, 307 West 36th Street, 11th Floor, New York, NY 10018 or info@skyhorsepublishing.com.

Night Shade Books® is a registered trademark of Skyhorse Publishing, Inc. ®, a Delaware corporation.

Visit our website at www.nightshadebooks.com.

10 9 8 7 6 5 4 3 2 1

Library of Congress Cataloging-in-Publication Data

Names: Rucker, Rudy v. B. (Rudy von Bitter), 1946- author.
Title: Million mile road trip / Rudy Rucker.
Description: First Night Shade Books edition. | New York : Night Shade Books, 2019.
Identifiers: LCCN 2018041191| ISBN 9781597809917 (pbk. : alk. paper) | ISBN 9781597809924 (hardback : alk. paper)
Subjects: | GSAFD: Science fiction.
Classification: LCC PS3568.U298 M55 2019 | DDC 813/.54--dc23
LC record available at https://lccn.loc.gov/2018041191

Cover artwork by Bill Carman
Cover design by Claudia Noble

Printed in the United States of America

For my Grandchildren

contents

"riding shotgun on the purple whale"

an introduction by marc laidlaw

S ome say the quintessential New Yorker is someone who moved to Manhattan from somewhere else, someone who arrived with their metropolitan fantasies infusing their lived experience. They will tell you stories of the streets as if they grew up on them; they have historical anecdotes memorized and would be happy to serve as your personal Baedeker; they gaze upon the City through love-colored glasses. In this sense, Rudy Rucker is a quintessential Californian.

Living nestled in the hills of Los Gatos (transreally transmogrified to Los Perros in his fiction), Rudy has for decades now been writing about San Francisco and Big Sur, Silicon Valley and Santa Cruz, sometimes on their own terms but more often as a jumping-off place for stranger destinations. California, grounded in the warm details of a beloved reality, is constantly refracted through his fiction, reinvented in terms Ruckerian.

When I first met Rudy, in the mid-1980s, he had just moved with his family from Virginia, crossing the country to take a job teaching computer science in San Jose, but also driven by dreams of surfers in gnarly Pacific waves and beatniks in North Beach bars and hippies in the Haight. No sooner had he plugged into his curriculum than he bought a wetsuit and a surfboard and jumped into an ice-cold current to teach himself how to surf— something I, a California native, had never bothered with myself. It is weird to admit that I caught the surfing bug from Rudy, when I had grown up in a Southern California beach town surrounded by surfers, but the mythic magic of a place can be stronger for a pilgrim than for a native, and Rudy's fervor was infectious.

Rudy, over the years I've known him, has given me many a high fervor. The very first time we dined at his house, I came away consumed by new interests in infinity, fractals, and chaos theory, all mixed up with Rudy's neophytic enthusiasm for surfing, which soon led to the first of our collaborative stories of crazed surfers Zep & Delbert. (Even our sole non-Z&D story, "The Andy Warhol Sand Candle," is set in Surf City.) Rudy brought his mathematician's rigor, and crazy Carrollian logic, to our stories; I'm too close to know what I contributed, but I certainly brought an ongoing enthusiasm to see what Rudy would come up with next. He always took my (to me) overfamiliar ideas and did something unexpected with them. This is Rudy's MO.

Collaborating with Rudy remains fun and surprising, but of course it is also work. On the other hand, reading Rucker, uncollaborative and unadulterated by my own hesitancies and half-measures, is just pure fun without any of the work. In collaboration, I always feel as if

I'm holding him back or down or otherwise boxing him in, when part of the joy of reading Rucker is watching an imagination that is absolutely unafraid of expanding without encumbrance . . . a pleasure fully indulgeable in *Million Mile Road Trip*.

Million Mile Road Trip starts, like so many of his stories, with a solid grounding in the local milieu and its affectionately observed inhabitants. We meet Zoe Snapp and her (maybe) crush Villy Antwerpen, surely heroes enough for the average science fiction adventure. But before long we have also met their extended families, who will all figure in the voyage ahead. And before much longer than that, the universe itself will have extended in novel ways, with the arrival of the first of an extremely varied cast of aliens. This being a Rucker novel, and Rudy being fond of reinventing some of SF's stalest staples, the first aliens arrive in a flying saucer, although not of the sort you might be used to. These saucers have *needs*. This being Rucker, the aliens speak in a variety of amusing accents. And, this being Rucker, we're barely into the second chapter, which is a signal that things haven't yet fully begun to get weird.

You can't spend much time in Rudy's presence without him mentioning Kerouac. He has written of his attempts to write in the Kerouac manner with a roll of butcher paper running continuously through his typewriter (one thing Rudy and I share is that we spent our formative years whacking on actual typewriters and were among the early adopters of word processors). So it's safe to say that Rudy's love affair with the literary road trip began with *On the Road*. In his early hilarious short story, "Inertia" (featuring the characters from his mind-bending—which is to say, typical—early novel, *Master of Space and Time*), there is an extended sequence involving a trip through space in a converted station wagon—but in that case, the car trip is more of a means to an end than an end in itself. *Million Mile Road Trip*, as the title suggests, is all about the journey. And what a trip it is.

Trust a mathematician to show you how to visualize, tangibly, a million miles—to make the drive seem doable. The journey, across a landscape I would not even dare to describe (not being a mathematician), is full of incidents and detours and stops at surreal diners, just like any road trip. By the end of the book, you will feel you traveled every mile of it yourself, a gleeful passenger in Villy's car, the Purple Whale. The sense of distance traveled, of sights observed in a rush through side windows, will be familiar to anyone who has ever driven cross-country, or sat in the backseat as a kid and watched unfamiliar landscapes unfold as their parents drove. Your fellow passengers chatter and laugh and sometimes bicker. Someone is hungry, someone else wants to push straight through without stopping. Someone has to pee! (This being Rucker, physical needs are rarely glossed over, let alone denied.)

So there's a sense of travel, a sense of constant change, a sense of continually arriving somewhere new and leaving it at the same time—and also an incredible sense of speed. There's a wonderful sequence in *Million Mile Road Trip* where Zoe and Villy just *floor it*. You know that time near the end of a long trip where you are tired of traveling and you just want to get there, so maybe you step on the gas a bit more and a bit more and hope there's no state troopers waiting on this long lonely highway? Covering thousands of miles in a rush, white-knuckled, driving so fast you'd have SS'1's eating your dust . . .

And at the end of it all, you arrive. You are *there*. The discomfort of days cramped in a car begins to fade as soon as you can stand up, walk around, stretch your legs. You scan the horizon and find yourself somewhere you never imagined. A place, in this case, only Rudy Rucker has imagined.

That's Rudy there, behind the wheel of the Purple Whale, waiting for you to get in, strap in, so he can peel out. There's a lot of miles to cover, so you'd better get to it, hit the road.

You don't even have to call shotgun.

He saved that seat especially for you.

million mile road trip

first kiss

zoe

Zoe Snapp is a total outsider, unable to finish anything on time, and unwilling to work society's games. She plays trumpet in her school's jazz ensemble. She refuses to polish her trumpet—she likes tarnish. She wears hoodies, T-shirts, and jeans. She makes her own jewelry out of crystals and rubber bands. Her best pal is skinny Villy Antwerpen, who lives a block or two away from her. Villy has zero ambition and poor self-esteem. But he gets what Zoe's about, and he'll always listen to her, and maybe she has a crush on him.

Often Villy gives Zoe a ride home from school. Today's not, strictly speaking, a school day—Zoe, Villy, and the other seniors just came for the afternoon to rehearse tomorrow's graduation ceremony. They didn't do the speeches, or the reading of the names, and they didn't mess with the gowns, so it didn't take long. And now, here they are in the parking lot, like the end of a regular school day.

Villy has an '80s beater wagon. He's pretty good at fixing things, but he has trouble with his math and science classes.

Villy says he's dumb, but that's not exactly what it is. It's more that he's too practical. Too into the physical world. He can pretty much figure out the inner workings of any gadget you hand him. Even so, there's still plenty of things wrong with his car. Because he's not in his garage all that much. More likely he's out surfing or riding his skateboard.

"All hail the purple whale," says Zoe, settling onto the ancient car's wide, bench-style front seat. She does a low laugh and shakes her dark hair. She wears it in a bob with bangs. And then she uses her lively eyes to shoot Villy a sideways glance which pretty much slays him, or at least that's what she likes to think.

"I might start calling this car the *puce* whale," says Villy. He has a straight mouth. When he smiles, it always starts with the corners. His hair is shades of blond—streaked from sun and surf. His tan skin is somehow salty-looking, in a good way.

"Puce?" says Zoe. She has a nicely shaped mouth, with precisely edged lips. She often makes faces while she's talking—as if she's miming a commentary on her words. That way, if she happens to say something uncool, the implicit irony gives her a fallback.

"Here's puce," says Villy and shows Zoe a colored patch on his phone's screen. Brownish purple.

"Very like your whale," says Zoe. "I always thought puce was a pukeful yellow-green."

"A common error," says Villy. He wiggles his dark eyebrows. He's wearing skinny jeans and a dark green T-shirt with a squiggle on it. Well-worn items, frayed and with just-so holes. Accidental chic.

"You know a lot," says Zoe.

"Anything I know I learned from games and comics and graphic novels," says Villy. "School is a hoax. Years of useless brainwashing." He has a low voice with a bit of a scratch in it. He's nodding his head to his phone's music.

"Graduation tomorrow!" exults Zoe. "I used to sit in class, looking out the window, and I'd envy the people outside doing things. Having lives. No teachers, no tests, and not being dissed by zerks like Tawna Garvey. At last we'll be free."

Villy's looking at her. Zoe feels she's too short and her breasts are nothing much. As for her butt, well, it's wider and rounder than it was when she was eleven, and boys have been known to stare after her in the hallway, brain-dead sexists that they are. But when Villy looks at her, she's glad. And she likes looking at *him*. He has these flowing surfer muscles. He's never out of balance, always in the now. So unselfconscious, so male.

All these unspoken intense thoughts in Zoe's head.

Villy starts the car. "I saw you arguing with Tawna before rehearsal today," he says. "She and her friends were imitating you later on. Laughing like hyenas."

"Really?" Zoe's both annoyed and pleased. "Usually I can hardly tell if Tawna even hears me. She acts like I'm a tiny dog, way down at the limit of visibility. A barking ant."

"*Snobby about what?*" says Villy, quoting. "That's what you yelled at Tawna today. For no reason. Right out of the blue. Like a crazy person." He laughs. His laugh is a weird high cackle. It's another thing that Zoe likes about him.

"Right," says Zoe with aplomb. "Snobby about what? Tawna's dim, she wears mall-store cougar clothes, she talks like a duck. So why snobby?"

"She's a suffering fellow clown," says Villy with a shrug. "Crying on the inside."

Villy has this annoying thing—at least Zoe thinks it's annoying—he has this thing of identifying with people and understanding their feelings and empathizing with them. So boo-hoo.

"People take advantage of you because you're nice," she tells him.

Meanwhile Villy guides his unwieldy whale towards the exit of the high school parking lot. Kids are all around— carrying backpacks, working their phones, bopping to music. Overhead the seagulls swirl.

"Look up ahead!" exclaims Villy. "Tawna beckons. She wants me, Zoe. Because I'm too nice." He guns his engine. A manly roar.

"Actually, she's giving us the finger," says Zoe. "Run her down."

Villy gets with the program. He veers in a menacing way so that his purple whale wallows very close to the curb where Tawna stands amid her coterie of friends. Squeals and yells. Someone lands a thuddy kick on the whale's rear fender. Villy honks and drives on.

"If we killed Tawna and I went to jail, at least I'd know what I'm doing this fall," says Zoe, gazing back at her enemies. "What set me off before rehearsal was the sound of Tawna making happy plans for a mall spree to assemble her college duds. Quack, quack. Strutting duck."

Los Perros Boulevard is crowded with seniors in their cars. Villy has some jagged surf music on the car speakers—it's a recording of the garage-band trio that he plays bass for. It's not a bad sound, although, in Zoe's opinion, strictly as instruments, guitars are lesser than horns.

It's the first week of June, and the misty blue sky is like a soap film. Palm trees line the wide street. Rats crawl up the palms and live in the dead fronds. Hazy forested foothills edge the scene. Homeless people live in caves up there. Maybe that's Zoe's fate.

"You need to get over being rejected by UC Berkeley," Villy is saying to her. "And by those other two schools." He seems genuinely concerned. "You haven't even looked into community college, have you?"

"I keep waiting for Mom to goad me into doing it, but she's crazy into being a realtor, and now she's even set herself up as a college admissions coach. As if. She started in March, and she has five clients."

"And you're not one of them."

"Mom nagged me for months to write my Berkeley application. The personal statement part. On the last possible day, I wrote that American life is a blockbuster movie with hiccup anthems, but I—I want a life that's a flip-card cartoon with sqwonky horns." Zoe smiles to herself and adopts a literary tone. "My mother grew incoherent. In tears, she cast me adrift. I savored the surcease of nag. In my heart, I knew the hipster admissions people at Berzerkely would fully understand. Like: 'Yes! Zoe Snapp!' I was so wrong. They wanted me to grunt an anthem. I'll never fit in anywhere."

"Tawna's essay for Berkeley says she wants to tutor at-risk minority middle-schoolers and monitor the environment for hidden toxins in our food supply," says Villy. "She showed it to me. Right before we did the deed on the padded bench in the weight room."

"Not funny," says Zoe, utterly dismissing this. "Speaking of desperados, my half-sister Maisie has really been craving attention this week. She's like this touching, boyish Oliver Twist lassie who makes the best of a bad lot. A love child, borne by the foul, home-wrecking Sunny Weaver. With whom my dad lived for, yea, unto sixteen years."

"Maisie has it hard," says Villy. "She has that funny bulge around her waist. It's not jiggly like fat. It's like she carries a rolled-up towel under her blouse."

"Maybe if I was closer to her, she'd explain herself," says Zoe. "I can tell she wants to pour out her heart. She sends me selfies and calls me *sistah*. I'm an outsider, but Maisie—wow. I do sit next to her in jazz band practice, even though she's a junior. If I didn't at least do that, I'd have to douse myself with gasoline. Got a match?"

"Stop it with the death-wish routines, Zoe. You're a better person than you admit. And some of us care about you."

Villy is looking at her. His pale brown eyes. Zoe feels something in her chest unknot. All of a sudden she reaches over and runs her hand across Villy's cheek. So close, so human, so real.

"Thanks," goes Zoe. "Thanks for saying that."

"Maisie plays trombone, right?" says Villy. Like he's not sure what else to talk about right now. "I like trombones. Honking into the sky. Loss of control."

"Maisie gets all impish and gleeful when she plays," says Zoe, enjoying the fancy words. "She likes to bump me with the brass slide. Sistah! But she plays really well. She was teaching me a new riff after practice today—even though I wanted to edge away. And right then she gave me this really pretty pearl and I was like too stunned to really thank her. I don't see how you can think I'm a good person."

"Also, you're hot," says Villy. "I like your skin. Smooth and kind of dark. I always want to touch it."

Zoe's sitting there with a total goofball smile on her face. "You're hot too," she says. She's completely not ironic, completely unprotected. It's okay. It's safe with Villy.

And now what? A silent interval ticks by.

"I never see Maisie on weekends," Villy eventually says. "Never at a party. It's like she leaves town."

"I wonder about that too," says Zoe. "I do know she's into that flying saucer cult that meets in the community center. The New Eden Space Friends. Dad's old group. He used to say there's good saucers and bad saucers, and it's up to us to help the good ones win. Why am I even talking about this?"

"It's okay," says Villy. "I like your voice. If we weren't in California, maybe your father could have been a Baptist or a birdwatcher. Instead of becoming a vanished saucer nut." Villy pauses, then restarts. "On the upside, if saucers are real, then it doesn't matter if we go to college. Because the end of the world is nigh."

"We're in a vortex of madness," declaims Zoe. "Living on borrowed time. Soon to lie beneath sad white stones in a grassy dell."

"Death-wish alert," chides Villy. "Nix, nix."

"Reset. At least I'm still making jewelry."

"At least I still surf."

"Have you taken note of my necklace?" asks Zoe, doing a geeky nineteenth-century-talk thing. "I found some stretchy-strong plastic to use for the string. The color of the string is—puce. Yes. And the crystals are faceted so they shatter light into colors. You think they're tinted, but they're not." Her voice catches, and her stream of chatter breaks. "Oh, Villy, what are we going to do with our lives?"

"You'll make jewelry and wail on your horn. I'll surf and work on my car. And sometimes we'll drive around together and get food. Can't that be enough?"

"Mom doesn't think so. And I've reached a point where I physically can't do anything she tells me to. It's like I'm paralyzed."

Villy makes a mystic pass with his fingers, as if awakening Zoe from a trance. "Arise! College or job! College or job!"

"I don't want a low job," says Zoe in a small voice. "Even if they think that's all I deserve. A salesgirl behind a counter. Submissively helping rude idiots buy embarrassing medical aids." She pokes at her phone. "I know there's a registration page for Waste Valley Community College someplace online. All you need is to be a high school grad. But I keep delaying. Get it together, Zee. Do it now."

"Me, I probably can't even go to West Valley," says Villy. "I'm failing math. I'm not graduating. I don't know why I even went to the graduation rehearsal today. It would be bullshit for me to walk across the stage and not even get a diploma."

"Oh Villy," says Zoe in true sympathy. "I didn't know. The grisly square root? The smelly log?"

"I always think I understand, but on the test I get a mental block. Also the teacher doesn't like me."

"Can you take math in summer school?"

"They have an online remedial course, but I don't want to do it. Studying online is for robots. My father—he pours every day of his life down the toilet of his screen. I want to be the opposite. If I can't graduate, maybe I should be a mechanic in a garage."

"Would your father let you do that?"

"He'd think it was funny. He doesn't care what people say. But—like you said—a job means regular work hours and a boss. Don't want. Plan B? I'll buy junker cars and fix them and sell them."

Zoe is watching a seagull float along with the car, like it's pacing them. The gull cruises over the town library, the minimart, the nail parlor, the Victorian mansions with flowering shrubs, the Route 17 overpass, the supermarket strip mall, and the flimsy old ranch houses that sell for two million dollars each, the gull guiding itself with feathertip flicks. Mindless. All-knowing. In the good old now.

"What if we two skip town?" Zoe suddenly says. "Like really soon."

"And, lo, they journeyed in the belly of a whale," intones Villy, doing an unctuous voiceover.

"I mean it," says Zoe. "A massive road trip."

Villy considers. "Well, okay, yeah, the brahs and I have used my purple whale for surfaris. Slept inside it with camping mats. You and I could roll across the country, sure. Why not? Drive on back roads. Sleep in haystacks. Trade cow chores for farmhouse breakfasts. Busk on sunset street corners. You'll play your horn and I'll juggle. Fully off the grid."

"Yah, mon," says Zoe, reggae style. "Maybe we hit Mexico for starters? I've never been there. I've never been anywhere but Los Perros and Santa Cruz and San Francisco and—gag—San Jose. Where Dad lived with Sunny Weaver."

"I'll bring a surfboard," says Villy. "We'll veer down the coast to Baja." He likes veering.

"One thing," says Zoe. "Would, ah, would this trip mean we're officially hooked up? And you'd be my boyfriend?" Her voice is cautiously flat.

Long pause. "We don't have to *officially* decide something like that, do we?" says Villy. "I'd rather drift into it."

"We're drifting and drifting and nothing happens," says Zoe.

"I'd like something to happen," admits Villy. His voice is husky. "But I can't fully visualize how we get there."

"Not that hard, Villy. Lots of people do it." Zoe rolls seductive eyes his way.

Villy laughs nervously, and brushes his hair out of his face. "Talking to you about sex—if that's what we're talking about—it makes me feel like I've been skating on an easy sidewalk, but suddenly there's a thousand-foot drop-off on either side, and the sidewalk has narrowed to a single-track trail, and pebbles are skittering off the edges and bouncing down the rocky cliffs, all the way down to the exploding sea."

"I'll call that a compliment," says Zoe, laughing a little bit. "Or maybe not? Here's my house, Villy. You're about to drive right past it. Rattled much? *Bouncing down the rocky cliffs*. Will you give me a ride to the talent show tonight?"

The high school's spring talent show is a night-before-graduation evening of wholesome fun. Not to be confused with the senior prom, by now a month in the past. And no, Zoe hadn't gone. Due to hideous, self-sabotaging bungling, she ended up without a date, and she hadn't been able to face the prom alone. She should have asked Villy. Whatever. At least she's playing in the spring talent show, ta-da! Tonight's show will include two numbers by the group Zoe's in: the Los Perros Jazz Howlers. Does it matter? Her life is slipping away.

"Uh, sure I'll give you a ride," says Villy. "But—"

"We'll talk more later." And now, just when the boy thinks he's safe, Zoe leans over and gives him the kiss that she's been thinking about for weeks or even months. She means only to plant her lips on his cheek, but at the crucial moment he turns towards her, and she arrives at his mouth. Kissing for real. Their teeth click, their foreheads bump. Awkward, awkward. But then somehow it's good. For a sweet long minute they linger. And then stop for breath. Enough for now.

Zoe slams the whale's door and skips up the sidewalk to her home with a song in her heart. The rhythm track is a metal riff from a punky girl group, a sound like crunchy surf. Behind the riff, an unseen female vocalist, possibly Zoe, is yelling incomprehensible words of joy. And above it all, a lone, serene trumpeter plays a soaring line of melody. The trumpeter is Zoe too.

The deed is done, the die is cast, her future has begun.

TWO

magic ladder

zoe

Inside the house, Mom is sitting at the kitchen table with her latest client, who looks to be a go-getting junior. A shrimpy boy with braces on his teeth. Papers all across the table, and Mom has reading glasses perched on her head. She gives Zoe a bright, infectious smile, like, "*Isn't this fun?*" Playing a role for the boy. Conning him.

Zoe feels oddly envious of the kid. "I'm gonna look at the West Valley schedule for this fall," she announces. "I'll register for a music class. And maybe cosmetology?" Throwing Mom a bone—and then mocking her.

The boy snaps his head around, staring at Zoe. He doesn't go to Los Perros High, but he's definitely taking in the fact that Zoe is a loner with a trumpet and no college plans.

"Heed my mother's counsel," Zoe tells the boy. She turns up her palms in a not entirely faked gesture of despair. "You may win where I so sadly failed."

"My daughter is—a pathfinder," says Mom in an even tone. "We wouldn't have her any other way. Right, Zoe?"

Acceptance and love. And Zoe's a little bitch. Red haze of shame. In silence, Zoe plucks a yogurt and an orange from the fridge. Retreats to her room, flops on her bed, and feeds. The walls in this house are hella thin. They're in this cheesy dump because it's one of Mom's house-flipping deals. It'll go on sale as soon as the market lurches higher again. And then Mom will move them into, like, a crumbling condo by the freeway. Mom's plan is that, as of September, Zoe will be gone.

Be that as it may, Zoe has made this room her own. She likes to keep her clothes in mounds, sorted by the fashion concept they exemplify, each concept a two-word phrase in Zoe's mind, like: Eff You, Fash Splash, or Goth Coma. She's accumulated a few musical instruments other than her trumpet—a cheap electric guitar she likes using for feedback, a tuba she got at a thrift store for laughs, the boring flute Mom made her play in middle school, a shimmering Tibetan gong, and this fetid African rattle that her father gave her.

Fetid in a good way. It's a big hollow gourd, stained a shiny dark brown, with a string net around it, plus one hundred and twenty little cowrie shells strung onto the net. The tops of the cowries are carved off so that you can see inside them—and so they make a louder noise.

Thinking about her stuff reminds Zoe about the pearl that Maisie gave her today. If it is a pearl. She digs it out of her jeans pocket. A smooth sphere, way larger than a normal pearl, but smaller than a marble. Incredibly valuable? A fake? It has an iridescent pale surface just like pearls do. Feels a little heavier than you might expect. Zoe's never seen anything quite like it. It's not drilled with a hole like a bead. If she were to use it in a piece, she'd need to fashion a setting to hold it, which isn't really a skill that she has. Lovely to look at, though. Odd of Maisie to give it to her. She sets it down among her normal beads.

All the while she hears the endless drone of Mom's voice indoctrinating the shrimp. Mom is advocating a seven-stage plan of attack. Many, many counseling sessions will be required. Soon after the divorce, when Mom became a realtor, she learned how to con people. Her girlish innocence long gone.

Conning people is not in Zoe's skill set. She hopes it never will be. But suppose, just suppose, that she were to hook up with Villy and maybe even marry him. And then he'd divorce her, and then she'd have to get all sly and hard like Mom. Years ago, Mom hadn't been all that different from Zoe. She liked painting and camping, and she even danced ballet. But then she handed her life over to a man. And she had a baby. And—

Whvenk, wheenk, wheenk. By way of escaping the squeaky gerbil wheel of her mind, Zoe gives her African rattle a sizzling shake. She has a special wiggly way of rattling it. With an effort of will, she manages to restart that happy I-kissed-Villy song in her head. So refreshing to think about the kiss. With more to come. But no rush. If they do this crazy trip, they'll have weeks and months together, just the two of them. Zoe hopes they can keep being relaxed with each other. Keep having fun. But then she's back on the gerbil wheel. What if she gives her whole heart to Villy, and then he leaves her like Dad left Mom?

Leaves her for a skungy, plastic Sunny Weaver. *Wheenk, wheenk, wheenk.*

Zoe gets out her trumpet, plugs in her practice mute, and begins to play, losing herself in the tune. Finding her path. The muted horn's sound is tiny and clear. Zoe is playing the smoky, understated melody line from Miles Davis's classic cut with that perfect title, "So What." Most kids don't know about him. His hoarse, gone bleat, with each note a fuzzy blotch, like an iridescent oil spot on rain-wet pavement. So what? So everything.

Under her solo, Zoe still has some pulsing, punk-metal sludge going in the primeval stem of her reptile brain. Not exactly the tootling background the Los Perros Jazz Howlers will play behind her tonight. Such a painfully groovy name for a band. But the school's mascot is a coyote, so there you have it. Someday she'll play in a real band.

Back in December, Mom made a video of the Howlers and emailed it off to the music department at UC Berkeley, in hopes that Zoe could waltz in as a performer, despite her inappropriate essay and her middling grades. Zoe was achingly embarrassed by this, and she yelled at Mom, but secretly she'd hoped the ploy would work. It didn't. And none of the backup schools had panned out— that is, neither of the two other places that Zoe had actually managed to apply to. None of them were into the Zoe Snapp worldview.

So what. Zoe has a plan now. She's going on the road with Villy.

Still into her muted trumpet solo, Zoe rises to her feet and sways like a snake charmer. She's veered away from

Miles's line, and she's on her own. Well, not entirely on her own. She's folding in the kinky riff that sistah Maisie was teaching her after practice today. An odd little stutter-stop. Like a glitch, or like a hip-hop sample. The skips make Zoe's solo more magical. Like a holy hymn.

Yeah. Zoe's gonna frikkin destroy the crowd tonight. They'll finally grasp how hip she is. Even Tawna Garvey will get it. Zoe sashays over to her desk and leans over her supply of beads, still playing. She's especially focusing on the awesome silvery pearl that Maisie gave her.

"Rise," she thinks at the pearl, as if she's a snake charmer.

And, now, for once in Zoe's life, a power fantasy works. Maisie's iridescent ball quivers and lifts into the air, slowly rotating. Its surface gleams. Almost like it's winking at Zoe. No way. Her heart is hammering in triple time, but she maintains her trumpet's tone and stretches her breath. Stutter-stop, stutter-stop. Coaxing the little ball higher. Not letting herself think. She leans back, horn high, supporting the mysterious pearl with her thin, wavering tune. The pearl's by the ceiling. And along the way it's grown to the size of a ping-pong ball.

Something flickers in Zoe's mind. Like an unseen new friend is saying, "Oh, there you are. Here I come." And then she's fully out of breath. She lowers her tarnished trumpet.

The lustrous swollen pearl hangs there, slowly turning. A tiny globe with north and south poles. And now all at once it's transparent. With things inside.

Something pokes out from the south pole. A pair of horrible insect feelers? No, no, they're sticks, and there's— rungs between them. It's like a tiny ladder that tapers to a point at its top. Well—not so tiny, no, the bottom part of the ladder is growing. The ladder is sliding out like a ramp.

The bottom end hits the floor with a thud. The ladder's rungs are spaced normally at the bottom, and they're closer and closer together towards the top. It's as if Zoe's seeing a much longer ladder in perspective. The top end is a point, and that's where it touches the transparent orb of the pearl.

And now—oh wow—someone is climbing down the ladder. A little yellow alien, very small on the highest rungs—humanoid, skinny, moving with a womanly sway. The alien lady waves to Zoe. Alien for real.

Zoe forgets about holding onto her trumpet. It clatters to the floor.

"Everything okay?" calls Mom through the wall.

"Don't mind me," sings Zoe. She doesn't want the magic to end.

Watching the alien descend the ladder, Zoe thinks of a circus acrobat shinnying down a rope. A moment later, the odd yellow figure is standing next to her, just her height. Somehow the woman seems like she's in her twenties. A bit older than Zoe. She smells of cinnamon and paint thinner, which is a little hard to take.

"I'm Yampa," says the alien woman. "Greet me." Her legs are very short, so she has a low waist. Her torso is a long column with a T-joint at the waist and bulbous shoulder joints where her arms come out. She's leathery and scarecrow-thin. Her voice is squawky.

Yampa holds out her hand as if to shake. Her hand has eight or nine fingers, all different kinds of them there, like the tools of a soft Swiss knife. Zoe braces herself and takes hold. The hand is sticky in spots, but not in a totally disgusting way. Drily sticky, like a lizard's toes.

"I'm Zoe Snapp," says Zoe. "And this is my room."

"Welcome to me and thanks to you," says Yampa. "You're scared?" The strange woman's face is in shades of orange and yellow, her large eyes are pale lavender, and her lips are red. Her lower jaw jiggles loosely. "I think you think I stink," she says. And then she laughs.

Nice to hear a laugh, if it is a laugh, but Yampa's smell is indeed bothering Zoe, who goes ahead and opens her window wide. There's no screen. She draws in a lungful of fresh air.

Yampa uses the moment to take a picture of Zoe's room. That is, she holds her hands up on either side of her face and makes a click sound.

"You and your room an eternal diorama dream," says Yampa. "A design to decorate Lady Filippa's drapes."

"Did I summon you with my horn?" asks Zoe, wanting to feel some control.

"Your unny tunnel twined to me," says Yampa. "Steered by your ooky squonk. Mediated by Maisie. She told me where to wait. This is ballyworld, yes?"

"Not sure what you mean," says Zoe. And—had the alien just now mentioned Zoe's half-sister Maisie?

"The onward landscape of your lawn and town and prairie and sea—it doesn't flow forever, yes?" says Yampa, gesturing towards Zoe's window. "It bends back, no? *Bally*."

"Well, yeah," says Zoe, kind of understanding but not really. "We're on a planet. Earth. What planet are you from?"

"What basin, you mean. What basin in mappyworld, you mean. Mappyworld is a cosmic candy sampler box. Or an endless egg carton. With a flat world-skin within each basin of the box. Mappy. Not bally. My guy and I are on a spree. Meandered a million miles to find Zoe Snapp."

"Guy? Drove?"

Yampa turns and stares at the high reaches of the pointed ladder. She calls out a name. "Pinchley! Pinchley!"

At this point, the oddness catches up with Zoe. She feels a sidewise-sweeping wave of unreality, as if the floor were the pitched deck of a ship. Catching her balance, she leans on Yampa. The alien woman's body is firm. Springy. She's stronger than she looks.

"Don't yell again," Zoe cautions Yampa. "We don't want Mom in here." Which reminds her to click the feeble lock-button on her door.

Meanwhile a second figure has started down the pointed ladder. A yellow-orange male, shaped more or less like Yampa, but with a bigger jaw, and with stubble on his chin. He too seems like he's in his twenties. An alien slacker.

Halfway down the ladder, Pinchley hops free and tumbles downward, doing a flip along the way. As he falls, he grows. His feet thud onto the floor. He's an inch taller than Yampa, and he wears a tool belt made of shiny dark leather.

"Showy and loud," says Yampa, her odd face bending in a smile. "Pinchley is my love oaf. I wish he were tidy for trim Zoe." She puts her hands up by her head and clicks again. "A someday souvenir," she says.

"Zoe!" Mom's voice again. "What's all that noise? Nelson's done with his lesson. Did you see I laid out some good clothes on your bed? We can—"

Mom is interrupted by the doorbell. Shrimp Nelson's mother. Volleys of maternal chatter ensue, fantasias on Nelson's prospects at the UCs or back East or why not try Stanford. San Jose State is a solid safety school.

Zoe smiles at Yampa and Pinchley. She feels miles above Mom's petty concerns. She's with the coolest two kids ever. "So you guys are visiting me from, like, I mean—how far does that ladder *go*?"

"Just high enough," says Pinchley. *Juust haaah enouuugh*. He has a country accent, like a friendly, good-time hillbilly. Not scary or mean at all.

"Your honkin made your pearl stretch out like a tunnel," continues Pinchley. "One end by you, and one by us. Your sis Maisie told us where to stand, you understand, and we was ready with our ladder. You ready to climb up and peek through?"

"I'm supposed to climb a ladder to the gate of an unny tunnel to an alien world?" says Zoe. "I don't think so."

"It'd be fun," says Pinchley with that drawl of his. *Fuuun*.

"Have Zoe leave later," says Yampa. "Better to bag the boyfriend and his ballyworld car. Then tease Zoe's tunnel bigger, and va-vooom we four thread through."

"My boyfriend?" says Zoe. "That's Villy. He does have a cool station wagon." She hardly knows what she's saying. "We'd like to do a big road trip."

"Now you talkin," says Pinchley. "You're gettin the plan.

You stay with Zoe here, Yampa. I'll go meet beau Villy. We'll talk cars."

And now, oh god, Mom's rattling the locked bedroom door. She wants in.

"Just a second," says Zoe though the door.

Pinchley somersaults out of Zoe's open window and drops onto all fours. In this position he looks slightly like a dog—a weird dog whose front legs are longer than his hind legs. A dog who's wearing a tool belt. A dog who's not a dog. He's golden in the summer evening sun and right now he's staring right at the sun, seemingly fascinated by it.

"Woof woof," says Pinchley, kidding around, and he trots off, still on all fours, heading in the general direction of Villy's house.

"He can smell your smeel trail," says Yampa. "The link of love. I'll be scarce."

Before Zoe can say anything else, Yampa folds up like an easel, telescoping her legs and folding her arms. She rolls under Zoe's bed, still giving off an intoxicating smell of spice and turpentine.

The doorknob rattles again. "Zoe!"

Meanwhile the ladder is still in place, stretching from the floor to the swollen pearl by Zoe's ceiling—and the pearl is the gate to an unny tunnel to mappyworld. Or something like that.

Zoe grabs hold of the ladder and shoves it upward. As smoothly as if on rails, it slides into the still-hovering pearl, shrinking as it goes. And then—*poof*—it's all inside. As if knowing its work is done, the lustrous pearl contracts to its old size and drops from the air. It's still kind of transparent. Zoe catches it in her hand and shoves it into her jeans pocket. And then she opens the door for Mom.

"Why's your trumpet on the floor?" is Mom's big question. "Why can't you ever polish that thing?"

"Tarnish is the tang of my tune," says Zoe.

villy's family

villy

Driving home from Zoe's after dropping her off, Villy thinks about the kiss. He taps his fingers on his lips, trying to renew the sensation. He's kissed other girls, of course. He's a senior and not a complete borg. He kissed Tawna Garvey last month, for instance, at a bonfire party on the beach. And last week Tawna said hi in a very friendly way when he saw her in the weight room. Not that he then had sex with her, like he'd tried to tell Zoe just now—and why had he even said that?

Villy's house is pretty decent, partway up a foothill and with a view of San Jose. Villy doesn't see his father Pete or his younger brother Scud, but he assumes they're both home, as Pop's curvy electric kit-car is in the drive and the house's front door is open.

Probably Pop is working on his computer in his home office, which is a separate little cottage in the backyard, a room decorated with seashells and African masks. Awesome stuff. Pop is a contract programmer, an ace, and he likes toys. This month he's upgrading the ad management tools sold by a marketing company called InYoFace. Making online ads ever more invasive, ever more conscious of who you are.

Villy's mother Marie was a high school English teacher, but she died of cancer last year—died at home the way she wanted to. Ever since, Villy imagines there's a low, dark cloud over his house—and that Pop, Villy, and Scud are three lost boys. They're walking on thin, clear ice with the dark currents of death beneath. If Villy yells too hard, the ice might crack.

Pop and Scud seem to feel the same way. Mostly they're being nice to each other. Although, yeah, Scud's something of a pain in the butt. Not really the kid's fault. Mom's death has hit Scud the hardest of all. He's a tenth-grader, and sixteen years old, not that you'd know it. Unbelievably immature.

Villy thinks back to his own tenth grade. It's only two years behind him, but it's like remembering a long-gone fever-dream. All the kids at their worst—pubing out, zitty, voices cracking, utterly without self-control, hating everyone. Something changed in Villy after his mother died. He had this realization that everyone's the same. We live, and we flail around, and we die. Every single one of us. So why bother hating people? Let things slide.

The downside of this enlightenment is that Villy doesn't have any kind of urge to do great things. He hasn't even managed to put any moves on Zoe Snapp yet, much as he would like to. But now, *bam*, Zoe had kissed him. He's glad.

And—yeah, baby, yeah—Villy and Zoe might take off on a giant road trip. Finally leaving Los Perros. The phrase "common-law wife" drifts through Villy's head. He's not exactly sure what that means, but for sure it involves sex. *Motel* sex. With Zoe? Could that actually happen? *It's not that hard, Villy.* Zoe was one for talking big. When would they be leaving? Tomorrow? Tonight?

There's still three hours till the talent show. Villy decides to do some fast work on the purple whale. Like, he has six new spark plugs he's been meaning to install. And a new oil filter. And maybe he can even fix the left front window so it closes when it's supposed to. Prime the whale for an epic run.

As soon as Villy pulls his car into their double garage, Scud pops out of the house door that's in the garage and starts hopping across the garage floor on his old super-high-bouncing smart pogo stick, yelling cowboy yee-haws. Scud's sixteen, right? And he's acting like he's twelve. Typical.

Scud has reddish-blond hair, worn short in a buzz cut. Sharp features. Mouth too big, spit on his teeth. Tall and awkward. It's like his nervous system hasn't caught up with his bones.

"Welcome to the Antwerpen ranch, podner!" Scud's cracking voice echoes in the garage. The pogo stick goes *thonk-squeak-thonk.*

"Idiot," says Villy, not without affection. "Is there food?"

"Franks 'n' farts round the campfahr," shrieks Scud. "If it warn't that the cook's gone zombie." He means that Pop is fully into his programmer mode, eyes glazed, mind locked into his screen, no inputs accepted, no outputs to be had. A computer-hacking frenzy.

"Stop being so hyper and immature," Villy tells Scud. "It's almost scary. Like you're nuts. If you act normal, I'll make our supper and I'll let you help me with the car. We can eat here in the garage. Two grease monkeys. Way hipper than cowhands."

Thonk-squeak-thonk. Scud is bouncing almost as high as the garage's rafters. But he won't hit his head. Scud is in fact very cautious, and despite all appearances, he always knows what he's doing. He's totally figured out the pogo stick. He's been known to bounce on it for up to an hour.

"I'll fix hamburgers and celery if you stop," offers Villy. "I'll rustle our grub right away. I'll even make a plate for Pop. So his brain doesn't fall out."

A trace of human empathy appears in Scud's eyes. He lets the heavy-duty pogo stick clatter to the floor. Basically, he's lonely. He hasn't been the same since Mom died.

"We're gonna do the spark plugs?" asks Scud, looking up at Villy. Wanting to be loved. "I'll start on the plugs while you fry the burgers." Seeing hesitation in Villy's face, Scud turns hyper again. "I can do it! I know how! I'll do it from underneath the car, where they're easier to reach."

"I trust you," says Villy quietly. "What's the worst that can happen? You set my car on fire and our house burns down. Better than dying of cancer, right?"

Scud cocks his head, processing this. "We're not anywhere near dying, are we? You and me?"

"You got it. See this socket wrench? The plugs are down on the side of the engine block with wires attached to them. Undo a wire from a plug, screw out the old plug, screw in a new plug, replace the wire. One plug at a time, or you scramble the wires. Be careful with your hands. The engine block is hot."

Just to bug Villy, Scud reverts to his twelve-year-old-kid routine, whooping and waving the socket wrench like it's a tomahawk. Did Villy ever act this lame when he was sixteen? Probably not. The socket extension tube flies off and rolls under the car. Scud flops onto Villy's car-mechanic creeper board and rolls under the whale, looking for the part.

Meanwhile Villy goes into the kitchen, makes three burgers, and washes some celery. He's hungry enough that he eats his burger standing by the stove, wolfing it the hell down, catching the runoff in his free hand, wiping the hand on his jeans. *Yaaar*. Munching on a stick of celery now, Villy takes Scud's plate out to him. Scud is under the car, zoning out, counting the parts, whatever it is he does.

"Grease monkey!" cries Scud, sliding his knuckled hand out from under the car. "I'll eat in my lair."

Villy goes and carries the other plate of food to Pop's cottage. It's like a fairy-tale gnome's house, with windows and a door and a roof and even a sleeping loft. Villy loves the bizarro African masks, so off-kilter and earnest and full of glee. Like ambassadors from cartoonland.

Pop doesn't turn around. Doesn't notice Villy. No frikkin way will Villy ever be a programmer.

"Hey, Pop! Food!"

"Uh, thanks," says Pop, snapping out of his trance. "Yeah." As a gesture of politeness, he turns off his monitor.

Pop can't really talk if there's a live computer screen in his visual field. He takes his plate onto his lap. "This is great. Your day okay, Villy?"

"I'm driving Zoe to the talent show tonight," Villy says. And then, what the hell, he tells the rest. "We're thinking maybe—maybe we'll go on a giant road trip."

"I like Zoe," says Pop, wiping his mouth. "She's smart."

"She didn't get into a college," says Villy. "And—I've been meaning to tell you—I'm failing math. So I won't actually graduate tomorrow. The teacher says I should log on for, like, thirty hours of online remedial math this summer."

"You don't have to do that," says Pop. "Don't listen to your teacher. Fact is, all you have to do is pass one single standardized math test, they call it a GED test, it's the same as taking the course. Do you think you could pass a test like that?"

"Maybe," says Villy. "A written test? Or do I have to go online?"

"It'll be written," says Pop, a little exasperated. "With a teacher watching you. They're not gonna trust slackers who have to sign up for equivalence tests." Pop is half smiling, half annoyed. "You've never, ever used a computer for anything resembling work have you? Is that your roundabout way of telling me that my career sucks?"

"We're different," says Villy with a shrug.

"Maybe not," says Pop. "Maybe I used to be like you. But now I'm stiff. We'll get you a frikkin high school diploma." Pop takes another bite of his burger. Swallows the bite. Zooms the hamburger around like an alien aircraft, making a humming noise. Bites the burger yet again.

"Can a person tell when they're mentally ill?" asks Villy, making his voice all innocent.

Pop takes this in stride. "Can a person tell when their planet is being overrun by flying saucers? Like Zoe's father used to say?"

"Not me," says Villy, not giving an inch. "I can't tell at all. You okay with our road trip or not?"

"Zoe's mother knows about it?"

"Uh . . ."

"She better know. Or she'll put the cops on you. Or, even worse, she'll come after *me*. Might not be so bad." Pop wiggles his eyebrows in a wolf-whistle way.

"Don't," says Villy. "Zoe and I are eighteen. We can do what we want."

Meanwhile, out in the garage, Scud is howling and shouting and making animal noises. Something about a dog.

"I wish I was better with Scud," says Pop, maybe thinking about how things will be when Villy leaves. "Marie had a special rapport with him."

"The guy is different," says Villy, with a shrug. He gives Pop a pat on the shoulder.

All of a sudden Pop gets emotional. "Thanks for telling me your plans," he tells Villy. "I'm always on your side. You're my hero, in a way. Take your trip wherever it goes."

"Thank you," says Villy, more pleased than he likes to let on. "You're a good dad." He hugs Pop and walks back to the garage to see what's going on.

A huge, crooked, yellow dog is standing there. But—is that really a dog?

Scud is on Villy's creeper board, out from under the car,

lying on his stomach, scooting around like a cockroach, yipping and growling at the dog-thing. As if trying to scare him away. The creature watches Scud and Villy. He has a weird head with almost a human face. His front legs are too long. And—he's wearing a tool belt.

This isn't a dog. The moment Villy realizes that, the thing rocks back onto his hind legs and stands erect, shaped approximately like a twenty-five-year-old guy.

"Monster!" shrieks Scud. So weird. After all the crackpot chatter about saucers in Los Perros—here's a genuine alien.

The creature has big eyes and a mouth with purplish lips. He's unshaven, with his stubble dark green against his yellow-orange skin.

"Pinchley's the name," he says, sounding like a grease monkey from Oklahoma. He shows his teeth in what might be a friendly way. Pats his tool belt with his many-fingered hand. "What say we soup up your wheels?" And then comes the kicker, "We gonna drive a million miles. You and me and our lady friends."

"You— you already know I'm planning a road trip?" asks Villy, completely thrown off track. "And you know about Zoe too?"

"A run to Szep City with Villy and Zoe," continues Pinchley, walking over to the purple whale. "My hometown. We've got what you need."

Scud has risen to his feet. "Where are you from, Pinchley?"

"What I said. Szep City. In mappyworld." Pinchley peers into the whale's open hood. He's all set to start tweaking it.

Even amid this rush of weirdness, Villy still cares about his car. He looks under the hood too, checking on the engine, and—oh no! "You pulled all six wires off my plugs at once," he yells at Scud. "It's a frikkin rat's nest."

"I couldn't get the first spark plug unscrewed," mutters Scud. "And then I was mad, and I wanted to teach your car a lesson."

"Yeah, you taught it what an idiot you are."

"*Stop calling me an idiot!* I'm smarter than you. I'm not the one flunking math." Scud is right in Villy's face.

"Don't lose the fun," advises Pinchley. He smells like cloves and gasoline. "Them wires don't make no nevermind. Watch me work out, boys. I'll use crawly slime, a peck bird, and a balloon of zilch." The alien smiles to himself.

"I'm coming on the road trip too," says Scud. "Please, Villy? Don't leave me with Pop. He doesn't like me."

"Oh hell," says Villy. He should have seen this coming. "Pop likes you fine."

"Does not! I can tell. I want to come! Why don't you have a flying saucer, Mr. Pinchley?"

"I'm a car guy," says Pinchley with conviction. He lays his tool belt on the fender. "Cars are what it is. And, yeah, the mappyworld saucers can fly, but you can't hardly ride inside them. They alive. All meat. They zap and bite."

"I want to come!" repeats Scud. "All the way to Szep City."

"Okay by me if Scud tags along," says Pinchley. "My pal Flipsydaisy said it'd be better to round up three. Cut your bro a break, Villy. We'll team up. Yampa, me, Scud, you, and foxy Zoe Snapp. Freaks drivin' fast."

"Yubba woot!" yells Scud.

"Be quiet or I'll choke you," Villy tells his brother. But he smiles as he says this. Deep down he's glad Scud is coming.

zoe's mom

What's going on, really?" says Mom. She perches on Zoe's bed beside the clothes she'd picked for her daughter. The sharp, tingly odor of Yampa is wafting out from under the bed. Mom is stagily sniffing the air.

The funny thing is that she looks almost exactly like Zoe. Two peas in a pod, but one of the peas has wrinkles. And Mom dyes her hair blonde. Not really a good look with olive skin and big dark eyes. But she's covering the gray. Also, it's kind of expected that a woman is blonde if she's a realtor.

"Are you vaping pot?" asks Mom. "Or is it something worse? I feel dizzy just sitting in here. Please don't tell me you're smoking crack! Not every musician has to be a junkie, Zoe."

Zoe hardly knows where to begin. She's about to leave home with Villy, she's met two aliens, and Mom is so totally out of the loop that she's calling her a *junkie*?

"Look at me, Mom," says Zoe. "I'm here. Next to you. Your daughter. You're not watching a troubled teens TV special."

"You're so distant with me," says Mom, "This whole college thing . . ."

"I want to leave home," blurts Zoe. "Go off on my own."

"You can be an intern at work-study summer charity camp," begins Mom. "I have the perfect contact. It would be a such great activity to list on your—"

"No more applications, Mom. That's over. Your daughter Zoe Snapp has been admitted to—the *now*! With a major in Nothing and a minor in Everything. No more future imperfect. I have some rather amazing activities in mind." She's talking fancy to try and sound big.

Zoe hears a rustle and a hiss from beneath the bed. It's Yampa. The alien is whispering, her voice so faint that only Zoe hears: "Sorry I'm smelly."

Meanwhile Mom is sighing and shaking her head, fixated on her crumbling fantasies of how her daughter should be.

Outside the open window, the honeyed light dims. Before long Villy will come to pick up Zoe. Maybe he'll have Pinchley with him. They might as well start their road trip tonight. Zoe is so over this scene. The trip will be rad with the two aliens along. Zoe feels brave and defiant thinking this, but for sure she's scared. It's more of a road trip than she was bargaining for.

Basically Yampa and Pinchley want to kidnap her. And sister Maisie sent them? How does that even compute? Maisie's been in with the aliens all along? Is this her revenge for Zoe's coldness?

Worse than this, what if Zoe is only *imagining* that an alien named Yampa is under her bed and saying that she knows Maisie? Creepsville central. Forming the quietest possible whisper, a mere modulation of her breath, Zoe leans towards the edge of the bed and says, "Are you there?" Naturally, just to make things worse, there's no answer.

If only she could talk things over with someone. But there's no way to talk about anything real with Mom.

"I don't know why you've changed," Mom is saying, her voice thin and unsteady. "I only want the best for you." She's crying. Oh, this is unbearable. Zoe is being smothered here. Wrapped in layer after layer of itchy, potpourri-scented wool.

"I need space," says Zoe, getting to her feet, feeling unsteady. "I need to get ready for tonight."

Mom sniffles, stands, dabs at her eyes with a tissue. Her face is damp and unfocused. Zoe's haughty pose weakens. What if she really and truly leaves tonight and she never sees her mother again? Oh god. Life is impossible. Zoe puts her arms around Mom and holds her.

"Look at me!" says Mom after a bit, trying to sound pert. She steps back and smiles at Zoe. "I'm completely going to pieces. Silly old woman. We'll talk about your plans tomorrow." Mom glances at her watch. "I need to go to the supermarket before I go to your show." She smiles, her eyes filled with love and concern. "I'll get some strawberries for you, Zoe. They're so good right now."

"Thanks," says Zoe. "Thanks for everything you've done. I hope someday you'll be proud of me."

"I'm happy with you right now, Zoe. I am. I can't lord it over you. I made a mess of my life. I—I just hope you'll do better."

Call it a wrap. Zoe kisses Mom on the cheek one last time. "Bye!"

Mom drives off in her vile white max-sized SUV, and Yampa pops out from under the bed. Yampa is real. Not a hallucination. But—

"What exactly are you doing here?" Zoe asks the odd yellow figure.

"Pinchley and I came for kicks," says Yampa. "A million mile road trip. And, more, we're on a mighty mission— thanks to the goading of Goob-goob and the mach- inations of Maisie."

"Why are you talking about my sister Maisie? She lives here in Los Perros. Not in the mappyworld."

"Your sister shuttles," says Yampa. "She's . . . similar to the saucers? She presented you the saucer pearl. She taught you the toot for the tunnel. She put Pinchley and me in place at your tunnel's termination. Why? Goob- goob wants to wrangle two or three humans like you—to win the wand for warring with Groon. The trip will be a thrill. If we don't die."

"Die?" echoes Zoe, quite unable to process the stuff about Maisie and the saucer pearl and the rest of it. But even so, she's smiling. This is the most exciting thing that's ever happened to her. And Yampa's spice and ether smell—it's jazzing her up. Like coffee or candy or—

"I have you high," says Yampa with a nod. "For happy talk."

"I don't want to be high," protests Zoe. "Despite what you and Mom seem to think."

Yampa's smell damps down to a faint whiff of baking

brownies. "Sometimes my smells are secret signals," says

the alien in a coy tone.

"I am so far from knowing what you're talking about," says Zoe.

"Chocolate," says Yampa, her voice a low rasp. "We want some."

"We can look in the kitchen cabinet," says Zoe. "But hold the glee. Before we get any further into this—why did you say we might die on the million mile road trip to Szep City?"

"Other odd aliens," says Yampa. "Not all of them friendly. We'll see Flatsies, giant ants, music cubes, Thudds, bubble-men, Freeths, thinking tsunamis, tottering trees—and the saucers. Some of the saucers are your sworn foes. Intending to invade."

"For some reason we hear about saucers a lot in Los Perros these days," answers Zoe. "Who's riding inside them?"

"They're not vehicles," says Yampa. "They're muscle and meat, with bumbling brains. The problematic ones are parasites who siphon people's smeel."

"You mean smell?"

"*Smeeeel*. Your scientists don't study smeel. It's mind stuff. You and I have heaps of smeel. Rocks—a rudimentary ration. Where's my ladder?"

"When Mom came, I slid the ladder inside the floating saucer pearl," says Zoe. "And the pearl shrank, and now it's in my pocket."

"Show me," says Yampa. "Later you'll play to the pearl again, and it'll make a tunnel to mappyworld. For now, I need to know no noxious critters have crept through the pearl's passage. Perhaps the saucers sense the significance of what Pinchley and I seek, and they sent small saucers for sabotage."

Zoe shoves her hand down into her jeans and finds the fat pearl with her fingers. And, oh wow, she must not have shut the pearl's gate tight. Because there's critters in her pocket. Tickling her palm and nipping her fingertips. She snatches her hand from her pocket and finds two little round disks stuck to her palm, blue in the middle with yellow rims, each with a tiny, baleful, red eye. Leech saucers?

Yampa makes a sound pretty much like *Aaaaak*! And now Yampa's many fingers are worming all over Zoe's hand, popping those two saucers. The popped saucers leave spots of blood on Zoe's palm. They were feeding on her like ticks, drawing off some blood along with the— smeel?

Without slowing down, Yampa wriggles a hand down into Zoe's pocket and does a search and pinch routine. To Zoe it feels like a micro mosh-pit in her pants.

Yampa's cleanup doesn't fully achieve its goal—a third tiny bright saucer squirms out through the seam of Zoe's jeans. It has a yellow dome set onto a floppy white rim— like a tiny fried egg. Like the others, the dome has a little red eye on it. In a heartbeat the saucer has zoomed out the window.

"Thudd dung," exclaims Yampa, and she pulls the pearl from Zoe's pocket. "The pearl is totally transparent. The gate gapes. Be quick and close it!"

"Smash the pearl with a hammer?" asks Zoe, frantically fumbling with her jewelry tools.

"No, no, no," says Yampa, talking very fast. "Toot your tune. You played the pearl open. And now you serenade it shut. Zip zap, Zoe Snapp."

"Why—why do you call it a saucer pearl anyway?" asks Zoe.

"Every saucer carries such a pearl at its private core," says Yampa, shortly. "The pearls help them levitate. Now hurry and close your pearl."

With shaking hands Zoe gets out her trumpet and plays one of her special bits—a sarcastic bebop lullaby. And then she tacks on Maisie's little riff—played backwards. All at once the saucer pearl isn't transparent anymore. It's solid and iridescent like it was at the start. The gate is closed.

"Good," goes Yampa. "As for the escaped small saucer, he'll try to trail us to mappyworld. He'll leech onto us when we leave. He'll be fat and full of stolen smeel. We'll do best to burst him, yes."

FIVE

augmented whale

scud

Scud watches Pinchley prepare to do his alien mechanic routine. Pinchley pats the dark tool belt he laid on the whale's finder. "It's made of genuine ant leather," he tells Scud.

Scud loves it. "Isn't this awesome, Villy? But, wait, ants don't have leather, Mr. Pinchley. They're stiff. And tiny."

"Ants in mappyworld got leather," says Pinchley, opening one of his belt's compartments. "They're wiggly, and they hella big. Don't call me mister. I'm twenty-three of your years old. My woman Yampa, she's twenty-six. With a powerful yen for cool mechanic-type guys like me. I got her dazzled! Not that Yampa would flat-out say so."

Pinchley takes something squirmy out of his ant-leather tool belt. It's a little tan pancake that's alive. He holds it at some distance from his body, using a pair of fingers that he's shaped into a claw.

"I'm upgrading you boys to what you'd call a dark-energy motor," Pinchley tells Scud. He adds a sound effect. "*Vooo-don va vooo-don.* Don't need none of that stinky gasoline for *this* rig. Your engine'll be smarter than six schoolteachers." He leans under the hood and tosses the pancake onto the top of Villy's old mill.

The pancake thins like a puddle of batter, running down onto every side of the purple whale's engine. The alien goo eats away at the Detroit iron, reshaping it, transforming it, bringing it to life. Scud's dangling wires are gone.

"Wait—" begins Villy, obviously worried. But already the change is done. The thin slime pulls itself back together, forming a tidy pancake resting on top of—

"That's your dark-energy motor right there," says Pinchley. He whistles admiringly. The smell of his breath is hard to take. "I bought this fancy flapjack off a Rubtan in Szep City."

The new engine has a glossy sci-fi look—it's a nest of gold and chrome tubes supporting a transparent sphere with soft green sparks amid a lavender glow. Branching sparks stream from the orb's center, and they spiderweb across the ball's glassy inner surface. A dark-energy turbine. An eccentric train of asymmetric gears runs from the sphere to the purple whale's earthbound grease-and-metal transmission.

"Good thing your whale's not in gear," Pinchley tells Villy. "My motor's ready to roll your heap at a thousand miles per. And then some. Look inside at the dash. That smart engine pancake upgraded your speedometer too."

"Jeez," says Villy, peering in. "The dial goes up to— three thousand miles an hour?"

"Well, the pancake likes to exaggerate," says Pinchley. "Truth be told, you'll be lucky to go faster than two K. And you'd want a nice clear stretch of land."

"My tires will burst," protests Villy. "The shocks will bottom out. My car will catch fire and burn down to the metal."

"Don't sweat it none," says Pinchley. "We not done tinkerin yet."

"But why do we have to drive so fast?" interrupts Scud.

"Do some math there, Scud. I already told you we're driving a whole million miles, didn't I? To hit Szep City in less than three months, we want to make ten or fifteen thousand miles a day. A wild mappyworld run." Pinchley craggy face splits in a reckless grin.

"What do you mean when you say your world is *mappy*?" presses Scud. He doesn't like mysteries.

Pinchley fields this one too. "It means we don't live on round balls. No planets. Our world's one giant continent with mountains cutting it into basins—and no end in sight. Each basin matches a settled planet of your world. But not like a twin, not even like a sister or a brother. More like a third cousin. Why? Nobody knows. Mappyworld grows itself, ballyworld grows itself, and they in sync. Chicken and egg."

"Icken and chegg," puts in Villy, maybe doing this to mess with Scud's head.

"Can you say our ballyworld is regular matter, and your mappyworld is dark matter?" persists Scud.

"You could say that if you wanted," says Pinchley. "But likely you'd he talkin' out your ass."

"Let me ask you this," says Villy, not wanting Scud to go off on one of his science tangents. "Does mappyworld have highways?"

"Hell no," says Pinchley. "Pretty much the whole million mile drive is gonna be off road. Which is why I'm fixing to make your mommy-wagon look like a bad-ass monster truck."

Villy looks annoyed. "If you want to dis my bitchin' purple whale, you can go and—"

For no reason in particular, Pinchley switches to a silly fake-Dutch accent. "Vait till you see, Villy und Scood van Antverpen. Zee mappyvorld iss voonderful."

It hits Scud that whatever accent Pinchley talks in, it's always going to be a goof the alien is running in his head. This guy is very far indeed from being any kind of local yokel.

Pinchley takes two more tools from his belt. One is a little orange bird. She has bead-bright blue eyes on either side of a black beak. Her beak is soft and moist like a dog's nose. The other tool looks like a birthday-party water balloon, long and waggy, pale blue with two glowing red eyes. The balloon is oozing slime on Pinchley's hand, with a putrid smell coming off the slime.

"Nasty but he's nice," says Pinchley, not at all upset. He flips the balloon onto the floor.

"*Splat!*" yells Scud, feeling joyful. But, no, the balloon critter doesn't burst. It humps along the floor like a worm, making his way beneath the purple whale.

"Gonna rock some quantum shocks," says Pinchley. "Smooth as snot on a doorknob, feller says." He's giving off an allspice smell with a rubbing-alcohol edge.

The balloon creature makes odd noises under the car: *ping*, *hiss*, and *gronk*. The left front corner of the whale rises at an awkward angle, with the fender way higher than the tire. And now the right front end of the car rises up as well, tilting the car's body backwards.

"Bucking bronc!" says Scud. He's feeling giddy from Pinchley's fumes.

More squeaking and whooshing, and now the whole car is up high, like the pickups that the mountain rednecks drive. The balloon creeps out from beneath the truck—damp, deflated, triumphant. Pinchley stashes it in his ant-leather tool belt.

"What was inside it?" asks Scud.

"Nothing but nothing." says Pinchley. "Call it quantum foam? It ate whatever rusty crud you had under there before. And now you got force fields instead. Quantum shocks. This permutated whale's gonna *haul ass* across them rocks and rills."

"But my feeble little tires aren't—" begins Villy.

"Watch the birdie," interrupts Pinchley. "She's gonna do like a magic marker. Physical graffiti, boys. Scribble on them tires and they get fat."

"Let me do it!" says Scud, and Pinchley hands him the marker bird.

Scud kneels down by the left front wheel and presses the orange bird's damp, dank beak against the tire. The creature twitches violently, gets halfway free from Scud's grip, and claws his hand. Scud hollers and drops the bird. She hops onto the tire and begins scribbling on her own.

"Likes to do it herself," says Pinchley.

"Why didn't you warn me?" whines Scud.

"Maybe I like to hear a greenhorn yell," says Pinchley flat-out. "Maybe I shouldn't admit it? We'll be friends anyway, and don't you mind my pranks. Long trip ahead."

The marker bird finishes the left front tire and moves on to the next. That first tire is shifting and swelling, filling in the space that the high quantum shocks have freed, and my god, the tire is nearly six feet tall, with heavy-duty corrugations sticking out like the teeth on a gear. Scud raps his knuckles on the transmuted, amplified tire. Taut, squeaky, firm.

"Tessellated carbon," says Pinchley. "Graphene. These tires roll true blue. I clocked a set at four thousand miles an hour on a desert. Woulda been fine, except I ran over a toothpick and went ass over teakettle. Lucky I landed on my head." He stares at Scud, with his weird, lumpy jaw working. "That's a joke, son."

"But what about accidents?" asks Scud, who's prone to worrying, even though he knows it seems wimpy. "What if you do crash going at a speed like that?"

"The space inside our car stiffens up with Truban inertia gel. It's like you're packed in bubble-wrap during the crash. And then you jump outta your car and yell at the other guy. Not that there's much left of him to yell at. Unless he's got that special Truban inertia gel himself."

With all the tires done, the marker bird perches on the purple whale's roof rack, which is nearly touching the garage rafters. Leaning over the door frame, the marker bird makes a choking sound—and extrudes a rubbery black rope that she affixes to the roof with a brisk peck.

"What you might call a bungee cord," says Pinchley. "For climbing in and out of this rig. We gonna be growing the wheels even bigger in mappyworld."

Meanwhile the marker bird hops around the roof and squeezes out a dangling rope for each of the car's four doors. By way of finishing off her work, she lowers herself down each of the ropes in turn, moving upside down like a nuthatch, fastening the four flexible cords at the bottoms of the door frames and leaving long ends dangling.

"Good girl," says Pinchley. He coaxes the bird to his hand with a morsel of food and stashes her in his tool belt.

"I still don't get what's in this for you," says Villy. He looks uneasy.

"The great Goob-goob hired Yampa and me to fetch back some humans so we could equip you for the cosmic beatdown comin' down," says Pinchley. "So we drove a million miles to New Eden—which is just a hop through unspace and a drive over the ridge from here—and we connected with Zoe's sister Maisie. Maisie recommended that we pick up you and your girlfriend Zoe. She said you two were meant to be intergalactic heroes."

"Oh come on," says Villy. "There's got to be another angle. Something that you yourself get."

"Wal, okay," says Pinchley. "Down to brass tacks. Would you have any caraway seeds in the house?"

"Caraway seeds?" echoes Villy. "Is this, like, the world's most complicated joke? Caraway seeds from rye bread?"

"Mom used to put them in her pork stew!" exclaims Scud. He's proud of remembering this. And glad for a chance to mention Mom. He speeds off to the kitchen, rattles around, and about forty-five seconds later he's back with a spice jar of curvy little caraway seeds.

Pinchley is exceedingly pleased. And now he comes up with another request. "Chocolate?"

"We had some last week," says Scud. "But I ate it."

"Never mind," says Pinchley. "Yampa will score chocolate from Zoe, no doubt. Yampa and me are wild about that stuff. It gets us high. And the caraway seeds make us healthy. Gimme, Scud." He holds out his yellow many-fingered hand.

"Maybe I keep the seeds for now," says Scud, and stuffs the jar down into his pants pocket. He wants to keep whatever leverage he has. He worries that Pinchley and Villy might get sick of him, and throw him off the trip. In certain moods, Villy can be mean. In the old days, Mom would always stick up for Scud. Now that Scud's alone, he has to be sly.

Meanwhile Villy's climbed up behind the whale's steering wheel. He bounces on the seat, turning the car's giant front tires back and forth. He looks eager to go—and perfectly happy with having Scud come too.

"Zoe's expecting us," Villy tells Scud as he hops down from the car. "We need to grab whatever we want to bring on the trip. And you should say goodbye to Pop."

Walking down the hall past his parents' bedroom, Scud wishes for the thousandth time that Mom might somehow be in her old room. I mean, sure, he went to her funeral and saw the horrible little box that was supposed to be her ashes, but maybe? How can a person totally disappear from one day to the next?

Going into his own room, Scud thinks of something that makes him stand stock still. Maybe there's a copy of Mom in mappyworld? Maybe Scud will see her. Thinking about this makes him feel sick with longing. Mom was the one who loved him, the one who cared. On the other hand, what if the mappyworld copy of Mom is some-how—wrong?

Scud does his best to close down that spooky thought. This trip is supposed to be science. It's his best subject at school. He doesn't flunk math tests like Villy. Villy is good with his hands and good at videogames and he can surf, but he's bad in school. It's not Scud who's the idiot around here.

Scud likes science because it's logical, with no chance of a horrible surprise darting out at him. A horrible surprise like Mom staying home from work with a sore hip one day, and two months later Pop is showing Scud a little can of gray ashes with bone chips, and that's supposed to be Mom? The can was so light. Scud wishes he hadn't touched it.

Okay, snap out of it, what is he supposed to be doing here in his bedroom? Oh, right, pack some things for this insane trip. Bring stuff he can barter with the aliens. He has a diamondback rattlesnake skin that he likes, and a box of foreign coins. Maybe his video drone with linked goggles? A few months ago, he used the drone to see the neighbor woman naked by her pool, not that he was spe-cifically interested in that particular woman in that way, but seeing her naked was something to brag about to his friends. Like seeing a black widow spider, or finding a tiny nugget of gold. *The female of the species.*

Rooting around his room and muttering to himself, Scud puts stuff inside his knapsack. His throwing knife of course. A sweatshirt. A second pair of underwear—for sure that's something Mom would have told him to bring. A pencil sharpener shaped like an Earth globe—he can astound the aliens with that. How can those guys be living on a flat, endless landscape? Where do they put their sun?

Scud would like to bring his binoculars, but his binoculars are hiding as usual. Scud hates them for that. And he'll leave the drone and goggles—they're too big.And the foreign coins are too heavy. But he'll bring a couple of his fossils. He collected them himself from cliffs near the beach. The fossils are like smooth black rocks with white patterns in them—primeval shells and crinoid stalks and crawly trilobites. Scud is good at finding things. Except for those bastard-ass binoculars. Never mind them. He grabs three of his best fossils. Supposedly they're three million years old.

"Let's go!" yells Villy, out in the hall. He's filled a knapsack of his own. "Did you tell Pop you're leaving?"

"Let's just go," mutters Scud. "Pop doesn't care what I do." It hurts to say this. It makes Scud feel hollow in the middle of his chest. But there's a certain resentful satisfaction in being bitter.

"Whatever," says Villy, who doesn't seem to be in a mood to indulge Scud's drama. He glances into Scud's pack. "You're bringing those stupid fossils?"

"Yeah. And I bet you're bringing your stupid surf-boards."

"My personal treasures, yes," says Villy, cracking a smile. "This is going to be fun. I can't wait to get on the road and see how our augmented whale handles."

"Be sure to drive carefully," says Scud. "I'm too young to die."

"So stay home, why don't you?"

"I'm coming! But I'm scared."

"I'll take care of you, little dude." Villy throws a brotherly arm across Scud's shoulder and they head down the hall towards the garage. Right at the door there, Villy pauses and scribbles a note for Pop on the family whiteboard—a note that says he's taking Scud.

"Just in case the old man does care some tiny iota about his younger son's whereabouts," says Villy. "Even though the rat-ass younger son can't be bothered to say goodbye."

"We might not even be gone all that long," says Scud, feeling ashamed for avoiding Pop. But mostly he's glad to be setting forth on an incredible journey.

SIX

unny tunnel

zoe

Zoe had expected to find baking chocolate in the kitchen, but Mom hasn't been cooking much this year. There is, however, a big can of cocoa, nearly full. Yampa is utterly thrilled with the chocolate powder. She makes a clicking sound to take one of her mental pictures, then pries the lid off the can and sits on Zoe's bed, dabbing up taste after taste with her thin, flexible fingers.

"Such a savor!" says the alien, trembling with pleasure. "So happily healthy. So smooth I feel—how sleek."

"Glad you're happy," says Zoe noncommittally. She's packing for the trip. Beads, threads, and wires. Jeans, pajamas, shoes, tops, sweaters. Her trumpet.

She's still planning to do her number with the Jazz Prowlers at the talent show tonight—before they head off into the neverland of mappyworld. Or maybe just to Mexico and the Midwest. As long as it's with Villy.

No way does Zoe want to look like a prissy groover in the pitiful white blouse and navy blue skirt that Mom laid out for the show. Instead she selects an outfit from her special Eff You mound, thank you very much. A thrift-store black cowboy shirt and orange toothpick jeans.

Just for kicks she gets Yampa to put on the clothes that Mom set out. And she hands Yampa one of her bead neck-lace creations— aquamarine glass spindles alternating with fake silver balls on stretch cord.

Yampa preens in front of Zoe's mirror, very pleased with her white blouse, blue skirt, and necklace. She shoots a holographic mental 3D selfie of herself—or whatever it is that she does when she makes that clicking sound.

Zoe supposes that Pinchley thinks Yampa is hot. Even though the alien woman is like a child's drawing of a per-son, so thin and crooked with her head way larger than it should be. Her lower jaw wags when she talks. But of course Pinchley looks that way too. Zoe hopes Yampa isn't reading her mind.

"Your clothes hang high on me," Yampa is cheerfully saying. "Glamour garb. May I haul them home?"

"Sure."

"Be sure to pack your saucer pearl," says Yampa.

"In my pocket," says Zoe. "And I have my trumpet right here."

"Perf," goes Yampa.

Where does this alien get her vocab and her style of speech? Before Zoe can ask, she hears Villy's car out-side—oh god, he's driving right onto the lawn, with his headlights raking across the house. She laughs to herself. Villy doesn't care what people think. That's yet another thing she likes about him.

It's just about dark now. The purple whale's body is fifteen feet in the air, somehow mounted above four insanely large tires. Like jet airline tires. So dumb—you have to use ropes to help you scramble in. As a final touch, Villy has two surfboards on the roof rack. Sweet. His favorite red one, and he's brought his blue one for Zoe.

The whale's horn is as comically weak as ever. *Toot toot.* Yampa hops out of Zoe's bedroom window onto the lawn, still wearing Zoe's outfit. The effect is jarringly strange. The clothes don't fit Yampa at all—after all, her body isn't much thicker than a human leg. The blouse hangs off one shoulder. Yampa wears the top of the skirt rolled, to keep it in place, but she keeps having to hitch it up anyway. She's got the tin of cocoa in her hand.

At the last minute, Zoe decides not to bring her phone. Probably won't work where they're going. And she wants to make a full break anyway. She locks up the empty house and runs out the front door to the funny car, carrying her backpack and her trumpet. She grabs hold of a rope and—*boing*—it pulls her right in. Yampa and Pinchley get into the back seat, and Zoe is alone with Villy in front, with her pack and her trumpet by her feet. Villy is smiling, very stoked, utterly gorgeous with his dark tan and his long, streaked hair. He gives Zoe a high five. But—hold on. *Scud* is in the back seat between the aliens.

"What is he doing here?" asks Zoe, her voice very tight and clipped. She can't stand Scud. The kid is hormonally imbalanced. Like, he'll see Villy and Zoe together and he'll totally lose it and shriek some rude word like "*boner!*" or "*booty!*" in his horrible cracking voice. The most immature tenth-grader ever. He's also known to be something of a perv with his drone camera—he's been seen shooting pictures of the cheerleaders doing warm-up stretches and then drooling over the video at lunchtime with his pubescent tenth-grade friends, not that Scud has any friends, but he *can* gather a knot of fellow losers with a ripe shot of, like, Tawna Garvey leaning way, way over for a leg stretch, with her butt like a grotesque Halloween prize pumpkin against the sky.

Pinchley has filled the car with a stony alien smell—which may be why Zoe's mental images are so vivid. Like when she rides with people smoking pot. Rides with surfers.

Zoe plays it cool. "Turn down the mind warp, Pinchley. And Villy, are you dropping off Scud somewhere? Or what?"

"I'm coming on the trip," says Scud. Usually he's totally unaware of other people's feelings, but maybe he can feel the blast furnace intensity of Zoe's loathing. The boy looks tentative. Like a feral mongrel longing for a kindly touch. "Villy and Pinchley said it's okay."

"I'm getting out," says Zoe, hardening her heart. "I'll walk to the talent show." She reaches for the door handle, but the monster whale has already lumbered away from her house and is rolling down Los Perros Boulevard with traffic whizzing by. Boy, are they far off the ground. And the monster car's engine seems to make no noise at all. All you hear is a gentle squeaking from, like, the Martian suspension and the Venusian tires, or whatever they are.

"Don't bail on me," says Villy to Zoe. He glances over at her, looking out from under his dark eyebrows all tender. He pats her hand.

"But—this was supposed to be about—the two of us," blurts Zoe, with a silly catch in her voice. "I mean, no, I'm not saying we're totally a *couple*, but I thought the trip would be for having fun, talking, being relaxed—and now we've got two aliens and your little—"

Scud makes some kind of noise right then. A suppressed giggle. Is he about to yell, like, "*sexual congress*"?

"I'll kill you!" Zoe screams, twisting around so that she's kneeling on the seat and glaring at the sixteen-year-old—who looks frightened and surprised.

"I've got a gun in my backpack," rants Zoe, totally lying. "One rude word and I blow your brains out, Scud, and I'll get away with it, too. These aliens are cannibals. They'll eat every scrap of your corpse."

"And gobble his fossils for dessert," whoops Villy. "Teach the boy some manners!" And now Villy and Zoe are laughing and it's starting to be the great crazy road trip it's supposed to be.

Only now Scud has to ruin things by starting to snivel. Totally caving. "I'm sorry I'm here," he wails. "I'm sorry I'm alive. I just wanted to have—to have an adventure." Gangly and rangy as he is, nearly as tall as Villy, it's odd to see him cry. You don't quite realize what a child Scud is until you talk to him.

"Me, I like Scud," puts in Pinchley. "He's good for the mix, Villy. Zoe is a little dark. Like she's carrying the weight of the world. Scud's a screwball. A wingnut."

"Don't go putting Scud down," says Villy. He gets edgy when people say things about his brother. But then he takes a dig at Scud himself, addressing him directly. "Can't you ever tell when someone's joking?"

"I'm sorry, Scud," adds Zoe, not that she really means it. "We can be friends." This is what she has to say. Life is an endless series of cages.

"Warning," says Yampa just then. "A flying saucer. A male. His vile vibration is scraping my skin."

"Pinchley was talking about saucers too," chirps Scud, all perky and interested again. "Zoe's father should be here with his New Eden friends." His tears have disappeared. Zoe wouldn't put it past him to have been faking.

"The saucer grubbed through Zoe's pearly gate," says Yampa. "Lousy leech from mappyworld. He's formed like a fried egg. We'll promptly pop him."

"I'll be the lookout!" cries Scud, crawling into the luggage-jumbled rear section of the purple whale.

"Are we still going to your talent show?" Villy asks Zoe. "The turnoff is pretty soon."

"*Yeah*, we're going," exclaims Zoe, meaning I-can't-be-lieve-you're-asking-me-that. "That show is the one single bright spot of my entire senior year. Pre-college dropout that I am."

"Fine, fine," goes Villy. "No problem."

"Also we should talk some more about our trip," says Zoe. "Is it really and truly a good idea to volunteer for alien abduction?"

"A rollicking romp," says Yampa.

"Not a butt-probe," adds Pinchley. "We're stoked to have three new ballyworld human friends. We might help you save Earth from a giant saucer invasion. And you'll do mappyworld some good too."

"Tell me more about saving Earth," goes Zoe. She'd dearly love to do something big. Without having to plan it and all. Just to have the big thing happen, with her in the center of it.

"You three will win a wiggly wand from Szep City," says Yampa, fiddling with her blouse.

"Aristo wand," adds Pinchley. "You'll have to show the wand some class."

"Are you sure it'll work?" asks Scud.

Pinchley and Yampa look at each other. Yampa shrugs and says, "It's your optimum option."

"These three are the chosen ones, right, Yampa?" goes Pinchley. "These kids are hero material."

"Whack-a-doodle wham," says Yampa, who keeps eating dabs of the brown cocoa powder, giving tastes to Pinchley as well.

"You're making no sense," says Zoe sternly. "You're slushed and delusional."

"Words fail us," says Pinchley. "Furds wail us."

"Will there be surf?" puts in Villy. "On the million mile road trip?"

"Yah, mon," goes Pinchley. "Living waves mile high."

"Corkscrew caves and zonked ziggurats," adds Yampa.

"I'm down with it," says Villy. "Are you good, Zoe?" He gives her a nice private smile.

"Maybe," she says, wanting to be wooed. At least Scud isn't butting in and yelling. He's busy staring out the whale's rear window. "Just don't forget that my talent show comes before the trip, Villy. If you don't want to see it, you can wait in the parking lot. Chew tobacco with the other monster-truck boys."

"Oh, of course I want to hear you play, Zoe. You're the—"

"Here he comes!" shouts Scud. The rubbery flying-egg saucer thumps onto the whale's hood. He's four feet across by now, a rich yellow dome set onto a twitching white disk. The headlights of the oncoming traffic glisten on the swollen saucer's bulge. Whoa. His eye is a glaring red orb, greedy and mean.

"I foretold he'd be fat," says Yampa. "Swollen with smeel. Wind shut the windows!"

"What's smeel?" asks Villy.

"Raw mind stuff, supposedly," says Zoe. "I'd call it hippie jive."

"No call for that," says Pinchley. "Consciousness ain't imaginary. It's real. It's smeel. Mind is a physical thing like atoms or electricity, even if your crude techs don't know that. Saucers eat smeel. Folks like us grow our own smeel, but certain lazy-ass vampire saucers leech it from people's bodies and brains. Battle alert!"

The saucer slides from the hood onto the windshield, possibly meaning to edge over to Villy's window, which is still wide open. This is the window that sticks, even with the whale's new upgrades.

Through the windshield Zoe can see the saucer's underside, which holds a nasty little mouth with a ring of raspy teeth. It's like the mouth of a lamprey or a sea skate. Horrid.

Villy's having trouble seeing the road, so he scoots over towards Zoe. At the same time, he's slowing down, even though the driver to their rear is tailgating them and honking his horn like a crazy person.

Pinchley crawls up into the front seat, reaches out Villy's window, and flails at the saucer, wanting to pop it.

He's bunched his fingers into a sharp hook—but the hook is bouncing off the saucer's skin. Meanwhile the saucer's leaning his dome over to one side so that his glaring red eye can see into the car.

Here comes the spot where the road bends to the right, just before the high school. Zoe can tell that the visibility-impaired Villy isn't turning the steering wheel far enough, and then—oh shit—they've veered into the oncoming traffic. A big-ass white SUV heads towards them with its brights flicking, and the uptight Los Perros woman at the wheel isn't slowing down one bit, no, no, she has the right of way, she's entitled. They're bound to collide. Zoe's so stressed that at first she doesn't recognize the woman, but of course it's—

"*Toot your trumpet!*" yells Yampa. Zoe has a visual flash of Yampa's words bright red with halos of jagged yellow lines. "*Honk the horn! Take us in the tunnel!*"

The trumpet is by Zoe's feet. She snatches it up and plays that vibrant Maisie riff with the special stutter-start flutter. Can her saucer pearl possibly become an unny tunnel so big that the whole car can drive through? Even as Zoe thinks this, the pearl in her pocket is swelling and warming, as if it knows what it's supposed to do. Things are happening very, very fast. Zoe plays harder. The responsive pearl wriggles its way out of her pants and hangs in the air.

Zoe plays with all her strength. The pearl swells to the size of a basketball and stops for an instant. Not enough. Her notes a rapid blur, Zoe gestures with the bell of her trumpet. The pearl zooms out of Villy's side window, gets out in front of car—and turns transparent. It's the gate of an unny tunnel. As the car approaches the gate, the transparent sphere of the pearl seems to expand—or maybe the car is shrinking? Either way, the tunnel's gate is the size of a garage door. The unflappable Villy tools right in, veering into the fourth dimension. All of this takes less than a second.

Inside the unny tunnel, their old ballyworld Earth dwindles to a distorted image. The unny tunnel is in some sense perpendicular to the workadaddy world. Zoe can see it through the transparent gate, which now lies behind them. Presumably their mappyworld goal is somewhere ahead. Zoe's still playing her horn. The whole amplified whale and its five passengers—Zoe, Villy, Yampa, Pinchley, and Scud—Zoe's transporting all of them with the lumpy, bumpy bebop of her trumpet's sound.

And—so refined is Zoe's touch—she's able to exclude that disgusting fat leech of a saucer that was on their windshield. The parasitic saucer isn't piggybacking onto them through the tunnel, nope, he's flying along on his preordained trajectory to—

Splat!

Yeah. Peering back at the warped image of her home world, Zoe sees the engorged saucer hurtle into the grill of the white SUV and burst in a spray of—what? It's like water, or mucus, or lymph—clear and glistening, deeply organic, evaporating into wriggly mist. *Smeel.* Raw consciousness, dissipating in the Los Perros night air.

For the fortunate occupants of the purple whale there's no crash, no collision, no contact with the white SUV.

They've made a sharp turn into unspace. They're on their way to an alternate universe. Mappyworld. Riding the burble of Zoe's horn. Stutter-stop, stutter-stop, jump-cut, jump-cut.

"You can quash the crooning now," Yampa tells Zoe. "We're on our way. The tunnel won't turn tiny."

So Zoe sets down her horn and catches her breath. Way up ahead are some lights. To their rear is a last tiny gleam of Los Perros. As for what's around them, here in the middle of the tunnel, well, it's most peculiar.

Like, Zoe is looking out her window—and she sees a purple station wagon that's keeping pace with them, and the driver is Villy, precisely and to a T. When she whips around to see if Villy's still driving her car—yes, he is. But when she looks past Villy and out through *his* window, she sees another image of the purple whale, and in the front seat there's a dark-haired girl who's looking away. And she definitely resembles Zoe. Zoe waves her arm, and that girl waves her arm in sync. Zoe turns her head and looks over at the purple whale on their right, and looks past the Villy to the wheel to see that same girl in the front seat with him—same hair, same clothes—but this other girl has her face turned away too. She's looking out her side window. It's like Villy's car is inside a rolled-up mirror.

"I see an idol ahead!" interrupts Scud.

"Goob-goob," says Pinchley quietly.

Zoe still sees those faint lights in the distance, but closer than that is an archaic figure, staring at them. She resembles a carving from a Mayan ziggurat, a primitive goddess with scrolled hair and curly fingers, a weathered, centuries-old glyph, but she's intensely alive, with an aura of supernal power. The august personage unfurls one of her hands and makes a gesture, pointing onward. Towards mappyworld.

"This way to the party, *amigos*!" goes cloddy Scud. "*Cerveza fria* means cold beer!"

"I hope Goob-goob lets us come back home when we're done," murmurs Villy. His face is serious, his mouth straight, and his tangled blond hair frames his eyes. He's gripping the steering wheel so hard that his knuckles are white.

Gradually the mirror images of the purple whale fade away. The road warps back to normal. The ghostly Mayan goddess is gone. They're cruising into a town. A shape like a shiny basketball tags along after them. It's Zoe's saucer pearl, still transparent. She calls to it with a bleat of her trumpet.

The pearl flies in through the car window and perches on Zoe's lap. She plays a diminuendo passage on her horn. Slowly, smoothly, the pearl shrinks down to the size it was before. Zoe ends the process by playing Maisie's riff backwards—and the saucer pearl is transparent no more. Gates closed. Zoe shoves the pearl into her pocket. It's their path home.

"Made it to mappyworld!" says Yampa.

"What a haul we got," says Pinchley.

"You mean the caraway seeds and chocolate?" says Villy.

"He means you!" says Yampa with an excited giggle. "Ballyworld beauties."

SEVEN

cruising van cott

villy

Villy's glad that his car window is open. It's a summer evening here, with the sky very black. Everyone's staring at Villy's purple whale. He feels proud of himself, sitting up high on his bitchin' wheels, tripping into what looks to be a fully off-the-hook scene. And Zoe—Zoe looks gorgeous with her lively face and her cute dark hair. She's peering this way and that, excited, taking everything in, although at some level she's got to be bummed about having missed her concert.

They're cruising down a city street among weirdly streamlined cars. An animated crowd fills the sidewalks, the scene lit by living street lights—tall, glowing calla lilies, with their blossoms aglow. About half of the figures on the street look human. They wear tight tops and baggy skirts. The clothing materials are fully natural—big flower petals, and leaves, and woven spider silk. When the humans greet each other, they often lift the fronts of their skirts and kick their legs like dancers. The person being greeted makes a polite squeal and acts surprised, like, "Oh ho," or, "Oooh la."

More striking are the many locals who aren't human. Skinny yellow Szep like Yampa and Pinchley. Chirpy futuristic ants three or four feet long. Lively little brown gingerbread men. And—they're passing him right now—a lizard man chewing on a hefty drumstick of—fried chicken? The guy's tail is ungodly thick, and he has muscular T-Rex-style haunches. He holds his tiny little arms up under his chin. Hell, he's not a lizard man—he's a *dinosaur*.

"A mini Thudd," says Yampa, doing tour guide. "Munching a fried momo bird."

One of the Thudd's clawed hands holds his momo drumstick, and the other balances a coconut shell filled with something pink. The Thudd's wife holds a fried momo breast by its crunchy wing. She wears a blue silk dress and sports a big floppy magnolia blossom atop her head. Not exactly a magnolia, it's bigger than that. Their two dinosaur kids trail behind, nipping at each other and nibbling ground meat from cones made of curled-up leaves.

"Not exactly like Earth," says Scud. "I wonder if we might find a copy of Mom here." His short reddish-blond hair glows in the city lights.

"That wouldn't be good," says Villy.

"Maybe not," says Scud. "But I really would like to see her again. Just once more."

"A fresh world here," insists Villy. "We can't keep circling back."

"I guess," says Scud. "System reset. All these aliens. Can you imagine when we tell the people back home about our trip? We'll be, like, world famous. Hollywood starlets will be humping me."

"This is a guy who's never had a date yet," Villy says to Zoe, by way of apologizing about his brother. "A rough peasant, untutored in social couth."

"I should have brought my phone," says Scud. "I could be taking pictures with it. Did anyone bring their phone?"

"I wasn't exactly expecting there to be a signal," says Villy. "Or a way to charge the battery. We'll just look at stuff and remember it."

"What's this place called?" Zoe asks Yampa.

"The title of this town is Van Cott," says Yampa, once again prying the lid off the powdered chocolate can. She and Pinchley go back to dipping and licking their fingers.

"Van Cott is a trading center," says Pinchley. "All sorts of folks."

"And it's me who brought us here," says Zoe. "With my saucer pearl and my trumpet." She seems on edge, but happy.

"You're amazing," Villy tells her with a smile. "The one and only Zoe Snapp. Playing the fourth dimension for your entertainment tonight."

Villy hopes that Zoe and Scud can start getting along. Mainly Scud needs to watch his mouth—he'll especially need to pipe down if Villy and Zoe start heating up. The thought of that causes Villy to raise his hand and caress Zoe's cheek. And right away Scud makes a hooting noise.

Zoe turns and glares at him.

"Boy is she touchy," says Scud, making it worse.

"I'm surprised they have cars here at all," says Villy to change the subject. "If those actually are cars. There's something kinky about them."

"You might say this basin and your Earth's surface are different views of one same thing."

"Think of a puzzle-piece mega mural," says Yampa. "Each piece has two sides. One side is a flat basin like Van Cott. And each piece's other side is a fancy planet like Earth. And the two sides mostly match."

"This side of this piece is like Earth if you peeled it and flattened out the rind and snipped out the dull parts," adds Pinchley. "And there's a gazillion more puzzle-pieces, each with a flat basin on one side matching a planet on the other side."

Mappyworld is a wild mosaic of worlds. A cosmic stamp collection. "But what's in between the basins?" asks Villy. "What's along the edges of the puzzle-pieces?"

"We got a big-ass mountain range round the edge of each damn one of 'em," says Pinchley. "Now, you fellas separate your planets with light-years of twinkle stars and empty space and dead rocks. And mappyworld crunches all that crap down into the mountain ranges between our kick-ass basins of awesome."

"There's two hundred basins between Van Cott and Szep City," says Yampa. "A million miles. Every basin yummy."

"Well, not every basin is exactly *yummy*," allows Pinchley. "Like for instance there's some stinky gas-giant basins. Kingdoms of the poot-blimps. But we'll bypass those."

"And after Szep City, the basins keep on going?" asks Zoe. "Forever and ever? An infinite world?"

"Debatable," says Pinchley. "I myself *do* see mappyworld as an endless boogie. A song that don't repeat."

"And that way I'm the one and only Yampa," says Yampa, swaying her long arms.

"Yeah, baby," goes Pinchley. "Let's dip some more of this powdered chocolate."

"But who makes the ballyworld and the mappyworld sides match?" asks Villy.

"Goob-goob!" says Pinchley. "You saw her just now. The worlds are like her body, son."

"Goob and goob," adds Yampa. She's laughing, and scarfing up the chocolate as fast as she can.

"You're talking about that idol in the tunnel, right?" says Zoe.

"I've rarely seen her so clear," says Pinchley. "She likes you three."

"I popped a picture of her," says Yampa. "I'll appliqué it to Lady Filippa's dress."

Yampa herself is still wearing the schoolgirl-type clothes that Zoe's Mom picked out—the white blouse with the little round collar and the tasteful blue skirt with a zipper in the side. The clothes hang on the alien like rags on a scarecrow. The necklace that Zoe gave Yampa is apparently lost. The powdered chocolate is making the Szep reckless.

"You might say mappyworld is *Goob* with a capital *G*," says Pinchley, holding up two fingers. "And your bally-world is *goob* with a little *g*. Ever the twain shall wheenk. Get it? Got it!" The guy is trashed.

The low beetle-like convertible in front of Villy slows abruptly, and he nearly bumps into it. Around now Villy realizes that the other car really *is* a beetle.

The driver, a piebald alien with an exceedingly long snout, makes a gesture that could be construed as giving the finger. That is, one of his stumpy limbs is holding out a hooked claw. Waving it at Villy.

"So rude," says Zoe, with a frown.

"Back up and ram him hard," says helpful Scud.

"No," warns Yampa. "That bad boy is an anteater. Never aggravate an anteater. They're cold killers. Bounty hunters, paid per ant antenna."

The anteater points his insanely long nose into the air and flicks his dark, snaky tongue. His fur is mostly black, with a big dingy white stripe around his middle like a diaper. His beetle car picks its way into a parking spot. The car walks on six legs. Looking at the traffic with new eyes, Villy flashes that *all* of the cars around him are beetles.

"Check out that snack stand," says Scud before Villy can start talking about his discovery. "Those little gingerbread men are selling crooked rainbow tortilla chips that are sitting in a bowl of—water? But—"

"Those mini men are Flatsies," interrupts Yampa. "They live in the Surf World basin. They link up with living waves. They're—"

"I wasn't done talking!" shouts the rude Scud. "I was trying to tell my brother that those nachos are getting all soggy. Who would ever eat something like that?"

"Those things aren't food at all," says Pinchley, coming back to his senses. "They're live sea critters you can use for telepathy. Teep slugs, we call them. Got special feelers on them. You buy a teep slug and you set it on your bod and then you can read minds. Teep slugs swim in the Flatsies' ocean. They'll settle onto anyone that'll have them. Draining off a little blood and maybe a little smeel. I don't want one. Don't want to know what everyone thinks."

"*Crooked rainbow tortilla chips,*" goes Villy, mocking Scud. "You think this is the midway at the Santa Clara county fair?"

Right then, two gleaming, waist-high ants converge on the Flatsies and snatch a bunch of those colorful teep slugs. All very dramatic, lit by the flowering streetlights beneath the black sky. The two Flatsies begin shouting for help. Seems like they're scared to go after the ants themselves. The gingerbread men have high voices, and they use weird old-time English. Like, "Sound the alarum! Seize yon footpads!"

The anteater from the convertible lumbers over to the Flatsies, extracts a payment in advance, and takes off after the ants, moving surprisingly fast. Scud is excited—he's yelling a real-time, blow-by-blow account, pretending he's a sportscaster—which is something he likes to do. High as they are, Yampa and Pinchley think Scud's routine is funny.

Villy rolls forward, keeping pace with the anteater.

"I can't believe we missed my show," says Zoe now.

"I know," says Villy. "Everything got so—"

"Oh well," says Zoe with a sigh. "My mental state is flip-flopping every thirty seconds. First you and I are running off together, then two aliens show up, then we're nearly killed in a car crash, and now we're in a seething parallel world. I'm like—" Zoe grimaces, widens her eyes, and holds up her hands with fingers widespread—as if in terror. Probably she means this to be ironic and devil-may-care, but that's not what comes across.

"Easy there," says Villy, a little worried about her. "Maybe you should play the solo you rehearsed for the show? It'll chill you out. And I'd love to hear it."

"Yeah," says Zoe, brightening up. "Miles Davis with the Maisie Snapp variations." Her eyes turn warm and alive.

She takes her trumpet from its case and leans out of the car window, blowing far-out choruses at the passersby. A woman smiles, a Thudd grunts, a Szep wriggles, a gingerbread man does a flip.

"This Van Cott is some kind of party town," remarks Pinchley. "We even hear about it in Szep City."

"We should sell some of our cocoa," Yampa tells Pinchley. "Before you eat it all, you mad bad boy."

"You eatin' more than me," says Pinchley. "Anyway it's a big can, and it's still nearly full. We'll just sell part of it."

"Right," says Yampa.

"The night market is right ahead," Pinchley tells Villy. "We'll park under a big funky tree with branches like colored snakes. And with floatin' yellow Freeth heads underneath."

"What about my caraway seeds?" asks Scud. "Do you want to sell them too?"

"We'll save the seeds for Szep City," says Yampa. "A treasure trove. They'll fatten our reward."

"If regular, average stuff from Earth is so valuable, why did you rush back here so fast?" Scud asks the Szep. "Why didn't you seriously load up the car?"

"Because Pinchley is a crafty canny conniver," says Yampa, cheerfully shifting her limp rag of a blouse from one shoulder to the other.

"Point is, this Szep called Flipsydaisy offered us a good reward to pick up Zoe and Villy," Pinchley tells Scud. "Getting you is a bonus, plus the cocoa and the caraways. And a smart guy knows to quit when he's ahead. Also we were about to have a head-on collision with another car."

"Flipsydaisy?" asks Scud.

"Flipsydaisy is like a maid for Lady Filippa, who's in with the great god Goob-goob," says Pinchley, as if any of this made sense.

Zoe takes her trumpet from her lips. "Did anyone notice the woman who was driving that car?" she asks. "Did any of you notice that the woman was my mom?"

"What!" cries Villy.

"Maybe we *didn't* miss hitting Mom's car," says Zoe, her voice getting spacy. "Maybe we rammed into Mom, and we're all dead. Maybe I killed my mother, and we're in hell."

"We did *not* hit your Mom's SUV," Villy tells Zoe in a flat tone. "Will you stop it with the morbid raps? We slid over the other car in hyperspace. I know about hyperspace from videogames."

"Look," says Scud, eager to explain. He holds his two hands out flat, with his palms parallel to each other. He moves the hands back and forth, keeping the palms an inch apart. "Plane, plane," he tells Zoe. And now he balls his hands into fists, and moves the fists around, not quite touching each other. "Hyperplane, hyperplane. See?"

Zoe flips over into giggling and for a while she can't stop.

On the sidewalk, that anteater has finally caught up with one of the ants who ran off with the Flatsies' telepathic slugs. The ant is chromium-shiny and five feet long. She's working her mandibles, and the anteater is striking at her body with his stubby claws. A circle of Flatsie gingerbread men and women stands around them cheering. One of Flatsies has already peeled off some of the stolen teep slugs that the ant parked on the surface of her elegantly curved rear segment.

"You've got to admit it's pretty great here," Villy says to Zoe. "You did good bringing us here."

"Maybe," says Zoe. Villy can see she's regaining her poise. Donning her default attitude: Bitter, yet willing to enjoy life, in a superior, ironic kind of way.

"What's so good about caraway seeds?" Scud is asking Yampa. Scud is always very dogged in his lines of questioning, which can be annoying, and Villy's talked to Scud about it, but Scud's response is always that he's more focused and alert than other people.

"Caraways are a mappyworld medicine," answers Yampa. "An excellent elixir. Szep City will welcome Pinchley and me like a duke and a duchess."

"You mean they'll chop off our heads in the public square?" says Pinchley. "Like they did with Lady Filippa's parents?"

"I mean like good old days duke and duchess," says Yampa. "Before saucers. Before Szep City was sad and cursed."

"How will the Szep treat *us*?" interrupts Zoe, putting some acid into her voice. "Like slaves? Like zoo animals? Like roast beef?"

"They'll mow you down with rayguns," says Pinchley. "Or try to. But we'll be fast and sneaky. We'll run to Lady Filippa. She'll have an Aristo wand. You'll act cool so the wand is willing to team up with you. And then you'll meet Goob-goob. Goob-goob cares about ballyworld Earth, you bet. That's why we saw her in the unny tunnel."

They're passing a lit-up Thudd club, with a dozen pairs of mini dinos dancing to the sound of a living bagpipe. Villy slows his jacked-up purple whale to a crawl, checking this out.

The bagpipe looks like a pig-sized Canada goose but with two necks and two heads. Both beaks are wide open: one is hissing, the other is honking. A mini Thudd rests his massive foot on the bagpipe-goose, kind of pumping it to keep the sound going. He looks serious about his work. Possibly this isn't a nightclub, but a church? One of the Thudd celebrants leans back and balances himself on his tail. His partner beats the ground with her heavy feet, and he paws ecstatically at the night sky.

Following the upward gaze of the breakdancing alien velociraptor, Villy takes a good look at the black sky. Even though it's not cloudy, there's no moon, no sun, no stars. Nothing up there at all. It's like they're in an endless basement. Forever in the dark.

Zoe is noticing this too, and Villy can see that she doesn't like it. He's afraid Zoe might suddenly say they have to go home.

"I want to do this drive," Villy quickly says before Zoe can open her mouth. "This is the best day of my life, Zoe. We kissed. And we've got these funky new Szep alien friends.

And they did an insane custom upgrade on my car. And mappyworld, it's like an old-time cartoon. And—"

"We'll be dead in a week!" cries Zoe, flipping into her panic mode.

"If things go sideways, you get out your saucer pearl and honk your magic horn, and you're home," says Villy, losing patience with her a little bit. "Me, I'm staying."

"But, Villy—"

"A million mile road trip!" cries Villy. "Come on, Zee."

"Maybe I *will* leave you," says Zoe. Her face is stiff and she's not meeting Villy's eyes. "You can do the drive alone. You and your precious little brother."

"If Zoe leaves, I'm going with her," puts in Scud real fast. Villy wants to kill the guy, wants it more than ever before. The thought of Zoe leaving—partly because Scud's here— the thought of Zoe leaving is like a hole in his guts.

"I need you," Villy tells Zoe. Not holding back. "Otherwise—otherwise there's no point. This trip is about *us*, Zoe. Look at me, will you? I'm your Villy. And I even brought condoms."

"Sweetly spoken," croons Yampa. "Listen to your lover, Zoe, and learn. And, early advice, if and when you *do* hop homeward, you'll need to—"

"Don't be bugging her with every little thing," says Pinchley. "Here's the night market! Park your car, Villy. And, Yamp, let's you and me go sell our powdered chocolate."

"And then, hooray, the million mile trip!" says Yampa. "We'll traverse a candy-box of two hundred bosky basins, Zoe. We'll be bugs among bonbons. Each sweetmeat a treat!"

EIGHT

night market

zoe

Zoe likes the market square—it's lit by those tall calla lilies with luminous blooms. Just about all the cars at the market seem to be beetles—spiky and curved, crawling around the edges of the square, putting their heads together, buzzing to each other, awaiting their riders. The beetles gleam in the calla lights. They're pale green and lavender, pink and yellow, orange and red—most of them with six legs, but a few with eight. The only other mechanical car is the one that Villy parks next to, right under that weird tree Pinchley was talking about. The other car is a worn and dusty yellow convertible with huge wheels and quantum shocks, just like the wheels and shocks on Villy's whale. It bears a red P&Y monogram on the hood.

"That fume bomb is ours," says Yampa. "We squired it from Szep City. Can't use a feeble beetle for a hero haul."

"A million miles," says Villy yet again. Like it's his mantra. And now, probably to bug Zoe, he switches to a Dutch accent like the one Pinchley had used. "I'm vant go your city vith my vooman."

Zoe elbows him as if to say, *enough already*. But she's softening. She's done with her most recent freakout, and glad to be out of Los Perros. Sensing an opening, Villy leans over and kisses her on the mouth, very calm and debonair. Their second kiss ever.

Scud whoops. Zoe savors the kiss anyway. After she and Villy break their clinch, she turns around, aims a finger at Scud's face, and raises her thumb like she's cocking a pistol, wanting him to truly get the picture.

"It's not nice to keep telling someone you want to shoot them in the head," whines Scud. "It makes them feel bad."

Zoe isn't moved by this. She's learned that Scud likes to state his feelings as loudly and as frequently as possible. He freeloads off other people's empathy. But that's not happening now.

"Can you clamp your freaking crack?" Villy says to Scud, very quiet and menacing. "Can you let us have a life?"

"Maybe Scud can ride in Yampa's and Pinchley's car," Zoe murmurs to Villy. Batting her eyes at him. Working her wiles.

Meanwhile Yampa and Pinchley are already standing in the parking lot. The three kids swing to the ground on the bungees. Yampa takes one of her clicking mental pictures of them in action.

Another one of those pestering little saucers starts buzzing around Zoe, like a horsefly poised to bite. With a smooth, quick motion, Zoe snatches it out of the air and pops it between thumb and forefinger.

"Good going," says Yampa. "Keep killing those buzz babies so the saucers sense you're a tough target."

Zoe feels proud of herself. "We're like the first astronauts with their lander on the moon. Nobody from Earth's ever been here before."

"Oh yes they have," says Yampa. "Folks like your father, and maid Maisie. They have fab gab with the good saucers."

"My *father*?" goes Zoe. "Maisie?"

Yampa could say more, but she's ready to go. "We'll reunite anon," she tells Zoe. She links her skinny arm with Pinchley's. "Time for our chocolate pep party, yes? Whoopee with friends. I'll parade my Los Perros lounge wear." She does a rusty-hinge giggle.

Pinchley waggles the big tin of powdered chocolate, very cheerful. "It's just as well Scud is holding our caraway seeds. Tonight's fest is gonna get crazy."

Fully comfortable with themselves, the two Szep amble off as if they're on a date, him with his tool belt, her with her floppy white blouse and rolled skirt.

The outdoor night market has sixty or maybe a hundred booths, each booth sheltered by a giant mushroom. Some booths sell food, and others sell—well, it's hard to say. Hovering eggshells, furry spiral tubes, sticks with sparks crackling from their ends, floppy sheets of twitching cloth, pots of ointment, seashells that glow—

"About that big tree leaning over us," Scud says to Zoe. It's like he's trying to start a normal conversation. The sixteen-year-old doesn't deliberately mean to be a pain in the ass all of the time. "Pinchley said the branches are like snakes," Scud continues.

"I like the dark, rich colors," responds Zoe, going for a pleasant tone. "I'm glad they're not moving. It's starting to seem like everything here is alive. Those glowing yellow fruits in the tree, for instance. They're bobbling around."

"Like balloons," says Villy. "I don't think they're even attached to the tree. I guess they just live there."

"They have faces," observes Zoe. She's holding her trumpet in her hand, just in case.

"The balls must be Freeths," says Scud. "Pinchley mentioned them." He waves his long, knobby arms and raises his voice. "Hi, Freeths!"

One of the creatures bobs closer. A jiggly blob, with a pair of eyes that seem painted onto the skin—cartoon black dots inside white circles. The creature has a toothless mouth, and cheeks that are yellow with touches of peach. Zoe notices that the cheeks could equally well be forehead and chin. She thinks of an ambiguous figure drawing that could either be a girl with a necklace or an old woman with a hooked nose.

The blob is about to say something to Zoe, but now a tall stranger appears from behind the tree. He seems to be a Szep. "Which of you has the unny tunnel?" he asks. He's lithe and lively, yellow like Pinchley and Yampa— and wearing an ant-leather tool belt.

"We're just here for a visit," says Villy, not answering the question. He gives Scud a sharp glance, lest his brother blab.

"We're about to take a walk," Zoe tells the Szep. "We're friends with Yampa and Pinchley, by the way." She hopes this might give them some clout.

"Know that," says the Szep dismissively. He stares at Zoe for a few long seconds, swaying his body back and forth, wriggling like a moray eel about to bite. "You're the one who tunneled across," he concludes. "Yeah. You've got a saucer pearl in your pocket. And you know how to open its gate." He stares into Zoe's eyes. "I'm Irav. You're gonna wanna ditch this crew and let me be your handler. Your pals are in for a run of bad luck." Irav chuckles and writhes. "Big trouble."

Zoe feels a pulse of fear. She has half a mind to play an I'm-outta-here riff on her trumpet right now. Assuming that'll open up the unny tunnel inside her saucer pearl—and get her back to ballyworld. But she's very intrigued with this new world she's in—and curious about Maisie and her father being here.

Also Villy kissed her just a minute ago. And he's standing right next to her, all poised and alert. The coolest boy she's ever seen. So handsome. She loves all the shades of brown and blond in his hair. And how low he wears his pants, and the shape of his butt. No, she's not leaving yet.

"Can you lock the car?" Zoe asks Villy.

"We can try," says Villy. He caroms up into the purple whale, rolls up the three working windows, and—with considerable effort—manages to close the driver's side window. Then, before rappelling down, Villy clicks the locks on all four doors. As if the locks are likely to stop the weird aliens.

"I'll be waiting," says the intimidating Irav. Unpleasantly flexible, he worms up onto the hood of the purple whale and lolls there, leaning back against the windshield, with his tool belt turned around to the front.

Zoe, Villy, and Scud hurry off.

"So creepy," says Zoe.

"Pinchley and Yampa will know how to deal," says Villy.

"I think they went this way," says Scud, leading the others towards a food stand beneath a gigundo red-capped mushroom.

Zoe likes the look of the stand. Free samples of pineapples, papayas, and oranges are on the soft white counter, which is the top of a smaller mushroom. The fruits are peeled, cut up, and ready to eat. Reassuringly, the booth is tended by humans—a weathered farmer and his son. They're both wearing loose skirts like the other men in Van Cott. The son watches them closely.

Villy reaches for a piece of pineapple. Always cautious, Zoe slaps at his wrist. But Villy wants to show off. He bites into the sweet-smelling lump of fruit and suddenly bends double and spits the food on the ground. He's moaning and slobbering and huffing air as fast as he can.

"Burns my mouth," he says indistinctly. "Like 'ot 'epper. Like acid."

The old farmer thinks this is funny, but his son hands Villy a cup of what Zoe hopes is water. Villy swishes out his mouth, and tries to spit, but it seems like he can't. A giant blob of slime dangles from his lips. The stuff in the cup has reacted with Villy's saliva.

"Don't worry," says the farmer's son. "This is what you need."

Scud is in paradise, cackling with joy.

"The water holds a dose of local germs," says a rough voice just over Zoe's head. "Probiotic. It's good for you. Tunes your system for the Van Cott grub."

Zoe looks up—it's that yellow ball creature from the tree. Evidently she's trailing them.

"What's your name?" Zoe asks her.

"Call me Meatball," says the cubist blob. Her voice is oiled gravel, with a British accent. "Fit name for a tough cookie. And yes, I'm a Freeth. An elder race, rather down on our luck. I enjoy rollicking, rough-cut laughs. I'd love to be your roadie gal pal."

"You call yourself a girl?" says Zoe.

"Let's pretend. Actually, we reproduce by fission. When we can get a spare saucer pearl."

Meanwhile, with much wheezing and hacking, Villy has cleared the rest of the slime from his mouth.

"Do you *have* to spit on the ground?" says Zoe. "It's crass."

"Try my food again," the farmer boy at the booth tells Villy. He holds out a fresh chunk of pineapple. Villy shakes his head, but the guy insists. "You'll like it now."

Villy's greed takes over and he pops the food in his mouth. Chews carefully, then smiles. "Tastes *good*." He takes a sliver of coconut as well.

"The germs in that water—are they parasitic or symbiotic?" asks Scud the scholar.

"These germs are friendly," says the guy. "The *parasites* are the flying saucers that Groon controls. They're getting worse all the time. A big battle's coming soon. You three just hopped here from ballyworld, right?"

"Yeah," says Scud.

"Perfect," says the young farmer. His allows himself a slight smile. "My name is Meno. I happen to know Zoe's sister Maisie. She's been talking about making this happen. She says you three are the heroes we've been waiting for."

"Heroes? I like that," says Scud. "I'm Scud and this is my brother Villy."

Ostentatiously chewing his food, Villy offers the gamy cup of water to Scud. "Take your vaccination, bro."

"You can stuff your gut proper then," chimes in Meatball the Freeth, doing her knockabout Brit routine. "This feed's on yours truly." She pops a little red pyramid out of her skin. Mappyworld money. The red shape drops into the counter by Meno, the farmer kid.

Zoe has to laugh. Why not enjoy this madness—why not be reckless? As Villy said, it's like being in a cartoon. And you never die in a cartoon—not even if a giant safe lands on your head. The pineapples and oranges are very tempting.

Zoe and Scud look at each other, sharing a rare moment of mutual understanding. They're in. What the hey. They take sips of the probiotic elixir. The reaction hits, they scrape the slime off their tongues and lips, and then it's time to feed.

The three kids chow down on mango, oranges, and baked tofu. Meatball is gumming down the goodies as well, spilling scraps from her loose lips. Zoe munches a yam, using its pointed end to spoon up dollops of fragrant coconut ice cream. Zoe grins at Villy. This is the kind of trip she'd been hoping for.

"Goob-goob be with you," says Meno as they move on. "We're counting on you three to fight in the cosmic beatdown. Coming soon."

Zoe doesn't want to know what Meno means. At least not yet. So many people here, so many aliens, so many competing plans.

The wide-skirted man in the next booth over is selling sticks and plant tendrils that are woven into cubes, with glittering berries on the strands. The berry patterns appear random, but they somehow activate the cubes, and each of these seemingly primitive gizmos is crowned by a glowing ball that holds a lens-like view of some distant landscape. The views are live, like video, and they change in response to the merchant's motions.

Villy is being quiet, but it's not a sulky silence. He has a way of relaxing and being part of a scene. And when Zoe talks, he's always willing to listen.

A young local couple have just finished buying one of the viewers. They're going to use it for navigating to the next basin. The guy wears a banana-leaf skirt and a blue jersey. The woman has an orange jumpsuit with a lavender ruffle on one shoulder. Purchase in hand, they move to the next booth, where a gingerbread man offers colored—pendants? Objects like oversized teardrops, like jellied gouts of liquid, about an inch long. Straining her ears, Zoe gathers that these so-called food mints serve as a long-term nutrition supply. You suck on one for just a little bit, like on a lozenge, and then you're full.

"You can really stock up for an expedition here," says Villy. "It's cool that those two are going it alone. Like we were planning to do."

"I have to admit I'll feel safer with Pinchley and Yampa driving in their car right next to us," says Zoe. "We'd get lost right away."

"Well, yeah," says Villy. "I just mean that you're right about wanting for us two to be a couple."

"Did I say that?" goes Zoe, toying with him. Acting as if maybe Villy's getting a little too possessive.

He comes over and puts his arm around her waist. "We'll put Scud in Yampa and Pinchley's car. And if anyone crowds in with us, we two can always sleep outside at night."

"We'll nestle," says Zoe. "Cuddle." And then, go for it, she gives him a kiss.

In the back of her mind, Zoe wonders why Scud isn't hollering about the kiss. Oh, he's busy eating coconut ice cream. And who knows, maybe he's getting over her and Villy a little bit. Their kiss tapers into a hug, and they just stand there with their arms around each other. Could they be reaching a new plateau where public displays of affection are normal? Like a girlfriend and a boyfriend? Is Zoe totally setting herself up for heartbreak like her mom with her dad? Why does she always overthink things? Trying not to be too obvious about it, she unwinds her arms from Villy and takes a step away.

Right about then Zoe notices a sinister open-air butcher shop nearby. It's run by a pair of gray starfish. Each of the alien echinoderms stands on a pair of its stubby legs—or maybe you'd call them arms. The starfish have saggy, expressionless faces in the centers of their bodies. The joints of meat on their counter bear an unpleasant resemblance to human legs.

So then, just like that, Zoe flips back to wondering what the hell she's doing here. Still no sign of Yampa and Pinchley. They'll be partying with their chocolate powder for a while. Zoe turns in a full circle, peering along the mazy paths of the marketplace, lit by the booths' multi-colored calla-plant lights. She sees a man swathing himself in wiggly cloth. An ant purchasing an urn of honey. Two mini Thudds are carrying a big beetle larva with glistening eyes and a pair of mandibles. They'll either roast it or grow it into a car. Off in the parking lot, Villy's purple whale is still visible beneath the Freeth tree, with that same oily Szep lounging on the car's hood. Alert to Zoe's gaze, the Szep makes a come-hither gesture. Ugh.

"Hate that cheeseball," says Villy, right in tune with Zoe's thoughts.

Meatball the Freeth is hovering above them. "Do you know anything about Irav?" Zoe asks her, surreptitiously pointing at the distant Szep.

"Well, I heard him talking to you," says Meatball. "I rather expect he's a yob who robs whomever he can. I don't mingle with Szep, generally. It could be that Irav is a cat's-paw for the less savory class of saucers."

"How do you mean?" says Zoe.

"Slavers. Irav would be wanting to capture you and sell you at Saucer Hall."

"What would the saucers want me for?" presses Zoe. She has a general idea from what Pinchley and Yampa have said. But she wants more detail.

"Are you as green as you are cabbage-looking?" says Meatball.

"What the hell does that mean?" snaps Zoe.

"Means I hope you're not as naïve as you pretend to be," says Meatball. "The saucers are smeel stealers. Vampires.

They'd drain you dry, sassy Zee. Empty you to a husk. And send you home to Mom as a saucer agent."

"Where is this Saucer Hall?" asks Zoe, very uneasy by now.

"Centrally located in bustling Van Cott. Like an elite city club, isn't it? You'll find good saucers and bad saucers there. The bad saucers nip over from New Eden and gather in Saucer Hall with an eye to feasting upon the unspeakably toothsome smeel of the Van Cott locals and—even better—the smeel of lost little lambs from ballyworld Earth."

"Me no like," says Scud in a gremlin voice. He turns to Zoe. "Do you actually have a gun? Please say yes."

"No gun," says Zoe absently. She's thinking about the place name that Meatball just mentioned—*New Eden*. Back in Los Perros, her father founded a saucer-nut club called *the New Eden Space Friends*. Crazy Dad was talking about something real. How very—unexpected. "Can you tell me more about New Eden?" Zoe asks Meatball.

Meatball gets all science class on her ass. "Unless I'm mistaken, the New Eden basin matches up with a ballyworld planet near Proxima Centauri where—"

"Oh spare me the windblown bullshit," interrupts Villy. "Do any of the booths in this market sell weapons?"

"Right enough, they do," says Meatball. "Not that you've any need for guns—if you've got a Freeth like me on your side. I can zap people. And I'm a shapeshifter. I'm formidable."

"You don't look tough to me," the obnox Scud tells Meatball. "You're a lumpy yellow balloon. Full of hot air."

As if wanting to demonstrate her shapeshifting skill, Meatball molds herself into a very convincing drag-on-head. She snarls so hard at Scud that he takes an abrupt step backward, trips over his own feet, and falls on his ass.

"Scud," says Villy. "Do you have to be so—" He looks up at the Freeth. "Don't be mad at my brother, Meatball."

"A spirited lad," says Meatball, turning all yellow and round, and smiling like a waiter.

"I want a gun so I can shoot Irav," says Scud, bouncing back to his feet. "Making scary faces isn't always gonna be enough, Meatball the blob."

"Front me a caraway seed, and I'll fetch you an atom-izer right enough," Meatball tells him. "An atomizer will make you a mighty man, eh?"

"How do you know I have caraway seeds?" asks Scud.

"Heard your Szep pals gabbing. Me lurking about, don't you know. All ears."

"Let's back up a minute," interrupts Zoe. "You're offer-ing Scud an *atomizer*? That's for spraying perfume."

"Do I mean vaporizer?" says Meatball, a little flustered. "Dematerializer? Death ray! I'm not fully on board with your patois." Meatball has drifted so close to Scud that she's touching him. "Give me that caraway seed now," she purrs. "And then I'll put the quietus on the foul Irav. You'll be pleased as punch with me in your service. Con-trariwise, I'm not one to be crossed."

Zoe picks up an undertone of threat in Meatball's last sentence. She glances at Villy, knowing he can be protec-tive of his younger brother. And now, sure enough, with no warning at all, Villy grabs hold of Meatball, digging his hands into her flesh.

"Oh, the big bad Freeth tingles!" he says, seeming to think he has the Freeth at his mercy. "She vibrates against my hands. Scary, scary."

"You'd do well to unhand me," says Meatball, her tone brittle and cold.

"What's your real game?" Villy demands, squeezing the Freeth so tightly that she takes on an hourglass shape. "Are you Irav's partner? He threatens us, and you offer to help? It's a protection racket, right? You think can push us around?"

The Freeth's expression grows dark and strange. Little sparks race along the wrinkles in her skin. She forms one of her bulges into a sharp cone and—

"Look out!" calls Zoe—too late. Meatball extends the cone, and her body clenches in a spasm. A flash of light, a furious buzz, a tingle of ozone.

Villy manages the start of a scream—then drops heavily to the ground, silent, his muscles slack. He lies utterly still, blank eyes clouded, limbs askew.

"You see?" growls Meatball, rising higher in the air. Her flat eyes are unreadable. "You see what a Freeth can do?" She turns her attention to Scud. "Now, little lad, are you giving me that seed?"

Clumsy with fear, Scud takes off running down an aisle between the booths, knocking stuff over. Quickly he rounds a corner and disappears from view.

Zoe is numb with shock, all alone here with the lifeless Villy at her feet. He's dead? And frikkin Scud is gone.

She needs to bail. She sets her saucer pearl on the ground before her and raises her trumpet to her lips. She's moving very quickly, but she's so wired that from her point of view it feels like she's slow.

The first note seems to drool out, with its sound vibrations like yawning gaps. Zoe pushes to play faster. It's like she's running in sand. Gradually her second note issues forth. Now comes the third. And to the locals listening, Zoe's riff is coming out as a frenzied squawk.

Whatevski. The saucer pearl's gate swells to the size of a plum, ready for action, hovering at waist level. And it's turned transparent—meaning the gate is open. Zoe walks towards it, blatting her horn. The closer she gets, the bigger the gate seems.

NINE

saucer hall

scud

Scud hurries past the garish booths, randomly making turns, keeping his mind blank, not letting himself think about Villy. He finds himself in a more exotic part of the night market. The calla lights are red and orange here, the fungal booths are aglow. An alluring girl cavorts beside a hut-sized puffball with an arched door and lavender light within. She moves in the slow figures of a snake dance, her outstretched arms like anacondas. She wears flat live creatures as clothes—they creep across her skin like slugs or live tattoos. Her makeup is phosphorescent; her tongue is patterned with polka dots. And on her brow she wears a pink Flatsie teep slug.

Scud is thunderstruck. He can't stop looking at her and wondering what she's like. Underneath all the makeup, she might not be much older than him. Like maybe seventeen. Weird, though, that she's working as a dancer at the night market. He's staring so hard at her that she comes to a full stop.

"Hello?" she says. "I'm a person. You got a name?"

"I'm Scud. I'm—I'm from Earth in ballyworld? We came here through unspace."

"Very fresh. Meno teeped me a message about you. There's this thing about the parasite saucers, see. A cosmic beatdown coming soon. If you ballyworld humans can work with us it'll be so—" The girl breaks off and laughs. "Info overload! I'm Eekra. Come into my floopsy den. I like your spiky hair." She lets out a throaty, musical laugh and makes a sweeping gesture, as if to usher Scud into her hut.

"I—I wish I could say yes," says Scud. His heart is going a mile a minute and his throat is parched. "But right now, I mean we just got here, and I'm—"

"Paranoid? Afraid of girls? A virgin? Come on, Scud. I might be the most important person you meet tonight. Nothing happens by accident in the cosmic script."

"Can—can I kiss you?" The words leap unbidden from Scud's lips.

"I don't think so," says Eekra, striking a pose, one hand on her hip. "Not out here."

Scud backs away, his face frozen in a stiff, embarrassed smile. "Sorry. I gotta go, Eekra."

"Maybe another time."

Hardly seeing where he's going and hating himself for being so shy, Scud stumbles further into the market. The next thing that catches his attention is a booth that sells cactus plants. Two teenage mappyworld boys are mashing lobes of the cactuses in a bowl and rubbing the cactus slime on each other's bare chests. The air tingles with the scent of the pulp—like ink and incense. The skinny woman running this booth warbles mazy Egyptian tunes on a crooked little horn.

As Scud turns away, still thinking about Eckra, a gingerbread man plucks at his sleeve. The little Flatsie wants to sell him one of those teep slugs; he's holding it in his hand. The slug is lemon yellow with a red stripe around its edge, and a bunch of green feelers on its back. The Flatsie has a teep slug of his own on the middle of his chest, a purple one.

"I seek a boon, young sir," says the gingerbread man. He bows. "And in return, I, the humble Filkar, offer this intrepid slug in return. I am honored to address a ballyworld trader of your ilk." Scud waves him off, but the Flatsie is not going to give up that easily. A group of the yellow slug's brethren lounge in a bowl of water at the booth nearby. The booth is run by a Flatsie woman, Filkar's partner. The two of them begin chorusing that Scud should strike a deal for the excellent yellow slug with the red stripe around its edge.

Egged on by the Flatsies, the yellow teep slug flutters out of Filkar's hand and undulates through the air towards Scud's face. It keeps itself airborne with cunning twitches of its edges, banking and gliding against all-but-imperceptible currents of the air. It's no bigger than a small leaf, and it carries a scent of the sea.

All of a sudden the slug lands on Scud's cheek and stings him. Hard. As if taking a sample of his flesh. And then it goes back to fluttering around Scud's head, making a high, thin sound, like an ultrasonic song. Scud can feel a bump on his face, as if he's been bitten by a spider. At this point he snaps—he swats the nimble slug to the ground and stomps it, or tries to, but it's too fast and slimy. It rises above him once again and continues its aethereal piping. The gingerbread woman is railing at Scud, but she isn't going to do anything more. Scud has the scary aura of someone who's running amok. He's ashamed to be acting this way near Eekra's hut.

Looking for a way out, he pushes his way between the cactus merchant and the Flatsies' booth—and finds himself in a field bordering the market. The sky remains completely, totally, utterly black—but even so, it's not fully dark in the field because the grass gives off a bit of a glow. Also, there's some light from the marketplace, and from the buildings lying beyond the meadow.

A few mappyworld locals are meandering around—chatting, doing deals, possibly connecting for sex. High in the air, two Freeth drift past. They don't seem interested in Scud, not that it's easy to read a Freeth's intent.

Scud's on his own in the soft night. The scene has a medieval feel. He likes it. Everything is alive, nothing's a machine, and the air is threaded with unfamiliar scents. He wouldn't mind staying here for quite a while—if he could. But mappyworld seems to be a dangerous place.

By way of confirming that, here comes a buzzing mini saucer the size of a bug. It lands on Scud's forearm, and with no preliminaries at all it bites him, just like the teep slug had done. *Damn*! Scud manages to swat the thing hard enough to pop its nasty little body.

Meanwhile, what about the overwhelming issue that Scud's been blocking out? Meatball may have murdered his brother. Villy may be lying dead on the ground right now. Scud was a rat to run off. Rats are the ones who survive. They squeal and scurry for the nearest hole. It makes sense to be a rat. But—oh, poor Villy.

Scud finds a dim spot beside a tree, where he leans against the trunk and easefully pees. His body still works. Even though he ate those alien germs and all that fruit—and got bitten by that flying yellow teep slug and by the mini saucer. Maybe he'll live through this. And maybe Villy's okay—maybe Villy's sitting up and rubbing his face and cursing, the way he always does in the morning. What tales Scud and Villy can tell when they get home.

Assuming they do get home. Assuming Zoe hasn't totally bailed on them. Right when Scud ran off, it looked like she was about to raise her trumpet. Scud was in too much of a squealing-rat panic to wait and see.

Maybe he'll go back and look for Zoe and Villy. In a minute. Give the crisis some time to play itself out. Wait for Yampa and Pinchley to get back into the mix too. If everyone's still here and alive, and they're still going on the road trip—well, then they'll wait for Scud, right? So what's the rush?

Looking out past the tree he's leaning on, Scud sees a decent-size flying saucer cruise by. This one is gold with a pale purple rim. It's fleshy and alert, like a round stingray, six or seven feet in diameter. There goes another and another, each of them a different color. Like tropical birds heading for their roost. Each of them seems to have a red eye or a black eye—not something often mentioned by human saucer fanciers. And their bodies' diversity of form is also something that's not well known.

Yes, many have the classic sombrero shape, but he also sees one like a lime-green pyramid, and one like a flying snake, and yet another is shaped like a short flight of stairs. "Saucer" is a catch-all category, it seems, with varying contents. Scud is excited and pleased to be observing all this.

The saucers' roost is a big old building across the field from the market. An impressive, even pompous, structure—like the US Supreme Court building, or the Parthenon, with fluted columns and a triangular pediment on top. The triangle is ornamented with glyphs that glow in gentle pastels—yellow, peach, pale red. At first Scud thinks the symbols might be Arabic script or Korean ideograms or Egyptian hieroglyphs—but, naw, they're even stranger than that.

So large is the building that its looming pair of bronze doors are a hundred and twenty feet tall. They gape wide open, spilling a soft blue glow that highlights the surfaces of the saucers gliding in and out of the hall. Scud hears a low, rhythmic sound from within. Music.

Surely this is the Saucer Hall that Meatball mentioned. With saucerian inscriptions on the pediment. So awesome. Scud longs to go inside—even if a goodly proportion of the saucers are vampiric, soul-sucking leeches. Scud is such a geek that he finds Saucer Hall less intimidating than Eekra's hut in the marketplace. His main question about Saucer Hall is simple: How is he going to sneak in?

Keying right into Scud's thoughts, the gingerbread man from the marketplace draws near. Filkar. He's wearing his purple teep slug on his chest, and he's still carrying that yellow one with the red stripe and the green tuft of antennae. Rather than walking erect, the Flatsie slides across the ground, his soft body undulating across the meadow's lumps.

"The boon I beg is but one caraway seed," chirps Filkar. The Flatsie comes to a halt upon the damp spot at Scud's feet. "In return I'll plant this teep slug upon you. Having tasted you, the slug is in readiness. You'll peer into others' minds, yes. *And* you'll learn to craft a cloud of unknowing. No saucer will ken your presence."

Another shoal of colorful, multiform saucers glides by overhead. Scud *has* to see their lair. Filkar's teep slug is kind of sick, but it's sick in a *good* way. Like skateboard art. But—

"What about my brother?" Scud has to ask. "Shouldn't I go back to help him?"

"Via my teep slug, I wit your brother was laid low by a Freeth." says Filkar. "And you took a coward's way out. Here's solace: oft a Freeth seeks only to stun, and not to slay. Let us therefore suppose that Villy is hale. How do you regain face? Return bearing the benison of a teep slug."

Scud goes for it. The slug is an add-on. A power-up. He extracts the dusty spice jar from his jeans and drops a caraway seed onto flat Filkar. The gingerbread man bucks and shudders, absorbing the seed's fragrant biochemical essence and, very clearly, feeling the better for it.

"Thankee, Lord Scud." Beaming with good will, the Flatsie peels himself up from the ground. "And your fine new sensor shall be implanted—where?"

"Uh, here?" says Scud, tapping his left wrist. "Like a watch. And does it have to be so big?"

"Teep slugs seek ever to please their hosts," says Filkar. "Think only of what you want." Filkar utters a command in a burbly, low-pitched tongue. In harmony with Scud's wishes, the teep slug reshapes itself into an elegant hemisphere, little more than an inch across. Scud sets the thing on his wrist.

The teep slug writhes delicate tendrils into Scud's flesh, connecting to his veins and nerves. The boy feels a joyous singing in his veins, a delicate flutter in his forearm. His surroundings take on an altered look. The people and aliens in the dark field, the saucers and the Freeth overhead—each of them wears a halo of aethereal light, and each halo has a unique individual hue. They're visible to Scud even when they're behind him.

The situation reminds him of a time when his science teacher made him to pretend to be blind for two days, walking about with his eyes covered. Scud learned he could build up a full mental image of the world even when he couldn't see. He patched his world-model together from the things he touched, from his memories, and from the rich cues to be found in ambient sounds.

Now, with his teep slug working for him, Scud forms a unified holistic sense of the beings around him in the mappyworld night. He knows where they are, and he knows what they're thinking.

"Sixth sense," says Filkar's voice inside Scud's head. "Omnividence."

"I like," says Scud without moving his lips. He doesn't even think the words. It's more like he broadcasts the feeling. *This is good.* He examines the minds around him.

The Flatsie is fifteen thousand miles from his homeland, which lies three basins away. Filkar and his partner—in fact she's his wife—have come to Van Cott to make deals.

Nearby, two dog-sized ants are conversing via scents and by taps of their antennae. Their thoughts have a geometric quality—like colored wooden blocks in a mound. The blocks stand for things like sugar, sex, larvae, and smeel. Apparently, ants like smeel as much as the saucers do. But they're not parasitic about it. Instead they gather those scraps of smeel that humans have freely cast aside—forgotten thoughts, abandoned plans, discarded dreams. Once they're formulated, ideas and emotions have a wispy independent existence of their own. And the ants—who have teep powers of their own—the ants scavenge for psychic scraps like for crumbs beneath a dining table.

A mappyworld boy and girl are lying on the ground a few hundred feet away, fully dressed, arms around each other in an embrace. They're cooing and kissing and giggling. Scud tastes the contents of their minds. Glowing lava, ferns in the wind, inner song. This is the first time these two have gone off together. They're happy and proud.

A mini Thudd is in a ditch, eating the corpse of a dog, crunching the dead animal's skull and bones, deeply satisfied by his meal. Scud can see the Thudd's recent memories as well. It was just a few minutes ago that the Thudd found the dog, drawn by the odor of its decomposition.

Tentatively Scud extends his awareness to one of the passing saucers. The saucers seem to have gender, and this one's a girl. Her name is Nunu. She's small, maybe four feet across, with the traditional saucerian shape. She has a green dome with a floppy yellow rim. There's a thickened spot in her rim.

Nunu's mind is like a concentric nest of glowing shells, each shell a different shade, each shell softly playing a musical line in harmony with the others. Her dome bears her single cartoony eye—a personable black dot set in a white oval. She has teep. Telepathy seems not to be unusual over here. Nunu senses Scud, and her eye rolls downward, assessing his scrutiny.

Scud withdraws his mental probe and crouches in the cover of the tree. He's playing way out of his league. Really, he should be using his new teep to check up on brother Villy—instead of obsessing about saucers. But when Scud turns his focus towards the night market, he finds that his teep slug's powers reach no further than Eekra's hut. That beguiling mappyworld denizen is still trolling for an audience—dancing, sculpting shapes in the air, milling her hands around each other like a cheerleader.

Scud can't stop wondering what exactly would happen if he went into Eekra's hut with her. She's not a really a close match for his fevered, fantastical notions of hookers. But maybe? Or maybe she just dances for a while and you give her a tip? Or maybe she clonks you on the head and takes all your money? Or she sells you to the saucers? Well, maybe not *that*. She'd talked about fighting the saucers. Oh, and what about Villy?

Filkar, who's still nearby, monitoring Scud's thoughts, repeats his opinion that Villy will recover.

"Fine," says Scud, choosing to believe the Flatsie. "So how do I get into Saucer Hall?"

"Hark," says the gingerbread man. In the blink of an eye, he vanishes.

Using his real eyes and his teep slug, Scud studies his surroundings. No sign of Filkar, who should be right here. No sign of the gingerbread man's body, and no sign of his mind. But wait. Upon closer examination Scud sees that, yes, there *is* something. A dim scribble where the Flatsie had been. Reaching out with his hands, Scud can feel Filkar's body, a flat sheet of flesh.

"I wear the cloud of unknowing," says the invisible Filkar, still able to send his teep into Scud's head. The Flatsie flips back into visibility, and he shows Scud how to cover himself with the cloud. It's like finger painting. You look at yourself from the outside—and then you smear your image around.

Scud does that and looks down at his hand—and, yes, it's all but invisible, not only to his teep slug, but to his real eyes as well.

"This is impossible," he says. He feels uneasy. "Is it safe?"

"Your flesh and fire are shadows of your soul," says Filkar, not quite addressing the point. "Life's teeming hordes are images in the air."

"I'm a pattern in the cosmic smeel?" suggests Scud.

"Thou sayest it, my liege. Drawing on the supernal power of your teep slug, you addled your warp and woof—and in this wise you've conjured a cloud of unknowing. 'Twill engulf you and your raiment until you relax your hold."

"You still haven't told me if it's safe," says Scud. "I mean—I look like a mound of black velvet spaghetti."

"Waver not, milord. Go where your heart listeth." Filkar gestures towards Saucer Hall. "And, may I say it, a supererogatory gift of a second caraway seed would be well received."

"When I get back," says Scud. "Maybe."

Wearing his cloud and feeling tiny, he climbs the steps of Saucer Hall, then darts through the vast entryway. He's like an insect invading someone's home. An invisible ant. The saucers sail past overhead, some big and some small, some faceted and some smooth, some like disks and some like pretzels, most of them in fancy colors, and each of them with a single bright, observant eye. As before, some of the eyes have red pupils, but others have black. A whole menagerie.

Scud gets the feeling that the saucers with the red eyes are the bad ones. He likes the black-eyed ones who have flexible rims that undulate like hula skirts. In some odd way, Scud finds them sexy. Some have their mouths on the edge of their rims, instead of on their underside, and those edge mouths are sexy too.

In short, the hall teems with exotic and alluring saucerian life—dozens or even hundreds of distinct forms. But if Meatball is to be believed, a goodly number of them are parasitic leeches—the red-eyed ones.

The music echoes and throbs. Perhaps it sounds different to each listener, but to Scud it's a funky, polyrhythmic gospel song with a throaty voice chorusing a single phrase over and over.

"I'll take you there. I'll take you there. I'll take you there."

Entranced by the chant, Scud visualizes the place the voice is singing of—a land of play and sex and power. Quite suddenly he forms the notion that the keeper of that heavenly land lies within an orb of clear white light that hovers at the far end of Saucer Hall. He sees a dark image within the orb, a sacred icon perhaps, a figure with odd projections near its head. Scud makes his way towards the glowing orb, utterly entranced. In his rapture he drops his cloud of unknowing—*oh shit*! He's standing there, fully visible.

"Ssst!"

It's that same saucer he noticed before. The one with the green dome and yellow rim and a lively cartoon eye with a dark pupil. Her name was Nunu? She homes in on him and hovers beside his head. He could wrap his arms around her if he wanted to. She's speaking to him with a pair of red lips set into her wobbly, lumpy rim.

"Careful, or bad ones drink your smeel," whispers Nunu. She speaks in a strange way, as if words were ideograms or postcards—with no need of articles, tenses, or inflections. "You go invisible some more, quick. Ride my back, no shy. I carry you off. I am long time want love a human boy."

Nunu has a set of long dark eyelashes around her single eye. Scud can't help but trust her. Nunu is here to save him, yes. With a quick motion of his mind, he restores his cloud of unknowing.

Now Nunu floats down low and Scud flops onto her, like a man mounting a child's swim raft. Nunu vibrates with something like a giggle. As they glide out of Saucer Hall, Scud feels a pang of sorrow to be leaving the music behind. And that half-seen icon within the glowing white ball—who or what was it?

Moments later they're with Filkar and his wife beside the tree. Scud drops his cloud of unknowing, then slides off Nunu to stand on his own two feet. He scatters a generous pinch of caraway seeds onto Nunu, the Flatsie, and his wife. He's like a wildly tipping tourist on a binge. The aliens are glad.

"You can know where your friends?" asks Nunu. "*I take you there*." Perhaps a hint of irony in her use of this phrase. She's a perky one. Scud's fairly sure she's reading his mind. That means she knows Scud is insanely wondering if there's any way that Nunu might become his girlfriend. She has such a pleasant voice. And his chances with real girls are so very slim. And she's not flinching away.

"I'll walk from here," he says, not wanting to seem weak. "But I'll be glad if you follow."

"Okay," says Nunu. "I am curious you. Sexy boy. Bye bye, Filkar."

"Fare thee well," says Filkar. "Be prudent, Scud."

This world is a maze. Scud will be glad to rejoin his team. With a teep slug to brag about, and with Nunu the saucer in tow!

And Scud is noticing an extra bonus: whenever one of those obnoxious, horsefly-like mini saucers tries to bite him, Nunu zaps it with a quick spark. It's good to have a saucer girlfriend.

TEN

three zoes

zoe

Let's backtrack and see what happened to Zoe.

The way it went down was that Meatball zapped Villy, Villy collapsed, Scud took off running, and Zoe tootled her magic tune. Her saucer pearl turned into an unny tunnel gate. She walked through it. And then—

Trumpet in hand, Zoe stands on Los Perros Boulevard with her saucer pearl gate behind her. She's tunneled back to the same place and time on Earth as when she left—except now she isn't inside the purple whale. She's on a spot where the whale *was*. The car and its occupants are inside their own unny tunnel, inside an older version of the saucer pearl, and they're traveling from Earth to mappyworld. Zoe can see into that old tunnel through its own transparent gate. Seeing through the old pearl's gate is like looking at a scene inside a crystal ball.

And yep, Zoe can see her earlier self in the front seat of the whale—that is, she sees the back of that person's head—a girl frantically playing her horn. The whale dwindles deeper towards the center of the old gate and out of sight, and then the old pearl goes opaque and disappears, leaving our later Zoe by herself on the asphalt street, there in the Los Perros spring night, with her current version of the saucer pearl still floating behind her. Looking up in the sky, she sees clouds, stars, and the moon. A sky like it's supposed to be.

All this goes by in a flash, but now there's the pressing matter of a careening white SUV. The SUV's headlights blaze, its tires squeal, its horn blares. It's bearing down on our Zoe with a gleaming splotch of spilled smeel on its hood, and the smeel's dissolving into smoke. And yep, that's Mom's face behind the windshield, Mom staring aghast at her problem daughter, version two—that is, the slightly more experienced Zoe Snapp who's just now materialized in the street holding her trumpet.

Zoe should dart off to the side of the road—but she's having a deer-frozen-in-the-headlights moment, even though her mind is racing. She shouldn't have bailed on Villy. He might even be alive. She shouldn't be here at all. Never mind running away from Mom in her SUV—instead she'll tunnel right back to mappyworld.

So okay, now where the heck is the—ah, yes. Her current saucer pearl is hanging in the air just behind her, and it's still a transparent gate, but it's getting small. Still feeling like the world is in slow motion, Zoe raises her horn like a gone goofball jazz cat coming out of a nod. Time for her chorus. She faces her pearl, hits her first note, and yeah baby, the funky pearl swells and gleams—it's a gate she can fit into again. Still playing, Zoe steps into the gate and she's safe in the unny tunnel. Looking back, she sees a warped panorama of Los Perros and the skidding SUV.

Zoe pauses to fully assess the situation. Her old self, Zoe #1, is in a different unny tunnel with the old version of the whale. Zoe herself is Zoe #2, and she's in her own unny tunnel, heading for mappyworld again. Fine.

But wait. To make things even more gnarly and effed up, a Zoe #3 enters the Los Perros panorama with her *own* trumpet in hand. It's an extra Zoe, with a guy right behind her. They're popping out of a *third* unny tunnel gate, their legs a blur. Running flat-out as fast as they can. They speed across the street in time to dodge the killer SUV. Evidently Zoe #3 is a future Zoe who thought ahead when she tunneled home.

Who's the boy with Zoe #3? Believe it or not, our current Zoe—that is, Zoe #2—is so boggled by the multilevel madness that she doesn't make a visual ID of the boy. He's sprinting fast, it's dark, and Zoe #2 is putting most of her energy into the bluesy horn solo that's keeping her unny tunnel open for her.

And now Zoe #2 is like: *Eff this. I'm outta here. Sayonara, SUV.*

She returns to the tunnel and goes back to mappyworld. On the way she gets another glimpse of that Mayan-type Goob-goob, the goddess of mappyworld. This time Goob-goob looks like a vine-covered pyramid as much as she looks like a woman. Seedy, imposing, beyond the mundane—and, for whatever reason, keenly interested in Zoe's activities.

Then Zoe's back in mappyworld, back to the same place and time in the night market. She lowers her horn. Her tunnel's gate collapses back down to a pearl. Zoe plays the lock-the-gate riff and pockets the now opalescent pearl.

Zonked Villy is still on the ground with that frikkin Freeth balloon overhead. Meanwhile, the Freeth is bitching at Zoe. Maybe she didn't even notice that Zoe just now flashed out of their shared reality for a sliver of second.

"Not my fault!" Meatball is saying, her tone aggrieved and self-justifying. Like she was right to knock Villy flat. "He borrowed trouble."

"Stupid stinky gas bag," hollers Zoe. She kneels beside Villy, ready to do some mouth-to-mouth resuscitation. She hadn't thought of that before. Villy's dear, noble face so pale. Zoe takes a deep breath and presses her mouth to his.

"Huh?" mumbles Villy at the first touch of Zoe's lips. He, groans, sits up, rubs his face.

"Oh, Villy," says Zoe, hugging him. "My lean flame. Poor darling."

"What happened?"

"The balloon gave you a shock," Zoe tells him. "Like a giant electric spark. She grew a special bump for doing it."

"Dark energy," says Meatball, drifting closer. "Emanating from a zapper node. Villy was brutalizing me. I take care of myself—goes without saying. *And* I take care of my friends."

"You're no friend to us," says Zoe. "You just want a caraway seed. Well, guess what, fatso, Scud ran off with them."

"Scud's gone?" says Villy, trying to sort things out.

"We both thought you were dead," says Zoe. "Your brother ran away. And I was trying to revive you."

"You hopped," says Meatball. "Can't fool me. I twigged. For a split second you were gone."

"Bullshit," goes Zoe.

"Dead sly, aren't you?" says Meatball. "I respect that."

"I strive to surprise," says Zoe.

"Hopped where?" asks Villy. "Sly about what?"

"Never mind. I'll explain later." Zoe glances up at the Freeth. "Happy now?"

"I'm happy we've had a gloves-off go-round," says Meatball. "With more to come, I shouldn't wonder. Never mind the caraway seeds. I'm chuffed to join your travel party. All the way to Szep City. And why stop there? Mayhap I'll roll onward—to soddy, ancestral Freeth Farm."

"Maybe this Freeth is okay," says woozy Villy, once again rallying at the thought of the Szep City run. He gets to his feet. "I'll admit I was squeezing you awfully hard, Meatball. I wasn't thinking of you as being like a person with feelings. But, yeah, it's better if we're friends. We can use help." He holds up his hand, like for a high five, and Meatball slaps a rubbery bit of her body against it.

Zoe pats Meatball and hugs Villy, and then the fully recovered Villy starts dancing around and singing, kicking his legs and shaking out his arms, glad to be alive. Zoe bops along, dancing with her man. She tilts up her horn and toots a few happy notes.

It's crazy in mappyworld, but it's fun.

But there's one new thing troubling Zoe. Was that Villy with Zoe #3—or was it someone else?

ELEVEN

leaving town

Villy's a little worried about Scud, but not that worried. Hey, Scud left Villy for dead, okay? Let the guy blunder his way back to them on his own. The ceaseless flow of strange people and alien creatures is getting to Villy. And, even though he's dancing, he's fairly wiped from that zap.

"Want to go back and wait in the car?" Zoe asks him.

"Yeah. Sorry to be a lightweight."

"You're the baddest of them all," says Zoe. "Don't worry. If you can stand just a *few* more minutes, I have this atavistic desire to do a big shopping for our trip."

"I'll treat," says Meatball, who's listening in. "I'm gravid with money, dearies. Like a fish full of roe."

"Let's buy the same stuff that we saw the other couple buy," suggests Villy.

"Yeah," agrees Zoe. "One of those long-lasting food mints."

"You'll want five," advises Meatball. "Three for you humans, one for the two Szep to share, and one for me. They come in seven fantabulous flavors. Raw sucrose, kippered herring, crankcase oil, sea cucumber, roast beet, viggy vloor, and tom turkey."

"Vloor and turkey," says Zoe.

"I'd advise against the vloor," says Meatball. "Vloor—well—viggy vloor eats *you*, in a certain sense. And that's fine for a Freeth, but for a wound-up little dolly like you . . ."

"Okay, fine, let's just get sucrose and two tom turkeys," says Villy, but Zoe glares at him. She's against sugar. "Roast beet instead of sucrose," says Villy. "And I want one of those vision balls that sits on a rickety cube made of sticks and vines and berries."

"A waste of time," says Meatball. "You've got me—and a Freeth always knows her whereabouts."

Although the Freeth won't buy a vision ball, she's by no means stingy. She sheds a series of red pyramids as they move from counter to counter. They get silky blankets, fresh fruit, and a potted daffodil that's a lamp. Their arms are full, and even Meatball is carrying a few things. They make their way back to the cars.

"Presents for me?" says Irav the thieving Szep, sliding down off the high hood of the purple whale.

"You'll be leaving now," says Meatball, setting down a blanket and a bunch of bananas. Her features take on a foreboding look. "Ta-ta."

"I saw them first," says Irav, drawing a conical snail from his tool belt. The shell is intricately patterned with chevrons. Two gemlike eyes, mounted on flexible stalks, project from the shell's pointed end. There's a tubular little snout as well.

"A whaler snail!" says Meatball. "Not much good

against *me*, Irav. *En garde!*" The Freeth emits a fierce yelp. Her war cry. Energy shimmers across her surface as she forms a zapper cone and sends a spark as thick as an arm. The bolt plunges into Irav's chest—and sputters in place for at least thirty seconds.

Villy feels a sympathetic twitch. That's got to hurt. But Irav takes the attack in stride. He's wincing, yes, but at the same time he's laughing at Meatball, snide sleazebag that he is. And now he deploys his whaler snail.

It spits a tiny dart from its snout. A dart like a free-flying harpoon, which sinks into Meatball's flank. Immediately a small region of the Freeth's flesh turns sickly green. Undaunted, the hearty Meatball pinches off the damaged region and drops it to the ground.

It strikes Villy that there's something stagy about this duel. It's almost as if Meatball and Irav are pro wrestlers performing a prearranged routine. Villy decides to step in and make his own move against Irav. The guy is within reach, and he seems a little dazed.

With a whiplike motion Villy snatches the whaler snail from Irav's grasp. For what it's worth, Zoe bugles a fierce honk from her horn. Villy aims the tip of the shell at Irav. The beady stalk eyes gleam and the snout flexes, as if drawing a bead on Irav's chest. But Villy's not sure how to make the snail shoot.

A shrill yell interrupts them. "Villy! Hey, Villy! You're okay!"

It's brother Scud, trotting across the parking lot with— is that a flying saucer tagging after him? Villy's too busy to look. He'll do the reunited-brothers thing in a minute.

For now, he just hopes the whaler snail doesn't turn against him. He moves it out from his body, like he'd hold a Roman candle. And now his finger finds a raised bump on the shell's side. A trigger?

"Don't you dare," says Irav. "Give me back my snail right now."

Villy presses the bump and—yes—the whaler snail fires a dart into Irav's body, catching him in his slender belly. For a moment Irav seems wounded—he totters to one side. He rips his shirt open. The flesh of his belly is green. But then, dammit, Irav does what Meatball did. With a certain peculiar motion of his body, the alien manages to shed a pound or two of his body mass—and thereby heals himself.

Not wanting to have the poisonous whaler snail in his pocket, Villy lets Scud take it and study it.

"Fight, huh?" says Scud, looking up from the shell. "I bet Nunu can help! She's not a vampire saucer, so don't worry. She's my new friend."

The saucer is hovering above them. Villy takes her measure. She's a cute little number, with red lips in her rim, like a movie-star mouth. Clearly, she wants to aid Scud and his friends. A downside is Villy's sense that Nunu can see into his mind.

The saucer tilts back and beams a wiggly green ray from her underside. It's another style of zapper ray, less intense than Meatball's, but with a broader swath. Nunu plays the ray across Irav's body. He flinches and edges away, not liking the sensation. Using her ray, Nunu tries to herd the alien away from Villy's car. In reaction, Irav runs forward and leaps up at Nunu. The saucer easily eludes his grasp, but it seems her ray isn't strong enough to knock Irav out.

"He's strong," murmurs Scud.

"I'm afraid he'll kidnap one of us," says Villy.

"Imagine Meatball and I make combo ray," suggests Nunu.

Villy doesn't know what Nunu means, but Nunu teeps an image. In his mind's eye, Villy sees Meatball and Nunu beaming rays at each other—with Meatball's thick yellow spark running down the center of Nunu's diffuse green beam.

"I'm game," says Meatball, who's picked up the image as well. She looks very wrinkly. Like she's slightly deflated by her intense but fruitless zap against Irav. "I can work with a saucer if I must. Draw closer, Nunu."

Irav is uneasy over the new development. "You come with me," he yells to Zoe. "Pronto." A last-ditch effort at bullying. "If Zoe comes, I'll let the rest of you go free."

By way of answer, Zoe lifts her horn and plays a peppy little tune, a repeating staircase of notes—like a nursery rhyme or a rope-jumping ditty. Meatball and Nunu face off in midair, six feet apart. Blobby Meatball is patronizing, Nunu eager. Each of them sends a ray towards the other, with neither of them putting too much force into it. The yellow spark and the wiggly green ray merge.

Just as Nunu predicted, there's a synergy to the combined beams. The combo ray makes a high, singing sound, like a buzz saw, like a vibrating wire, like a dark-energy garrote.

"To hell with you freaks," says Irav, making as if to walk away. "I don't need this jive."

At this moment Nunu and Meatball drop to waist level and dart forward, Meatball to the left of Irav, Nunu to the right. It almost seems like Irav could have ducked under the beam—but he doesn't.

Dzeent!

The upper half of the Szep comes loose and thuds to the ground. They've literally cut him in two. Or, no, into *three* parts—for at the last minute Irav moved his right arm towards the beam, and his right hand was cut off at the wrist. Is he dead? No such luck. Irav's legs are still balanced, still upright. His upper half is rolling around, righting itself. And his hand is walking on its fingers like a nimble spider. Irav isn't bleeding. Perhaps he's somehow sealed off the cut surfaces of his body? Or maybe he has no blood at all.

"Quite unexpected," says Meatball. "By no means a usual thing for a Szep. One wonders if Irav is an imposter. Some other kind of being—who happens to have *disguised* himself as a Szep."

Theatrically yelling, Irav worms his upper half over to his legs. He wraps his arms around the legs and clambers up, balancing his torso sideways on top of the legs. The hand is scuttling around on its own—but it's hard to keep track of it, what with Irav hollering so loud. The alien's intensity is scary.

Staggering a little, weaving to balance the load, the legs make their way to Pinchley and Yampa's car, which is parked only a few yards away. It's a dirty, beat-up jalopy, mostly yellow, and with those red initials on it: P&Y for Pinchley and Yampa. The beater stands high, with spoked wheels even bigger than the ones on the purple whale. It's open on the top, although it bears a solid-looking roll-bar. Luxurious ant leather on the seats. Several racks of water bottles and some quilts in a wad. Still balancing the torso, Irav's legs stand beside the Szep's car, as if wondering how to open the door and get into the seats.

Zoe doubles the speed of her tune and raises its pitch, goading Meatball and Nunu towards another attack. The saucer nods. The mouth on her rim smiles, as if she's enjoying the deadly game. She and Meatball rise above the stalled Irav—and angle through his torso like the blade of a guillotine.

Dzeent!

Irav's legs manage to sidestep the guillotine, but his upper half is cut in two. One chunk has his head, a shoulder, and his right arm—which lacks its hand. Another piece has his chest, belly, and left arm. The legs are running around in circles. And that stray right hand is running all over the place on its twinkling fingers. No way Irav is dead.

"I sorry!" cries Nunu. "We goof."

Working together, the pair of legs and the pieces of torso somehow wallow into the front seat of Pinchley and Yampa's car. They get the beater started and—

"Catch that hand!" screams Scud. "It stole my caraways!"

Yes, the creepy hand crawled up Scud's leg and picked his pocket, and now it's up high on a thumb and two fingers, holding the jar of caraway seeds against its palm with two of the other fingers. To make things worse, Irav's little whaler snail is riding on the back of the rogue hand. Like Captain Ahab on his ship. The frikkin hand bagged the snail too.

Villy charges after it—but there's no catching the hand. It skitters to Pinchley and Yampa's top-down convertible and—with a single, startling leap—it springs to safety inside.

The stolen space-jalopy peels out, slewing wildly across the sandy lot. Propped behind the steering wheel, Irav's head and half torso cackles, exults, and shrieks insults in what Meatball says is the Szep tongue.

Meatball and Nunu fly after the car, but yet again, the four-part Irav proves cannier than expected. Irav's free-agent hand undoes his tool belt. Creatures like gauzy butterfly nets flit out of the fleeing car—and wrap themselves around the Freeth and the saucer.

Arcane energies sizzle along the enveloping meshes. It's all that Meatball and Nunu can do to fight their way free. Loath to pursue the wily pieces of Irav any further, they settle to the dust of the parking lot, as if licking their wounds.

"Unheard of," says Meatball. "A very curious affair."

This is when Pinchley and Yampa show up. Yampa has lost her borrowed clothes in the course of the evening, but Pinchley's still wearing his tool belt. He's still got his cocoa tin, and at this point it's only about half full. Even now, the two wasted Szep are still dipping at it.

They don't seem very upset about their stolen car. And the kids don't immediately tell them about the lost caraway seeds. The Szep refuse to believe the story about the separate pieces of Irav staying alive. They seem to think the kids are telling them a recondite parable or joke.

"When Pinchley squats, he splits in two," says Yampa, making a rude sound with her mouth. "If we conjecture kac is conscious."

"All hail the followers of the One True Rump," adds Pinchley. He bows so deeply that he falls onto the ground, but somehow he manages not to spill the precious cocoa.

"Mighty Truban titans we," says Yampa, helping Pinchley to his feet. Obviously these two are loaded from their cocoa party. They lean together, propping each other up like a pair of seedy clowns.

Pinchley screws his face into a parody of deep thought. "Now tell me this," he says to Villy. "Does a turd have smeel?"

"You're not listening to us," says Villy. "This Szep gangster called Irav—he split into four."

"We thought we killing Irav but not happen," puts in Nunu, abashed.

"I should tell you that the Iravs stole all the caraway seeds," Villy now confesses to Pinchley and Yampa.

"What the hell?" shouts Pinchley, his mind suddenly in focus. He's apoplectic, turning red. "Robbed by a piece of crap?"

"The caraways are crucial for Lady Filippa," wails Yampa. "You were stupid to squander the seeds."

Pinchley points a finger at Zoe and roars, "Get more caraways! Go to Los Perros and get more!"

"I won't," says Zoe. "I hopped back to Earth today, and then back here. I'm not sure I'd be able to go back and forth again. I don't want to get stuck on Earth with no road trip."

This is the first Villy's heard of Zoe's hop, but he's staunchly on her side. "If you want the caraway seeds, Pinchley, why don't we just catch up with the pieces of Irav and, uh—"

"And kill them," says Meatball.

Yampa squints at Meatball and Nunu as if only now noticing them. "You're extra," she peevishly says. "Extraneous. Why a fat Freeth? Why a silly saucer?"

"These two floaters—they want to come with us," Villy says. "You think that's okay? I guess they can help with the chase." He talks slowly and clearly, hoping the stoned aliens will understand him.

"I expect I can stand a Freeth." says Pinchley after a moment's pause. "If she's not some kind of double agent. But a saucer? Don't you get the part about half the saucers being enemies?"

"Nunu's eye is black," says Scud, as if this decides it. "Not red."

"You never know," says Yampa. She grabs hold of Nunu's rim and bends it, exaggeratedly lowering her head to peer at the saucer's underside. "No teeth beneath," she reports. "Not set up for siphoning smeel. She's safe. But—" Yampa pauses, staring at Scud and at Nunu—and reaches a conclusion. "Scuddy's sweet on her!"

Villy starts laughing. The situation is *so* Scud. At age sixteen the guy finally gets a girlfriend—and she's a flying saucer. Scud will definitely have to stop razzing Villy about Zoe now.

"I'm worried we won't all fit in the purple whale," puts in Zoe, reminding Villy that they'd been hoping for a caravan of two cars—with Zoe and Villy alone together. "Is there some way to get a second car?" asks Zoe, directing the question at Pinchley.

"Done told you," says bleary Pinchley. "No real cars in Van Cott at all. Only thing they driving here is beetles, beetles, beetles. Can't road-trip no million miles in no beetle. Thing's gonna pupate, or some shit like that."

"It's larvae and caterpillars that pupate," corrects Scud. "Not full-grown beetles."

"Our pet professor," Yampa says to Scud, with a little bow. "Egg, larva, pupa, adult. Lady Filippa's folk fashion that same flow."

"What-frikkin-ever," blusters Pinchley. "So maybe a car-beetle spawns a ribbon of eggs and keels over dead and the eggs hatch out larvae that eat the flesh of the passengers, which would serve you right if you're stupid enough to road-trip in a beetle."

"Jabber jack," says Yampa, hit by another wave of intoxication. She lurches over to the purple whale, bungee-bounces wildly up, collapses into the back seat, and falls asleep.

"Just great," says Villy, eyeing the sprawled-out Szep. "That leaves us the front seat and that little tiny space in the way-back."

"The pig's nest," says Scud. That was what he and Villy called the cargo area of Dad's station wagon when they were kids. "Are we supposed to put four of us in the pig's nest?"

Villy looks at Nunu and Meatball. "Were you two actually planning to ride *inside* the car? Can't you can't just fly along above us?"

"I can hover and bob and fly up to a thousand miles," says Meatball. "But never so as far as Szep City. Let *Nunu* fly above the car. If she comes at all."

"My father and uncle very big," says Nunu. "Lifted by fat saucer pearls. Small saucer like me, small pearl, not fly high. I want hitch ride with you, yes. I go in pig nest with Scud." She bats her eye.

Scud grins at this, then asks one of his endless questions. "If you have a pearl inside you, Nunu, does that mean you can tunnel over to ballyworld?"

"If I tunnel through the pearl inside my body—I turn inside out."

"Whoa," goes Scud, deeply intrigued. "I love hearing about topology."

"We discuss all cozy in pig nest."

"That shy and coy crap doesn't cut it for me," says Meatball. "I don't trust Nunu."

Nunu giggles, as if embarrassed by such a rudeness.

"You don't know how hard I can zap," Meatball tells Nunu. "I'll turn you into a heap of ash if you leech on our Scud."

"I not bad one saucer," pipes Nunu. "If I maybe kiss Scud, I get tiny taste of his smeel and that plenty for me. No need excite." Earnestly she rocks her rim up and down, as if nodding her head.

"Your call," Villy says to Scud, who smiles and nods his head in sync with Nunu. Villy can tell that as far as Scud's concerned, the main point is that Nunu wants to kiss him.

Pinchley accepts the decision. "Looks like I gotta upgrade the dang whale," he slurs. "Make her bigger inside. A land yacht. I can do it. I'm the man." He fumbles at his ant-leather tool belt. He first manages to close his powdered chocolate tin and stash it in his belt. Then, digging deeper, he produces a dark green crustacean. Its shell is mottled, with shades of red and blue and green.

"A lobster?" says Villy. "But—he has a *handle* in back instead of a tail? And his claws are—fuzzy?"

"A stretch-crawdad," says Pinchley. "He grabs onto raw empty space and I pull on him. Like doming up a pie crust. Lend in your weight, Villy. Like we're a tug-o'-war team. We want a long, steady pull."

The two of them haul themselves up to the car. Pinchley tosses his stretch-crawdad inside. The critter clamps his furry claws onto the empty space within the purple whale and hangs there in midair, quizzically twitching his antennae. With his foot on the door sill and his hand around the bungee, Pinchley grabs the handle on the lobster's rear. Villy puts his arms around Pinchley's waist, and they pull. It's hard getting started—like extracting a nail from a board. But then, all at once, the space in the car loosens—and they're stretching it like chewing gum. They jump free of the car and pull even further.

"We done," says Pinchley after a few seconds of this. He feeds some dried meat to his stretch-lobster and returns the little beast to his tool belt.

Seen from the outside, the whale looks the same as before. But when Villy goes back up and looks in through the open door, it's like a distorted spherical fishtank in there. Like looking through a weird lens. The car is much, much bigger inside.

Yes, relative to the car's interior, the back seat looks tiny, and so does Yampa, asleep on it. The seats and the passenger didn't change size. It's like they're fixed-size coins taped to the surface of a balloon that swells. The bloat of the car's interior space means there's big aisles along the sides of the seats, and there's tons of room between the front seat and the back.

As for the pig's nest—it's the size of a bedroom. And the car roof is so high they'll be able to walk around inside without bonking their heads. Meatball and Nunu hurriedly push into the pig's nest and bobble against the padded ceiling like party balloons.

Villy swings into the front seat and he's at the wheel once more.

"Will the car handle the same?" he asks Pinchley.

"No problem," says the Szep, taking a blanket and making himself comfortable on the wide strip of floor behind the front seat. "Wake me if we catch those four Iravs who stole my car."

"Which direction should I go?" asks Villy.

Pinchley makes a weary gesture with his hand. "Call it north. Yampa and me didn't come in that way, but word is, you can turn left at Alaska and drive across some water. Then you hit this basin's ridge. There's a pass—Borderslam Pass—and people can get through." Pinchley yawns so wide that the top of his thin yellow head tilts backwards like it might fall off. "Details later."

"How much later?" persists Villy.

"Couple of hours till you hit that Borderslam strait. Put the hammer down, soon as we out of town. Get her up to five hundred miles per—or why not a thousand. I double damn guarantee you can trust our shocks and tires. This amplified whale don't really need a road at all. A road's just an opinion about which way to go."

Villy honks the horn—that same feeble *toot*—and they roll out of the night market's lot. He's exceedingly proud of his amplified and enlarged whale. And he's got hot Zoe Snapp in the front seat beside him.

Zoe is bouncy and excited, Yampa's out cold, and Pinchley's drifting off as well. Scud is in the rear with Nunu and Meatball. The Freeth is in a talkative mood, issuing snide, funny put-downs of Nunu. For her part, Nunu's still acting meek and demure.

One thing Villy finds a little disturbing is that Nunu is telepathic. He can sense her thoughts brushing against his mind, continually checking that everything's cool. Oh well.

Scud wads up some quilts to make a comfortable lounge seat in the pig's nest. Nunu settles onto him like a blanket, letting her rim droop across his body and smooching her red lips against his cheek. Scud's never looked happier. He knows that big brother Villy is watching, but he doesn't care.

Villy begins making his way through the maze of Van Cott. Zoe offers driving suggestions. Villy knows by now that she likes telling him what to do. It's more or less her default way of talking to people. Not that most people listen to her.

"Go over to a parallel road," says Zoe. "I see a street party up ahead of us. Mini Thudds. Look how they throw their heads back and roar. Why don't humans ever have that much fun?"

"I do," says Villy. "Especially when I surf."

"I'm glad you brought two boards. You can teach me how to roar!" Zoe smiles over at him, completely happy. "Turn right here and then turn left, Villy."

Villy enjoys the sound of her voice. "You're so alert," he says. "Dialed up high."

"I'm glad I stuck with you," says Zoe. "When Meatball knocked you out, I panicked and hopped back to Los Perros."

"What was it like?"

"I went through the pearl and it led me back to the same spot and to the same moment that we left from. Hopped into the past, you could say. But I didn't stay."

"*I don't care about history*," sings cheerful Villy. "*'Cause that's not when I want to be.*"

"With *you* is where I want to be," says Zoe.

Villy burps the car's accelerator, watching the lit buildings of Van Cott stream by. They go about twenty blocks on the parallel street that Zoe steered him onto—and now he spots another crowd in the street. Could the four Iravs be among them? Planning an ambush? The shoulder with a head and arm, the torso chunk with just an arm, the pair of legs, and the stray right hand. Grisly foes. What kind of creature *was* the original Irav if not a regular Szep?

To be on the safe side, Villy edges to the right and drives partly on the sidewalk. The whale *thumpity-thumps* over a couple of parked beetles and bombs past the dim group—it's a party and not menacing after all.

"*Buh bye!*" Zoe calls to them, doing a teener accent. She and Villy laugh. They regain the street and speed on.

Van Cott is huge. Villy has his speed up to a hundred miles an hour, according to the thin wobbly needle of his revamped speedometer. Zoe leans against him. The city blocks strobe past. Insane, to drive like this in a town, but so far it's going okay. The beetle cars scuttle out of his way, most of them, and the ones that don't—well, Villy just rides over them, like he already did before. He's springy and light on his quantum shocks, and probably he's not damaging the beetles or their drivers. Everything's cool, everything's smooth.

The streets grow darker on the north edge of Van Cott, as there's none of those tall streetlight lily-plants. But the streets and houses and empty lots do give off a bit of light on their own. Meatball says they have glowons stuck to them, whatever that means. In any case, by now Villy's headlights are on.

Finally, they reach the open countryside. Low rolling hills, once again faintly luminous. An ocean somewhere in the distance to the left. An occasional settlement of mappy-world humans. Villy stays quiet, concentrating on his driving—and on Zoe. This is how the trip was supposed to be.

A bright dot appears far ahead. It grows, looms, and rushes towards them. Wary of a collision, and once again worrying about the Iravs, Villy edges onto the grassy shoulder of the road. His whale is rolling so steady that he doesn't bother slowing down. A beetle car whizzes by, with headlights of its own.

Back on the road, Villy nudges the whale up to seven hundred miles per hour. The landscape is a dark blur. When they hit the top of the next rise, they fly quite some distance through the air. Like skating off a ramp. Zoe laughs a little too hard, edging towards hysteria.

The landing is gentle. The tires make a comfortable squeak as the whale regains its purchase upon the road. Villy cranks the whale up to eight hundred miles an hour. The sense of speed is insane. He has to maintain a pinpoint focus on the farthest reaches of the faintly lit zone ahead. If his gaze deviates even slightly, his attention will be swept into the cascading rush of dim fields on either side.

"Reckless driving," says Zoe, trying to keep her tone light, but not quite managing. "Like those doomed stoners they always showed us in the driving-safety videos at school. You're overdoing it, Villy."

"If we crash and die, then at least the vampire saucers won't get you," said Villy, going for gallows humor.

"Slow. Down."

"Not to worry, dear," interjects Meatball. "You're safe as houses." She's crept along the car cabin's ceiling, making her body long and snaky. A yellow bulb of her flesh rests on the back of the front seat between Villy and Zoe, with an eye-spot and a slit mouth. "Your quantum shock absorbers have an aura," adds Meatball. "Loom what may, we're likely to go over or around or through. Do you call that the— nowhere principle?"

"I think you mean the uncertainty principle," says Zoe, very dubious.

"Yes," says Meatball. "And it means we won't ram those trees up—*ahead*!" Her voice shoots up high on the last word, but by then the dark redwood grove is already behind them. "With quantum shocks, even a thousand miles per hour is tea and crumpets," insists Meatball. "We wave and we don't matter."

"Hear that?" says Villy. "I'm not slowing down, Zoe."

"Wishful thinking," says Zoe, who's taking a dislike to the overbearing Freeth. "We missed the trees because you didn't steer into them. And if we hit a rock, we hit a rock."

"I'd not care to test that," admits Meatball. "But do keep in mind that we want to cover a million miles."

Villy races onward, hypnotized by the unseen landscape's rushing flow. A forest flies past, a mountain, a lake, endless fields. Everything is faintly aglow, as if in a winter snowscape. The surfboards on the roof vibrate, sounding a matched pair of treble tones.

A squadron of large saucers flies past overhead, perhaps fifty them, bizarrely shaped and wildly colored. Commuting to one of the neighboring basins? Villy has a distinct sense that the saucers are aware of him and the others—including Nunu, who's totally making out with Scud in the pig's nest.

Oh, never mind that. One thing at a time.

For the moment, Villy's just grateful the saucers in the sky don't approach the whale. He bombs onward, and Zoe falls asleep against his shoulder. They really are becoming a couple. Worth the trip.

TWELVE
weird dream

zoe

Zoe has an unusually strange dream, and no wonder, considering this has been the weirdest day of her whole entire life.

At first she's imagining the dark landscape streaming past with little blips of color off to the sides—random faces, shiny cars, flying saucers—and then she flashes on the head-on crash with Mom's car. Cut.

She's onstage at the jazz performance. She's supposed to play her trumpet solo, and she's naked, and the idiot behind her is bumping her with the slide of a disgusting trombone. It's half-sister Maisie. Maisie is naked too, and Zoe sees that Maisie has a flap of skin around her waist. Like a skirt. That's what Maisie's been keeping rolled up under her blouse for all these years.

Maisie's skin flap has images on it, like on a squid. Letters of the alphabet. HI ZOE. Zoe has a sense of stepping backwards off a ledge. *Thud.* An electric jolt goes up her leg.

Maybe this isn't a dream. Maisie is focused and intent. The bell of her trombone rests on Zoe's shoulder.

Everyone is quiet. Zoe's supposed to play but she's blank. Maisie hums, prompting her. It's that stutter-stop riff Maisie taught her yesterday. Zoe raises her horn. Her notes—she can see them—they're tiny glider planes, like origami. They drift out and rock their wings, wanting to fly to the crowd—but they're sucked into the hungry brass bell of Maisie's horn.

Maisie followed Zoe up here, and she's teeping to her. This is real. And—

"*Uuuunnh!*"

Zoe comes awake with a groan. She's lying on her side on the seat. Villy pats her leg.

"You okay?"

"Um, yeah, it was just that I saw . . ." Zoe trails off. She's not quite ready to talk about her creepy dream. The car tires hum. The others are asleep, except for Meatball. In silence Zoe looks out the car windows, contemplating the unimaginable place that she and Villy have come to.

"We should talk about Maisie," she finally says. "We haven't talked about Maisie yet at all."

"What's to say?" goes Villy.

"She gave me that magic pearl, and she taught me the riff that opened it into a tunnel to mappyworld? And Yampa claims she saw Maisie up here? And she says Maisie told her where to look for the gate of the tunnel I made?"

For a moment Zoe can't tell if Villy even hears her. He's staring straight ahead, out into the indistinct landscape, gently controlling the steering wheel to keep them on the road.

"I wonder if we're going to find her here," Villy presently says.

"Maisie's been coming to mappyworld all along," says Zoe. "She's not a regular human. That lump around her waist? It's a rolled-up flap of skin."

"How do you know that?" asks Villy.

"I saw Maisie just now. In my dream. We were trying to play the Jazz Howlers concert, and everything was wrong. We were naked, and I didn't know the music, and Maisie told me what to play. My notes flew out of my trumpet and into her trombone."

"Some dream," says Villy.

"Worse than that," says Zoe. "I think Maisie teeped it to me. A message."

Villy slides his eyes over to Zoe for just a second and smiles. "Calm down? We'll figure out Maisie later. For now, I mean, this is already the craziest trip ever."

"You and me," says Zoe. "Do you mind when I sit close to you? You won't think I'm sleazy and desperate and a clinging vine?"

"I won't think that," says Villy. "I like being near you."

They ride along in a companionable silence, with Zoe's leg touching Villy's. They're not worrying about seatbelts. Pinchley's installed some better kind of safety feature, which Zoe doesn't quite understand, but Pinchley says it will work. Zoe's heart rate settles down as the memory of her dream fades. She's really here, really on a giant road trip with—can she think of Villy as her true love? Okay, sure, but keep that to herself.

"It's getting light," is all Zoe says.

"That figures," says Villy. "It had just gotten dark when we came yesterday, and it feels like I drove all night. Can you see the sun? I can't take my eyes off the road."

Villy's got the whale goosed to a steady eight hundred miles an hour, but Zoe isn't even going to think about that. At least the road's straight and level. They're way up north in Canada. Or someplace like that. It's getting brighter all the time. The fields are a fresh green, speckled with wildflowers, and there's he sees sawtooth mountains on the horizon. Shiny ocean waves far to their left. But nothing in the sky.

"No sun," Zoe tells Villy. "I mean, how would it rise and set, if this world is flat and endless? Would it drill through the surface? And you'd need lots and lots of suns for such a big world. Like grow lights in a warehouse."

Once again Villy doesn't immediately answer. Sometimes when he's so quiet for so long, Zoe wonders if there is, in fact, anything at all going on in his head. Wonders if he's dumb. But then he'll say something interesting, and, yes, his stream of consciousness was flowing all along, like an underground river.

"Maybe the light's in the air itself," is what Villy says now. "Like we're inside a neon tube."

"I like that," says Zoe. "Remember how Meatball mentioned—glowons? I figure they're particles of light. Like phosphorescent plankton. The glowons float around all day, and at night they settle onto the ground and go dim."

Zoe cracks open her window, sampling the fresh dawn air. The slipstream rustles the scraps of paper in the car, stirs Zoe's clothes, tousles her hair—and clears away her images of Maisie.

Feeling more like herself, Zoe smiles at Villy. "Dare I utter a ladylike *yee-haw*?"

"Our special road trip," says Villy in a really nice way. Zoe snuggles up to him some more. It's fun being kittenish, and clearly Villy digs it. Zoe is silk-spinning him into her web.

"You have to turn left rather soon," puts in Meatball. She's got her nosy bulb-head atop the back of the seat again.

"What'll we find in the next basin over?" Villy asks the Freeth.

"I'm not quite sure," allows Meatball.

"I thought you said we don't need a map because you always know exactly where you are," says Zoe.

"I was building myself up," says Meatball. "Beating my own drum. I'm prone to doing that." Somehow this admission makes Zoe like Meatball a little better.

"What are you Freeth doing in the human basin anyway?" asks Zoe. She touches Meatball's yellow skin, pushing it in and out, playing with it.

"Scrounging for scraps," says Meatball. "Hoping to profit from the cosmic beatdown."

Zoe shakes her head. "You aliens keep coming on all heavy and meaningful, but—"

"But we have no frikkin idea what you're talking about," says Villy, his eyes continually fixed on the road. "Or whether you're putting us on." They're among mountains now, some of them with snow on top. The mappyworld Alaska.

"Allow me to expand upon my remarks," says Meatball. "The parasitic saucers plan to escalate their forays to

Earth. They want to open a huge unny tunnel between the worlds. With one gate near Saucer Hall and the other gate in your Los Perros. Motivation? Their ruler, Groon, wishes to emigrate to your planet Earth, and to mastermind a full-on invasion. I share this emerging information as a token of my good faith."

"Invade Earth?" says Villy. "Pinchley and Yampa were talking about that. Somehow we're supposed to stop the invasion."

"Curious that you're now driving a million miles in the wrong direction," says Meatball with a short laugh. "Away from the upcoming war. But perhaps it's not entirely idiotic. The Szep Aristos are well connected with Goob-goob."

Zoe glances back at Nunu, wondering what she thinks about this conversation—but the saucer's eye is closed and she's plastered against Scud's body like an overcoat. Asleep. Or pretending to be.

"You're losing me again," Villy tells Meatball. "Right now, all I want is to catch those Iravs, and get our caraway seeds, and find the monster waves that Yampa was talking about."

"Stout fellow," says Meatball in a hearty tone. "Soldier on. No need to fight in every possible battle, eh? You'd do well to sit out the cosmic beatdown. We can journey past Szep City to Freeth Farm."

"Have you been there before?" asks Zoe.

"I must confess that I'm a gutter Freeth, a third-generation immigrant, born in that manky parking lot beside the night market, and compelled, as I say, to beg for boons. A Freeth of low estate. I'd gain renown, were I to divert you from the cosmic beatdown. If not—" The Freeth pauses, as if embarrassed. "Well, otherwise, Pinchley and Yampa say you're destined to become intergalactic heroes."

This is when Zoe realizes that Meatball isn't really their friend. But Villy's not picking up on that. He's sleepy and amused. He goes, "Talk about heavy, bogus, primo grade gibburish—"

And just then Meatball's eye-spot bulges and her whispery voice rises to a shrill buzz. "Turn left, turn left, turn left!" They're rocketing towards a sharp fork in the road—with a solid wedge of rock straight ahead.

Villy cranks the steering wheel, and the whale goes into a prolonged skid, barely making the left turn. Zoe clings to him for dear life. Momentum sends the whale rolling along the face of the bare, rocky bluff—thumpity-bumping across ledges and scrubby pines, a hundred feet above the ground, the passengers held in their seats by centrifugal force.

Everyone's awake and making noise, especially Yampa and Scud, but Zoe's screaming the loudest, and it feels good. She's got a lot of scream bottled up inside her. Especially after that trippy dream. But then Yampa raps Zoe on the back of her head with her knuckles, and she shuts up.

Villy angles back down to the road, and they're speeding along between two cliffs, with the other end of the cut in view. The ocean is out there, and a crooked thin island, and beyond the island, a mountain range that towers into the pale blue sky.

"We're driving over that?" asks Scud. He's clambered forward from the pig's nest to join Yampa and Pinchley.

Enough room for everyone. Scud pushes Meatball's bulbous tendril to one side and shoves his own head into the front seat. "God, you're going fast, Villy. Give it a rest. It's time for a stop."

"Not yet," says Villy, unwilling or unable to look away from the road. Zoe's seen him get like this playing videogames.

Zoe turns around so she can see what the others are up to. That floppy, sneaky Nunu is glued to the ceiling now. Pinchley and Yampa are rubbing their faces, looking hungover. And Scud looks weirdly content. What was he doing with Nunu during the night? *So nasty*. She breaks into wild giggles.

"What's your problem?" Scud snaps, probably using his teep slug to read Zoe's mind. "Slow the hell down, Villy!"

Finally Villy eases up. The tires' frantic whining abates. What a relief. The whale coasts out of the canyon into an open landscape. Up ahead is a rickety frontier town with inns and outfitters. A cold, rough sea lies beyond—deep green with lacy whitecaps. The thin island splits the strait into two channels, the first one narrow and the second one wide. On the other side, foothills and bluffs rise into the highest mountains Zoe has ever seen. The range runs north and south, as far as she can see. It's a wall between them and the next basin.

Villy drives another quarter mile and then, with a spray of gravel, he slews the whale to a halt beside a ramshackle establishment called Borderslam Inn. It has a porch, but nobody's on it. Villy seems dazed from the long drive, but he smiles at Zoe and helps her clamber down from the high seat. It's majorly cold here. The thin, dry air feels good in her nose and lungs.

Nunu and Meatball hover by the car, working their surfaces against the icy ocean breeze, with Meatball pretty much giving Nunu the cold shoulder, not that Meatball has a shoulder. Yampa and Pinchley swing down their door-ropes like pirates, skinny and gnarly as a pair of fresh-dug roots. The Szep don't look excited—they've driven across lots of basin ridges before, even if this particular one is new to them. They're sharing one of those food mints, a kippered-herring one. Maybe Zoe should look for her roast beet one. Meanwhile Scud wants to pee on the ground by the car, but Pinchley warns him not to.

"Word is there's feisty folks running Borderslam Inn," the Szep tells Scud. "Zeke and Lucille? They get all kinds of trash rolling down from Borderslam Pass. Best not rile them. Be a gentleman and use the indoor facilities. And buy food in there. We're gonna wait out here." Pinchley gives the kids of those little red pyramids that they use for money here. "Me and Yampa made out real good with that cocoa sale last night."

"I can't stand saucers," says the bleary Yampa, squinting at Nunu like she's never seen her before. "Whence, whither, wherefore?" She's completely forgotten about last night.

"Nunu's my good friend," repeats Scud. "And she's *not* after my smeel." With that he takes off alone, trotting into the Borderslam Inn.

"That saucer is Scud's *good friend* because he made out with her for *hours*," Zoe tells Yampa. "In the back of our car." It feels good to gossip.

"You don't talk that," intones Nunu, bumping against Zoe with her leathery rim. Zoe again notices that the saucer girl's mouth is set into her rim. Her plump lips are as red as if she wore lipstick. "Scud and I like married now," adds Nunu.

Zoe is dumbstruck. Like, *whoa*. Does Nunu actually mean that—

"You can always count on my little brother," says Villy with a sigh. Obviously, he too saw Scud kissing Nunu in back. And clearly he's upset. He makes a show of checking that his two surfboards are still holding tight on the roof rack. Then he stares out at the island, the flat sea, and at the impossibly high peaks ahead.

Zoe can't see any mountain passes up there at all. Is their road trip doomed? Another thing: she sees glints of light in the sky. Two heavy-duty flying saucers, hovering very high. Zoe wonders if they know about Scud and Nunu. And then right away she knows that the answer is yes. She feels the cool, inhuman touch of the high saucerian minds. They know about Scud, Nunu, Zoe—and about Maisie too.

Zoe gets a flashback image of Maisie in her dream. The girl's skin sticking out like a stiff little skirt around her waist. Like the rim of a flying saucer.

"I better go into Borderslam and wash up," says Zoe, all gaiety gone.

THIRTEEN

borderslam inn

scud

Inside the inn, Scud sees a bar, some shelves of goods, a communal dining table, and a grill. A tall, lanky man is at the grill. A sweet-faced woman with long dark hair tends bar. A long-haired mountain man with a prominent Adam's apple sits at the common table eating fried meat. Unlike the city slickers in Van Cott, these folks are wearing ordinary jeans.

To enhance the scene, an alien creature stands at the bar. He resembles seven or eight soap bubbles stuck together like the segments of a centipede. Colored gas swirls inside the bubbles. A cartoony, black-outlined eye floats inside the blue-gas-filled top sphere. Almost as an afterthought, the second sphere sports a pair of thin, flexible arms. The alien is nursing a mug of—green liquid soap? He's not actually drinking it—he's dribbling the stuff onto his bubbles. Never mind.

Scud turns to the cook at the grill. The man has his name embroidered on his heavy shirt: ZEKE. "Got ice cream?" asks Scud.

"Nope," says Zeke. "Try toast."

"French toast with syrup?"

"You got it, friend. Coffee with that?"

"Sure," says Scud, feeling manly. Maybe he's just a sophomore in high school, but he's on an adventure in the far North. Actually, he's almost a junior now. And last night, he made out with Nunu for ages, deeply kissing her mouth. Not quite the same as losing his virginity, but it's a start. Up till now he's never gotten more than a dry peck on the cheek. Nunu had felt really good on his lap.

Scud doesn't like the way Zoe was laughing at him just now. Nosy little goth. Scud's still wearing his new teep slug on his wrist, and a quick check on Zoe reveals that she thinks he actually had sex with Nunu—which would have been a little over the top. But kissing the cute saucer for a long time? Why not? But maybe not something he'll brag about to his friends.

In the bathroom, Scud feels compelled to examine his face and his neck—he's slightly worried that Nunu might have done something weird to him. Like bitten him, or inscribed some insane saucerian tattoo. But no, he looks the same as ever. If anything, he looks more grown-up than before. Rough and tough, a man of the world. Like a secret agent in an intergalactic SF novel. He cocks his head, giving the mirror a cool stare. He's the man.

When Scud comes out of the bathroom, there's Zoe and Villy. They're giving him odd looks and thinking bad things—like he's a disgusting pervert. Zoe's vibes are particularly edgy. She scoots past Scud and goes straight for the bathroom. Villy corners Scud by the bar.

"You and the flying saucer?" says Villy. "It's true?"

"I, uh, I mean, who says? Zoe? She's completely—"

"*Nunu* says," hisses Villy. "Do you have any idea what you're in for? Nunu's says you're married now. If you can wrap your tiny mind around that."

"Listen to me," says Scud, feeling flustered. "I did not have sex with Nunu. No way. I kissed her for a while. That's it. End of story. And if Nunu thinks kissing makes us married, she's wrong."

"Vedding?" puts in the alien bubble creature. "You should zelebrate! Tchampagne, Lucille!"

"No, no, no champagne," says Scud. "I'm having coffee."

"Coffee for me too," Villy calls to Zeke the cook. "And scrambled eggs."

"No eggs," says Zeke.

"Steak?"

"You got it."

"No tchampagne for you?" the alien asks Villy. "I see you're vondering vhat I am, and vhy I talk to you. I am a Bubbler. My name is Gunnar." He doesn't have a visible mouth. He talks by vibrating his head-level bubble like a loudspeaker.

"Thanks for offering champagne, Gunnar. I'm Villy. I'm already wasted. From being up all night. Hoping to drive through Borderslam Pass today."

"Open bottle anyvay, Lucille. Scood vill pay. And give a towel. Bubbler man vashes vith bubbly—vhy not! Vhere you go, Villy?"

"A million miles," puts in Scud, trying to recover some of the swaggering bravado he'd been feeling before Zoe and Villy came in. "All the way to Szep City."

"Zaucer trouble there," says the Bubbler.

"We'll help out," says confident Scud. "My brother's driving a souped-up car. I might drive it too."

"I'd trust Zoe to drive before you," says Villy. "You still haven't managed to get your driver's license, Scud, which is kind of unbelievable. And obviously your judgment is not exactly—"

"Don't pick on me!" yells Scud. He can't take the contempt that's bubbling out of his big brother's mind. "I'm a man. Not a nerdy, clumsy little brother."

"With a sex thing for flying saucers," Villy smoothly adds.

"Zaucers very bad," says Gunnar the Bubbler. "Ve glad they don't come into our Bubble Badlands." He's splashing champagne onto his spheres and toweling himself at the same time. Like washing windows. Each of his bubbles encloses a pastel gas: pink, lemon, lime, lilac. "Noble elements," Gunnar says. "Xenon, argon, neon, krypton. My mind is gassy vhirls and svirls."

"Getting back to the saucers, I see Scud's girlfriend floating outside there," says Lucille behind the bar. "Plus a Freeth and two Szep. Motley crew. They can come in if they want. Everyone's welcome at Borderslam Inn. A car full of *really* strange critters came by an hour ago. Three or four of them, sort of deformed? They didn't stop. Heading for the pass. Were they running from you?"

Scud would like to discuss this info, but Villy won't let him start. "Our other friends will wait outside," is all Villy says.

Zoe emerges from the bathroom looking refreshed. Villy heads in there for his turn.

"We're eating?" Zoe brightly asks Scud. Like she's a social worker talking to an institutionalized sex offender.

"Thanks a lot for spreading rumors about Nunu and me," says Scud. "How does it feel to be so mean and catty?"

"Let's not even start," says Zoe. "We all know that you're an idiot, but let's you and I pretend we're friends. For Villy's sake."

"What about for *my* sake?" says Scud. "I have feelings too. And don't forget that I can read your mind. Which makes it even worse."

"Me, I'm having a big time watching you three," says the mountain guy with the plate of meat. "Name's Hungerford. I bring down pieces of starstone from the peaks. And I stock the Borderlands larder with fresh game. You should try one of these steaks, little lady. You're Zoe?"

She nods.

"It's mini Thudd meat," says Zeke the cook. He lays a forefinger over his smiling lips. "Don't tell a soul. Specialty of the house."

"We only eat mini Thudds after they're dead," says Hungerford, chuckling. "Wouldn't be humane otherwise. What with them having some rudimentary intelligence. Fortunately, a lot of them mini Thudds die on their way down from Borderslam Pass."

"Hungerford kills and butchers them," says Zeke with an evil grin.

Thanks to his teep slug, Scud can tell that the two of them are just teasing the greenhorns.

"I think I'll have whatever my friend Scud ordered," Zoe is saying in a small voice.

"French toast," says Zeke with a shrug. "But I have to tell you I'm using ant-jelly instead of egg-batter. And why not eat a little smoked Szep meat on the side? Gamy, oily, and ropy—with an unforgettable tang. Makes great bacon. Wish you'd get one of your Szep friends in here with us, so Hungerford can freshen up my supply." Hungerford cackles.

Zoe seems to wilt. And now Scud takes pity on her.

"Stop scaring Zoe," he yells at Zeke and Hungerford. In his head he's casting himself as a scrappy newcomer—like in an old-time Klondike gold-rush film. He longs to impress Zoe—just this once. Truth be told, he admires her. "Admit that you're lying!" adds Scud.

"Listen at the lad," says Hungerford. "He's got grit."

"The boy's right," says kind Lucille from across the room. "Don't pay Zeke and Hungerford any mind, Zoe. These two clowns get bored and they think they're funny. We don't eat Szep, we don't eat Thudd, and we use real eggs."

"Come on and set down with me," Hungerford says to Scud and Zoe. "You done passed your initiation into Borderslam Inn chapter of the Order of Exalted Sourdough Tale-Trappers."

"Can you show me one of those starstones you were talking about?" Scud asks Hungerford, taking a seat. "What are they? I have some ballyworld fossils in our car. Millions of years old. Maybe we can do a trade?"

"Ballyworld?" exclaims Lucille, coming out from behind the bar and pulling up a chair. "This is a gala day. Which one of you found the way over?"

"Me," says Zoe with quiet pride.

"But I might learn how," says Scud.

"What's up?" says Villy, emerging from the bathroom. "I thought I heard Scud yelling. As usual."

"Everyone's being nice to me now," Scud tells his big brother. "I'm a greenhorn hero, old buckaroo."

"Whatever," says Villy, as Zeke sets down three plates. "Is that my steak?"

"Thudd meat," says Zoe, giving Scud a wink, and the two of them crack up. Exalted Sourdough Tale-Trappers that they are.

They have a friendly breakfast while the bearded Hungerford makes some remarks about Borderslam Pass. There are special rocks on the mountains along the basin borders. Especially in the passes. These are the starstones. A starstone has light-years of space scrunched up inside it. And that's how widely separated planets can be right next to each other in mappyworld. All that extra junk is bunched up inside the starstones on the ridges.

Villy steers the conversation to the topic of where the hell they're going to end up when they cross Borderslam Pass. Turns out there's two different basins on the other side of the pass. That is, three basins meet here, making a corner like a Y. The first basin is the Earth-like Van Cott basin they're in right now. The second basin is New Eden, a home base for the flying saucers. And the third basin holds a primeval jungle called Thuddland. In Thuddland, according to Hungerford, the full-size Thudds can bulk up to forty feet tall. Kind-faced Lucille confirms Hungerford's claim that the big Thudds eat anything they consider meat, including people and Szep. But the most direct route to Szep City is, nevertheless, through Thuddland.

Piling on the wonders, lean Zeke says that the New Eden and Thuddland basins match ballyworld planets that are, respectively, fifteen and twenty light-years from Earth. Looking to fill out the picture, Scud goes over to the bubble creature Gunnar and tries sounding him out for more info.

"Crabs in next basin," declares the zonked Bubbler. "Big, smart crabs. Not Thudds." But then he pauses, with his single eye staring down into his mug of green liquid soap. "Oh, vait, Crab Crater is near Flatsie Pass by vhere I live, not here by Borderslam Pass."

"Where do you live?" asks Scud.

"In basin called Bubble Badlands, other side of Surf World basin. I going home there soon. I came all the vay here to Borderslam to get a starstone for my vife Monika. I vas scared to collect them myself, zo I traded Hungerford a bubblegun for one. But my vill vas veak. Yesterday I ate the new starstone on my own, and had a crazy good time, and now I got nuttin. Dot's vhy you paying for this tchampagne, Scood."

Meanwhile, Villy has four cups of coffee, amping himself up. And then they're outside with Nunu, Meatball, Pinchley, and Yampa. It's cold as hell, but none of the four aliens seems to mind. They're sitting in the sun on the inn's ramshackle porch. Yampa is showing them her pictures. The images appear in midair, solid-looking and fully 3D. Like spliced-in volumes of space. There's a shot from the Szep's party last night, with Yampa throwing her blouse across the room. Yampa says she might put this photo on Lady Filippa's pillowcase.

Scud's busy worrying about the trip. He edges around Yampa's holographic, animated super-picture and goes to Pinchley. "You know about Borderslam Pass, right?"

"Wal, I told you that Yampa and me came to the Earth basin by a different way. But we did hear things, hanging around the market. And we've crossed a buttload of passes before." Pinchley points at the steep slope across the windy strait. "See that faint zigzag line? That's gonna be our road. Or a piss-poor excuse for one. A mini Thudd last night told me the road peters out at the bottom end of a rockslide up top. We'll have to gun the whale up that slide and then weave through a field with big, chunky starstones. You know about them?"

"I'm trying to get a starstone from one of the guys inside," says rock hound Scud.

"Good," says Pinchley. "Here's the deal. The ridges between the basins are squeezed-up space. And the parts with stars in them bulge into starstones. Hundreds and thousands of stars in a rock the size of your leg. Giant nebulas. Light-year volumes of space."

"Are the starstones alive?" wonders Scud.

"Not exactly running around doing push-ups," says Pinchley, "Not alive like that. But you get a feeling they're—payin' attention. Don't you think, Yampa?"

"Old gold souls," says Yampa, who's studying her picture of Zoe's room. "Clots and knots of smeel."

"How about the next basin over?" asks Scud. "It's really giant Thudds?"

"Thudds bigger than houses," says Pinchley. "Trees like skyscrapers. We gonna be tiny vermin, son. We gonna move fast. Did the innkeepers say if Irav has been by?"

"A car drove by, yeah," says Scud. "With the four *pieces* of Irav. Do you remember that we cut him up, and that all the pieces are alive?

"Seems like if you chopped up a Szep, the pieces would be dead," says Pinchley, really doubting him.

"Therefore, Irav wasn't a Szep," says Scud. He's been thinking this over.

A long pause. Scud can't guess what Pinchley's thinking. Scud's teep slug isn't all that good at probing the hidden recesses of alien minds. It's like staring at walls of moving hieroglyphs.

"Did Nunu seem surprised?" asks Pinchley presently. "About the pieces coming back to life?"

Scud shakes his head. "Nunu—she never says much. We could ask her now."

"Waste of time," says Pinchley. "I just wonder if Nunu and this Irav thing are working together. Maybe that fight with Irav was an act."

"And how would Meatball fit in?" says Scud.

"Hard to be sure where she's at," says Pinchley. "Freeth have been known to work for the saucers. I'm not sure we should have Meatball and Nunu along. Could be they're out for sabotage."

Now here comes skinny Hungerford, running out of the Borderslam Inn. He's holding out a chunk of starstone—impossibly beautiful. Transparent, polished and rounded, with brilliant specks of light at its dark center—a vision of vast, empty space. The primeval cosmos. Thanks to his teep slug, Scud can hear the starstone in his head. It's sending out a low, slow sound, like an organ note that never stops. An endless *Om*.

"Hang on," Scud tells Hungerford. "I'll get my fossils." And then he's in the back of the whale rooting around. He extracts his specimens from his pack.

"Come kiss me more," Nunu whispers to Scud. Once again, she's glued herself to the underside of the car's roof. "We make real sure we like married."

Zoe is watching them from her perch in the front seat, secretly full of laughter, and Meatball's watching too. Scud feels wildly uneasy. Worse than that, he feels ashamed.

"I don't want to make out with you again," he tells Nunu. "It's not right. It's not what a human is supposed to do. I mean, you're nice, but—"

"Okay dokey," flutes the saucer. "I sure last night was enough!"

Enough for what? Scud doesn't care to contemplate that, nor does he try teeping into Nunu's cryptic mind for clues.

He hurries out of the car, eager to complete his trade with Hungerford. A fitting activity for an Exalted Sourdough Tale-Trapper. Hungerford is very taken by an ossified brachiopod shell that Scud found at the base of a crumbly ocean cliff near Los Perros.

"Done deal!" says Scud, and hands the fossil to the mountain man. He gets a pretty starstone in return. And then he hauls himself back into the car, sitting between Pinchley and Yampa on the rear seat. He's so aware of what everyone's thinking that he's embarrassed to go back into the pig's nest with Nunu.

"Good luck with the pass," calls Hungerford as the whale pulls off.

"Why did he say that?" Scud asks the others as they roll on.

"The big starstones can get a little pissy," says Pinchley. "If they don't like your looks, they don't let you through. But first we gotta cross the water and climb that steep-ass hill. Meanwhile watching out for any chopped-up Iravs."

"Question," says Zoe, as they approach the cold sea passage between them and the mountain. "There's no bridge here. Won't we sink?"

"Don't overthink," says Pinchley. "All Villy's gotta do is *drive fast*."

Villy floors the accelerator. The dark-energy smeel engine makes a rising whine as they rocket forward. The whale skips across the channel—*pap pap pap*—like an artfully thrown flat rock. They reach the skinny island in the center and tear-ass across that, scattering a great flock of screaming birds. Then they zoom off the other side of the island—and bog down in sandy shallows.

Eventually the shallows end, and they're in deep, frigid water. The whale has slowed its pace. They're floundering along, buoyed by the car's enormous tires, with seawater sloshing in through the windows.

"Screw this," says Villy and cranks the engine speed to a chattering scream. The spinning tires throw up a monster rooster tail. The whale rises up and hydroplanes the remaining half mile to the far shore. And then they start the climb.

Right before that second hydroplane run, when it's looking like they might drown in the icy sea, Scud slithers into the way-back to be with Nunu. She plops down onto him, pressing him flat on his back against the floor. He feels safe, and happy, and turned on. And maybe a little bit trapped. Nunu does come on strong. She twitches her disk, wrapping herself ever tighter around him. With Scud pinned in place, she bats her single eye, puckers up her red lips, and begins kissing him again.

Scud and Nunu canoodle for over half an hour. They've survived the passage across the straits, and they're steadily slewing up the twisty gravel road that runs up the flank of the mountain. In fact, they're almost at the top. Regular life seems likely to continue as before. Nunu begins suggestively squirming against Scud's crotch, and now he feels he should tell her to stop.

"No," he whispers to Nunu. "It's wrong."

"You not enjoy last night?" says Nunu. "We make something good." She rolls her big dark eye towards the car's ceiling, then adjusts the angle of Scud's body so that he can see what she's looking at. He can't quite figure out what it is, but then the car jiggles, and, *oof*, the back of his head bonks against the floor, and with the bonk comes an understanding of what Nunu was doing this morning on the car's ceiling.

She was laying eggs.

Yes. It's a clutch of pale white capsules up there, nestled together like the cells of a honeycomb, three or four dozen of them, shiny and smooth, moist-looking, with faint dark patterns beneath their translucent skins and— oh my god—please tell me they're not twitching.

"Our children," whispers Nunu, and she plasters another warm, sticky kiss onto Scud's mouth. By now he very badly wants to get away, but her tightly wrapped saucer disk encases him like a cloak. Or a straitjacket. And now her long kiss intoxicates him once again. Their bodies jiggle with the whale's wild motions.

"Don't tell the others about the eggs," Scud hisses to Nunu.

"You not proud our kids?" murmurs the saucer. Flirting. Pretending to be annoyed.

"Please don't tell."

The saucer giggles.

FOURTEEN

nunu's father

villy

Do you see what Scud and Nunu are doing back there?" Zoe asks Villy. "They're making out again. So skeevy."

"Scud's always been different," says Villy. "And he took Mom's death really hard. Let him be. Help me drive. Sing out if you notice I'm heading for a boulder. There's hardly a road at all anymore."

"You really should slow down," says Zoe, even though she doesn't like to nag. "You're going two hundred miles an hour. We're practically at the top."

Villy doesn't slow down. He's loving this drive. It's like a video game, but better, because it's real-world-and-no-kidding dangerous, which adds spice. And thanks to the quantum shocks, the fat whale handles like a sports car. Villy's using controlled drifts to scutter around the switchbacks. He speeds like a madman on the straight-aways, with the whale beating up clouds of dust that twinkle in the mappyworld light.

The green bowl of the Van Cott basin stretches out behind them, perhaps five thousand miles across. It's like they're in an airplane, or a spaceship.

"Go, man," says Pinchley from the back seat. "Keep gunnin' it. All the passes are like this. It's hard to switch basins. Sometimes, at the top, the big starstones decide not to let you through."

"In Borderland Pass, the starstones stop dumb Thuddland dinos from hunting the humans of Van Cott," puts in Yampa. "A good deed indeed."

"Don't spook the kids, honeybun," says Pinchley. "One crisis at a time. The rockslide is first."

Even though Villy knows he shouldn't take his eyes off the sketchy road, he glances back at the two Szep. Pinchley calls Yampa *honeybun*? They're leaning against each other, cozy, with their arms around each other's shoulders and their legs propped against the front seat. They're giving off a spicy, contented smell.

Once again Meatball has draped a tendril into the front seat. It has a mouth and an eye. Behind them all, in the pig's nest, the green and yellow Nunu has Scud wrapped up like a burrito, with his head sticking out. They aren't kissing just now. The saucer happens to yawn—and Villy notices the tips of some retractable fangs set into Nunu's upper jaw. Like on a rattlesnake. Nunu's got her red-lipped mouth right next to Scud's neck, and it just might be that—

"Hey!" Villy yells. "Meatball! Stop Nunu from biting Scud!"

Meatball fastens onto Nunu, as if meaning to peel the alien away from the youth. Villy has his full attention on them, although meanwhile the purple whale is speeding blindly forward and—

Zoe screams. Huge thumps against the bottom of the car. The steering wheel twists like a live thing. There's an odd subliminal *pop*—and the enhanced space inside the car fills with Truban inertia gel. It's like an immersive quantum airbag, holding everyone in place. The bright landscape tilts and keeps tilting. An outcrop knocks against the windshield, which spiderwebs into crazed cracks. Rocks hammer the car's sides and roof. The whale rolls over, once, then twice, improbably tumbling uphill. And then they're upright, in a skid. With a terminal crunch, the purple whale slams into a hunk of solid stone.

The space within the car relaxes. All the windows are cracked, but none has shattered. The whale's puny horn is stuck, endlessly bleating. Villy's okay, and Zoe too. She's hugging her trumpet like it's her only hope in the world.

"What if we get stuck here?" she asks Villy. "Maybe we should go home before it's too late."

Villy can't quite come up with an answer. The others are crawling around the car like hornets in a fallen nest.

Meatball has finished prying Nunu loose from Scud, and the saucer has glued herself back onto the pig's nest ceiling. Scud is fine—maybe Nunu wasn't really planning to bite him. The leathery, weathered Szep work to open one of the rear doors. The front doors are totally jammed shut. The whale is lodged between two fifteen-foot boulders, as if stuck in a gate—wedged, tilted, and with hood askew. Foggy fumes pour from the engine. Dark energy.

"This'll be an interesting repair," says Pinchley as the left rear door partly opens. "Let's have a look-see."

The two skinny Szep squeeze out. Meatball ushers Scud out of the car's back hatch. Villy and Zoe exit via the hatch as well. As for Nunu, she stays plastered on the ceiling of the pig's nest, which suits Villy fine. Even if she's not a vampire, he's seen more than enough of her. He slams the hatch, leaving the saucer on her own.

It's windy up here, and seriously cold. Zoe stands off to one side, still holding her trumpet. Two of the car's tires are flat, and the body is gouged. One of the surfboards is cracked in half—the red one, Villy's fave. He takes the pieces down, with an eye to patching them back together, and takes down his blue one as well, just to be handling it.

The light up here is dim, like an all-day twilight. Maybe there are fewer glowons at this altitude. The car is less than twenty yards from the level crest of Borderslam Pass—the slope rises up just a little more and then you see the sky.

Lots of big pointy boulders around here, almost like Easter Island monuments. Starstones. Stern, slanted, unspeakably ancient. And with an intriguing vibe.

Villy goes over to Zoe and puts his arm around her. "Are you okay?"

"What if I lose my power to turn my saucer pearl into an unny tunnel?" says Zoe. "Maybe if we drive and drive and drive, the connection will be too far. We'll be out of range. I think I want to go home, Villy. Let me see if we can hop right now."

"Please, Zoe, we *gotta* see what's on the other side of Borderslam Pass. And you and me—we've hardly started. Give us a chance." He goes to kiss her, but she twists

away. Even so, her body's a little less tense. She stands at
his side, silently watching the scene unfold.

Grease-monkey Pinchley's already busy with the car. To
start with, he opened the hood all the way and discon-
nected that lamenting horn.

"Can we drive it again?" calls Villy.

"You screwed the pooch, son," says Pinchley. And then
he smiles—that is, he lets his lower jaw hang loose and
he wobbles it back and forth. "Damn good thing I've got
my tool belt. We'll have this junker on the road in half an
hour."

"I'd vote to banish that little saucer," says Meatball.
"She says she's not a smeel leech, but she could switch
allegiance anytime. That's how saucers are. Born parasites. Let's give this little snip her walking papers. And if
she won't clear out, I'll use a zap to fry her proper."

"I'm fine with that," says Villy. He turns to Scud. Poor
kid. "What do you say?"

Scud is downcast, almost in tears, his voice very low.
"Thanks for wanting to help me, Villy and Meatball. But
I—I *like* having Nunu kiss me. I don't—I still don't think
she's evil. She's nice to me. Nobody's ever nice to me.
Especially not girls. I don't know what I do wrong. I wish
so much that you'd stop thinking I'm a loser." Scud pauses
and takes a trembling breath. "And there's something else.
About what Nunu's doing on the ceiling. She, she—"

Before Scud finishes, here come two more flying sau-
cers, hefty guys, the size of a big car and a very big truck.
One of them has a green dome and a yellow rim like
Nunu, the other one is done up in shades of dark purple.

Rich, painterly hues. The saucers make a low, intricate hum, a drone with subtle curlicues within. They hover above the wrecked car. The tendrils of their telepathy comb through the crannies of Villy's mind.

"Don't make me kill you," Meatball yells at the saucers, trying to sound tough. Her surface sizzles with dark energy. But maybe that's not enough. Next to these guys, Meatball is like a dog barking at alligators.

"I want my daughter," booms the green saucer. "They call me Pa Saucer." He has no visible mouth. His deep voice emanates from the resonant vibrations of his disk. He's twenty feet across and he must weigh over a ton. And he's the smaller of the two. At least his single eye is black, which is supposed to be good.

"Your daughter?" squeaks Scud. Pa Saucer is quite intimidating.

"Nunu," bellows the saucer.

Villy hears a chirping—it's Nunu closed up inside the whale, saying something in response, but he can't make out the words. And he doesn't dare step over to open the hatch. This scene could turn grim if he makes the wrong move.

The other saucer, the big purplish one—he goes and hovers right over the whale. He teeps that his name is Boldog. His single eye is red, which is bad. Villy almost expects Boldog to carry the station wagon away, like a raptor with a lamb.

But no. The bruise-colored saucer stabilizes himself, bracing his thick, muscular rim against the steady wind. And then he sends down a beam. It's not a cute, wiggly, green beam like little Nunu's—no, man, this four-ton dump-truck-sized saucer has a beam that's a brighter-than-white industrial laser that Villy can barely stand to see.

With quick, efficient motions, the beam cuts a circle in the battered whale's roof, about where the surfboards had been. As if on cue, Nunu rises through the hole, still upside down, bearing the freed disk of roof above her like a platter. And then she flips herself upright, using her rim like a suction cup to hold the piece of roof against her bottom.

"Greeting, dear father and esteem Uncle Boldog," goes Nunu, very demure.

"We return to Saucer Hall," thunders Pa Saucer. "Where you belong, Nunu."

"I love her!" Scud for some reason feels impelled to yell. As so many times before, Villy longs to choke his brother into silence. And then, suddenly remembering that Scud is teeping his thoughts, he feels horribly guilty. Why shouldn't poor desperate Scud find a scrap of love?

Pa Saucer's green shade darkens, and the lumbering Boldog tilts back, as if lining up the sights of his X-ray laser beam.

"I lay eggs!" bursts out Nunu. "They seed by him kiss! I no go back Saucer Hall. I go New Eden for hatch eggs. Mother Meemaw will love to see. Is allowed, dear father and esteem uncle?"

The three saucers touch down, and Nunu exposes the section of car roof so her father and uncle can ooh and aah. They're not angry—they're excited. Gloating, even. A fine hatch.

Villy moves closer to get a look, and Zoe hops atop a rock. Scud's on a rock too. He's clutching the polished bit of starstone he got from Hungerford. Like that's going to help anything. Take it easy on the kid, Villy.

In silence Villy, Zoe, and Scud study the dingy, flexible eggs. They wobble from side to side on the round bit of roofing.

"Scud saucer caviar," says Zoe, wanting to make a joke. Nobody laughs. The kids are scared. It's hella alien here, on this cold shadowy mountain, with the starstone monoliths on the top of the ridge, the frikkin enormous heavy saucers—and Nunu's eggs. Several dozen of them.

"What do you think happens when they hatch?" Scud asks Villy. "Will the babies follow me around?"

"I wish we could rub out the eggs right now," says Villy. "They're disgusting."

"Don't say that," protests Scud. "I mean—in a way, they're cute. They're mine."

Zoe unleashes a shrill, nervous laugh.

"Keep your voices down," calls Pinchley. "Don't rile them big saucers. We act right or they kill us. What it is."

Villy rises to the occasion. He clears his throat and faces Nunu's father. "Handsome eggs," he goes. "I suppose this makes us relatives."

Pa Saucer offers no response.

"You and me," continues Villy, taking a step towards the huge, bulbous dad. "Kinfolk." He makes a sweeping gesture that includes the eggs, Zoe, Scud, Nunu, and the monstrous elder saucers. "All one clan."

"You like to come visit New Eden?" asks Pa Saucer,

as if suddenly warming to the humans. He speaks better English than Nunu. "We can give you a ride. Some other Earthlings live there in a village called Berky. Just over the ridge from Van Cott. Your crew can settle in with Nunu and me if you like. We're good saucers. I'm divorced, but my ex-wife Meemaw lives nearby. Nunu's mother. Near Berky. We're working for freedom. Not like my pinhead brother-in-law Boldog here."

"Freedom is bad," rumbles Boldog. "An insult to our great master Groon."

"Groon is garbage," says Pa Saucer, his voice very clear. "He uses saucers like slaves!"

"Oh yes, you come to Berky us!" cries Nunu, fluttering close to Scud's face. "It nice for humans there. Very dangerous if you chase after Iravs."

Villy looks at Scud. Almost imperceptibly Scud shakes his head. And Zoe's very strongly against the invitation.

"No way!" she yells. "Leave us alone!" She raises her trumpet to her lips. Once again, she's on the point of hopping to Los Perros.

Nunu's Uncle Boldog tilts back, clearly longing to zap Zoe into a white-hot gas of plasma. But if Zoe hops fast, she'll be able to duck him. And she'll tell everyone on Earth about the saucers. She's already got her trumpet in action, boop-de-beeeping the start of her magic spell, tootling a sketchy rhythm.

The hop could work. After all, Zoe's already gone through the unny tunnel three times—first when she brought them here, and second when she did her panic hop from the night market to Los Perros, and third when she came right back to Van Cott. Maybe all she needs to do is lean on the notes a little harder—and her pearl will pop out of her pocket and open its gates and she'll be gone. Villy senses that Pa Saucer and Boldog are thinking this too—and they don't like it. They don't want Zoe to hop home and warn everyone about them.

"We'll go now," intones Nunu's father, drawing back from the standoff. His serious voice rolls across the stony wastes. "It's not for us to interrupt their mission, Boldog. It is well if they succeed."

Nunu fastens onto her scrap of car roof once more, with the eggs safe beneath her rim. She puckers her cartoony red lips at Scud, as if blowing a hopeful kiss.

"Bye, Nunu," calls Scud. "I'll miss you."

"Get the hell out of here," hollers Zoe.

"You're like the little dog that starts barking after the big dog walks away," Villy says to her with a smile. Teasing her a little.

The three saucers rise into the dull sky, and Nunu settles onto the wide rim of her father's disk, catching a lift. Rather than heading back towards Van Cott and Saucer Hall, the saucers fly over the Borderland Pass, veering to the left and towards, presumably, the New Eden basin.

"You'll miss Nunu, huh?" Villy says to his brother. "Even if maybe she *was* planning to drain your smeel. Dangerous friends. For sure her uncle wanted to blitz Zoe."

"Nunu's nice," repeats Scud. "I trust her."

"I saw the tips of her fangs," says Villy.

"Oh whatever," says Scud. "I've already teeped your redneck opinions. Fact is, Nunu has no reason to bite me.

She got what she needed by kissing me. A person's mouth is full of loose skin cells, see. Nunu scored as much of my DNA as she needed."

"DNA?" says Villy, not quite getting it.

"For fertilizing her eggs," says Scud.

"Oh wow!" exclaims Zoe. "So you didn't actually need to have sex with her."

"I *didn't* have sex with her," says Scud. "Can you get that through your tiny head?"

Zoe's loving the banter. She's in a good mood again. "Those big saucers were stoked about Nunu's eggs. Baby shower, anyone?"

"Maybe saucer-human blends are rare," says Villy. "Maybe there aren't all that many human males as funky as you, Scud. When the eggs hatch, you'll be like a sixteen-year-old hillbilly with about forty kids."

"I hope I see my saucerbabies," says Scud, off in his own world. "Will they look like me? I wonder if it's nice in New Eden."

"That basin's crawling with saucers," says Pinchley. "Not my scene. But if you gotta go there, be sure to stay in Berky. A farm town with good saucers. And there's skungy humans from ballyworld Earth mixed in. Freakers and seekers."

"The weird thing is that I've heard of Berky," says Zoe slowly. "Not only did my crazy father name his UFO group the New Eden Space Friends, he talked about Berky like it was a holy city. He had this T-shirt about it: *Where swain / and saucer miss / share bliss. / Visit Berky.* It's like we've fallen down a rat hole to a land where my dad's demented ravings are true."

"Your father lives in Berky right now," Pinchley now tells Zoe.

"How would you know that?" she cries.

"Mappyworld is mammoth, but words have wings," says Yampa. "Dad is glad to hear you're here."

"We all expect you three to stop Groon and his slaves from trashing Earth." says Pinchley.

"I hate how everyone keeps saying that," says Zoe, kind of shrugging it off.

For just a moment Villy forgets all the crazy hassles and looks at Zoe. The wind is blowing back her hair, uncovering her brow. A high rounded forehead, full of thoughts. Her voice is sweet, slightly draggy, and full of force. He can't quite believe she stood up to Nunu's uncle.

"You're on an epic quest," Pinchley continues. "And we're your helpers."

All this brave talk makes Villy feel weird and shaky. Like he's in a funhouse with mirrors that aren't mirrors. Also the car accident has him pretty warped. Also he drove all night. Also he's bummed about his broken red surfboard. He sits down beside a big rock, collecting himself. Zoe's father's lives in an actual saucer settlement in mappyworld?

Villy's never felt so tired and wrung-out in his life.

Dear Zoe comes and sits beside him—strong, rapid, adroit. Her ears are like delicate shells. He loves her.

FIFTEEN

maisie

zoe

Zoe, Villy, Yampa, and Meatball rest in the lee of a boulder while Pinchley works on the car. He assures them he can get the whale back into shape, maybe better than ever, so they can continue the trip via Thuddland. Meanwhile they make good use of pillows and blankets. Villy's asleep, his head in Zoe's lap. Naturally Yampa takes a picture.

As for Scud, he's at Pinchley's side, working on the car, seemingly in tune with the Szep, exclaiming over the cool, animalistic tools that Pinchley produces from his ant-leather tool belt.

The crawling pancake fixes the engine again. A giant tongue heals the cracked windows by licking them. A twinkling green spider weaves a taut cover across the drilled-out hole in the roof. The skinny water-balloon creature reappears to freshen up the quantum shocks—he makes them twice as powerful as before, which lifts the whale's body a full twenty feet off the ground. The bird with the black beak reworks the tires, expanding them until they tower high above everyone's heads—and while she's at it strengthens and extends the doors' bungee-ropes. A six-legged trowel creeps about on the whale's surface, patching the rips and buffing the finish. As a bonus, the trowel even fixes Villy's broken red surfboard. The whale is a best-in-show monster surfmobile for true.

Zoe smiles, looking down at her Villy, fast asleep. There hasn't been nearly enough laughter and fun so far. And not enough kissing. At what point did they decide their languorous road trip would have be an insane save-the-world rush? Because of the saucers? But the saucers have been a threat for centuries and centuries, right? Worrying about threats—that's for old people. That's all they do.

Oh, and they're also hurrying because of the Iravs and the caraway seeds. So dumb. I mean—caraway seeds?

Why not just relax, and drive a million miles—and who cares if they arrive a million days late? Put that on your tardy reports, all you teachers and bosses. *Zoe Snapp was one million days behind schedule!* Idly she wonders if a person lives a million days. Maybe not. She doesn't feel like doing the math. School's out.

"Take a gander at that rock," says Meatball, who's puddled on the ground beside Zoe. She's talking about a penguin-shaped boulder about thirty feet uphill. "It's watching us. And it's not the only one."

Meatball's right. Zoe can totally imagine that the big star-filled stones up there are watching them. It almost feels like the starstones are craning for a better view. Anything seems possible, once you accept the concept that this ridge is garnished with wadded-up light-years of space.

So far, nobody's had the energy to walk up to the top of Borderslam Pass and see if there's really a pair of basins on the other side. New Eden and the Thudd jungle, right? Zoe decides to go for it. She feels too hyper to sit around. She slips a pillow under Villy's head, wraps a spare blanket around her shoulders, and, trumpet in hand, walks towards the penguin boulder. It's fatter on the bottom than the top, and its cocked at an angle. The top is fully transparent, like a crystal, with swirls of stars within.

"Can you talk?" asks Zoe.

No spoken answer—but the starstone is putting out a nonverbal telepathic vibe. At first Zoe imagines it's a warm greeting. Like, "Hello." Or, "You're important." Or even, "You guys are the ones."

As if. Would an entire sector of the galaxy be rooting for three particular Earthlings? Would an Earthling root for three germs? The stone's vibe is one of serene indifference. Peaceful void. And Zoe's just reading things into it. But let her read.

She glances back at the others—Scud and Pinchley fixing the car, Meatball lounging, Villy and Yampa asleep. Her crew. She feels a rush of love for them. For once she belongs. Here at the ass-end of nowhere.

As Zoe proceeds further up the hill, she encounters more and more of the starstones. Each of them has one or more clear crystalline patches with spills of stars within. It's like she's looking out through the portholes of an interstellar ship.

But when she reaches the top of the ridge, she forgets the stones. She's standing at a triple point: the Earth basin behind her, the New Eden basin to her left, and the Thudd basin to her right. The Thudd basin looks maybe a little smaller than New Eden.

The lighting in the New Eden basin is pale and cool. Almost like what you'd see in an office. But the lighting in the Thuddland basin is warm, with a touch of green. Perhaps the glowons adjust a given basin's light to match that of the ballyworld planet that's somehow paired with it. Thus Van Cott's light matches Earth's, the light of New Eden matches a planet near Proxima Centauri, and so on.

New Eden has oceans and cities and green fields, a little like Earth. Unlike the blocky boxes that humans build, the New Eden buildings are like vertical parking lots or multilevel birdhouses, consisting of open shelves. The rack-like structures are topped by towering spires with saucers tethered to them. Looking along the base of the ridge separating New Eden from Van Cott, Zoe can make out a farm town with a human-scale look on the New Eden side of the ridge. That must be Berky, where Pa Saucer wanted to take them. Supposedly Zoe's dad has been living there since he disappeared. So strange.

The main thing about New Eden is of course the resident saucers. Thousands of them crowd the New Eden sky, in shapes and colors so various as to beggar description. It's like seeing one each of every flying insect species in the world. To call them saucers is simply a linguistic shortcut. They're spheres, dumbbells, donuts, cubes, snakes, zigzags—whatever. They nest in the cities, parade on the fields, and bathe in the seas. Zoe feels a little sickened by the sight of so many of them. Pinchley and Yampa insist that many of the saucers are good but, for Zoe just now, looking into New Eden is like seeing maggots on rotten meat. Ugh.

Studying the overall motions of the saucers a little more closely, Zoe notices a curving band above New Eden. It's a river in the sky, an air channel filled with saucers, a jet stream flowing into New Eden from who knows where. At the spot where the stream strikes the ground of New Eden, saucers boil outward across the landscape. Oddly, there's a steady inward flow of saucers towards the spot as well. It's hard to make out the details, but it may be that the stream is sucking up old saucers at the same time that it blows new ones out. Staring hard at the two-way river of saucers for several minutes, Zoe begins to imagine that she's hearing an eerie tune—a thin, incessant piping.

Turning her attention to the steamy and more intimate Thuddland basin is a relief. It's primeval and misty, with enormous trees and bright, splashy flowers. Really, really great light. Like full summer beside a fern-crowded stream. Sky vines snake into the atmosphere, buoyed by lighter-than-air pods on their stems. Leather-winged reptiles wheel in flocks, swooping among the trees and tendrils, their hoarse cries a cacophonous sonata. In the distance Zoe sees a colossal pink flying saucer, an intruder from New Eden, a mile wide and with a glowing red eye in her underside. The monster drags limp, dangling arms across the jungle, extracting smeel from plants and animals alike. Further in the distance is a giant blue saucer, presumably the first one's mate.

An enormous toothy serpent swoops past like an airborne express train. Fat green dinosaurs reach into the trees with necks a hundred yards long. An unseen raptor roars a joyful thunder that vibrates deep within Zoe's chest. Prehistoric raptors *always* have a nice day.

A broad dirt track slopes down into Thuddland, leading from the cold, windy ridge to the jungle and the rot and the green light and the bellowing and the mist. The path is dark and loamy, with fresh ruts—which suggest that the Iravs are somewhere ahead.

The wind is like an icepick up here on the eerie, stony pass with the starstones. Starting back downhill towards the purple whale, Zoe considers the fact that with each step she takes, she's crossing untold light-years of emptiness in her native ballyworld. She steps carefully, holding her blanket tight around herself. She's ready to rejoin her friends and to resume the trip.

But now one of the starstones blinks and lights up—as if it has an incoming call for Zoe, a call from someone who's very much at home in the mappyworld. A call from Maisie.

Zoe studies the ghostly image of Maisie within the stone. She's not naked anymore; she's wearing yellow tights and a crop top, and she's carrying a little clutch-bag cloth purse. Her dishwater-blond hair is in a ponytail. Her lithe seventeen-year-old body is outlined against the stars. She still has that floppy horizontal disk of skin jutting out from her bare waist, right above the tights. Maisie takes hold of her disk with one hand, gently bending it up and down. It's like she's waiting for Zoe to take the hint, but the hint is—what? The disk patterns itself with polka dots, then with paisley teardrops, and then it's blank skin again.

Maisie's thin voice vibrates from the stone. "Hey there, Zee. You and Villy and Scud are moving right along."

"Where are you?" demands Zoe. "Are you following me?"

"I'm in New Eden right now," says Maisie. "With Dad. I tunneled over a few minutes after you did. Right before our concert. And now I'm using teep to talk to you. I'm pretty good at telepathy. I learned from the saucers."

"Why are you calling?" says Zoe. "What do you want?"

"The cosmic beatdown's coming soon," says Maisie. "You and I and the Antwerpen boys will fight. Those two Szep, Yampa and Pinchley, they showed up in New Eden looking for some likely human heroes, and they asked Dad and me about it, and we thought of you three. That's why I gave you that saucer pearl and taught you the riff to open it. I took Yampa and Pinchley over to Van Cott to wait at the spot where your tunnel would come out."

Zoe asks three questions closest to her heart. "Dad's really in New Eden? How come you get to hang out with him? And how come you never told me?"

"I didn't want to upset you," says Maisie. "As for why he lives in New Eden, are you sure you want to know?"

"Not sure," says Zoe uneasily. Maybe, just maybe, the answer is starting to dawn on her. But no. She glances downhill towards her crew. Villy's awake, sitting next to Yampa on the ground, Meatball's watching Zoe, and Scud's behind the wheel of the purple whale, joyfully revving the engine. The car is twice as tall as before, and it's shiny all over. Pinchley makes last-minute checks. Inside the purple whale is where Zoe wants to be.

"Your father's second wife—Sunny Weaver—she's not my mother," Maisie is saying. "That's what you have to understand. My real mother—well, she has some connections over here in mappyworld. That's why I can work both sides. And that's why we four will be so important in the cosmic beatdown. You guys should hurry. Fetch that wand from Szep City!"

This is a lot to process, and really Zoe should talk to Maisie some more. But Zoe has had it with being guilt-tripped by her half-sister's lonely little voice. So she loses her temper and yells—that's what she does when she feels trapped. It's not a nice way to be, but it's how Zoe is.

"Don't tell me to hurry!" she shouts, more or less at random. "I am so frikkin tired of hurry!"

Without waiting for an answer, Zoe turns her back on the glowing starstone and picks her way down the slope. Down to her boyfriend. That's what Villy is by now, right? Even though they haven't really had a chance to say it. He's looking towards her, like he's wondering what she was hollering about just now.

"Let's go!" calls Zoe, trying to sound all upbeat and enthusiastic. She waves her trumpet in the air. "Let's ace this gig!"

On the hill above her, Maisie's image goes dark.

SIXTEEN

thuddland

scud

Scud's turn at the wheel," says Pinchley as they bounce—it's sort of a reverse-rappel now—up into the car. "You need a rest, Villy. And, ahem, don't forget you just now wrecked us. Don't want that again. Not with our car as shiny as it is."

"*Yeah*, I'll drive," says Scud, thrilled to be helming the monster-truck purple whale. "Even if I haven't gotten my license yet, we had a traffic-safety class at school. You sit up front with me, Pinchley."

"Reason the car's so gleaming bright is that I gave it a slipstream supershine," says Pinchley, settling in. "Meaning that we won't hear no air beating at us no more, even if the windows are open. We smooth as silk. We'll overhear whatever tryst or fracas or hooty squonk we're passing by."

"It'll be like we're riding an electric car through a talking diorama," says Scud.

"Just about," says Pinchley. "The way I've doctored up this car, she practically drives herself. But keep in mind the diorama has teeth. Be glad I finally fixed that driver side window so it's easy to close."

Villy and Zoe get in the back seat, and Yampa crawls past them into the way-back.

"The soiled, sordid swine nest for me," she says. "Yampa and Meatball—the voluptuous vixens of vengeance."

"I'm more what you'd call the bouncy blob of bulge," says Meatball. "With a zing of a zap." She thumps a pseudopod against the taut spider silk covering the hole in the roof. "What say we doff this lid, Yampa? That way I can be a pop-up tail-gunner."

"Not now," says Yampa. "It's cuttingly cold."

"I saw the Thudd jungle from the top of the pass," announces Zoe. Scud can tell that she's happy sitting in back with Villy. "It'll be hot down there. Teeming. And I had a conversation with Maisie, but to hell with that. I want to go, go, go! I hope you drive better than your brother, Scud." She winks at Villy, but he doesn't think it's funny.

"The accident wasn't my fault," he mutters. "I got distracted because I thought Nunu was about to bite Scud."

"There there," says Zoe, teasing Villy and babying him at the same time. "Put your wittle head on my shoulder and get some more sleepy-bye."

"Not yet," says Villy fighting back a yawn. "I want to see." He turns and looks at Yampa. "Can you do something to pep me up?"

"I'll exude some attar of Szep City rat," says Yampa, extending a gnarled, witchy finger. Tingling musk fills the cabin, and everyone catches a lift.

Thanks to Pinchley's stretch-lobster, the whale's interior is so big that Scud needs to lower the seat so he can reach the pedals. But his view out the windshield is still fine. He drives slowly up the stony slope to the pass. They roll over one waist-high boulder and then another—*poomp poomp*. Thanks to the gigantic tires and the maxed-out quantum shocks, the whale barely even tilts. Scud steers extra carefully around the larger starstone sentinels at the top of the pass.

Scud has set his own starstone on the dash for good luck, the one he got from Hungerford. And now he's driving past a really big starstone with those glints of light inside it. He slows down to stare at the thing—kind of gloating over the wild concept that there's stars and light-years and nebulae inside of it. He notices a kind of flaw in the shiny surface of the rock, as if a little piece of it is missing. And then comes a wild clatter.

It's his starstone going apeshit. It's bouncing around inside the closed-up car like a bird looking for a way out. The little starstone caroms off the windshield, off the seat, off the ceiling, off the side of Scud's head. Before it gets any wilder, Scud manages to catch it in both hands and stuff it way down inside his pants pocket.

"That starstone was lookin to go home," says Pinchley. "That's how they do. Hard to keep one for long. Especially when you're crossing a ridge. Good snag, Scud."

So okay, fine, and on they roll. Scud's awed by the jungle basin—it's the best thing he's ever seen. Toothy airborne reptiles, utterly primeval. An armored creature like a living tank, with a spiky club at the end of his tail. A flying green manta ray. A foul-smelling flower devouring a wildly squealing pig. Well, sort of a pig. More like a tapir, maybe. Its snout is a short, flexible trunk.

"Watch the road," cautions Pinchley.

They coast down along the black dirt road into Thuddland and—hooray!— it's Scud who's driving. What with all the tweaks, the car's hella smart. You barely have to steer, and Scud's managing a decent speed. Palms, tree ferns, and sky vines arch overhead. The leaves glow like stained glass in the Thuddland light.

"Keep a lookout for the Iravs," says Zoe from the back seat. "I don't think they're that far ahead. See how fresh the tire tracks are?"

The double-rutted trail winds on. By now they have the roof hole and the car windows open. Thanks to Pinchley's slipstream supershine treatment, there's no clamor of beating wind. The rich jungle speaks to them—an articulated chorus of life in full bloom. The humid air is laden with rich scents. Gardenia, cinnamon, and fig. Rot, dung, and blood.

The Thuddland creatures walk, crawl, and flap—six-legged deer, fist-sized spiders, tiny flying worms, naked rodents, striped pig-tapirs, waddling moa birds, lizards with beaks, leather butterflies, and a carnivorous puffball like a collapsed house beside a mound of bones.

"So sick," says Zoe. "I love it."

"Somewhere in your ballyworld there's a planet like this," says Pinchley.

"Did you guys say it's Goob-goob who makes your basins match our inhabited planets?" asks Scud, still hoping to get a straight answer.

"Nobody makes everything do nothing to everybody," says Yampa. "Mappyworld and ballyworld are two views of the same face."

"Hea-*veeeee*," says Zoe, drawing out the second syllable. Kind of mocking Yampa down. Villy laughs at the Szep too. The three kids are tired of never knowing what the hell is going on here. But what can they do? It's part of the trip.

Scud drives for several hours, doing his best to maintain a good pace. It's a kick, having these huge tires with the quantum shocks. The hulking car is as nimble as a rabbit. And thanks to his teep slug, Scud's aware of everyone's feelings. A big change for him. Pinchley's impatience that they aren't going faster is in balance with Zoe's worry that their speed is too high.

Not that Zoe's worrying all that much. She's mostly focused on Villy, who by now is too excited to sleep. He and Zoe are happy together, and they're holding hands. But Scud's not going to tease them. What with the Nunu business, he's in no position. He keeps wondering what his and Nunu's hatchlings will be like.

Meanwhile he's hearing an insistent gurgling, and now it grows into a splashy roar. A jungle river, easily a hundred feet wide. Sandbars and stony rapids separate the stream into channels, some shallow and some deep. Lively, muscular flows of water out there. Scud halts on the bank, not sure what to do.

"Let's take a break and go for a dip!" says Zoe. "I keep thinking we're throwing this whole trip away. Can't we relax and forget the Iravs?"

"I got a bad feeling them Iravs not gonna forget *us*,"

says Pinchley. "But, sure take a break. Not that swimming would be a cool move. Bound to be some biters in here."

"Got it," says Zoe.

A herd of squat, peevish dinos can be seen downstream, looking ready to charge. Closer in, the surface of the water is rippling with the motions of—Scud's teep helps him make out the shapes. Eels with legs, leeches with fins, and nautilus-like ammonites with tentacles and shells. A leathery turtle head darts out of the water and snaps a dragonfly from the air. Not exactly a turtle, more like a halibut with legs. And not exactly a dragonfly. It's one of those flying worms. The worm screams in a horrible, tiny voice as it dies.

"Whets the appetite, eh?" says Zoe, doing her gallows-humor thing. "Let's skip the swimming and have a picnic." Villy obligingly gets out their food mints, hands Zoe the roast beet, takes a tom turkey for himself, and gives the other tom turkey mint to Scud. When Scud puts his mint in his mouth, the surface melts off and turns into, well, slimy jelly. But the jelly tastes like meat, and it's easy to swallow. Scud eats another layer, then stashes the rest in his pocket with his starstone.

A flock of small winged reptiles skims along the river's surface, screeching, clacking their beaks, and devouring the tiny flying worms. Something pokes out of the stream near where they're standing—two extravagant feelers and a substantial pair of eyestalks. No, this wouldn't be a good place to swim.

Scud focuses his teep on the submerged creature and gets a sense of its mind. Slow, writhing, implacable. Its vision is in black and white. It's thinking of crawling out of the water and scrambling into their car. Crude fantasies of bathing in gray blood.

Upstream, the trees by the river begin to sway.

"Something big," says Pinchley. "We better roll out."

"The jungle Thudds aren't civilized one bit?" says Scud. He's teeping, but he can't make out for sure what's shaking those trees. "The Thudds in Van Cott were almost like people. They wore clothes. They had families. They talked."

"They was *mini* Thudds," says Pinchley. "Like I told you. Traders and diplomats. A different species, really. A full-size jungle Thudd—there's no chatting with that fella. Big appetite. Back in the car, guys, seriously. Then drive on across this stream, Scud. Crank up the power if we bog down. Whatever you do, don't stop."

"Rushing me again," grumbles Zoe, getting in the back seat with Villy. "Tonight's going to be different, okay? When we're out of this jungle."

"We'll cuddle up in private," Villy assures her. "We'll find a way."

"I'm not saying we're going to be sexually intimate," cautions Zoe in a low tone. Scud has to use his teep to hear her. "I'm not that easy."

"Nobody's every going to say you're easy, Zee." Villy is punch drunk with exhaustion. But even now he won't let up and go to sleep. Scud can tell Villy doesn't like to see his kid brother drive. Bossy know-it-all that Villy is.

Brutally Scud slams the car into gear, and they crunch over whatever was waiting for them in the water by the river bank. The thing writhes, snaps a supersized scorpion tail out of the water, and expires in a flutter of gassy burbles. Scud rumbles into the main part of the stream. It gets steadily deeper, rising to the top of their enormous tires. But the water's not coming in the windows.

Scud feels damn good about how well he's doing. And then those trees upstream part, and out charges a monster that's—not a Thudd after all. It's a giraffe with a giant beak, and with leather wings between his body and his long front legs. Like on a flying squirrel, of all things. The creature takes a few long-legged steps, bends his knees, and glides low along the river, plopping down in front of the purple whale.

Sound effects: *ker-splash* and a huge, discordant *caw*.

Reflexively and foolishly ignoring what Pinchley told him, instead of speeding up and veering around the attacker, Scud halts the car. It stalls. The raptor's beak is the size of a rowboat. Naturally he aims a hearty peck at the whale's windshield—which shatters into bits. The zillion tiny pieces of glass shower onto Scud and Pinchley, safety-glass cubes tumbling in a slow-motion cascade.

"Smooth move," jeers Villy, slouched in the back seat.

Scud is a devoted amateur student of dinosaur science, and in his opinion the ungainly assailant is akin to a little-known Earth dinosaur known as a *hatzegopteryx*. Scud's always wondered how it would be to meet one. And here it is—no, it's something even better: an *alien* hatzegopteryx! The tip of the monster's beak is in the front seat between him and Pinchley. It smells like rotten garbage.

Meatball enters the fray. She surges forward like rubber lava, envelops the point of the flying dino's beak, and feeds it a blast of dark energy that drops the behemoth to his knees, leaving him draped across the hood of the car. Meatball delivers a second zap and now the hatzegopteryx-thing is lying on his side in the river, possibly dead, with joyful, many-legged scavengers setting their pincers and feelers to work.

"Drive on, my man," says Pinchley, making a chilled-out gesture with his hand. Doing a billionaire-in-his-limo routine. "Don't linger to gawk at the rabble. We need to exit this jungle before nightfall."

"Um—how far *is* it to the next pass?" asks Scud as he rolls over the neck of the poor hatzegopteryx.

"Maybe three thousand miles," says Pinchley. "They call that gap Galactic Pass—on account of so many starstones there. You want me to take the wheel, kid? Or we could bring in Villy again, or let Zoe drive."

"I can do it," insists Scud. He can sense that Villy is eager to resume control, but no. This is Scud's chance to shine. He lurches and splashes across the rocky river, finds his way back onto the rudimentary dirt road, and powers the whale up to a completely reckless three hundred miles an hour. He uses his teep to do a quick mental scan on the passengers. Everyone except Zoe is fine with his driving. All of them want to be on the move.

It's annoying, however, to have those crooked little chunks of glass all over his lap, and to have the wind intensely beating in through the hole where the windshield used to be. Flying worms keep splatting onto Scud's face and bursting, leaving a foul-smelling residue of venom and blood.

"Not a tenable situation," says Scud.

"I'm on it," says Pinchley, all smooth and urbane. "Don't

need to slow down one tit or jottle, son. I've got me a deluxe model glassblaster beetle. Better than the healer tongue I used for the cracks after your brother rolled the car."

Pinchley draws yet another tool critter from his belt. It's like a transparent glass cockroach, but with too many legs—like everything else around here. It scurries around the car seats and the floor, gobbling up every bit of the windshield glass. By then it's the size of a bowling-ball, kind of scary almost, like a fat tick after a big meal. The glassblaster beetle drags itself onto the dashboard, and—

"Do it!" says Pinchley.

Ting—the beetle makes a move that's almost too rapid to follow. It pops out a sturdy little transparent umbrella and, bracing itself against the wind, twirls the umbrella very fast. The umbrella spreads out like tossed pizza dough spinning in the air. Its edges take hold of the windshield frame. The sheet oscillates back and forth like a drumhead and then—second *ting*—it locks into shape, having analog-computed its optimum surface curvature. The beetle glass is stronger and clearer than the windshield they had before. Pinchley feeds the glassblaster beetle a treat, then returns it to his tool belt.

Scud bombs on. He uses his teep to sense the myriad of minds in the jungle and, equally important, he senses the relatively empty zone wherein lies the road ahead. He can do this so well that he feels he could drive with his eyes closed, not that he actually tries it. He doesn't want to freak out the others, not when he's blasting along at four hundred miles per.

A humane bonus to Scud's teep technique is that he can

telepathically warn off all the minor critters that remain in their path—such as the clueless six-legged fawns and the ubiquitous flying worms, not that all of the worms listen.

"Why winged worms?" says Zoe around now. More and more of them are appearing, and despite Scud's efforts, they're splattering against the windshield at a growing rate. "What do flying worms have to do with the Age of the Dinosaurs?" Zoe adds.

"Remember that this isn't actually prehistoric Earth," says Scud. "It's Thuddland. It matches an alien planet that's twenty light-years across our galaxy."

"Oh."

Pinchley supplies an additional fact. "Those two sloppy mile-wide saucers that we saw from the ridge, those guys are *not* Thuddland natives. They slipped over from New Eden. I think they're called Bo and Peep?"

"Poppo and Bombo," corrects Yampa. "Groon's goons. Here from New Eden to scavenge stacks of smeel. Their oral arms ooze burning slime."

Pinchley speaks again. "Anyway, Poppo is feeding nearby, and she's the one stirring up the flying worms. I hope you kids kill Groon and Poppo and every one of those vampire saucers. I hate parasitic crap that flies."

"Do keep in mind that the flying Freeth are kind and noble," puts in Meatball. She's bulged part of herself out through that now-open hole in the roof. She has to push the surfboards apart a little so she can fit. "Poppo's off to our right and drawing closer!"

"Pink Poppo will waft past our party to be with blue Bombo," says Yampa. "Perhaps we lie low."

"Hell, if we keep takin' breaks and screwin' around, then Groon's invasion will be a done deal by the time the kids bag that Szep City wand and drag-ass it back to Van Cott," says Pinchley.

"If your famous wand is so great, then maybe it can fix things no matter *when* we get back," snaps Zoe. "I, for one, would like a good look at Poppo. Let's stop, Scud!"

As if on cue, one of Poppo's damp, dangling tentacles sways out of the undergrowth and slaps blindly into their car. Meatball goes ahead and zaps the oral arm, but the behemoth saucer couldn't care less. The goo on the tentacle is sticky, and the car is pulled a little way off the road before it lets go. Scud skids to a stop just in time to miss crashing into a tree.

"There's a clearing right over there," says Villy. He leans into the front seat, pointing. "See that really dense tree? Let's hide under there until the monster is gone. I don't want her to get interested in us."

"Fine," says Scud, doing his best to sound put-upon. But he'll be glad to take cover. He inches the car onto a sandy spot under the big tree. They lower themselves to the ground and stretch, enjoying the break from frantically zooming at hundreds of miles per hour.

The tree has numerous trunks, like a banyan. There aren't many animals to be seen here just now—the sloppy, titanic saucer's oral arms have drained the smeel from most of the critters in grove, which was furiously active just minutes ago. Meanwhile they can track where Poppo is because she's—singing. It's a hideously sweet sound, like the soundtrack to a namby-pamby kiddie cartoon featuring rainbows and unicorns. Weird to have the song emanating from a slobbering tent of death, up there in the sky with a red eye in her underside.

The many-trunked tree has a huge crown, which is still dripping with stinging saucer mucus in certain spots—but that just means you have to watch your step a little bit. The light is a luscious shade of yellow-green. It's interesting to study the crazy little flowers and mushrooms that grow around here—the ones that the avid saucer didn't happen to destroy.

Scud goes behind a tree trunk to take a pee. And that's when he spots the weird toadstool. It's waist high, a glistening shade of pale orange. And— how random is that?— it's got bunch of glowing words on its top surface. Like a credit screen.

"Hey!" Scud yells to the others. "Look at this!"

And here's the text they see:

COSMIC BEATDOWN
PRESENTING
ZOE SNAPP, VILLY ANTWERPEN & SCUD ANTWERPEN
VERSUS
GROON & HIS FLYING SAUCERS
CO-STARRING
MAISIE SNAPP
YAMPA & PINCHLEY
MEATBALL AND THE IRAVS
AND A CAST OF HUNDREDS OF THOUSANDS
DIRECTED AND PRODUCED BY
GOOB-GOOB

A big, snot-like gout of saucer slime dribbles from the tree onto the toadstool and it withers. The words on its surface are gone. For a moment nobody says anything—their minds are too blown.

"For real?" says Zoe. "A tweaked, sinister credit screen for a show with us in it—and we see the credit screen on a luminous toadstool in a jungle in a parallel world?"

"Maybe this world is talking about itself," says Scud. "And that means we're in a virtual reality. Like in one of those movies where—"

"*Screw* that stale you're-inside-a-game bullcrap," yells Zoe. "Look!" She tears off a chunk of the toadstool where it's not withered from saucer snot. She crumbles the chunk open, and within a hollow in the toadstool flesh are three tiny striped bugs, sitting around a berry that they're eating for dinner. The bugs stare up at them, twitching their damp feelers, not overly alarmed.

"This is not some lame-o cheap-ass videogame," continues Zoe, as if vindicated by the sight of the bugs. "Not some feeble piece of code, drawing piles of colored blocks inside a dipshit digital computer."

"You go, Zoe," says Villy, enjoying the rant.

Zoe gestures at the space around them, taking in the fat-trunked trees, the jewel-like flowers, and the timid flying worms who are only now starting to reemerge. A nearby sky vine dangles from its mile-high hovering float, not far from skeenky Poppo, who is drifting away like a cloud.

"This is my real life," cries Zoe. "I'm on a million mile road trip in a wonderful alien world. So don't frikkin try to bring me down into your world of bogus bullcrap vidcogames, Scud!"

Scud teeps into their surroundings, testing out the feel of what Zoe says. This world is rich with smeel, incalculably dense and strange, filled with minds large and small, scattered like grains of sand. "Maybe you're right," he says. "But, still—"

"You said *bullcrap* twice," Yampa remarks to Zoe, focusing on that for no real reason. "Not *bullshit*?"

"Bullcrap is flatter," says Zoe, winging it. "A dry pie. Not as smelly."

"Listen at the farmgirl," goes Villy, putting on his country accent.

"So, okay, fine," goes Scud. Giving in to Zoe. "Let's suppose this is real. But why did we see those words on the mushroom? How can things get all meta like that if we're not inside a videogame?"

"Simple," says Pinchley. "The frikkin Irav wrote on the toadstool."

"You shouldn't keep saying *the Irav*," goes Villy. "There's four of them, okay? We cut up that first one and all the parts stayed alive. Get it through your head."

"The Irav's in four pieces, fine," says Pinchley. "But probably he's still got just the one mind, shared four ways. Whatever he is, he's not a Szep."

"Could he be a saucer?" asks Villy.

"I expect he's in cahoots with them leech saucers," says Pinchley. "But naw, he's not a saucer. When you cut up a saucer, it dies. They have innards and all that good stuff, including a saucer pearl in their middle to help them fly.

This chopped-up Irav is some special kind of shapeshifter alien."

"Okay," says Villy. "And why would the Irav or Iravs write the fake credits on the toadstool?

"To pique us," says Yampa. "So we pursue them with pulsating passion."

"And why do they want us to chase them?" asks Scud, always one for another question.

Pinchley sighs. "I figure they're settin it up so we're nice and far from home when they—or their friends the vampire saucers—ambush us and kill us. Not that we're gonna let em do that."

"If the bad saucers want to kill us, then one of them could have zapped us as soon as we showed up in Van Cott," protests Zoe. "Or in the pass. Or they could tell Poppo to flop down onto us right now. Why stall and play cat-and-mouse?"

"They not sure how quick you are," says Pinchley. "They don't want Zoe Snapp making a last-second escape and warning the ballyworlders back home."

"I hate to say it, but I sort of doubt if I could tunnel home from here," says Zoe. "We've already come too far. If that's what you're talking about."

"Maybe you can, maybe you can't," allows Pinchley. "Your saucer pearl's mighty small. Pearl like that won't grow no really long unny tunnel. Wouldn't be much good for levitating neither. But you never know."

"How does the levitation thing work?" asks Zoe. "If I can possibly switch our conversation's topic away from my impending doom."

"If you ever get hold of a decent-sized pearl, I'll teach you to fly," says Pinchley. "But for now we gotta drive."

"Mount the jolly whale and drive like jiggly maniacs," cries Yampa. "Further fun before Yampa dies!"

Right about then they hear a blast of hooting and honking. It's the four misshapen Iravs themselves, peering back at them from a bend in the road ahead. They've been waiting there in their stolen car. Evidently, they want to gauge the effect of what they wrote on the toadstool. And they're eager to goad their pursuers even more.

Scud can see from here that the disembodied pair of Irav legs has grown a pair of eyes in his thighs, and a mouth in his crotch. Call him the legs-Irav. The chunk of torso with an arm has formed a slit mouth and a pair of eyes in his chest. Call him the chest-Irav. The scrap of torso with a shoulder, an arm without a hand, and the original head—he's the head-Irav. The free hand is still here too, the hand-Irav, looking pretty hefty. Perhaps the hand-Irav has grown an eye and a mouth? Hard to see, as he moves so fast—like a fat tarantula scrambling across the dash and seat-tops of the stolen Szep convertible.

Scud would really, really like to kill that hand. The hand-Irav is the one who stole the caraway seeds that were supposed to pave their way when they got to Szep City. Which is still one *hell* of a long way off. Hard to believe they'll ever get there.

As before, the Iravs make rude gestures. And now they're hollering what must be curses. They have very high voices.

"They're talkin' Szep," says Pinchley, cocking his head. "But they got a weird accent. And they're makin' filthy insults."

Focusing on his teep, Scud can just manage to decipher what Pinchley hears the Iravs as saying. They're telling Pinchley that he's a parasitic intestinal worm perched atop a fresh-laid turd.

"*Skorkers*!" cries Pinchley, losing his cool and dropping into the Szep tongue himself. "Drive, Scud! And Meatball, get ready to zap those *sneevers* where it hurts!"

"Why we no got gun, Pinchley?" Yampa asks Pinchley. "No *sneever*-shooter in our stash, for why?"

"I did bring a poison toad," says Pinchley.

"Guns are snug," says Yampa, pointing one of her fingers. "*Boom*! Why we mooch along so mild?"

"This way it's more of a—challenge," says Pinchley. "Doing a million mile road trip unarmed. This way we have to do wilder moves. I like that."

"Irresponsible idiosyncratic irresistible idiot," says Yampa. "My partner Pinchley."

They're in the whale and rolling again, and the Iravs have sped another few bends down the road. The giant saucer Poppo is gone. The car comes to a miles-long straightaway through a grassy prairie. Way up ahead the Iravs pause, flaunting themselves and making obscene signs. Scud can teep the slyness and the low cunning in their minds, but he can't make out what precise trick they're planning to pull.

Meatball is ready to help the kids—her body crackles with dark energies. She has a fat pseudopod sticking out of the roof's hole between the surfboards. She's prepared to pulse a jolt at anything that physically attacks the car, anything that's smaller than a giant saucer, that is. The chase is still on. Scud rockets forward, the Iravs take off, and the jungle closes in on both sides.

Now it's time for a giant jungle Thudd. He steps forth from the tree ferns beside the road ahead. He has high thighs, a restless meaty tail, and finicky forelimbs folded high on his chest. His head is like a tractor-trailer truck with saber-sized alligator teeth. In anticipation of a tasty kill, he leans back his head and does his roar.

Scud gooses the purple whale's engine and shoots past the Thudd before the monster can fully block the road. "Lost him!" Scud prematurely cries.

"You'll be surprised how fast the damn animals can move here," says Pinchley, looking out the back window. "We got our own kinds of natural laws."

Thus begins a five-hour chase across two thousand miles. As the end nears, full night has come on. The glowons dim as they settle onto the dirt and the plants. The jungle and the interspersed savannahs are pale ghosts of themselves. The only spots of color are in creatures' eyes—luminous eyes in the trees, on the vines, under the bushes, on the prairies. Yellow, puce, and violet eyes.

Scud depends heavily on his teep slug for navigation. He avoids the minds to the sides of the road and aims for the thoughts of the fleeing Iravs. Not that he can see very deeply into their minds. They have a mirrored, reflective quality that, Scud now realizes, reminds him of Meatball's consciousness. Might the Iravs be shapeshifting Freeths?

But the Iravs don't fly, and Meatball does. Things make less sense all the time.

Be that as it may, for now Scud's main job is to stay ahead of the relentless Thudd. The monster guides himself by sound and smell, and perhaps he has night vision. Now and then he stumbles off the path with a crash and a chagrined bellow, and when that happens, Scud is able to gain some ground. In the occasional stretches of savannah, Scud extends his lead by driving a frenzied, reckless thousand miles per hour, at least for short bursts, with the car all but airborne, bouncing from tuft to hummock to swale.

But the Thudd always catches up. He's like a monster in a nightmare, like a lumbering Frankenstein who never sleeps. The Thudd is obsessed with them. It's like having a kaiju chase your car from New York to San Francisco. Soothed by the fact that Scud has his teep working for him, Villy ends up sleeping through the whole thing, but Zoe and the others stay alert. There's one particularly close call when the Thudd actually claws the back of the car. Meatball sends an arm of slime through the hole in the roof and past the surfboards. This time her zap has its intended effect. The Thudd collapses with a meaty shriek of pain—wonderful sound. But half an hour later, the alien dino's on their butt again, and it's only Meatball's power of zap that keeps them alive.

Zoe reaches her breaking point. She gets out her saucer pearl, brings her trumpet to her lips, and toots her special tune. Observing her via teep, Scud senses that the connection isn't there. The pearl doesn't turn transparent. It doesn't become an unny tunnel gate. They really have come too far. Scud senses Zoe's sense of despair. But then the Thudd trips over a herd of wildly squealing pig-tapirs and the great beast pauses to devour them. Maybe fate's on their side.

Finally, they're tear-assing up the final steep patch of road that leads to Galactic Pass—at the far side of the Thuddland basin. Scud hopes something is going to change up there. The Thudd thunders at their heels. Meatball pokes a pseudopod body out through the car's roof hole yet again, and fires more bolts of dark energy. But these zaps don't amount to much. Meatball's power is running low. All Scud can do is drive faster.

Steering mostly on instinct, Scud wallows the whale past a stand of especially large starstones and into the saddle of Galactic Pass. Gigantically, ponderously, the Thudd leaps through the air towards them, ready for the final kill, and—

He slams into an invisible wall. A beautiful crunchy thud, a heart-warming bellow of pain. The starstones have thrown up a force field. They're more than wadded-up star fields. Just as the Szep and that guy in the Borderslam Inn had hinted, the starstones can function like club bouncers, barring the most obstreperous guests.

"*Thank you!*" says Scud, pulling the whale to a stop. He's numb and shaky. Up ahead of them, the crazy, misbegotten Travs are already driving down into another basin, like a car full of evil, indestructible clowns. Scud just stares after them, his body slack. He's utterly wiped. Jungle landscapes stream inside his eyes. He can't drive another inch. But he doesn't like to admit it. Using his teep, he nudges brother Villy—who's been asleep for about five hours.

"Let's stop for the night," is the first thing Villy says, and that's just what Scud wants to hear. "I need some *peaceful* sleep," says Villy. "We don't want to barrel into some other goddamn basin in the dark, do we?" He stretches and looks around. Once again, the air is thin and cold. "You did good, huh, Scud?"

"What's in that next basin?" Scud asks the two Szep.

"Alien ants," says Yampa, sniffing the air. "Smell them? Like vinegar. Alien ants and aphids and anteaters with white patches like diapers."

"We'll be taking the other basin, though," says Pinchley. "This is another three-way junction, you understand. A monkey saddle."

"Monkey?" goes Villy.

"He's talking about a shape," says Scud. "It's math. A saddle with, like, a third trough for an imaginary monkey's tail."

"Wait," says Villy. "I thought we were chasing the Irav to get back our caraway seeds."

"Screw the Irav for now," says Pinchley. "The point is to get to Szep City. And it's shorter through that third basin. Also I don't like ants. And you know those frikkin Irav are hell-bent on messing with us. For sure we'll see them again. And that's when we'll get back our seeds."

"What's *in* the third basin?" asks Zoe. "The one that's not ants."

"You'll see tomorrow," says Pinchley, doing his stupid *mysterioso* routine. "Your boyfriend's gonna flip."

"Who says he's my boyfriend?" says Zoe, shooting Villy a look.

Villy isn't paying the right kind of attention. "Zoe and

I will sleep in the car's front seat," he says. "Pinchley and Yampa in the back seat. Scud and Meatball in the rear. Move it, Scud."

"I am *not* going in the pig's nest," wails Scud. "It would be sad there with no Nunu. Anyway, I drove all day. I deserve the front seat all to myself." He knows he sounds bratty, but he's not going to be pushed around.

"Oh god," says Zoe. "Let's just sleep outside on the ground, okay Villy?"

"Backpacker-style," says Villy. "Could be rad. Keeping in mind that it's like the high Sierras in these passes. We can expect insane wind, and subzero cold, and we'll be lying on sharp stones. But that's fine—just so precious Scuddy is happy." He pauses. "I wonder if Pinchley here can—"

"Yaar," goes Pinchley, as if reading Villy's mind. "I got the kit. My water-balloon worm will make you a quantum-shock pad, and my spider tool can weave you a tarp for a tent. We'll make a lean-to against one of those starstone sentinel rocks. Won't take but a minute. You'll see a glow from, like, the Horsehead Nebula inside that rock, no doubt."

"Romance," says Zoe with a hopeful smile. "About time."

"Have fun," says Scud, trying to sound like he understands that other people have feelings. Wearing that teep slug on his wrist continues to make the process easier. But Scud's own comfort still comes first. "Toss me a blanket and a pillow, will you, Yampa?"

Scud conks out on the front seat and dreams of Nunu.

SEVENTEEN

surf world

villy

I t's dark on the ridge, with exquisite glows of starry light from the stones. Exciting. And in the distance, off to the left, Villy can hear—

"Surf?" he asks Pinchley.

"You know it, brah. You gonna get some extreme action when the light comes up."

"Big waves?"

"Planetary, my man. They got wall waves a mile high."

Villy has half a mind to go stumbling towards the roar, but Zoe wraps both arms around his waist. Like she's anchoring a zombie. The cutting wind is back.

"Make our tent?" Zoe says to Pinchley.

"You got it," says the friendly Szep. He hunkers down beside the most imposing of the stones. Villy catches a glimpse of the balloon thing and the green spider.

And then Pinchley's done, and Zoe leads Villy into a freshly assembled lean-to. They lie down on the invisible mat of a quantum shock absorber. The starstone and the shaped spider silk shield them from the wind. They have their quilts from the car. The bower is gently lit by the Horsehead Nebula. Or whatever you want to call that apparition inside the crystalline rock. The quantum-shock mat is firm and warm. Score.

"You're beautiful," Zoe whispers to Villy, smiling up at him from within the circle of his arms. But, as always, there's something a bit sly about her. Awaiting his move. Two or three steps ahead of whatever he plans. Never mind.

He kisses her for a while, and it's good. He slides his hand under her shirt, and that's okay. She's with him when they slip off their jeans. But when he puts his hand between her legs, she says no.

"We've got time, Villy. Don't spoil it." Girl talk. Spoil? Her breath is warm in his ear.

"What if we die tomorrow?" goes Villy. "Fried by the saucers."

"Then it won't matter either way."

Villy doesn't really mind being pushed back. Obviously, he has to try. And he'll try again tomorrow. But right now, relax.

"This trip," says Zoe after a bit. "It's so much more intense that I could have imagined."

"Too true," says Villy. "I thought we'd be eating corn and fried pork chops in Kansas. Camping by a bend in a lazy river."

"Maybe we should turn around now?" says Zoe. "We went over the Borderslam Pass like you wanted, and we saw all of Thuddland today, but couldn't that be—"

"I don't want to bail," says Villy. "I mean, I've given up so many times in my life. And there's gonna be surf tomorrow, right? And there's this angle that we might save the Earth. And—"

"It's so insanely dangerous here," says Zoe. "And if we do the whole crazy million mile drive to Szep City, that means we'll hit, like, two hundred more basins on the way."

"And we barely survived the first two basins," says Villy. "I get your point. But you can always save us, right? With your trumpet and your pearl?"

"Not from this far," says Zoe. "I tested it in Thuddland. You were totally asleep, but when the Thudd nearly caught up with us, I tried to open up the unny tunnel, and it didn't work at all. I'm really not suicidal, you know. That's a pose. Please understand that."

"If you had crawled back through the tunnel would you have taken me along?"

"I think so. Sure. But right now, that's not an option. We're too far. So now I'm thinking maybe we drive back to Van Cott?"

A fresh wave of fatigue hits Villy like a heavy drape. "Hush and cuddle," he says. Zoe wriggles onto her side, and he spoons himself against her back. "Gotta do the Surf World basin at least," he says.

"We'll talk," says Zoe, her voice rising at the end. She's clearly jazzed about being in bed together. "We're two bad mice," she murmurs. "In a cute dollhouse. We'll chew up everything in sight."

"Squeak," says Villy. And then he's asleep.

When he wakes, the glowons are doing their thing, shedding pale daylight across the Galactic Pass. Zoe's standing outside the lean-to, playing a bebop reveille on her horn. Villy rises and joins her beside the slanting sheet of spider silk. Zoe stops playing and hands him a food mint.

"Behold the Valley of the Ants," she says, gesturing to the right. She's chirpy and fey. Seems like for the moment she's put her fears away. "How would you like to go down there?"

Villy sees hundreds of the ants from here, shiny colored critters crawling on muddy nests. Some of the anthills are shaped like sandcastles, and some have the form of gothic cathedrals with balconies and hidey-holes and lacy passageways, all of mud. Among the anthills are gardens of tan moss and fungus, edged by clusters of dun aphids. A wild twittering drifts up from the Valley of the Ants. Also the smell of pickles.

"Is there such a thing as brown light?" Villy asks Zoe. "Ant light."

"But the ants themselves are like brooches made of precious gems," says Zoe.

"They bite," says Villy. "And four Iravs are down there waiting to jump us. I'm not going into the Valley of the Ants."

Zoe laughs, unsurprised. She's definitely in an up mood. "No ants? Well, *that* means you're today's radio KFJC dream surfari winner!" She's using a college-radio-deejay voice. She gestures grandly to the left. "*You're* going to Surf World, Mr. Villy Antwerpen of Los Perros, California!"

Yes. The Surf World basin is edged with huge, crumbly cliffs and a wide beach. And from there on out, it's nothing but sea—filled with bizarre, unnatural surf.

Monstrous glassy combers, lively pup-tent waves scooting off at angles, and—in the distance—waves like pyramids with staircases on their sides. And out past the horizon, if Pinchley is to be believed, they'll find unimaginably high walls of water, thin and wobbly, steaming along like express trains.

"So—you and I will ride those on our boards?" says Villy, still not sure if Zoe is serious about going along with his big plan.

"Me, I'm staying in the car all day," says Zoe. "It's my turn to drive. But you, Villy, you've got to surf. That's who you are. It's why you're here." And she means it.

"Yaar," says Villy, covering his fear and excitement with a facade of brain-dead surfer cool. "Tasty tubes."

Their gang is gearing up to go. At the cliff's edge, Yampa takes a picture of Scud and Pinchley standing under the massively tweaked purple whale. The car's frame is nearly twenty feet off the ground.

Scud proudly tells Villy that he still has his starstone. He let it sit next to one of the sparkling elder starstones for a while this morning and, according to Scud, his pet stone made a personal decision to stay with Scud for now. Supposedly it likes him.

Meatball is gung-ho about crossing Surf World. "Far more suitable than the Valley of the Ants," she opines. "Surf World is optimal." She hovers high in the air, flexing her body against the steady wind. Big beaky birds fly by in lines, like biker gangs on a run.

"The waves are going the wrong way," Zoe now observes. "Did anyone notice that?"

Um, yes, most of the waves are rolling outward from the shore to the open sea. Scary and strange. Catch one of those suckers, and you're not coming back.

"No problemo," intones Villy, masking his fear. "Easier that way. The idea is to get to the other side of Surf World, right?"

"Come see what we did," calls Scud from under the car. "Pinchley made a rudder, and I got him to shape it like a skeg. Like the fin on a surfboard?"

"I hope it rotates," says Villy. "We'd want to maneuver."

"Pinchley knows that," says Scud. "He's been here before. Just come and look, Villy."

Villy knows his little brother is hungry for praise. So why deny him? Why be a prick *all* the time? Especially if you're about to die. The rudder is in fact very nice. It's like half of a boomerang, a shiny, fifteen-foot rudder that sweeps back from the underside of the purple whale. Quantum vortex tubes connect it to the car's steering system.

"Excellent," says Villy.

"We rode through Surf World on the way here," says Pinchley at Scud's side. "Only we didn't go through Galactic Pass."

"Did you like Surf World?" asks Villy. "Do you surf?"

"At home, I ride the sky. We have this permanent gale, high above Szep City, a windy layer between us and a cloud that's thousands of miles high. You can skysurf the gale when you're there. And you'll want to see the cloud above the gale too. That's where Goob-goob lives."

"One freakshow at a time," says Villy, waving off the chatty Szep.

He makes the trek up to the whale's roof rack so he can check the two surfboards. Villy's red one has a funky crufty patch from Pinchley's trowel tool. He pushes the patch hard, testing its strength.

"Quark bonds," Pinchley says from below. "The best."

"I just hope my board's soul didn't leak out," says Villy. He's half joking, but he kind of means it. "I've ridden it so much that I feel like it's alive."

"Got you covered," says Pinchley. "I honked some smeel outta my nose and rubbed it onto your board's repair patch. This red mofo's soul is whole."

The Surf World light is a honeyed gold, like the light you get in Santa Cruz an hour before sunset. As for the surf—the waves keep looking bigger, though from up here it's hard to judge their size, given that their shapes are so strange.

There's no consistent swell, and the waves surge through each other, with no apparent regard for physical law. Staring at them does something unpleasant to Villy's head. In the weirdness of the moment, he feels like everyone's voice has gone high and tiny, and like he's seeing through binoculars turned the wrong way.

"Too gnarly?" says Pinchley, waggling his lower jaw in a savage Szep grin. "Know something else about them waves? They alive."

"You mean alive in the broad, stoner sense that *everything* is alive?" says Villy, trying to sound all ironic and calm.

"Alive in the sense that the Surf World ocean is ten percent smeel," says Pinchley. "A cocktail of consciousness, old son. Trippiness a la carte."

Zoe is perched in the driver's seat, looking cute and petite. "Let's go!" she calls. "Meatball spotted a track that goes down to the beach."

"Hey, *I'm* supposed to be the driver!" yells Scud.

"Not today," says Zoe calmly.

"I want a picture of the boys with the boards," says Yampa, holding her hands by her head and rocking her skinny body back and forth. "Surfari shot. Get the blue board, Scud, and stand with your brother."

So they do that. *Click*.

"Scud's going to suuuurf!" calls Zoe from the car. Sweetening her voice and warbling the last word. Mocking Villy's little brother again. "This is going to be *such* the epic day,"

"*Not* going to ride," Scud mutters to Villy. "Don't want to learn. I'll navigate. Me and my teep." He drops Villy's blue board roughly onto the ground and scrambles into the front seat of the car next to Zoe.

"I doubt I'll ride either," Zoe calls down to Villy. "Not in this mess."

"So *I'll* surf," says Yampa, inquisitively bending over the blue board. "Stand center? Eee-Zee. I'll virtualize viggy visuals."

"You mean shoot videos?" says Villy.

"Teep tracks," says Yampa. "For Lady Filippa's rug."

Villy puts the boards back on the roof, and ends up stuck in the back seat with Pinchley and Yampa. At least he gets a window. Meatball squeezes into the pig's nest. Scud is annoyingly happy to be in front with Zoe. Triumphant almost. Villy would like to choke him from behind.

The winding road down the cliff isn't bad, given that the cliff is an insane two thousand-foot drop. But others have traveled this path before. And the whale's immense tires get superb traction. They descend through a series of vegetation zones—lichens, grasses, shrubs, ferns, and fat-leaved succulents akin to ice plants.

Seen from the beach, the waves are ungodly big. Much larger than Villy had estimated from the top of the cliff. The ones he'd been thinking of as pup tents are the size of barns. The combers are a hundred feet tall. And the staircase pyramids—they're the size of villages. There are puffball waves too—great churning spheres upon the water. But he doesn't yet see the wall waves that Pinchley mentioned. The waves huddle, jostle, consult, and rush out to sea.

Villy and his crew open the car doors. The wall of sound rushes in. The cliffs echo the clashing chatter, doubling its force. Louder than a rock concert. The friends have to yell to talk to each other.

"It's two or three thousand miles to the pass we want," Pinchley tells them. "We're not going straight across the middle of the basin, so it's not as far as it could be. The place we're headed is called Flatsie Pass—on account of the Flatsies have a village there. You don't see them much on this side of the Surf World basin. Too close to New Eden. I'm gonna tweak the tires one more time. Shape all four of em into paddle-wheels. Like we did last time, hey Yampa?"

"Frontwheeler sternwheeler," sings Yampa. "Water-wheel."

While they stand on the forlorn beach, Pinchley produces a tool critter shaped like a large clamshell with black
edges and runs it across the treads of the tires. Graphene
shelves pop out. Not that Villy's focusing on this. He's
busy staring at the sea.

It's not remotely like anything he's ever seen. And the
waves do seem alive. Quirky, willful, and no two of them
the same. Shape, shade, speed, size—everything's up for
grabs. These waves do what they want.

"I'm teeping them," hollers Scud. "No words. Feelings
and motion. Like body gestures. They sense the car and
our boards. They want us."

"Great," answers Villy. "I'll be a tuna in a shark tank."
Increasingly wired, he jounces up and down. The amped
Yampa leaps into the air and does a double flip. And Meat-
ball soars back to the top of the cliff. Checking things out.

At Villy's side, Zoe holds her pearl and plays her trum-
pet, which is barely audible through the ocean's roar.
Obviously, she's testing if she can open her unny tunnel.
And obviously she can't. She shakes her head and shoots
Villy a look. Looks at the ocean. Looks back at him.

"Don't," she shouts. "Let it stop here. We get back
home, regroup, and drive to Iowa."

"Apple pie," says Villy, halfway to agreeing with her.
"Ice cream."

"Car's ready!" yells Pinchley, extremely loud. He can
puff up his throat like a bullfrog's. No end to this guy's
weirdness. He's put fins onto all of the wheels by now.
"Them waves aren't so bad," he booms. "They's good old
boys and gals. They only act rough cause they shy."

"Heard that line before," Villy says to Zoe, putting his mouth right by her ear. The wave sounds are stacking up inside his head. And that last line of Pinchley, it reminds him of the bad time last year after his mother died. He sings a little song, pumping himself up, inventing the words on the spot.

Kid in school picked on me, teacher said bullies are shy.
Kid said I was a mamma's boy, because he'd seen me cry.
It had only been a month, a short long month, a month since
poor Mom died.
I didn't hit the bully cause that's not my style, I'm a quiet loner
on the side.
But now I'm in the open and I'm ready for a wave.
I'm rocking with my girlfriend and Mom's one year in the grave.
I'm gonna face the reaper and help my posse rave.
I'm an epic bad-ass surfer who's gonna make the save.

Villy pauses for breath. He's got himself so stoked that he's shaking.

"You've got nothing to prove!" Zoe yells at him. "You're already my hero!" Awkwardly she embraces him, and they're kissing with their mouths off-center.

And this is when Meatball comes spreading panic, bobbling down from the cliff's edge. "Saucers up there!" the Freeth booms. "And the giant Thudd got past the star-stones! We've no choice but to press on, chaps. Do or die!"

"We'll cross the water!" Villy yells to Zoe. "We can do it. We'll make it to Flatsie Pass. And then we'll drive back to Van Cott along the ridges and hop home. I promise!"

He can't really hear Zoe's answer above the waves, but her expression is answer enough. She's on his side. She's morphing her fear into fire and grit. It's like Villy and Zoe are undergoing chaos-driven catastrophe-theoretic personality transformations—this being lingo that Villy knows not from science class but from videogames. Zoe flashes a wild smile and makes a steering gesture with her two hands. She's gonna drive.

Then they're all in the car again, with the roof hole closed and the windows rolled up tight. Pinchley offers Zoe his carefully thought-out advice about how to launch a paddle-wheel car into massively chaotic surf: "*Bomb in there like you batshit crazy, Zee.*"

Zoe unleashes a long, rising scream and revs the dark-energy engine to a quark-busting level that sends them tearing across the beach and well into the sea, plowing a gully through the waves. And then a gigundo pup-tent wave blindsides them like a brutal enforcer at a scurvy roller derby. They're on the point of capsizing. Wearing a thin, abstracted smile, Zoe swings the rudder like she's been a sailor all her life. She rights the ship— that is, rights the car—then speeds through a jiggly stretch of lively puffball waves and slopes up onto the backside of a monstrous comber rolling away from the shore.

"When you get to top, drop and ride," counsels Villy, leaning forward from the back seat.

"*Yeek yeek!*" goes Zoe. She's laughing and bobbing her head. She looks batshit crazy-as-a-fox, fully into wild-girl mode, and feeling the better for it.

"We're *on*," cries Villy. "Riding the now."

Zoe churns to the top of the hundred-foot comber, tee-ters on the lip, and slips onto the tube's clean, smooth face. With the engine on idle, the purple whale skims endlessly down the self-renewing hill of water. It's like she's riding a titan at Mavericks, with no shore-break in sight. Sweet.

For a while all is mellow—the big wave is swallowing everything it hits, sweeping a path through the living sea. The greens and blues of the ocean are beautiful in Surf World's golden light. The whale rides the wave for nearly two hours and, if you can trust the car's tweaked speedometer, they're moving at five hundred miles per. They've already covered a thousand miles.

At Zoe's side, Scud's got his window wide open, and he's hanging out like a tongue-lolling dog on a car trip. "*Blub, blub, bloo!*" yells Scud, wanting to be a cool surfer too. "Here comes a pyramid covered with rice paddies."

Yes, it's an immense Incan ziggurat made of smeely seawater, a water-pyramid with stairstep escalators for its sides. It's five times as high as the enormous comber, and it moves much faster. As the pyramid angles into their big wave, vicious eddies swirl towards the purple whale. The water's surface is so turbulent that it's, like, *pocked*.

Skillful Zoe trims their rudder and jiggers the pad-dle-wheels until—behold! She's maneuvered them off their disintegrating wave and onto the rising terraces of the epic ziggurat.

"I *say*," Meatball says to Zoe from the pig's nest, mean-ing to commend her. "Well done, missy."

"We're champions!" screams the overexcited Scud, still hanging out the window. "The wave-tamers."

"Ride the terraces to the peak," Villy advises Zoe from the back. "Then gun it down the other side."

"What a lift," says Zoe, shooting him the briefest of glances over her shoulder. A pert devil-may-care smile. Okay, fine, Zoe's not suicidal, but she does have a reckless side. Which is, of course, one reason why she hangs with Villy.

"All set for you and me to surf?" Yampa asks Villy. "We'll crawl atop the car and go bonkers on our boards."

"Not yet," says Villy, feeling a visceral twitch of fear. "Too, um, blown-out. Let's wait for those big clean walls that Pinchley talked about. Ultra surf."

The ziggurat picks up speed, swallowing a platoon of mammoth combers. Cathedral-sized pup-tent waves spawn off and come pinballing up the pyramid's terraced steps. Zoe is riding the stairs to the top as well.

"Rock it, sock it," says Pinchley approvingly, "By the way, y'all, we're flat-out unsinkable with these fatso tires. No matter how deep we sink, we'll bob back up. But a wave *could* wash a dumb-ass out one of our car's windows— if they was greenhorn enough to have the window open and to be leaning out. Talkin' to you, Scud." Pinchley pronounces the name like *Scuuuuud*. He's steadily amusing himself with his country accent routine.

Scud closes his window just in time. For when they get to the top of the ziggurat, it turns out that the very highest level—the square on the tippy-top—well, it's a hole, an insane suspense-movie elevator shaft running down into the dim, churning core of the ziggurat. Villy glimpses some things like whales down there, each with a single long horn. Narwhals.

"Jump it!" shrieks Zoe. She floors the accelerator and the responsive dark-energy engine spins the paddle-tires like buzz saws. They rocket upward and arc through the air across the ziggurat's central hole—

And, um, nosedive into one of the blocky pyramid's terraces on the other side. They spend a full two minutes underwater, tumbling in the grabby currents. When they bob up, they're on that same terrace—descending towards sea level at an escalator's stately pace.

"I'll nip out and gander what's in the offing," says Meatball. She slits Villy's window partway open and oozes through, drifting high into the air.

As far as Villy can see, the waters ahead hold—not much of anything. It's a curiously calm zone, the size of Los Perros. Ranged along its edges there lurks a menagerie of living waves, peering in like hungry animals. The pool's dark, cryptic surface is marked with folds and puckers. Definitely something under there. A giant squid? A primeval kraken?

As if piqued by their arrival, the submerged form flounders upward and—oh shit—it's a leech saucer that's nearly as big Poppo and Bombo. A flying, red-eyed, green-bodied, vampire jellyfish. It lurches towards them, rocks back, and fires a white-hot ray that turns the water beside them to steam. The saucers are done with holding back. They know Zoe can't hop from here.

Zoe shrieks in fear and fury. Perhaps the saucer means to fire again, but for the moment it's just wallowing there, halfway out of the water, off balance and bloated from feeding all day. Zonked on smeel. Doesn't have its shit together. The kids have a chance to attack. A window of opportunity.

"Kill it, Zoe!" screams Villy. "Ram the saucer!"

And here to aid them are those alien narwhals, swimming towards the half-submerged saucer with their tusks held high!

Zoe revs the paddle-wheels once again. The purple whale skims across the ziggurat terrace, goes briefly airborne, and tears into the saucer at two hundred miles an hour.

At the moment of impact, the space inside the passenger compartment stiffens up again, same as it did when Villy rolled the car at Borderslam Pass. They're safe inside a buffer of that Truban inertia gel. And once they've come to rest, the space relaxes. So, cool.

Zoe's getting all creative now, doing rapid donuts and figure eights on the body of the leech saucer, chewing up as much acreage as she can. Saucer lymph all over the place. A smell of fish and mold. The narwhals are in the mix too. They're feeding within the monster's flesh like two-ton worms.

The mortally wounded saucer flaps in spasms. It lifts itself twenty yards into the air, shudders, collapses into the sea, goes limp. Zoe guides their car free of the remains. Meanwhile the ziggurat wave has chuffed far past them, leaving an empty wake. A random pup-tent wave ripples across the car's roof and hood and across the surfboards, rinsing away the gore.

Scores of narwhals are feeding upon the saucer's deflated flesh, tearing off chunks of meat and fat. Great schools of smaller fish twinkle in the pellucid water, feeding on congealed tendrils of blood. Hundreds of hefty crabs busy themselves at the saucer's center, devouring the tissues with mandible and claw.

A twinkling cloud of smeel rises from the saucer's exhausted remains and releases a fine mist of vivifying rain. A final bubble of gas blorps from the vast corpse. Slowly, and with an evil majesty, the great form heels to one side and descends into the abyss.

Only one sign of the oppressive monster remains—an opalescent ball the size of a softball, bobbing upon the surface of the sea. The creature's saucer pearl. Meatball— who's been safely out of the picture—drops from the sky like a falcon, meaning to snatch the prize. But the narwhals are faster. A big one with dotted spots on his back seizes the pale orb in his mouth and swallows it whole.

And then, how strange to see, the narwhal rises into the air and hovers, weightless, flapping his tail in glee. A large pearl really does grant the power of levitation. The narwhal's fellows whistle their approbation. He twists, turns, and dives back into the blue depths. The rest of the horned whales turn flukes and follow.

Villy and his party are alone in the great lagoon, with the living waves around the edges jostling in. Zoe slumps wearily in her seat, letting the car engine idle.

"Zoe zoo zone!" says Yampa, unconcerned with making sense.

"See now, honey," Pinchley tells Yampa, wobbling his chin as if in senile glee. "It's fun with no gun."

Meatball oozes in through the side window and resumes her perch in the back of the car.

"What the hell were you doin' up there?" Pinchley asks the Freeth. "Calling the shots for that saucer?"

"I retreated as a matter of prudence," says Meatball, going for a careless tone. "I confess I had some doubts about how the confrontation might play out. I must say I'm sorely miffed that I failed to acquire that large saucer pearl."

Villy isn't much paying attention to Meatball. Zoe looks so beautiful to him just now, so smart and powerful, her eyes so full of life. He leans into the front seat and kisses her. "You're a goddess," he tells her. "I love you."

Maybe that's more than is safe to say—but he means it.

"So saucer pearls really *are* for flying?" Scud asks Pinchley, wanting to be the center of attention as usual. "As well as making unny tunnels?"

"Whoops!" says Villy, dragging Scud over the back of the front seat and scrambling up there to take his place. "My turn in front!"

"No fair!" howls Scud. Zoe and Villy are already sharing another hug.

"You was asking about saucer pearls," Pinchley says to Scud, who's next to him now. "And, yeah, they're good for unny tunnels, and for flying, and for the power of the zap."

"Where can I get one?" asks Scud.

"From dead saucers is a good place," says Pinchley. "Like you just saw. Also, believe it or not, folks can harvest saucer pearls from a certain spot back in your Los Perros. They grow like mushroom puffballs on muddy ground. Or, yet again, a saucer might *give* you a pearl. If you was an agent workin' for them."

Yampa cranks her weird neck around and glares into the pig's nest. "A mercenary mooch like Meatball maybe."

"I'll thank you not to nose into my personal affairs," says Meatball, very snippy. "As for you, Yampa, I rather doubt you'd have the mental capacity to use a saucer pearl for any of its higher functions. If you had a saucer pearl you'd be like a dog chewing the leather cover of a book."

"I raise my longest finger in salute, oh, Great Lady of the Royal Buttbite," Pinchley says to Meatball. "And don't let the door hit you in the ass on your way out."

"So sorry," says Meatball in a frosty tone. "I'm not ready to leave. I'd like a ride to shore. But I'll keep mum if you find me so galling."

"What was that big saucer doing here in the first place?" Scud asks Pinchley. Once again he's into his robotic question-asking routine.

"Them tanker-leech saucers sneak over to Surf World from New Eden and guzzle smeel from the Flatsies' sea," says Pinchley. "They slosh around in the water and tank up. The smeel gets them buzzed. When they rise up and go to wallow home—the Flatsies say that's a good time to rip into one."

"Why?" persists Scud.

"Wake up, kid. Everyone hates them parasite saucers."

Villy and Zoe are tuning out most of this. Villy's staring into Zoe's face, drinking her in. Zoe takes Villy's face in her hands and kisses him.

"I'd so hate for our lives to end," she says. "Just when we two are getting started."

"Faint heart never won the battle!" butts in Meatball from the back of the car. So much for her keeping mum. "Soldier on, Zoe Snapp."

"What a crock," says Zoe to Villy, not even bothering to turn around and look at the Freeth. "According to Meatball, it was gonna be safer down here than up on the ridge. According to Meatball, there were saucers and a Thudd on the cliff." Her voice is rising. "Know what? I call bullshit on that. And—how convenient—Meatball was way up high in the air when that big vampire saucer down here was trying to blast us."

Meatball addresses her next remark to Villy. "Your sweetheart has a case of the heebie-jeebies, young man. The whim-whams. Quiet her down."

"You have a stupid accent," Villy tells Meatball. "And I hate you." The car falls silent.

"That line is destined for the *Cambridge Compendium of Clever Comebacks*," Zoe remarks after a bit. "So vitty he is, my Villy!"

Meanwhile the purple whale is still adrift in the calm patch left behind by the giant saucer.

"Which way is Flatsie Pass?" Villy asks the group at large.

"That way," says Scud, pointing somewhat towards the right. "I can just barely teep the Flatsie village. Really far. But my teep slug works better here than in Van Cott. More ambient smeel."

"You the man," says Villy, reaching into the back seat to give his brother five. "Sorry about unseating you."

"You're not sorry at all," says Scud. "Never mind. Have you guys noticed there's teep slugs in the water here?

Pastel slugs with feelers at one end. Some of them are pretty big."

"Surf World is their home," says Pinchley. "That's why you see the Surf World Flatsies selling those slugs in Van Cott."

"Why don't you and Yampa wear teep slugs like me?" asks Scud.

"Pinchley can't bear being bothered by my musings," says Yampa. "He shields his self."

"And why no slug for you?" presses Scud.

"A slinky seductress has sex secrets," says the rawhide-tough Szep with a toss of her thin head. It's very hard for Villy to visualize her involved in sly passionate love affairs.

Anyway, with the ziggurat and the saucer gone, waves are moving into the smeel-rich waters around the becalmed purple whale. Combers, pup tents, puffballs, ziggurats, and—

"A corkscrew?" says Zoe. "Look at that. It's like a corkscrew lying on its side. And those slanting waves are its blades. All made of water?"

"Ride it!" says Pinchley. "Those twisty suckers can carry you a thousand miles non-stop express. Get the car up to speed, Zoe, and edge onto a blade of that corkscrew while it's drilling by."

"Yah, mon," goes Zoe. "Even though I have the whim-whams."

Meatball remains silent. She's sulking. Villy is glad.

The corkscrew wave is a half-submerged helix, with its central axis on the surface. A low bulge runs down the axis of the corkscrew, like the shaft of a ship's propeller, and the helix is like a ship propeller's screw. The slanting, rotating faces are linked by powerful underwater currents. The visible sections of the blades form a wave-train many miles long.

Zoe has more than a little trouble getting the whale onto one of the blade-waves. At one point the car is totally submerged again, tumbling at random like a surfer in a wipeout.

Villy itches to take the wheel, but he lets Zoe persist. And, who knows, he might not do any better. Eventually Zoe finds a sweet spot. The car is endlessly sliding down a glassy face whose vortical motion is lifting them as fast as they descend. It's like trotting down an up escalator. Zoe puts the paddle-wheels on idle, and they zone out for three or four hours, covering well over a thousand miles.

"Is rudeboy ready to ride?" says Yampa eventually. "Wall waves coming up." She's leaning forward from the back seat to put her head right into Villy's face. She's parroting Villy's surf slang. As usual, she smells like curry and gasoline.

"I guess."

"*Buk-buk-bwawk*," goes Yampa, imitating a chicken.

And now Villy sees the giant moving walls of water. This is it. "Okay," he tells Yampa. "We'll do it. Zoe can tow us in."

"Righteous," says Yampa. "Ready the ropes, Pinchley mine."

Pinchley produces his green spider, and the indefatigable tool critter spins out a pair of lines that Pinchley rolls into two coils, each with a spider-woven tow handle on one end.

"Need foot straps, too," says Villy.

Pinchley's tire-making marker bird pops his head out of the tool belt and coughs out four excellent padded foot straps with sticky fasteners. Easily on par with primo Dakine tow-board gear.

They're approaching those towering wall waves very fast. In fact, the first of them fills the entire horizon. Although it's moving away from them, the forward-drilling corkscrew wave is faster. Indeed, up ahead of them, the foremost part of the corkscrew wave has already drilled through the first wall wave.

Villy forms a plan. He and Yampa will jump into the water before the wall wave, and the car can sling them onto the great wall. They'll shoot upward, and the car will ride the corkscrew through the base of the wall.

"That wave is gonna to have a tube on its front side," says Villy. "Up at the top, where it curves over. We'll shoot that tube, right, Yampa? Mucho smeel in there. The one true light."

"Yah, mon," goes Yampa. She tosses the two loops of spider rope over her shoulder and grabs the foot straps with one of her complex hands. She gives Pinchley a hug and opens her window. With surprising nimbleness, she crawls onto the roof of the car with the boards.

Meanwhile Zoe's holding a steady course on the slope of the corkscrew wave. Only minutes till they pass through the wall wave's base.

"So, uh, goodbye for now," Villy tells Zoe. "Right before you punch through the wave, be sure to veer. So that you, like, slingshot us?"

"You'll fall down off that big wave. It's too steep to

climb." She gives a nervous giggle. "You'll be skittish as a hog on ice."

"The wave will have a current in it," says Villy, hoping this is true. "And, um, surface tension. We'll be water-striders on an upwards waterfall. The wave is alive. It'll want to carry us. For kicks."

"Don't go."

Villy can think of no better response than to quote his song. "I'm gonna face the reaper and help my posse rave. I'm an epic bad-ass surfer who's gonna make the save."

Again Zoe giggles.

"Too corny?" goes Villy.

"No idea," says Zoe. "My head is exploding." She's flicking her eyes between Villy and the nearing wall wave. "How will we find each other afterwards?"

"No sweat," says Pinchley from the back seat. "Yampa and Villy ride that gigundo wobbler as far as they can. Meanwhile Zoe and the rest of us ride the corkscrew to shore. And we meet at the Flatsies' village. Beach party."

"I'll be able to locate everyone with my teep," says Scud.

"And if there's a prob, the gingerbread men can round us up," says Pinchley. "Them Flatsies surf these smeely waves real slick."

"I'll be an observation blimp," declares Meatball. "A spotter." She synthesizes a jolly chuckle, but nobody responds. "Villy, I pardon you for your rude remark," Meatball adds after a bit. "It won't do to part on a sour note—if this should be the end."

"Whatev," says Villy, completely uninterested in Meatball's mind games. He levers himself out his window. Take one last look at Zoe. Sees stark sorrow on her face.

"Hey," he says to her softly. "I'm gonna shred this wave. And tonight we'll sleep together. For real."

"If only," says Zoe. Her hair flutters in the wind. She fastens her eyes on his. "My Villy."

At this point Yampa grabs Villy's hand and yanks him onto the roof. The skanky Szep is stronger than she looks. And more organized. She's already attached the straps to the boards and she's tied the two tow lines to the whale's roof rack. The big wall is coming up fast.

Scud leans out the window for a farewell look at his older brother. "You're brave," he says.

"Thanks, Scud."

Villy snugs his feet into his foot straps, grabs one of the spider-woven tow handles, and—*yeek*—he hops off the tilting roof of the car.

The water hisses beneath his speeding board. He hunches and sways, feeling for the one true line of optimal motion. He's tobogganing down the steep pitch of the corkscrew wave, with the purple whale still ahead of him. Behind him, Yampa lets out an exultant, ululating cry.

Even in this intense moment, the Surf World light makes things look mellow and somehow nostalgic. As if this scene is something he's remembering back home, years from now, a doddering forty-year-old. The greatest ride of my life. Glancing down at his feet, Villy sees that a sizable teep slug has just now affixed itself to his ankle. An orange nudibranch with a cluster of lavender feelers. Let it be.

The plan is to have the car's tow rope fling them off the edge of the helix blade so fast they'll coast onto the big wall. The otherworldly wall wave makes a creepy sound—a deep, endless roar, like the soundtrack in a horror film just before some mind-destroying monster appears. But that's just a sound. The teep, on the other hand, is good.

Thanks to his new slug, Villy is mentally in touch with the waves. The corkscrew is purposeful, gleeful, and happy about drilling through the immense wall. As for the wall itself—it's chanting a single cosmic *Om*, or some such—a sacred syllable with no beginning and no end. Like the starstones. Also, Villy senses that, beneath the *Om*, the wall wave is mildly amused. Like a woman noticing two tiny ants on her nail-polished toe. Ants with nearly invisible antennae.

Focus! Villy tells himself. *Hold the tow handle tight!*

And just as he thinks that, *zonng*, the slack plays out and the tow rope is like a steel cable, with drops of water flying off it. Zoe is accelerating outward across the blade of the wave. Villy clings to the tow handle for all he's worth. It feels like it's pulling his arms from his sockets.

He catches a glimpse of Zoe's determined face glancing back at them from the car up ahead. He can't wave, but he nods. He can't believe he's doing this. Zoe is rushing down the corkscrew blade's slope, steadily angling away from the corkscrew's axis. In her wake, Villy and Yampa sluice up great fountains of water.

And now the surfers are approaching the edge of the helical wave—nearing its sharp cusp, woven from a hundred thousand flow lines. Abruptly Zoe cuts back towards the axis of the traveling wave. Like she's cracking a whip.

The whip is Villy's tow line, and the tip is him. As he reaches edge of the wave, he bends his knees and jumps, carrying his board with him. He releases his hold on the tow line. Yampa does the same. They're on their own, thrown like stones from catapults.

Villy sails through the air for maybe a hundred yards, then *slaps* down and goes skimming across the eerily calm patch before the sky-high water wall. The patch slopes slightly upward. He's is going faster than he thought humanly possible. His brain can't keep up. His body is doing the thinking.

Come to me, says the mighty wall wave.

Villy crouches low. It's hard for him to see, what with the stinging spray in his eyes, but his teep is helping. He feels and hears a rapid chatter of pulses from the water's washboard surface. The sound is echoed by Yampa's board nearby.

And then they're on the vertical face of the spooky *Om* wave and it has a flow to it, and a special kind of surface tension—just as Villy hoped. The wave's internal currents raise him up and up and up, like a mother lifting her child. And Yampa's still beside him.

Far below, Zoe and the purple whale disappear through the rumbling cliff of water.

EIGHTEEN

beach party

zoe

Uneasily Zoe watches the deeply roaring wall sweep Villy into the sky. In seconds he's the size of a fly, impossibly high on the wobbling cliff of water. But now she has to look away and trim her course to ride the corkscrew through the cavernous hole in the great wave's base.

They emerge to see another wall wave looming a few miles ahead. The space between the two walls is oddly peaceful. Like a nature preserve, with calm glassy water—calm, that is, except for the corkscrew wave. The sea gleams with colorful slugs and silvery fish. Birds like pelicans loop and dive. Alien narwhals poke their heads above the surface and whistle. They gather in groups and rub together their unicorn tusks together, watching the outlandish purple whale upon the helical wave.

"You drive for now," Zoe tells Scud and lets him take the wheel. So now it's Zoe and Scud in the front seat, with him on the left and her on the right. Pinchley's alone in the back seat, and Meatball's way back in the pig's nest.

Zoe leans out the right front window, staring at the wall wave behind them, hoping to get a glimpse of Villy at the top. The long lip is adorned with a breaking crest. Zoe squints at it, with the wind beating at the back of her head, and then, off to the left, yes, she sees two spots of color. Red and blue, Villy's and Yampa's boards, deep inside the curling tube. They're maybe a mile above sea level, two miles behind Zoe—and falling further behind.

"You guys think we can maybe circle back?" Zoe asks the others. "I'd like to be there for Villy after he slides down that skyscraper. And for Yampa too."

"Negatory," says Scud, fully into his sixteen-year-old asshole mode.

"Just jump off the blade of the corkscrew," says Zoe. Scud acts like he doesn't hear her. Maybe he's scared to try. Probably he doesn't understand how to surf the car. He's never ridden a board in his life.

"If we slide off the blade, we'll coast onto wall wave number two," says Pinchley, annoyingly taking Scud's side.

"Shit," says Zoe, focusing on what's ahead. Indeed, the next goddamned wall wave is nearly upon them. With its own big corkscrew hole in the bottom. Scud has a white-knuckled death grip on the steering wheel and his face is a frozen blank. He's got them aimed at the wrong angle. He's going to frikkin miss the hole.

Zoe seizes the boy's shoulders, drags him away from the wheel, and resumes control. She changes the angle as sharply as she can without capsizing, then gives the paddle-wheels all she's got. Even so, they nearly eat it. As they enter the tunnel, the car slides way out along the corkscrew blade and, oh wow, up onto the tunnel's arched water ceiling. The surface tension and the centrifugal force hold them in place but—strictly speaking—they're upside down.

"*Damn* you, Scud," mutters Zoe.

"You look hot when you're mad," says Scud. Like, with Villy gone, Scud's seeing what he can get away with, leering sophomore horndog that he is.

"I don't give a shit what you think is hot," snaps Zoe.

And then, sigh, she's made it through this difficult passage. How many more will there be? They're riding across another calm nature-preserve-type zone, this one between the second and the third monster-wall waves. Turns out there's going to be seven of them in all.

Okay, now they're emerging from the tunnel through that seventh wave, and by now Zoe isn't especially mad at Scud anymore. The corkscrew dies down, and the nearby waves aren't so big as before. It's dusk. But some distance ahead of them is a *really* high dark shape—

"Please don't let that be waves," says Zoe.

"Cliffs," says Pinchley reassuringly. "Leading up to Flatsie Pass."

"Hope we can make the beach," says Zoe. "Such effing gnarly surf." Although not huge, a lot of the waves are heading out from shore, same as before. Fubar. Zoe jiggles the rudder and tap-dances the accelerator, hoping to thread her way through the darkening maze. And all the time she's worrying about Villy.

"I teep some Flatsies over there," announces Scud, pointing towards the right. He's clearly glad not to be driving, but he relishes his role as navigator.

"It's dodgy being a Freeth," says Meatball out of the blue. As if she's trying to apologize. "That's why I'm a maverick."

"*Maverick* isn't the right word," says Zoe. "*Traitor* is more like it. You're on the side of the leech saucers." She's not taking her eyes off the waves. If it gets much darker they'll be screwed.

"Perhaps it seems that way, but my actions are not of my own volition," says Meatball. "The Freeth do sometimes act as mercenaries. But, aside from that, we're jolly, we mean well, and—"

"Beat it, Meatball," interrupts Pinchley. "Told you already. Amscray. Last thing we frikkin need is a leech-saucer spy in our car. I got a feelin' you're gonna call down another hit on us."

"That's unfair," says Meatball. "I—"

"I said *git*!" cries Pinchley in a sudden access of rage. He draws a new critter from his tool belt and places it on his palm. Zoe steals a quick glance. It's a toad with glowing eyes. Its mouth is partway open. Zoe has a sense that you don't ever want that toad's tongue to touch you. Pinchley extends his arm towards Meatball.

Meatball wedges herself into the farthest corner of the pig's nest and forms one of her bulges into the conical shape of a zapper node. She and Pinchley glare at each other.

"Look out!" yells Scud right then.

A rogue ziggurat rams into the hood of their car—a wave as big as the pyramid of Cheops. It sinks them into the swirling depths of the inky sea. And just as they begin to float back up, something grabs hold of them. Tentacles, faintly luminous, creamy white against the windows of the car, dragging them down and down. Zoe's ears pop. Water seeps in around the doors and windows.

"The mandatory attack of the giant alien squid," says Zoe, almost too fried to care.

Moving with alacrity, Meatball presses herself against the rear window and tries sending a zap through the glass. Not all that much *oomph* to it, but it's enough to make the squid flinch. But still it maintains its hold. The squid's foul beak scrapes against the windshield, as if wanting to break through. Its enormous eye peers in. They sink deeper. The air in the car grows dense and cold.

Meatball makes her way around the car's interior, sending warning zaps through the windshield and through the side glass panes. None of the jolts are that strong, but they're starting to bother the squid. The beak clacks, the eye squints, the tentacles contort and writhe. *Zap, zap,* and *zap.* Finally, tiring of Meatball's routine, the abyssal monster sets them free. Slowly, with maddening aplomb, the car begins to rise. Zoe dares to let herself wonder if she'll ever see Villy again.

"Good save," Pinchley tells Meatball. He sets his poison toad aside.

But they're still not done. Everything around them is getting dark. It's like an enveloping shroud is growing up from the sea-bottom and closing in on them.

"A Neptune's tablecloth!" Pinchley yells. "Quick, Zoe, head straight up!"

Zoe revs the paddle-wheels once more. They lurch against a big, rubbery, seaweed-like sheet that's reaching up around them. It's a great disk with wrinkles along its sides. The disk's edge is above them, and it's starting to pinch closed. Like a kerchief closing around a melon. A flexible living sheet that becomes a pouch.

Yet another lucky break for our cosmic heroes: the purple whale's paddle-wheels propel them out of the shrinking mouth of the sack before it shuts. And now the whale's absurd finned monster-truck tires are churning the sea's heaving surface. Overcome by the stress and the chaotic motions, Zoe leans forward and pukes between her feet.

"Flatsies!" sings out Scud after a moment of intense mental scanning. "On the comber wave over there. They know we're here!" He opens his window and hollers.

It's hard for Zoe to see the Flatsies in the dim light. They're small, and they're lying on surfaces of the waves. These little dudes don't *ride* surfboards, they *are* surfboards. But now—*whoosh*—one of them whizzes along the comber's long barrel, goes airborne like a Frisbee, skims in through Scud's window, and lands gracefully on the front seat. A three-foot-tall gingerbread man.

"I hight Madclaw, milord and milady," he says with a bow.

"Is he speaking olde English?" asks Zoe.

"That's what they do," says Scud. "It's like each mappy-world alien has to be weirder than the one before."

"Can you help us reach the shore?" Zoe asks the Flatsie. "Please. I'm losing my mind. And there's two more in our party, still out to sea."

"Knowing not thy name, I am hard put to hear thee," says Madclaw.

"You're talking about etiquette?" cries Zoe. "Can we cut through the effing bullshit before another zillion-ton pyramid of water lands on us? I'm Zoe, and the idiot next to me is Scud. And that's Pinchley and Meatball in back. Meatball's a traitor. Even though she saved our butts just now."

"I'll be off your hands as soon as we land," puts in Meatball.

"High time," counters Zoe. She turns back to the Flatsie. "The missing two members of our party are my boyfriend Villy, and Pinchley's Yampa—I guess you'd say she's his wife?"

"Don't make your info so intricate," Pinchley warns Zoe, pushing his head into the front seat. "Flatsies are dumb."

The Flatsie glares at the Szep. "I mislike thy tone, thou wasted, liverish man."

"Please, no quarreling," says Zoe, laying one hand on Madclaw's chest and using her other hand to give Pinchley a good hard shove—sending him back to the rear. With the Flatsie in the car, the waves around them have already begun to calm.

"Thy touch is warm and cogent," says Madclaw, patting Zoe's hand with one of his paw-like gingerbread-man mitts. "Thou and thy retinue shall be guests at this eve's feast."

"Guests meaning that we're sitting around eating with you?" puts in Scud. "Am I teeping the image right? It's confused. It's not that you Flatsies want to kill us and roast us, is it? I feel like I'm seeing that too."

"Fret not, oh timorous youth," intones Madclaw. "Veils of ifness do ever billow in the teepful mind." He makes a commanding gesture with his stubby arm, directing Zoe to steer towards a gap in the waves. "Onward, milady. At my behest, the ensorcelled waves do grant fair passage. All will be well, and all will be well, and all manner of thing will be well."

"What about my Villy?" asks Zoe as she steers through the parting seas. "You'll save him, too?"

"There is one who even now seeks your mate, milady. She is a woman like you, and yet unlike. Villy will be at your side anon. Onward now, say I."

"Fine," says Zoe. "Excuse the mess in here . . ."

She risks opening the car door for a second so she can sweep most of her puke out the door with her foot. A lively gout of water splashes in to finish the job. That's a relief. Her stomach feels fine again. She likes Madclaw's vibe. The waves here are like friendly, rambunctious dogs. Pinchley is mellow, Scud seems more or less human, and they're almost rid of Meatball. Onward.

What with Madclaw's high-flown manner of speech, Zoe is expecting a turreted castle with pennants and crenellated battlements, but the Flatsies' village is a dump. Four-foot-high huts assembled from washed-up flotsam—junk like smelly narwhal hides and the shells of giant crabs, with the pieces lashed together by leathery squid tentacles. A bonfire roars, fueled by dry seaweed stems. Gingerbread men and women caper in the flickering light.

"Home sweet home," says Zoe. She pulls the purple whale to a stop on the hard-packed sand.

Exhausted and a little wobbly-legged, she and Scud and Pinchley lower themselves to the sand. Almost

immediately Meatball silently disappears into the sky.
Gone for good? Zoe hopes so.

The fire is warm, the Flatsies are jolly. Several of the
them are tending a pair of spits with something heavy
on them—oh my god! Zoe's blood pressure shoots up to,
like, a thousand. "They're roasting Yampa and Villy!" she
cries. But she's only picking up on the same hallucination
that Scud briefly had.

"Two giant crabs, milady," says calm Madclaw at her
side. "Be merry, I implore you!" He strides over to the fire
and joins his fellows.

"Them's definitely crabs on the fire," Pinchley reas-
sures Zoe. "You was just trippin' off the crabs' teep. They
trying to mind-game you. To show you that this really is
kind of a cannibal-type feast. Seeing as how those giant
crabs are as smart as that fella Einstein. Real good eatin'
though—if you set your scruples aside. Thing is, the crabs
sneak over here from another basin like the saucers do.
Foraging. And Flatsies figure anyone's fair game if they's
not native."

"In other words, the Flatsies *would* eat us!" exclaims
Zoe.

"Naw," says Pinchley. "They don't like Szep meat nor
human meat neither. They say we taste like oily rags, and
they call you fellas long pigs—and not meaning that as a
compliment."

"Pigs are delicious," protests Scud, much louder than
necessary. "Bacon, ham, pork chops . . ."

"I'd put a lid on that if I was you," goes Pinchley. "Not
a real good idea to piss off the Flatsies."

At least they're on dry land. And there's no red-eyed saucers in sight. And, hell, they've got a gala crab dinner coming up. Over by the fire, Madclaw makes some kind of speech to introduce them. He's uses gestures, song, and teep.

"So rich and cultural," says Zoe, feeling comfortable enough to be ironic again. "Like a Renaissance Faire."

"I bet Villy's lost," says Scud. "I bet he's dead."

"Thanks for that," snaps Zoe. "For, like, one nanosecond I was almost happy."

She turns and stares out to sea, reaching for Villy with her mind. This place is so wacked out with mappyworld teep—it's like being at a party where all the other kids are on shrooms—Zoe's picking up on this mind-reading thing. She can sense the rough playful minds of the waves, the giddy excitement of the Flatsies, and just now coming into visible sight—is that her weird sister Maisie? With Villy and Yampa close behind?

"Yes," says Pinchley, right in sync.

A perfectly formed wave approaches, lit from within by phosphorescent plankton. Clearly outlined in the sweet spot of the wave's slope are two archetypal surfer silhouettes—Villy and Yampa. And flying ahead of them is a glowing woman with a disk skirt like a saucer's rim. She's carrying a clutch purse.

The wave breaks into a gentle wash of bubbly foam. Villy and Yampa stride ashore, bearing their boards. The woman who led them—now she's gone. Was that really Maisie? Is she hiding? No matter. It's a day of miracles, with too many wonders to explain.

Zoe runs to Villy and they embrace for a very long time. His skin is cold.

"Don't leave me again," Zoe whispers to him. "Don't leave."

"Same here," says Villy, no Shakespeare with the love talk. But his hug says enough. Zoe holds him for a while, glad to know her body is warming him.

And then she leads him to the Flatsies' bonfire. The little gingerbread men and gingerbread women cheer. This is a big entertainment event for them. Scud is cheering too, and here comes Pinchley carrying Yampa, cradling her sideways in his arms like he's a groom carrying his bride across a threshold. Stop obsessing on marriage, Zoe.

Did she herself think that, or someone else? Hard to tell, with all the teep.

Zoe and Villy find seats on some big spiral shells close to the water, and the Flatsies bring them chunks of cooked crab meat.

"So delicious," says Villy, his mouth full.

"E equals m-c-squared," says Zoe, eating crabmeat too.

"Huh?"

"Never mind. Was your ride . . . *epic*?" Even as she says this, Zoe scolds herself for being sarcastic. Like, what is her problem?

"The best," says Villy, gamely playing along. "Beyond words." He teeps her a memory of his ride. It's like an immersive video. It's like Zoe is seeing through Villy's eyes, with Villy's arms and feet at the edges of the field of view, and with the gnarly Yampa up ahead, surfing the tube atop the wall wave. The hollow barrel of the tube is filled with pale light. The sound is a rich hum. Everything is in slow motion. And there's a numinous presence all around. The one mind.

"Yes," murmurs Zoe. She watches for a long time.

The Flatsies are serving up some kind of drink now, very sweet and aromatic. They call it *tuj*. Scud and the two Szep are going for it, but Zoe and Villy turn it down. The Flatsies are tapping the stuff from a large iridescent bladder. A seaweed float? A squid's ink sack? No telling what the juice actually is, nor what its effects might be.

Despite her various false moves, Zoe has pretty much decided that tonight's going to be the night for her and Villy. And Villy—she's sure he feels the same way. They're holding hands. In a way, a handclasp's as good as teep. A rich channel.

Right then two narwhals come wallowing across the shingle to join the party. Actually, one of them's not wallowing—he's levitating. Their wheezy whistles are a form of speech, and Madclaw is talking to them, making some kind of deal. The floating narwhal coughs a shiny iridescent ball onto the sand, then thuds to the ground.

"That's the saucer pearl from before," says Villy. "I recognize that narwhal too. With the leopard spots on his back? Look how excited Madclaw is. He's putting the ball in his body-pouch. He has a pouch at his waist like on a kangaroo. And dig it, he's already hovering in the air. That must feel great. I wonder what the narwhal gets in exchange."

The answer comes quickly. Madclaw drops back to the sand and drags out a still-living giant crab who's been lying there in the shadows, all tied up. A powerful specimen with lively eyestalks, and a dappled green shell, he's—much more than an ordinary crab. He's chirping and clicking like he's talking. Highly intricate and sophisticated sounds. Zoe recalls Pinchley's remark: *as smart as that fella Einstein.*

Oh lord, what have they been doing here? To make the rapidly unfolding scenario worse, the crab is teeping to them. Broadcasting his complex emotions and his despair. Villy, with his teep slug, seems to feel it even more strongly than Zoe. Not caring to witness the climax of this scene, Madclaw floats into the air and flaps towards the bonfire, flexing his little body like a manta ray.

The two narwhals attack the crab, stabbing him with their horns and twisting off his legs and his pincers and his claws. The crab's screams are truly horrible. Villy and Zoe are sharing in the psychic experiences of a sensitive, highly evolved being who's being torn apart by ruthless predators.

Villy peels off his teep slug and casts it far from his body. The crab's pathetic cries go on for a bit longer, but then, finally, the noble creature is dead and mostly consumed. The sated narwhals splash into the sea. A wave sweeps the crab offal away.

Not that the rowdies by the bonfire notice or care. They're singing a drinking song, with the Flatsies' voices like a youth choir, and Scud yodeling in his cracking voice, and Yampa and Pinchley doing multilevel alien laughs. Some of the Flatsies are staggering around with this giant, like, Alpine horn made of a long shell, and they're letting Scud blow into it. *Fwooonk.*

"Man," says Villy, solemnly eyeing a leftover scrap of the crab's shell. "That's what we were eating, Zoe? And you *knew*? And that's why you made the Einstein joke?"

"I'm sorry," she says. "I didn't understand how it really is. I'm always trying so hard to be tough and cool. I want to be a better person, Villy, I do."

"It's—I don't know," says Villy. "I'm not blaming you. All the rules are so different here."

"At least in Los Perros there weren't all these things trying to kill me," says Zoe. "Flying saucers, dinosaurs, Iravs, giant squid . . ."

"If the giant crabs had a chance, they might kill and eat us too," says Villy.

"Not this last one," says Zoe. "He was a gentle philosopher. Nobler than us. More evolved. I mean—just compare him to Scud and to the Szep and the Flatsies. So drunk and stupid."

The Flatsies are in a pyramid with Madclaw on top, his body fluttering like a flame. The celebrants are chanting *oof oof oof*, chanting in a steady rhythm like someone having sex. Meanwhile Pinchley and Yampa have hoisted the giant tuj bladder onto their shoulders, and they're squirting a stream of the foamy liquid across the crowd. The Szep are juggling their tin of cocoa powder too. Scud is hooting like a great ape.

"Might be the first time Scud's ever been drunk," says Villy. "Remember sixteen?" He shakes his head. "Let's bail."

But they don't stand up quite yet. It takes few minutes to shake off the mental echoes of the crab's screams, a few minutes for their jangled minds to settle down. Slowly, hesitantly, Zoe touches Villy's cheek. He gives her a melting look. Kisses her. Yes. Tonight.

"In the car?" murmurs Zoe. The car would be private for a little while anyway. But in terms of a lovers' bower it's not the best. It's grubby, and Zoe threw up on the floor, and Scud might burst in and say something—and then Zoe would really and truly have to kill the boy and feed his body to the narwhals.

What other options do they have?

"Prithee lodge in my manor," says Madclaw, gliding over to them all unctuous and polite. His motions are a little wobbly from the tuj. Evidently, he's been monitoring their thoughts.

"He means his hut!" exclaims Villy. "We can borrow it."

"Crab shells and narwhal skin," says Zoe. "Lovely. Especially after those screams."

"Is there a bed?" Villy asks Madclaw. "And—excuse me if this is rude—but can we have your place all to ourselves?"

"I offer a bedtick sack of dried ferns," says Madclaw. "With a comforter to match. Freely my lodging is fit for a covert tryst. I'll dance till sleep with my tribe and with your boon companions. It is well."

"Sweet," says Zoe. She smiles at the floating Madclaw. "How do you use a saucer pearl to fly, anyway?"

"One ponders a certain spell," says Madclaw. "Well known in this land. *Upsy downsy inside out.*"

"Easy as pie," says Villy. "But let's focus on the hut. Whither, dude?"

"Follow me, gentlefolk."

Scud leers at them as they pass the Flatsie party. The boy is leading a snake-dance conga line, with the Szep beating on the emptied tuj-sack like it's a bass drum. A few of the Flatsies lie motionless on their backs, overcome by drink.

Madclaw's hut is a few hundred feet along the beach. He ushers Zoe and Villy in, briefly opening the slit in his belly to let his saucer pearl light the room. And then the young lovers are alone.

Villy collapses onto the rustling sack of dried ferns, and Zoe lies next to him, on her side with her arms around him and her cheek on his chest. It's dark in here, with the hubbub of the party blending into the steady crashing of the waves. The bed smells okay—salty and earthy with a touch of cinnamon.

"I love this trip," says Villy, running his hand over Zoe's hair. "I never thought I'd have a ride like today."

"Today was amazing for me too," says Zoe. "Surfing the car. Who knew I could do that? And I didn't even tell you about the giant squid."

"Tomorrow," says Villy. "I'm too tired to talk."

"But there's something I have to say," goes Zoe. "We've made it through three basins, okay? And this morning you promised that would be enough. Like I said before, crossing two hundred more of these worlds—it's not realistic. For sure we'd die."

"But—*driving a million miles*," says Villy yet again. "I'm obsessing on that."

"I'm obsessing on you," says Zoe. "Maybe a little too much."

Villy turns on his side so they're face to face. He kisses her for a while. "Let's make love," he says. "Go to the next level."

"I want that too," says Zoe. "But can we please talk about tomorrow?"

Villy inhales and exhales a deep breath. Sighs. Yawns. Releases his grasp on Zoe.

"Too tired to talk?" she says, a bit of acid in her voice.

"I surfed a mile-high wave," says Villy.

"I know. It was magnificent. But until I know that we're going home tomorrow, I don't feel comfortable enough to—"

"Hell with it," says Villy. "Too much. I'm going to sleep." He rolls onto his other side, curls up, and he's gone. Deep, steady breathing with a hint of a snore.

No *wham bam*. No *thank you ma'am*. Villy's a selfish baby. Zoe would hop back to Los Perros on her own right now if she could. Maybe she shouldn't have pushed Villy so hard? But, look, a person ought to be willing to make some plans if they expect to stick one of their personal body parts inside of you. *Way* inside. *Sigh*. It would have been fun. Truth be told, this would have been Zoe's first time. And she ruined it by nagging him. So typical of her. But can't he see they have to go home? Etcetera.

She twists and turns for hours, uncomfortable in the cruddy alien bed, now and then giving Villy a really hard poke, but he never wakes up. No hope of sleep for her. Too many things in her head. Nunu laying eggs, the Thudd dino chasing them, the wall waves, the hideous scene with the giant crab. And that vampire saucer in the ocean. It had been waiting there to blast them.

There's definitely a correlation between the saucers' behavior and Zoe's distance from Van Cott. The further she goes, the more aggressive they get. Wanting to think this out, she forms the image of a map in her mind, can't quite get it straight, and then, what the hell, goes outside, intending to draw a diagram on the beach.

It's not totally dark. There's a light dusting of glowons, like new-fallen snow. The ocean is faintly luminous. Down the beach the embers of the Flatsies' bonfire gleam.

The revelers are sprawled on the ground asleep—Scud, the two Szep, the horde of Flatsies—all of them passed out from the tuj. On an impulse, Zoe postpones her map-drawing and slinks close to the sleepers. There's Madclaw in the middle, lying atop a female Flatsie. Zoe picks her way over to Madclaw and flips him like a piece of French toast, thereby exposing the slit of his kangaroo pouch. She slips in her hand and finds the hefty saucer pearl, meaning to steal it. No dice. Madclaw may be asleep, but he's reflexively clenching the slit of his pouch so tightly that Zoe feels her hand going numb. No way he's letting her pull out that big pearl. It's all Zoe can do to extract her hand intact. Damn. With a sleepy grumble, Madclaw flips onto his stomach and slumbers on.

The waves crunch and burble. Perhaps they can see Zoe, perhaps they're discussing what she does. Anything's possible here. It strikes her that if she were to play her special tune, then the big saucer pearl in Madclaw's pouch might well open into an unny tunnel, right where it is.

Maybe she could push Madclaw through the tunnel and make her way through it too. But somehow, just now, she's not quite ready to try that route. Come to think of it, an unny tunnel from Madclaw's ocean-harvested saucer pearl might not lead to Earth at all. Might lead somewhere like Alpha Centauri.

Zoe glances up the beach towards the hut she's sharing with the tyrannical, cold, vain, and thoroughly worthless Villy Antwerpen. *Sigh*. She finds a clean damp spot on the sand by the water and hunkers down. Using the gentle light of the glowons, she draws a cluster of five hexagons. Like a scrap of honeycomb.

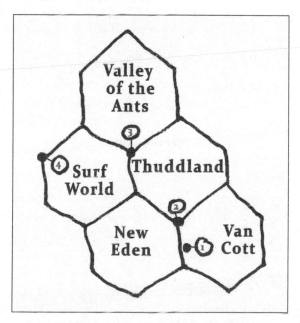

ZOE'S MAP OF THE LOCAL BASINS

Each hexagon stands for one of the basins they're traveling through. They started in Van Cott, the basin with the mappyworld version of Earth. Next to Van Cott is New Eden—the saucers' local base. And then comes Thuddland, the Valley of the Ants, and Surf World. Zoe numbers four dots to stand for the four nights they've spent here.

She has three hypotheses.

- It's easy for her to tunnel to Earth from downtown Van Cott. If she had a little more strength, or if her saucer pearl was bigger, it just might be possible to tunnel from a basin that touches Van Cott. But tunneling is flat-out impossible from basins further than that.
- The local saucers tend only to be in the New Eden basin or one of the basins that touch it.
- The saucers want to kill Zoe, but only when they're sure she has no possible option of dodging their death rays and hopping home.

And this leads to a conclusion.

- The saucers are most likely to zap Zoe while she's in a basin that *doesn't* touch Van Cott, and which *does* touch New Eden.

And, as it happens, Surf World is that kind of basin. Meatball was very keen on them visiting Surf World, traitor that she is. From the saucers' point of view, Surf World is a free-fire zone. Yes, Zoe managed to kill that big saucer lurking in the ocean. But another will be coming soon.

Peering upwards, Zoe sees something that confirms her fears. It's a flashing yellow beacon, some two thousand feet overhead. It's frikkin *Meatball*. Signaling for a saucer attack, the bitch. The next bad-guy saucer might take a couple of hours to fly here, but, yeah, he'll be coming soon. Maybe before dawn.

Somehow Zoe feels very calm. Logic is a beautiful thing. She's done with floundering and emoting. She sees two options—other than the dubious possibility of trying to tunnel through Madclaw's pearl to who knows where.

- Villy's choice: Keep heading towards Szep City. They should be relatively safe from the saucers along the way. Szep City itself will be iffy, but with any luck, they can pick up that anti-saucer wand there.
- Zoe's choice: Go back to Los Perros as soon as possible. They can circle back along the ridges to Thuddland, then push through the jungle to Van Cott, then use Zoe's pearl to tunnel home.

Either way, Zoe needs to get them off this beach and up to the Flatsie Pass ridge before the next saucer comes. She just hopes they'll be safe up there. Only one way to know: do it. Once more it's time to run.

Zoe smiles to herself. She's going to make a big scene, an epic scene. She'll rouse those three zonked idiots by the burned-out fire, get stupid Villy, and drive the purple whale up the cliff. She'll be calm and in charge. Villy, Scud, Yampa, and Pinchley will be whining and bewildered. But eventually they'll be grateful. Hooray for Zoe Snapp. The way it should be. Yeah.

Zoe goes over to the car. It's a comfortable silhouette, with the two surfboards back in place. And guess who's standing there waiting? Maisie, in a thin T-shirt and gauzy pants, with her meaty, skin-covered rim sticking out all around. She still has her little purse, plus two large folded sheets of—seaweed?

"Hey there," says Maisie. "I was expecting you."

"I need to leave Surf World," says Zoe.

"Right. A big saucer is on the way. One reason I flew here from New Eden was to warn you."

"You can fly?"

"I fly like a flying saucer," says Maisie, and she gives Zoe a significant look. But Zoe isn't sure what the look is supposed to mean.

"So many secrets," says Zoe. "Tell me about the saucer coming after us."

"It's Nunu's Uncle Boldog," says Maisie, setting down the seaweed. "The stupid dark-purple one. He plans to kill all of you. That's, like, the one and only thought in his tiny mind. Pa Saucer tried to stop him, but Boldog—you can't argue with him."

"Will we be safe if we make it up the cliff to the ridge?" asks Zoe. This is something she's not sure about.

"Smart question. Sad answer: *no*. Yes, the New Eden saucers aren't that likely to go on past the Surf World basin. It's a lot of work for them to fly over the basin edges. And Groon doesn't want them to get too far away from his music. We can't easily hear it, but Groon pipes his song into New Eden via a jet stream. Maybe you saw the stream from Borderslam Pass? It's full of saucers being rushed back and forth. Along with that horrible song. Groon's local slaves like to stay in New Eden or in a basin touching New Eden—so that they can keep hearing their master's voice."

"Wait, wait—what kind of music is it?" asks Zoe.

Maisie giggles. "Bagpipe, of course. The one instrument that's more squealy and horrible than anything else you ever hear in your entire life. Such a nasty sound that you never want to stop throwing up."

"Nothing makes sense," says Zoe.

"Why should it?" goes merry Maisie. She seems happy to be confiding with Zoe. "Anyway, Groon's slave saucers won't follow you into the next basin after this. But they'll still zap rays at you if they see you on the ridge. You have to keep back from the edge once you're up there."

"What are the basins on the other side of Flatsie Pass?" asks Zoe.

"Those would be Crab Crater and the Bubble Badlands. Various probs with each of those. Better to drive along the ridge between those two basins. It's bumpy and twisty, but if you go just a little way the saucers can't see you from Surf World."

"I've been thinking I might follow the basin ridge around Surf World and back to Thuddland and then drive back through Thuddland to Van Cott," says Zoe. "So I can hop home."

"Don't do that," says Maisie.

"I need some convincing," says Zoe. She clambers into the car. She needs to go pick up Scud and the two Szep. "Come on, Maisie. Ride with me and tell me more. Like—just for a random start—why are you lugging those two giant sheets of seaweed?"

"These are Neptune's tablecloths," says Maisie, still standing outside. "They're predators who live in the Surf World sea. Basically, they're big disks that bend around things and then pinch in their outer edge to make a pouch."

"Know about them," says Zoe.

"I just now dove down near the bottom and bagged these two," says Maisie. "They can stretch to a kilometer across. The outer edge acts like the drawstring on a sack, right."

"Who cares? Get to the point."

"We're going to use this pair of Neptune's tablecloths to trap Groon," says Maisie, very intense. "This happens during the cosmic beatdown in Los Perros. And I'll tell you the rest later."

"I never get the full picture here," gripes Zoe. "Everyone's always in a rush—I'm like Alice following the White Rabbit. Why do *you* know so much when you're a year younger than me?" Angrily Zoe thumps her hand against the outside of the door. "Get in the car, damn it."

"Only for a minute," says Maisie, taking a seat beside Zoe. "Action item: the giant saucer Boldog is on his way. He's ready to fry us all, including me. My situation with the saucers, by the way—it's kind of complicated. I mean, fine, I'm half saucer myself, but—"

"Wait, wait, wait," goes Zoe. Things are clicking into place. "*Your mother is a flying saucer?* That's what you're saying?" At some level Zoe already suspected this, but it's the first time she's let the idea into her conscious mind. "You're saying *my dad had sex with a flying saucer?* And that's how you came into the world?"

"A saucer can get pregnant from a kiss," says Maisie. "Like with Nunu and Scud. But actually our father and Meemaw really have done the full-on hump-o-rama. Lots of times. In fact, they still do."

"Oooo," says Zoe, breaking into shocked laughter. "*Meemaw?* What a name." She still hasn't started the car. "Is Meemaw hot? I mean—hot for a flying saucer?"

"Don't mock," says Maisie. "Meemaw is a good mother. She's not a slave of Groon. She has a strong, independent personality. She's divorced. And she just so happens to be a flying saucer. She's Dad's real love. His marriage to Sunny Weaver was for show. And yes, yes, yes—I'm half flying saucer. My parents are Meemaw the saucer and our common father Kirkland Snapp. Can we get past that?"

"Sorry."

"Meemaw is Nunu's mother too, by the way," says Maisie. "Meemaw and her ex-husband Pa Saucer are Nunu's parents."

"So Nunu is my *relative?*" cries Zoe. Another shriek of laughter escapes her. "I'm sorry, Maisie, but I'm utterly and completely losing my mind. Put me in the rubber room. Get me a straitjacket."

"Nunu is your half-sister's half-sister," says Maisie calmly. "So you're still inviolate and without stain—okay? The

Immaculate Zoe Snapp. As for my mother Meemaw—another reason not to mock her is that she's handicapped. Some narwhals attacked her two years ago when she was on vacation in Surf World. The narwhals didn't kill Meemaw, but she has scars now, and she flies crooked. Kind of sad."

"Sorry to hear that," says Zoe.

"Dad still loves her, and so do I, and Pa Saucer likes her too. Anyway, you better start the car. Because I'm picking up vibes from Uncle Boldog. He's not far. I totally hate him, by the way. He sold himself to Groon on purpose, just to get paid some extra smeel. So it's perfectly fine with me if you and the Flatsies kill him. But I don't want to be here when it happens. Or somehow I'll get blamed."

"How would the Flatsies kill Boldog?"

"They do this special routine with the narwhals and a ziggurat wave. Boldog should know about that, but he's too dumb to inform himself. Have you ever noticed that stupid people never doubt themselves?"

"I doubt myself a *lot*," says Zoe. "Especially I keep wondering if I should bail on the million mile road trip and go back to Van Cott and tunnel home to Los Perros."

"Listen to me and go to Szep City," urges Maisie. "Do it! And now please start the car."

"Why is everyone pushing for Szep City?" complains Zoe. The purple whale's dark-energy engine pops into life. Pinchley didn't get around to taking off those paddle fins last night, but that's okay. She bumps quietly along the beach towards the snoozers by the Flatsies' dead fire.

"I don't know why I have to explain this over and over again," says Maisie. "Goob-goob says that if you go see

Lady Filippa she'll have a special wand. Lady Filippa is an Aristo, which is a big deal. And supposedly an Aristo's wand is good against saucers. I'm not exactly sure what the wands *are*. I do know that they're alive, and that they won't actually help you unless they meet you and approve of you. The other big thing is that you need to connect with Goob-goob while you're in Szep City. With Goob-goob on our side, we'll *really* have a chance."

"A chance at *what* exactly?" Zoe holds herself back from screaming this into Maisie's face. "Sorry to be slow, but I'm not able to guess the parts that none of you ever bothers to tell me."

"Here we go again," says Maisie. "You should learn to listen when people talk to you, Zoe. Groon wants tens of thousands of his slave saucers to invade Earth, and then he wants to crawl over to Earth himself—greedy, skungy, scrotum-like bagpipe that he is. Earth will become a planet of zombies. A race with no wit and no love. Even more than now."

"Okay, I remember," says Zoe. "And this when I say it's too dangerous for me to go to Szep City."

"You *won't* die," says Maisie. "You, Villy, Scud, and me are cosmic heroes. We can't lose. We're living myths."

"Even Scud?" protests Zoe, although she does like the idea that she herself might be mythic.

"There he is," says Maisie, her voice soft. They've reached the spot where Scud lies asleep beside Pinchley and Yampa. The two Szep are twined around each other like a pair of woody vines.

"I've come to think of those two Szep as cute," says Zoe.

"Scud's cute too," says Maisie. "Even if he is a year younger than me."

"Hate to repeat myself, but—*Scud*?"

"In some ways Scud's like me," says Maisie. "A complete outsider. And we both like fossils."

"I didn't know you liked Scud."

"Oh—*you*," says Maisie. "There's a lot about me you don't know. You just think about yourself, and not about your family."

"Let me try and fake it," says Zoe. "Just now you told me that my dad's really and truly alive. He lives in New Eden with a hot but decrepit flying saucer named Meemaw. And Meemaw is my half-sister's mother." And now Zoe's giggles are starting up again.

"Our father is working with the good saucers for a revolution," says Maisie, her voice firm. "This really isn't funny, Zoe."

Zoe gives Maisie a rambunctious shove, and finally Maisie lets up and starts laughing with her.

"All this crazy shit you told me," says Zoe after a bit. "I feel like I just watched a two-hour movie in ten seconds."

Abruptly Maisie hugs Zoe. "I'm so glad I told you. My whole life, it's been like nobody can see me. And now I have my sister for true."

"I'm happy," says Zoe. "And now? Any more advice?"

"You have to kill Meatball," says Maisie, turning intense. "If Uncle Boldog doesn't kill you, then Meatball will. That's her mission. Her and the Iravs. You have to kill them all."

"Pinchley might find a way to do them in," says Zoe, studying the gnarly, sleeping Szep. "He's tough."

"And be nice to Scud," puts in Maisie. Unexpectedly she kneels down and kisses the sleeping boy on his cheek, and then on the mouth. Scud shifts, smiles, murmurs—and keeps sleeping.

"I've wanted to do that all year," adds Maisie, getting to her feet. Valentine hearts flicker on the rim of skin around her waist. "Can't you see at all that Scud's lovable?"

"Scud? He's too young."

"*Stop* that. He's almost a junior. One year younger than me. So what?"

"So—let it be Scud," says Zoe. "I honor your decision, sis." Although privately she still has doubts about ever being nice to Scud.

"We need to wrap this up," says Maisie. "Boldog draws nigh. We'll connect in New Eden or Van Cott. I'm glad to be important for once. I may be half saucer, but I'm fully on Earth's side. And I'm telling you, Zoe, if you don't get that wand, Earth's going under."

"Got it."

Zoe studies Maisie, her mousy hair and her intent, modest expression. She's odd, but, yes, Maisie is a person like Zoe, hoping to fit in, longing for love, wanting to do right. Full of hopes for her upcoming senior year.

"I'm sorry I've been cold to you at school," Zoe adds.

"I understand you better than you realize," says Maisie. "You're not as bad as you want people to think. You were nice to me plenty of times."

"Sisters," says Zoe.

"Sistahs!" echoes Maisie with that accent she puts on. She raises her hand. "Gimme five!"

A slap of their hands and Maisie goes on her way, a cryptic moth flying low across the dim waves, clutching her pair of folded Neptune's tablecloths to her chest and holding her purse that has—Zoe now realizes—a big saucer pearl inside.

NINETEEN

riding the ridge

scud

Someone is shaking Scud. He has sand in his eyes. His head hurts. Last night—he was dancing with the gingerbread men and the Szep. Chugging tuj while the Szep ate chocolate. Madclaw with his saucer pearl. Madclaw told him how to use a pearl to fly. Upsy downsy inside out. Like looking at rotating cube and flipping its perspective? Aside from all that, there was something more important. In Scud's dreams, a girl had kissed him.

"Wake up, idiot!"

It's Zoe, poking him with her foot. Bitch. Why doesn't she like him? It's still dark. Pinchley and Yampa are standing over him too.

"Scud!" Weird-smelling Yampa leans down to his face. She's worried. Pulling on his arm. "You are able to arise?"

What a question. With some effort, Scud gets onto all fours and—retches onto the sand. His stomach spasms two more times and then it's empty.

"Get him in the car!" says Zoe. "That killer saucer's almost here."

Pinchley and Yampa walk Scud towards the monster-wheeled whale.

"I can do it myself!" says Scud, twisting free and clambering into the back seat with the Szep. Away from Zoe. His pulse is pounding in his brain, like *tuj, tuj, tuj.* Yampa hands him a pod of water. Thank you.

The car roars, cruises, stops. Zoe runs into a hut, screams at someone for a while, then comes back with Villy, who's clearly in a bad mood. He swings into the front seat next to Zoe. Zoe peels out and slews the car onto a mountain trail resembling a fire road.

"What's the panic?" Scud asks the company at large.

"Zoe says a big saucer is flying here to zap us," goes Villy as the car rumbles around a first bend. "Nunu's Uncle Boldog? Maybe he'll spare you, Scud. Since you're in the family and like that. Careful, Zoe. These are serious cliffs. You're driving like a crazy person."

"Jerk," says Zoe. "Why am I even saving you?"

"Because you think you own me?" says Villy, his voice cold.

"You don't love me one bit, do you? Stupid gearhead surfer test-flunker."

With the paddle-fins still on the tires, the car is vibrating really hard. In Scud's opinion, Zoe's driving very well: accelerating on the straight bits, doing stuttery four-wheel skids in the hairpin turns, and monster-trucking over obstructive boulders. But he doesn't say that to Villy.

Way down below them, the Flatsie village is a cute cluster of lights, as if seen from a plane. The glowing sea slants to the horizon. It's pale green, streaked with combers, pocked with ziggurats, and—*uh-oh*. What's that glowing violet spot?

"Uncle Boldog," says Pinchley, also spotting the saucer. "Faster, Zoe."

Even though they're going several hundred miles an hour, Scud opens his window. Above the steady shuddering of the finned tires, he hears the Flatsies in their village. Shouting, chanting, and blatting on that giant seashell horn of theirs. *Fwhooooo!* They know Boldog's coming.

Just as the car's about to reach the top, Boldog's zap-ray sizzles into life, hard and white. The ray looks to be aimed at the hut where Zoe and Villy spent the night. The zap beam sizzles for thirty seconds, profligate with its dark energy, digging so deep that—oh wow—an immense thousand-foot facing of stone begins to teeter loose from the very cliff they're driving on—and there goes the support for the dirt track that the purple whale has been barrel-assing along.

Zoe screams and mashes the pedal. The paddle-finned tires kick savagely at the loosened plinth. The whale claws its way upward, nimble as a goat, slamming its fins against one ledge after another, scaling the final sixty feet to the cliff's crest. They come to rest at a weird angle up there, nearly rolling back off the edge, but not quite. *Whew.* Huge roar from the ongoing avalanche below. But the collapsing face is off to one side, and most of the Flatsies' village is spared.

Meanwhile the whale's overclocked engine has stalled. And frikkin traitor Meathall's right overhead, blinkety-blinking her light. Calling in the hit. *Here they are!*

Uncle Boldog homes in on them, no doubt recalibrating his death ray as he comes. Tremulous Scud manages to cover his eyes as the zap hits the front end of the whale. But even so, the long flash is so bright that it goes, like, inside his head, under his skin, into his flesh, and through his bones. Relative to the apocalyptic zap, Scud is transparent. A puny microbe doomed to die.

But then, *phht*, the light stops. Something's knocking the fat maroon saucer off-kilter. What? No time to look. Scud's the first one out of the trashed whale, hitting the ground on all fours with his butt high in the air, running like a primeval hyena.

The whale's flaming front tires light the scene. And Scud's eyes do still work. Looks like Boldog's blast blew the whole frikkin engine off their car, vaporizing part of the roof as well. Thank god Boldog missed the passenger cabin. Villy's prized surfboards are charred, melted scraps.

Scud spots a drop-off just a little way ahead of him— this ridge isn't more than thirty feet across. Dreading another blast from Boldog, he makes it to the far edge in, like, three seconds.

Without so much as a downward glance, Scud swings his legs over the edge and lets himself drop. Dwindling downward scream? Naw. He jolts onto a ledge five feet below. A solid, abrupt thud that clacks his teeth. His head is just barely peeking out across the ridge now. He's like a soldier in a trench. Perf.

Bloated Boldog is still out there, a Las Vegas-neon-sign shade of lavender, but there's something screwed up with him, and he's still not firing a follow-up blast. The ocean beneath him is aglow. Something has just darted up into Boldog's belly.

Scud focuses on his companions. "Hey! Over here! Move it!" Villy is leading Zoe by the hand—she's in a daze—and Yampa's holding Pinchley's arm. The four are vague and wobbly.

For his part, Scud feels sharp and on point. Maybe this is an upside of having a hangover? It's like the world around him is in slo-mo. He scuttles up onto the ridge and helps the others to his nook, and then the five of them are lined up on the ledge.

Pinchley is such a grease monkey that he's already obsessing about fixing the car. He digs into his tool belt and sends a pair of two-inch-long fireman beetles buzzing over to the blazing front tires. The beetles poot out some kind of bio-nano-pixie dust that quenches the flames.

Meanwhile the Flatsies' giant alpine horn is steadily booming. And now Scud understands what's happening to Boldog. A patch of the nearby seawater has flared to luminous yellow-green, chartreuse. It's a titanic ziggurat right offshore. The Flatsies have mobilized the waves.

"They're shooting him!" exclaims Villy, getting the picture. "The ziggurat is spitting narwhals into the air, see? Like submarine-launched missiles. The narwhals are using their fins like wings, and they're —"

"Arrowing into Boldog and getting inside him and chewing him to bits!" cries Scud. "*Sweet!*"

With a stolid, subsonic groan, Boldog pitches to one side and skims unevenly towards shore. He slams into the beach and bursts—with chittering toothache-white sparks of zap energy dancing across his goo. As with that ocean saucer, the victorious narwhals root in the dead flesh, wheezing to each other, waving their tusks—and now they're batting the dead saucer's pearl back and forth. Scud wishes he could get that pearl.

"Come on and help me with the car," says Pinchley, interrupting the boy's reverie. The Szep is already back onto the flat part of the pass. Scud shakes his head. He doesn't like to say so out loud, but he thinks Pinchley's crazy. The car is junked.

Meanwhile the air around them is starting to turn light. Daybreak. No sign of Meatball. She's wafted off. Readying another ambush? Damn her.

"Let's eat breakfast," goes Villy, pulling himself up off the ledge. "Throw us our packs from the car, Pinchley."

So there they are, the five of them—three humans and two Szep—happy to be alive and not all that sure what comes next. Flatsie Pass is yet another triple point, another vertex where three basins meet. One of the three basins is of course Surf World, and the other two are supposed be the homes of the crabs and the Bubblers. This ridgetop trail runs along Surf World, with a fresh branch going off between the two new basins.

"That's where we should go," says Zoe, pointing down the branch trail. "We need to get off the Surf World part of the ridge before another saucer comes. I'd thought we might stay on this ridge, but it's like being a target in a shooting gallery."

Pinchley has thrown Villy and Scud their packs by now, and Villy is digging inside his. "You want a hit of this tom turkey food mint, Zoe? Or roast beet?"

"I'd like to say yes," goes Zoe. "But I'm not speaking to you."

"Why?" says Villy, actually sounding confused.

"I, uh—I forget?" says Zoe, and she starts laughing. "Because we yelled at each other in the car? Because we didn't have sex last night? Because we were fighting about whether to give up and go home?"

"Look, if you really want to head back to Earth, we can do it," says Villy, throwing his hands in the air. "Who knows, man. Maybe you're right. Why should we do a suicide mission? I was overamped last night. Ripped on surf glory."

Zoe turns her face towards him like a flower. The glowon dawn's light is sweet on her skin. Scud hangs back, just plain watching. He'd be happy to look at Zoe all day. Happy to have a girl love him.

"I've changed my mind," Zoe is telling Villy. "I think we should go for Szep City after all. Find Lady Filippa. Get an Aristo wand. Talk to Goob-goob. Stop the saucers."

"Yeah," puts in Scud, longing to be part of their conversation. "Go for epic."

"I was talking to Maisie last night," Zoe tells them. "She pretty much convinced me. She says we're destined to succeed. And Scud, did you ever know that Maisie has a crush on you? She was looking at you while you were sleeping."

Scud flashes on that ghost of a memory he'd woken with. The dream that a girl had kissed him. Maisie. Score! He stands there smiling.

Zoe studies Scud for a minute, her expression almost kind—but then she flips back to being mean. "The reason

Maisie has a lump around her waist? You ever wonder about that, Scud?"

"I don't know," mutters Scud. "I'm not really that observant of, like, girls' clothes."

"That lump is a saucer rim," says Zoe, slapping down the words like cards on a table. "Maisie is half flying saucer. Maisie and I have the same father, see, but Maisie's mother Meemaw is a flying saucer. You might say that my father Kirkland is the same kind of perv as you."

"I'm not a perv," says Scud weakly. He's totally confused. And, wait, did Zoe just say *Meemaw*? Wasn't that the name of—

"Meemaw is Nunu's mother too," says Zoe, seeing the question in Scud's eyes. Zoe looks as happy as a cat tormenting a rat. "Me and Maisie—half-sisters. Maisie and Nunu—half-sisters too. Get it?"

"Stop harshing on my brother," says Villy, interrupting her. "Let's go see if Pinchley can actually fix the car," The two of them join Pinchley beside the bombed-out front end of the soon-to-be-even-more-highly-modified whale. The Szep is kneeling beside the trashed front end, holding a crooked little ant from his tool belt. He's talking to the ant and telling it what's what.

"Just wait now," Pinchley says to Villy and Zoe. "This here's a fractal ant to help the car remember how it used to be. It's gonna take us some time to get this trick straight."

Meanwhile Scud and Yampa are staring into the closest of the new basins. Scud keeps his face blank, trying to hide how badly Zoe hurt his feelings.

"Bobbling ball beings," says gnarly yellow Yampa, pointing.

It's light enough for a good look at the Bubble Badlands. It's a maze of spires and arroyos, vaguely Wild West, but more eroded and with sharper points. Colorful critters bob among the towers and cluster upon the mesa tops.

"Bubblers," says Scud, wrenching his attention into the now. So good to have something besides Maisie and Nunu and Meemaw and stupid old Kirkland to think about. Focus, Scud. Get out of your head. Forget that Zoe hates you.

These new aliens, they're just like that bubble man at the Borderslam Inn—he'd called himself Gunnar. The smaller Bubblers are like little balloon animals, and the larger ones are like Chinese dragon kites, made of a dozen or more bubbles each. Each of the bubbles swirls with colored gas, and each Bubbler has a "head" bubble with an eye inside it. Two of the larger Bubblers drift over to Yampa and Scud and, oh my god, one of them actually *is* Gunnar.

"Scood!" exclaims Gunnar. "Vhat you got to trade?" As before, his head sphere contains pale blue gas along with his wobbly eye. His voice is a sonorous buzz.

"It's really you?" says Scud. "Gunnar? How did you get here so fast?"

"Qvantum qvick," says Gunnar. "Please meet my vife Monika." Monika's headmost sphere is pink and glistening, like a very large salmon egg. Her eye is softer than Gunnar's, more humane.

"Trade what for what?" says Scud after introducing Yampa. "In the Borderslam Inn you talked about trading something called a bubblegun?"

"Gotta get a gun," says Yampa. "Kick crash bash lash."

"Bubblegun!" exclaims Monika. Her voice is an octave higher than Gunnar's. "I am toting vun in my hindquarter. Can't trust vith my husband." She wags her body and indeed there's something shifting back and forth inside her rear-most sphere. Thumping her taut hide like a tambourine. She bats her warm eye at Scud. "Zo? Ve make deal? What you got?"

"I have a ballyworld fossil—"

"Wery many fossils here in our canyons," says Gunnar, cutting off Scud. "Pinchopods, dungosaurs, blahceratops, squatoons, and bone-bones. No vanting more. You know vell vhat we vant."

"A—a starstone?" says Scud, reluctant to give his up.

"Starstone!" trills Monika. "I am liking vun, yes, you sveet dumbbell, I vant."

"Why don't you just collect them from this ridge?" says Scud. He glances around, but now that he looks, there don't seem to be any starstones here at all.

"Ve ate all," says Gunnar. "Ve vent vild on the starstones for years, hey Monika? I already told you, Scood, I was supposed to bring new starstone from Borderland Pass this veek. I got vun from dot trapper vith beard, but, vell, I ate the whole starstone alone. Ate all the zuns inside it."

"Wery greedy boy," says Monika. "But now with Scud's starstone ve can party together like old time." She's cheerfully wriggling her chain of spheres.

So it seems like they're set for a deal, but then a swarm of smaller Bubblers comes flying over from a nearby mesa, clamoring in high thin squeals, circling around Monika, nudging her as if wanting to nurse on her. They resemble toy balloon snowman-figures that a circus clown might make. Cute little guys.

Gunnar, however, is insanely strict with them. Swinging his tail segment, he whacks one of them so hard that the poor little fellow pops. Shrilling in terror, most of others flee. But one of them clings to mother Monika with all his might and main, pressing so hard against her that her skin makes a *smorp* sound, and then the baby Bubbler is inside one of Monika's spherical body segments, with his muffled voice sounding through the sphere's wispy yellow gas.

"Daddy bad!" shrills the tot.

"Too many tchildren," says Gunnar, twitching his segmented body as if in a shrug.

"You are wery horrible," Monika tells him. "Vhy I live vith you?"

"Give Scud your bubblegun, then he is giving you his starstone, hunky dory, and you are feeling happy, ja, Monika? Not hard to spawn wery many more small fry if you vant."

"But that vas Sven-77 you popped. Alvays viggling so cute."

"Sven-78 is yust as good," says Gunnar. "Now make vith giving Scud the bubblegun, okay?"

"All *right*!" yells Monika, angry with Gunnar. She flips her tail forward like a scorpion's and—the bubblegun flies straight at Scud's face, going about sixty miles an hour. Fortunately, he's so wired that he catches the gun in midair.

It's a plump little derringer, a good fit for his hand, almost like a toy. It's made of a flexible yellow material like soft plastic, and the yellow is patterned with varicolored polka dots. Scud aims the stubby pistol out over the Bubble Badlands and gives it a squeeze. A firework-gush of bubbles whizzes out, maybe thirty of them, glowing hot, like balls from a Roman candle. On the way down, one of the balls bumps into the cliff below, and it explodes with a heavy concussion that shakes Scud's feet. Not taking a chance with another collapse, Scud and Yampa scramble over to the midline of the ridge.

"My turn to toot the root," says Yampa, holding out her hand. Zoe is watching too. Yampa levels a shot at a boulder on the ridge some fifty feet off. The festive bright bubble-sprinkles dynamite the rock to dust.

Meanwhile Villy is over by the car with Pinchley. The trashed whale has its charred passenger cabin in place and its mammoth rear wheels intact. The engine and hood and the front wheels—they're gone. And the vaunted fractal repair ant is sitting on Pinchley's hand thinking.

The exploding boulder gets Villy's attention. "Yah mon," he whoops. "We'll be ready when we see Meatball again. Can I try the bubble gun too?"

"Don't you guys be beatin' up dust and making a hooroar," says Pinchley. "This here ant's a-ponderin her specific moves."

"Aw—"

"You vandering wandals should know dot a bubblegun only shoots five times," puts in Monika. "You got three shots left."

Scud quickly recovers the gun from Yampa.

"Fork over starstone now to my vife!" Gunnar tells Scud, going so far as to nudge him with his tail segment.

The Bubbler's touch is unpleasant—it's like his body carries an electric charge that tingles against Scud's skin.

Scud fishes the stone out of his knapsack—he's a little sorry to let it go, given that this sparkly pebble is in fact a mega-light-year volume of star-sprinkled space, warped and twisted into a tiny package. But before he can mull this over any further, Monika has snatched the starstone out of his hand—kind of pinching onto it with a fold in her head sphere. Toothlessly biting it, you might say.

"What will you do with it?" Scud asks. "Use it for jewelry?"

"Hah!" says Monika with her resonant membranes. "Ve gobble it up like smörgåsbord. And have some bliss."

Monika now makes a gesture that's hard to understand—it's like she turns the starstone inside out. In a flash, the entire vast Bubble Badlands basin is filled with bobbling—suns. Little suns. Fortunately, some beneficent mappyworld force is keeping things under control. That is, the unpacked suns aren't insanely large and hot, no, they're quite manageable, with each sun about the size of Scud. There's at the very least a thousand of them, scattered like grains of sand, decorating the Bubble Badlands from hither to yon.

Villy, Zoe, and Yampa stand by Scud's side, goggle-eyed. But Pinchley is still busy conferring with his crooked ant.

Bubblers emerge from every cranny of the creased Bubble Badlands landscape. A mighty legion of Bubblers. They join in a mass feeding frenzy, pouncing upon the starstone suns, draining energy from the bouncy orbs, growing fat and bright. Gunnar and Monika are in the thick of it.

One by one, the drained suns shrivel, go dark, and wink out of existence. Scud has to wonder about the mirrored effects of these events on his home universe. Swaths of stars becoming black holes? Nebulae deliquescing to dark dust?

Once the starstone suns are quite gone, the Bubblers switch gears and begin a wild orgy—mating in pairs and triplets and n-tuples. Glittering drifts of spawn spread from the amorous clusters, comprising tens of thousands of new "tchildren." Slowly the passion ebbs. Scud spots Gunnar and Monika resting upon a nearby mesa. Languidly Monika waves.

"Looks like the party's over," says Zoe.

"Wait," says Scud. "I got a question." He raises his voice to reach Gunnar. "Did you say you ate a starstone *all by yourself* at the Borderslam Pass Inn?"

"Ja. Dot's vhy I vas tired."

While all this has been going on, Pinchley's crooked ant has been standing on his fingertip, poised on her six little legs, twitching her feelers, and letting her compound eyes play repeatedly across the remains of the purple whale.

"So how about it?" Villy says to Pinchley. "When's that ant going to frikkin do something?"

"It's a matter of refining the quantum vibe, is what you gotta understand," Pinchley tells him. "It's like—what's missing from this picture? This here ant is teeping with the matter-wave souls of me and the car, you see. She's grooving on our entangled quantum-space history, and— whoa Nellie, here we go!"

The little ant chirps, makes a funny little wiggle—and her antennae thicken up and become small, second-order ants. The antennae of the second-order ants shape themselves into third-order ants, whose antennae plump into fourth-order ants, and they're off to the races.

In seconds the one ant has turned into a branching fractal tree of—maybe not *infinitely many* ants, but sure enough a *huge buttload* of them. It's like a wobbly broom. Delicately, Pinchley pinches the rear gaster segment of the original ant between thumb and forefinger. The multiply branched antennae of the ant are like a tiny whiskbroom that Pinchley now brushes across the ruined front end of the purple whale. It's like Pinchley's holding a magic paintbrush made of quantum matter-printing ants—a purposeful formic fractal.

A few minutes later, the engine is going *vooo-don* and *va-vooo-don* again. Just like back in Villy and Scud's garage. It's all good. The narwhals killed Uncle Boldog, Scud has a cool gun with three shots left, the Bubblers ate a galactic subsector's worth of stars, and the purple whale's standing proud on four fat tires, ready to run the ridge. And Pinchley's even cleaned those bumpy paddle fins off the tires and removed that ocean-going rudder he'd had under the whale.

Scud gets back into the back seat with Pinchley and Yampa. Zoe is still driving, with Villy in front with her. The two of them are all lovey-dovey again. Zoe follows the ridge's narrow track away from Surf World, with the festive Bubble Badlands on the right, and Crab Crater on the left. Big, thoughtful crabs wander around in there, lugging pieces of wood and stone, and mounding them into intricate crab-logic designs. The crabs give off a salty low-tide smell, with a touch of decay.

"Let's not get into anything with those guys," says Zoe. "I'm worried they'll know that we ate two of them last night."

"Crabs don't *know* anything," says Scud, in a mood to contradict whatever Zoe says. "They have no minds."

"That's so wrong," says Villy. "You were too drunk to notice, Scud, but these particular crabs are incredibly advanced and intelligent. We're, like, savage unclean cannibals to have eaten them. I don't even like to think about it."

"Hell, *everything's* intelligent," Pinchley says carelessly. "You eat what you catch."

"I hardly know where to begin with that kind of—" Zoe loftily begins. But then she breaks off, staring forward along the ridge. "What's that up ahead?"

Leaning forward, Scud sees a figure standing in the road. A woman, it looks like. Insidiously familiar. Waving to them. She wants to flag them down. Her face is warm, tired, kind.

"No," says Villy. "Impossible."

Scud feels like a bomb's exploding in his head. "Mom!" he yells. "It's Mom!"

TWENTY

not mom

villy

Villy is suspicious. And scared. This whole scene—it's like a scary surreal movie. The godforsaken ridge, the featureless sky, the giant crabs and talking bubbles, the gnarly Szep, the saucers with zap-rays—and now an alien creature is posing as his dead mom.

Zoe glances over from the driver's seat. "Should I stop?"

The mother-thing points at Villy, calling to him. Her face isn't right. A stiffness around the eyes. An odd tilt of her head.

"A trap," says Villy.

But Scud won't stop hollering, and Zoe slows down. Scud tumbles out of the car while it's still moving, regains his footing, and starts hugging the—woman? By now the car has come to a halt. The mother-thing is talking to Scud, embracing him, and keeping a weather eye on Villy, obviously hoping to put her emotional hoodoo on him as well.

The creature's voice is just like Mom's, chirpy and excited, bursting with love. The sounds pluck at Villy's heart. Resonant vibrations. He lets out a deep sigh that's almost a sob.

"Yampa and I have figured something out," says Pinchley from the back seat. "Meatball and Irav—they're both Freeth, and they're working for Groon and his slave saucers. The saucers paid Meatball with a saucer pearl back in Van Cott, and the split-up Iravs are trying to earn pearls too. The Freeth are shapeshifters, remember? This isn't your mother, Villy. It's Meatball."

"Where's our new gun?" asks Zoe.

"Scud has it," says Villy.

"I'll get it from him," says Zoe. "Scud has a thing for me. He'll give me the gun, no problem."

Villy looks at Zoe, so smart and poised and beautiful. The most important person in his world. "Please stay in the car," he tells her. "You're the one they're really after."

"Zoe and I stay in the car," orders Pinchley. "Villy takes the gun from Scud. And Yampa helps Villy."

Zoe accepts this. "Don't waver," she tells Villy. "That mother-thing has to die. I'm sorry that sounds so weird. I'd never talk this way about your real mother. But—"

"Got it," says Villy, not yet moving. The mother-thing keeps smiling at him. This is like the worst nightmare he's ever had. But if it was a nightmare he could wake up. And he can't. Why are they even here?

Yampa pokes him. Get going, Villy. Villy and Yampa hop out of the car and slam the doors tight.

"My darling Villy," says the mother-thing. Her expression is utterly and completely wrong. How can that idiot Scud be going for this? "You look gloomy," she says. "Aren't you a tiny little bit glad to see me?"

"I—" Villy can't manage to produce a sentence. Too many emotions. Love, nostalgia, grief, pity, loneliness—and fear.

"It is *too* her!" yells Scud, as if willing his words to be true—even though he knows the others don't believe him. Scud's staring up into the mother-thing's eyes. He begins babbling questions like he's ten years old. "How did you stop being dead, Mom? Did you fly over here like a soul going to heaven? Or were you always here, even before you died? How did you know to wait for us on this road? Can we bring you back home?"

Slowly, steadily, Villy edges closer to Scud. Yampa is fully in tune with him—it's like when they surfed the wall wave together.

Villy sees a bulge in Scud's left pants pocket. The bubblegun. All he has to do is lunge and grab. But what if he's too slow? Meatball will zap the crap out of them. Kill all five of them, maybe. Perhaps the only reason she hasn't started is that's she's not quite sure if they're armed. Or maybe she's slightly worried that Zoe can still tunnel to Earth from here.

"*Yeek!*" screeches Yampa and tumbles over like a collapsing ladder. A classic distraction move. Faster than it takes to tell, Villy has the squishy little bubblegun in his hand, and he's holding it pressed tight against his imitation mother's chest. Tearful Scud starts pummeling Villy, but Yampa grabs Scud and, with surprising strength, flings him away. For good measure, Yampa knocks the mother-thing off-balance as well. Alien judo. Villy flops onto the fallen Mom.

So here he is, kneeling on the chest of a very accurate replica of his mother, holding a stubby polka-dotted gun against her head, trying to get the nerve to pull the trigger and kill her in cold blood.

"Do it!" calls Zoe, getting out of the car.

Mom/Meatball begins to blubber. "We Freeth aren't to blame," she says. "We're in hock for the saucer pearls that we need so we can zap and fly. In days of yore, we could pay for our pearls. But our resources ran out and now—now we're slaves of the saucer-master Groon. I've been a slave since birth. You and I—we're not meant to be enemies, Villy. I'm jolly and you're sweet. I'll find a way to postpone killing you."

Villy is almost beginning to waver. Meatball/Mom stretches a supplicating hand towards Zoe. "Talk to this boy. You're a woman too—"

Villy notices a wiggle around the outstretched hand's fingers. Like the wavering air above a hot summer road. Dark energy gathering for a zap. God help him, it's time. He presses the gun tight and pulls the trigger.

Villy's surrounded by smoke and sparks and exploding bubblegun balls. Meatball's remains are on fire. He rolls away from the flames and lies on his face, groaning.

A minute later, all that's left of Meatball/Mom are wispy ashes and a shiny sphere the size of a softball. Villy can't help but think of his real Mom's ashes after they cremated her. He feels like a fist is squeezing his heart.

"Looky there," says Pinchley, joining them. "The saucer pearl that the leech saucers gave Meatball when she was born in Van Cott. Our jolly pal. Yampa had Meatball's number all along."

"The pearl is mine!" yells Zoe, rushing forward to scoop up the iridescent ball. It's hot to the touch, and she has to juggle it—so in the end she holds it with the tail of her shirt.

Villy feels slightly annoyed with Zoe. Maybe *he* would have liked the pearl. And now Scud starts screaming in his face like a psycho. "*You killed Mom!*" As if this scene wasn't bad enough.

Yampa and Pinchley work on Scud, and finally he snaps out of it. The five of them stand by the car, tired and dispirited. At this point Zoe produces her trumpet and crouches over Meatball's big saucer pearl, gently tooting. The pearl's surface turns gauzy, then transparent.

"What the eff are you doing?" snaps Villy. "You're going to bail?" His voice is cold and empty. He feels zero empathy just now. He's a guy who killed his mother. He wants to die.

"I never said I was the bravest person in the world," goes Zoe. Her face is anguished. "I wish I could do the big mission, yes. Maisie won me over last night. But now, the next thing I know, here comes this, like, fake ghost of your mother and she tries to kill us, and—"

"So leave," says Villy. Even though, more than anything, he wants Zoe to stay. But right now his emotions aren't working. "Go ahead into the tunnel. Who cares. I'm sick of your scenes."

Zoe is silent for a long minute, as if disappointed. Waiting for Villy to beg. She leans forward, studying the unny tunnel gate that the saucer pearl has become. Looking into the mouth of the unny tunnel, with her trumpet held at the ready. And then, quite abruptly, she plays a falling pattern of notes, and saucer pearl goes opalescent again. The gate is closed. Zoe glances over at Villy. Her expression is hard to read.

"What?" goes Villy.

"This pearl's tunnel—it goes to a bad place," says Zoe, her voice shaky. "Spiky things with red eyes in there. One of them was starting to come through. I can't use this particular pearl to go home. I'm stuck here. And you hate me."

"I don't," says Villy, dragging himself back into the light. "I love you, Zoe. I love you more than anything in the world."

"That's what I needed to hear," says Zoe with a tremulous smile. Villy wraps his arms around her and hangs on.

"We can still use the pearl to levitate," puts in Scud. He's flushed and hoarse from his freak-out, but he wants to be part of the gang again. "I can use this big saucer pearl to lift our car. I know the trick."

"You say *upsy downsy inside out*," goes Villy, remembering Madclaw's words.

"Yeah!" says Scud, "I had a dream about that. Or, no, I was teeping with Madclaw."

"In the tuj haze," says Villy, getting in a dig. He's very upset about his mother, and some of those feelings are coming out as resentment towards Scud. The kid had made this latest scene even worse than it needed to be.

"I think it's more than just saying *upsy downsy inside out*," prattles Scud, off in math magic land. "Madclaw teeped me something about a line drawing of a cube. And you flip it back and forth in your head. Changing the perspective. Like when you look at a wire-frame cube and you say to yourself—which is the closest corner? Your perception flips back and forth, and each time you flip, it's like you're mentally rotating the cube in the fourth dimension, and that's how a saucer pearl flies."

"Huh?"

"You spin the cube in your mental hyperspace. *Upsy downsy inside out!*"

"Hearken to the Learned Pig," intones Villy, stressing the second syllable like it's *Learn-ed*, the way an old-time carnival barker might do. "Tap your trotter, Learn-ed Pig. What's three plus two?"

"I hate you, Villy."

"I *love* you. Especially when you almost get us killed. Especially when you make me shoot my mother in the head." A little unfair to blame Scud this way, but that's how Villy is feeling.

"Don't fight, boys," interposes Zoe. "We've got a long road ahead." At least she sounds like she's back on board with the trip again.

"Give me the pearl," Scud says to Zoe. "Then we can fly instead of driving."

"Greetings, humans of ballyworld Earth," says a crackly, hissing voice.

"Oops," goes Yampa.

"One of them giant crabs!" exclaims Pinchley. "Way bigger than our car. Keep the bubblegun ready, Villy. But don't shoot unless you have to. We ain't got but the two shots left." Pinchley makes his voice loud. "Hey thar, Mr. Crusty Crab. We gonna be friends?"

The crab's mandibles are in ceaseless motion, like a man chewing his mustache. His folded claws are the size of canoes, his stalk eyes like bowling balls. His long, finicky legs move on tiptoe in a brittle ballet. His low-tide odor is laced with a sharp tang of iodine.

"My name is not Crusty Crab," he says with a creaking hiss. "It's Klactoveedsedstene. Give me that saucer pearl."

"No way in hell," says Zoe.

"I'm going to use it to fly," prattles Scud.

"I doubt you'll be able to," hisses the crab, then echoes Villy's teasing phrase. "Learn-ed Pig."

"Don't you call me that!" yells Scud, already on the point of losing it again. "I'm not an idiot! I know about math and the fourth dimension!"

"You go, savage swine," says Villy, regaining some of his family feeling. He and his brother are *both* crazy, okay? He pats Scud on the shoulder.

"Back in the car, guys," says Zoe, poised in the driver's seat. "Hurry before it's too late."

"No need to fear me," clicks Klactoveedsedstene the crab. "I'm nonviolent. I eat seaweed and the dead bodies that I find." But by now the kids and the two Szep are all in the car with the doors shut tight.

Unwisely, Zoe feels she has to unburden her conscience. "I feel guilty because we ate two of your brothers or sisters," she tells the crab through her fully open window. "Last night."

"At the Flatsie beach party?" hisses the crab. No hope of reading any expression from his gleaming stalk eyes.

"That's right," says Villy, leaning across Zoe to talk out the window. "And then the Flatsies let a narwhal kill a third big crab. What are you going to do about it, shiteater?" In Villy's freaked-out state, enraging the crab seems like a sound move. Lay everyone's cards on the table, right? "You should have heard that third crab scream," adds Villy, waiting for the reaction.

"We do indeed scream when we're being tortured to death," says Klactoveedsedstene mildly. Taking the high road. Being all philosophical. "That's the way of the world, eh? Nature red in tooth and claw." He produces a long strand of dried kelp and delicately nibbles it. His mandibles are busy and intricate and disgusting. He tiptoes closer, his mouth at the level of the car window framing Zoe's face.

"You're making me paranoid," goes Zoe.

"Your bad conscience is at work," says the crab in a lulling tone. "You worry I might be as callous a killer as you."

"Step on the frikkin gas," Pinchley tells Zoe from the back seat. "This crab is working his way up to a rampage. That's how they do."

"Wait," says Zoe, seemingly unable to stop talking. "I know you're very smart, Klactoveedsedstene. Like Charlie Parker. Or Einstein. So tell me this. Is mappyworld real?"

"Meaty question," clicks the crab. His shell bumps against the car.

"Give me the gun," Scud whines to Villy. "I'm the one who got the gun from the Bubblers, and I want to be the one who shoots the crab."

"Human minds are like nests of snakes," says the crab, resting one of his claws atop the car. "Snakes swallowing their tales." He churns his mandibles so rapidly that they make a whining buzz.

"Go!" Pinchley implores Zoe.

"Wait for your answer," singsongs the crab. "Is mappyworld real? Is ballyworld real? Yes and yes. Yes and no. No and yes. No and no. And I prove these propositions thus—"

The crab digs the tip of his great claw into the car's roof, opening it like a sardine can. Zoe snaps out of her trance.

"*Yeek!*" She peels out and they roar off along the ridge.

Klactoveedsedstene stands there, furiously waving his claws. All signs of philosophical detachment are gone.

"Folks do take it hard when you eat their relatives," Pinchley tells Zoe. "Especially if you come mooching by to say you're sorry."

They speed on, passing through another three-way intersection. A new basin appears on their left—Yampa says it's called the Teetertotter Forest. The sprawling Bubble Badlands remain on their right, but none of the Bubblers are in the vicinity.

"Let me hold that saucer pearl," says Scud yet again.

"It stays with Villy and me," says Zoe. Indeed, the lustrous orb is in Villy's lap. He's kind of falling in love with it. What a beautiful luster it has. And a nice heft. And it's wonderfully smooth. He feels like he can figure out how to make it levitate.

"No pearl for you," says Villy to Scud. "But I'll give you back the bubblegun, okay? And let's try to remember there's only two shots left for the Iravs." He passes the murderous thing over the seat. He's glad to be rid of it.

The trees of Teetertotter Forest are in constant motion—flexing their limbs, swaying from side to side, ambling about on mobile roots. They have friendly-looking eyes set into their trunks. One of the redwoods beckons, but Zoe's into driving. She's got the big-wheeled whale cranked to damn near a thousand miles per hour. Somehow she's gotten past her fear of high speeds.

As for Villy, the cumulative stress is caving in on him. He slumps in his seat. He feels boneless. "Falling off the gallows with the noose around my neck," he says to Zoe. "Deep fried in rancid fat."

"Relax," Zoe says, glancing over at him and patting his hand. "You're safe."

Villy smiles at her touch. "Maybe." he says. "But— weren't you the one saying this whole expedition is doomed? And that every time we turn around, something tries to kill us? It's true."

"I flip-flop," says Zoe with a shrug. "You know that. Right at this moment, I cheer myself with the notion that we're invincible. Maisie told me we're mythic cosmic heroes. Predestined to win."

"Maybe she was shining you on," says Villy. "Building up your confidence, and who knows why. I mean—Maisie's not even human. Not a hundred percent."

"Redneck much? Take your nap, Villy."

They bowl along. Thanks to the car's streamline supershine treatment, Villy can hear everything outside. The fluttering leaves of the Teetertotter Forest are like the soothing susurration of a crowd. The saucer pearl in his lap is like a glowing, cozy cat. He nods off.

When he awakes, the car's at rest, and the others are outside. It's dusk, and the glowon light is warm yellow. Motes of dust hang in the air. Gnats jitter. Villy has slept through most of the day. They're parked between two basins, with the Teetertotter Forest on their left, and a new basin called Birdland on their right.

Birdland features a symphony of cheeps and peeps,

produced by big birds on low, sturdy oaks with wonderfully long and twining branches. The birds are six feet long, all kinds of them, in many colors. Sitting on the branches, they remind Villy of notes on musical staves.

Zoe, Scud, Pinchley, and Yampa stand by the car in conversation with a six-foot robin and a two-hundred-foot redwood who balances himself on a tangle of flexible roots. Scud has managed to get hold of the saucer pearl, and he's cradling it against his belly.

"Hi, Villy," says Zoe. "Check out these two. The robin is named Pickpeck. And the talking tree is Farktooth. Pickpeck seems a little dim. They're warning us that the Iravs are up ahead along the ridge, maybe five hundred miles from here."

"The Iravs are still driving Pinchley's car?" asks Villy. "And do they still look like pieces of a chopped-up body?"

"Word is they still got my car, yeah," says Pinchley. "And they haven't smoothed out their shapes, nor merged back together. Maybe they suppose they're scarier if they look that way."

"I'm—I'm worried we can't ever beat the Iravs," says Villy. That thing with Meatball imitating his mother has blown most of his confidence away.

"Farktooth and Pickpeck can teach us how to use our saucer pearl for flying," says Zoe. "Then we can, like, raise the car up into the air."

"Why would the bird and the tree want to help us?" asks Villy. "Do they want something?"

"Powdered chocolate," says Yampa. "Cocoa. The crazy cup that cheers."

"And I said as how we can give them some of our caraway seeds," adds Pinchley. "After we get that little jar back from them damned Iravs."

"You're optimistic," says Villy.

Pickpeck squawks her shorthand version of the Irav problem. "Jerks lurk!" She twitches her wings and bobs her head as she talks. Each of her feet is an orange claw with four scaly meaty toes—three in front and one in back. To Villy's eyes, the feet are like some monstrous murderer's hands. He can't stop staring at them. Paranoia, *the* destroyer. But Pickpeck's glassy black eyes seem somewhat friendly, thanks to her pale-yellow irises. And her muted red breast feathers are downy-soft.

"Cocoa loco," says Pickpeck. Villy wonders if she really has to talk this way. Could be her routine is a joke, in that odd mappyworld way. Or, as Zoe says, maybe she's not very intelligent. She is, after all, a bird.

"We should save our powdered chocolate for Szep City," objects Scud. "Instead of dishing it out to these two. We don't need the bird and the tree. Like I already told you, I teeped with Madclaw back on the beach. So I already know all about how to fly with a saucer pearl."

"But you *don't* know," says Zoe. "I'm letting you hold the pearl—and you're just standing on the ground talking. If you frikkin knew how to frikkin fly, you'd be in the air."

"I understand the *theory* of how to fly," says Scud, quickly covering his ass. "And later, when I'm ready, I'll put theory into action. You get the pearl to do a four-dimensional rotation. As if it's turning inside out. And the 4D rotation puts a kink in the gravitational field. And you ride the kink."

"Or maybe the kink rides you," says Villy, not entirely in mockery.

"Scud supposes he sketches the solution's shape," rustles Farktooth. "Silly to submerge the senses in science symbols. The simple secret is to sail the sky. I say send sturdy Villy on superb swoops." Farktooth has a bark-groove face and knothole eyes. Maybe he's smiling.

Villy stretches out his hand. "Give it here, Scud. The magic ball."

"No."

Scud's about to go all wild-eyed and irrational again. Truth be told, both the boys are a little crazed from the horrible encounter with not-Mom. Scud clutches the iridescent pearl to his chest as if it's his last worldly possession. But now Pickpeck delivers a brisk, well-aimed poke of her yellow beak—and the orb springs into Villy's grasp.

So that's sweet, but then, a lot faster than Villy is ready for, Pickpeck grabs his legs with her claws and lifts him into the air. Not digging into his flesh or anything, but she's holding him really tight, and he's hanging upside down. At least Villy manages to hang onto the grapefruit-sized saucer pearl as Pickpeck flaps upwards, bearing Villy up along the full height of Farktooth's woody body, passing an oversized bird's nest that rests on a thick, forked branch at the top—and then proceeding into the sky.

Villy's dangling there with the blood rushing to his head, holding the saucer pearl very tightly between his cupped hands. He has a sense of what's coming. It'll be a variant of that callous old routine: *Throw him in the water and he'll learn to swim.*

Far below, Zoe is berating Pickpeck. Scud is jabbering about the fourth dimension. Yampa has her arms out and is trotting back and forth, angling from side to side, perhaps by way of encouraging Villy to fly. Practical Pinchley has deployed a self-inflating, cushion-like creature from his protean tool belt. Quite large by now. It's scooting back and forth, as if hoping to be in the right place when Villy hits the ground.

"Try fly!" chirrups Pickpeck in her throat—and then she releases her hold on Villy's legs. Thanks a lot, robin. Villy drops from the sky like a crippled cow. Mandatory soul time.

He starts with Scud's jumbled ideas about reversing a wire-frame cube and visualizing a hyperspace rotation. But this doesn't seem to work for Villy at all. He mouths Madclaw's mantra: "*Upsy downsy inside out.*" Still no good. In desperation, Villy turns to the wisdom of his peer-group culture.

Flying doesn't have to be so different from surfing, right? Which reminds Villy that, thanks to Boldog, his good old red surfboard is gone. He takes a moment to be glad that Boldog is dead. And now—back to the crisis. That is, back to this pressing issue of falling hundreds of feet to the ground. And the question of how to solve it by surfing. Why can't the pearl be a surfboard?

Something begins growing out of the saucer pearl. It's a nacreous, transparent wriggle in space, like a three-foot-wide rim around the pearl. A circular fin drawn forth by Villy's ongoing prayer that the surfer god Kahuna save his ass. Or maybe the help's coming from Goob-goob.

Either way, it's working. The saucer pearl shifts in his hands, hyperdimensionally turning. Its saucer-like rim is gaining substance. Villy cries out in a loud voice—like a surf-shredder entering the holy eye of a mile-high wall-wave's upper-edge tube. Villy focuses on the saucer pearl like a bodysurfer leaning into a handboard. He's getting some traction. Cutting into the air.

All this is happening very fast, you understand, like in the first thirtieth of a second of Villy's fall. He's just short of skronking into the topmost branches of old Farktooth, the ones that hold the nest. But now—*yah, mon*—Villy does a full one-eighty, veering upwards like a skywriter sketching a J.

Villy's integrated himself with the saucer pearl. Its virtual disk is like an edge around his body. He's like a flying squirrel, or like Da Vinci's glyph of a man in a circle. He's controlling the osculating plane of his space curve, as brother Scud might say. And this means that Villy can, ah yes, swoop and loop and barrel-roll all around the towering spikes and branches of the Teetertotter trees, an ascended master of curvature and torsion.

One slight prob—here in the deepening dusk, it's a little hard to see where he's going. A head-crunching collision with a tree trunk is a very real possibility. So now, as the last dim, drowsy glowon settles onto Farktooth's limbs, Villy spirals down to rejoin his crew.

It's a magical scene beneath the faintly lit branches of the great tree. Zoe flings her arms around Villy and, yah mon, she lays a deep tongue-kiss on him. "Like a god," she says after a bit, stepping back and beaming, just barely visible. Both of them are breathless from the big smooch. "My Villy."

"I could fly too if you'd let me have a chance," whines Scud.

"Spectacular shaman Villy," rustles Farktooth. "Soaring with supple strength. Small Scud shall style a secondary stunt: shooting sparks."

"I can learn to zap?" says Scud. "The same as Meatball and the saucers? How?"

"Sense the subdimensional seething in the saucer pearl. See sizzle within your soul. Sally against the seamy Iravs!"

"Let's go after them right now," Scud exclaims. "I want to get even."

"Nest rest," chirps Pickpeck. "Dawn best."

"There's a nest on a wide forked branch at the top of Farktooth," says Villy. "I saw it." Pickpeck bobs her head.

"We can all get in the car and Villy will fly it up there!" exclaims Zoe. "Fun!"

"No way my brother can lift our car up there," says Scud. "We'll sleep here on the ground.

"Snorting savage swine stampede this sylvan scene soon," says Farktooth. "Seek safety atop my summit."

"Pigs bite," adds Pickpeck. "All night."

Zoe smiles at Villy, and her expression makes Villy bold. "I'm ready!" he cries.

"Yes indeedy," says Pinchley. "Get in the car, and let pilot Villy do his thang. I don't want to be standing around with my thumb up my ass when no herd of killer boars thunders in."

"The terrible trotters of Teetertotter," says Yampa. "Heinous hams."

"I'll balance the car on that nest," says Villy. "Let's just hope Farktooth doesn't sway too much."

"I shall surely sway," says Farktooth. "As I spear squalid swine for supplemental sustenance. But I'll strap your sedan with secondary sprouts. Shall we savor some of our powdered chocolate?"

"Dandy candy," sings Pickpeck.

"You got it," says Pinchley, and rummages in the back of the car. He emerges with a spoon and the battered tin of chocolate powder, which is still a quarter full. "Open wide, birdie."

Pickpeck presents her maw, and Pinchley tosses in a dose of the brown dust. Farktooth smacks the barky sap-damp lips in his trunk, and Pinchley serves him a portion as well. Farktooth sways in delight. Pickpeck chirps some very high notes, scratches the ground, and turns in a circle. Pinchley and Yampa take a quick couple of tastes from the cocoa tin and put it away.

"Fun for all," says Zoe. "What a bunch of freaks. I'm ready for bed."

Villy sits in the driver's seat with the saucer pearl in his lap. For a moment he's stilled by doubt. But then he feels the ball doing its hyperdimsional twist, like a lioness rolling beneath her trainer's touch. The power flows into him again. Thanks to the pearl, the car feels like part of his extended body. Lifting it is no harder than raising his eyebrows.

He blunders up through the glowing branches, feeling his way. Sudden fierce snorting from down below. Dim porcine shapes. Glittering tusks. The Teetertotter boars already! Villy wonders how high those pigs can jump. He redoubles his pace.

And then their car is in the clear night sky, hovering above Farktooth, their new friend the walking and talking tree. Gracefully Villy sets the car into the nest, putting its weight onto the forked branch that lies beneath the nest's length. Helpful Farktooth sends smaller branches whipping up, and the pliant shoots wrap across the car's hood and rear bumper. Additional sprouts twine around the wheels and quantum shocks. A solid connection. They're safe.

As for bedding—Pickpeck and two of her friends settle down into the sticks and straw of the big nest, allowing the two Szep and the three Earthlings to find nooks amid the great birds' downy breasts and bottoms.

Villy and Zoe go around to the far side of Pickpeck the redbreast robin—away from the sight and sound of Scud, Pinchley, and Yampa. Pickpeck is already asleep. The two lovers are alone amid the treetops, with the steady, warm grunting of the wild pigs below. Now and then Farktooth sways slightly to one side and stabs a root through some over-bold pig who then—very briefly—screams.

"That's mappyworld for you," says Villy. "Red in tooth and claw. Like the crab said."

"Never mind all that," says Zoe. "It's time for *us*."

Soon the two of them are lying in a warm embrace amid soft feathers, billing and cooing, their clothes cast aside. Naked at last.

"Now we do it?" says Villy.

"Now," says Zoe. "Yes." A soft kiss. "I want all of you." She giggles. "I looked in your pants pockets when you were asleep. I saw your condoms."

"I brought a lot of them," says Villy.

Villy readies himself and lies upon her. Their bodies fit together like the pieces of a puzzle—a puzzle Villy's been wanting for so long to solve. Zoe's breath is sweet and spicy. She's luscious all over. Her honeyed scent is nectar.

They rock slowly at first, savoring their bodies' all-over touch, knowing they'll finish soon, wanting to make it last. And then the full wave of passion overtakes them. Kissing and moaning, they ride the primeval rhythm into the flashbulb white light of the gods.

"I'm coming."

"I love you."

Together at last.

TWENTY-ONE
harmony

zoe

When Zoe wakes, it's dawn, and here she is in a downy nest with Villy, cuddled against Pickpeck's rust-colored breast. Feeling Zoe move, the great robin raises her head and peers at the lovers, eyes alert, beak large.

"Shhh," goes Zoe, rising onto her elbows. "Not yet."

Pickpeck tucks her head down to snooze some more. Three birds in the nest, plus Yampa, Pinchley, and Scud, who remain conveniently out of sight.

Zoe looks down at Villy. He's awake, watching her.

"We did it," Zoe whispers to him. "I'm glad." She flops onto his chest and they begin to kiss. Morning breath, but what the hey. They're in love.

"More?" whispers Villy. Such a good-looking guy.

"Yes," says Zoe, reaching down to feel him with her hand. "Let's do it again to be sure."

"Sure that we're lovers?" Villy's mouth is a straight line with curved corners. Keeping a straight face.

"Yes," says Zoe.

This time it's slower and smoother. Deeper. Zoe lies on her back, with Pickpeck's red breast like a cozy wall beneath the ceiling of the sky. Perhaps Farktooth senses they're making love. It feels like he's swaying to match their rhythm. And then—*oooo*—they're done again.

"Dear Zoe," says Villy, kissing her. He smiles, draws back, and licks her eyelids. Why not?

Happy Zoe is wondering how it would be to wake up every morning in bed with Villy. But then the tiresome wide world starts up again.

"Hey thar!" It's Pinchley. "Ready to waste those *skorker* Iravs?"

As they begin bustling around. Pickpeck flaps to the forest floor and returns with a giant blackberry, sweet and inky, holding it near Zoe's face until she bites into it. An earthly delight. And one of Pickpeck's bird friends fetches a fresh pork steak, torn from the carcass of a wild pig that Farktooth stabbed last night.

"Not going to eat that raw," says Zoe.

"Let's see if I can cook it with zap!" says Scud. "Let me hold the saucer pearl, Villy. Please?"

"Okay," says Villy. "How do you think you'll make a zap?"

"I'll do what Farktooth said. Sense the subdimensional seething. I bet I can do that. I seethe a lot."

Scud lays the chunk of pig meat on a leaf, takes the saucer pearl in both hands, and scrunches up his face in a scowl. Moments later Zoe sees a shimmer of dark energy around Scud's fingers. Sparks dance across the meat. Not killer zaps, but hot. Scud rocks his head, keeping the flow going. A minute later the Teetertotter swine steak is seared to fragrant perfection.

"I channel energy from the saucer pearl's quantum vibes," says Scud. "I have to feel angry for it to work."

Scud peels a bacon-like strip off the pig meat, chews, and fails to drop dead. So, okay, Zoe eats some as well. Energizing. Tasty. Goes well with the juicy blackberry.

"I'll drive today," says Villy after a bit. "If that's okay with you two."

They hoist themselves into the car. Villy levitates them off the branch and down to the dirt road atop the ridge.

"It would be nice to know *exactly* where the Iravs are," says Zoe. "So they don't surprise us. Can you tell us, Pickpeck? Or Farktooth?"

"Sneakily skulking," says Farktooth, which is totally unhelpful.

"Scout tout." goes Pickpeck, perching beside the car. "Need seeds." Her red breast is downy in the daylight, and her eyes are bright. She stands a bit taller than Zoe. Impressive that she was able to lift Villy into the air yesterday.

"Pickpeck means she's gonna fly along with us," says Pinchley. "She imagines she's a native guide. And she'll be wanting those caraway seeds we promised. Not sure how much help Pickpeck will actually be. She's got a brain the size of a pea. I'm just glad we have our bubblegun."

"And I can use the saucer pearl to zap," says Scud.

"And I'm ready to kick physical ass," says Villy.

"You be careful," Zoe tells him. "I don't want to lose everything. Our romance is just starting."

"I want what you want," answers Villy. "But if we turn back, the Iravs will hunt us down. We have to end it today."

They bid Farktooth farewell and set off down the road, winding the speed up towards a thousand miles per hour.

"Can you fly the car like a plane?" Zoe asks Villy. "That might give us an edge."

Even though Zoe's holding the saucer pearl while Villy drives, he's still able to use the pearl to levitate. He can manage little jumps—that is, he can drive the car pretty fast, then levitate it into the air—and then drift through a nice long arc, powered by the car's previous momentum. But the pearl isn't powerful enough to seriously accelerate the car forward while it's in the air.

Scud keeps begging to be the one with the saucer pearl, so Zoe lets him hold it, and Villy can still levitate the car anyway. Pickpeck flies along with them. Even though she's just a giant robin, she has no problem keeping pace. Pinchley wasn't kidding when he said the animals here are fast.

Pickpeck squawks raucously with the other big birds they encounter, but it's not at all clear that she's asking about the Iravs. At one point it does sound like a big robin chirps about the Iravs, and that she mentions a specific place.

"Did she say *amami*?" Zoe asks.

"*Harmony*," says Yampa. "Melody music land."

"It's the next basin over," says Pinchley. "Big wobbly cubes of jelly live there. Called Harmons. A Harmon can play like an orchestra. They do it for fun, but it's more than fun."

"Of course music's more than fun," says Zoe. "It's divine. The voice of the unknown."

"The ecstasy of empathy," echoes Yampa. "Ending ere

you expect." Something odd in her voice. She takes Pinchley's face in her two hands. "Lingering love of my long loop of life."

"We not done yet," says Pinchley, almost embarrassed. Like he wants to brush the foreboding moment away. "I love you, too, Yampa."

Zoe hears sweet sounds in the distance, coming and going with the slipstream's damped breeze. "Lift us real high so we can see," she tells Villy. He gets the saucer pearl from Scud and levitates the car a hundred yards into the air, smiling at Zoe all the while. Zoe feels proud of Villy's power, although it's maybe a little unsettling to be this high and to know it's only him holding them up. It's like dreaming about flying and at the same time dreaming that your power of flight might suddenly go away.

"I see Harmony," declares Villy.

Up ahead the ridge forks in two, with Birdland on the right, Teetertotter Forest on the left, and a new land in the middle: the Harmony basin. To Zoe it looks like an enormous summer salad bowl, with big cubes of colored Jello and mounds of whipped cream and twitching sprigs of mint. Not that those are accurate descriptions, but it's what Harmony reminds her of. A festive dish at a summer wedding buffet. They can hear the wonderful calm music of the Harmon cubes.

"Paradise," says Zoe. "Let's go there."

Villy lowers the car down to the trail, and they roll into the clearing where the three ridges meet. They get out of the car. Pickpeck flies into the distance, surveying the terrain, excitedly chirping.

And this is when the Iravs attack. They were hiding just over the ridge, right at the edge of Harmony, with their car squeezed down into a giant drift of the foamy white stuff that Zoe thought looked like whipped cream.

The Iravs still look like four pieces of a chopped-up body. Hand, legs, chest, head.

The hand-Irav is the size of a turkey, with big heavy fingers. He's been eating well. He has an eye on the back of his knuckles and a toothy mouth in his palm.

As before, the chest-Irav is a chunk of a torso plus an arm with a hand. He has beady eyes and a frog-like mouth in his chest. And he's added a pair of nimbly shuffling feet. As he rocks along, he leans back for balance, with his arm projecting like a crane. He's got that poison-stinger whaler snail riding atop his hand.

The legs-Irav has a baby-blue eye in the front of each thigh. His crotch opens into a toothy mouth.

And then the head-Irav appears. He's got the full-size head, plus the neck, a shoulder, and an arm with no hand. He's balancing himself on thin stork legs with knees that bend backwards, so creepy. He's grown a sea-anemone clump of tendrils to replace his missing fingers. The writhing little stalks are translucent and boneless.

The main thing about the head-Irav is that he's running straight towards Zoe—and he's holding a heavy hunting-knife in his sea-anemone hand. He's out to kill her.

Villy dives at the head-Irav, knocking the creature's long bird legs out from under him. The head-Irav screams in fury. Villy tears the knife from the creature's sticky fingers and tosses it to the side. Villy begins pounding the head on the ground, meaning to knock it unconscious or even kill it.

But now the legs-Irav joins in, getting a scissors-lock around Villy that pins his arms to his side. At the same time, the legs-Irav is trying to work his crotch teeth towards Villy's neck. For the moment it's a standoff.

The head-Irav wriggles out from under Villy and manages to stretch his arm far enough to seize the knife again. It's a heavy-handled thing, with a long blade, well balanced. Moving very fast, the head-Irav squints at Zoe and flings the knife as hard as he can. Zoe drops to the ground, but the head-Irav knew to aim low, and the knife is coming very fast. It's going to hit her.

But wait. Here comes Yampa running in from the side. The smart, lively, courageous Szep has seen what's coming, and she's getting in front of Zoe, intent on plucking the knife from the air. But now, a hideous misfortune. Yampa stumbles—and the heavy, hard-thrown knife gets past her hands—and the knife strikes Yampa's thin neck, severing it entirely. The Szep's head thuds to the ground. Pinchley screams. The full volume of the blood in Yampa's body gushes out and, just like that, she's stone cold dead.

Scud fires the bubblegun and vaporizes the head-Irav.

In the ringing silence after the blast, the vile hand-Irav scuttles over and starts—unbelievably—to feed upon Yampa's remains. He starts with her feet, grinding them up with the mouth in his palm. In fast-forward motion, he works his way upwards, swallowing Yampa's legs from bottom to top. The hand grows fatter and heavier as it proceeds. Before anyone can stop the hand, he's swallowed Yampa's whole body.

And then, with an obscene hiccup, the creature distends his mouth wide enough to swallow Yampa's head. The hand-Irav is ten times as large as he was two seconds ago. He's swollen like a well-fed tick. Unspeakably foul. The hand trots off on the tips of his fat fingers, circling the car, readily evading the weeping Pinchley's maddened pursuit.

Meanwhile Villy's still in the grasp of the legs-Irav. Sensing an opportunity, the chest-Irav enters the attack. He shuffles rapidly towards Zoe, holding out the whaler snail. Zoe scrambles towards the car, thinking it can shield her, but the chest-Irav is too fast. He lurches another step closer and aims. His whaler snail fires a dart into Zoe's breast.

A stinging coldness spreads along her arms, down her legs, and into her head. She collapses to one side, her body twisted so that her head is facing the Iravs. Her glassy eyes are open. She can't speak or move, but she can see.

Mad-eyed Pinchley snatches the whaler snail from the chest-Irav—and smashes it on the ground with his foot. Nothing daunted, the chest-Irav grabs Zoe's trumpet and scoots away.

Zoe is so paralyzed that she can't generate the nerve impulses that would expand her chest and fill her lungs. So she can't breathe. Pinchley knows this. His Yampa is gone, but he's going to save Zoe. He leans over her, giving her artificial respiration, pushing on her chest. And still Zoe can see what's going on.

With an angry lunge Villy twists himself free of the legs-Irav's clasp. The chest-Irav darts towards the freed

Villy, but Villy sidesteps the creature and topples him onto the legs-Irav.

Scud takes this chance to fire again. A two-in-one. He blows away the chest-Irav and the legs-Irav with the bubblegun's final charge. The blast vaporizes Zoe's trumpet as well, and certainly she'd bewail that if she could, but she has no voice.

Only the distended hand-Irav remains. Zoe can make out the bulge of Yampa's head, intact within the hand-Irav's body. The hand heads towards the purple whale, walking high on his fat fingers, plump, proud, insolent. Clearly he means to finish Zoe. The Iravs are implacable.

Coming up on the waist-high hand-Irav from behind, Villy grabs two of his heavy fingers and wrenches at them, as if wanting to tear the monster in half. The hand-Irav squirms, getting ready to bite Villy with the mouth in his palm.

Moving fast, Scud fetches the big saucer pearl from the car. He glares at the hand-Irav, still wrestling with Villy. The air around Scud's body wriggles with dark energy. The charge is building up. The hand-Irav is on the point of biting into Villy, but now Scud zaps the monster with a jolt of dark energy.

The hand-Irav goes limp and drops to the ground. But he's not dead. He's faking. He's poised to launch himself at Villy again. And Zoe is powerless to warn him. But Pinchley sees.

"Finish him!" screams the Szep, even while he continues pushing and releasing Zoe's chest. "Kill the *skorker* who ate my wife!"

Scud wreathes himself with a fresh corona of dark energy, twice as strong as before.

"It's not my fault," wheedles the hand, suddenly breaking into speech. He has a high, thin, insistent voice. "I've still got your caraway seeds. Take them now and please let me go." He bends one of his fingers and—*pop*—the jar of caraways emerges from his spongy flesh.

Villy grabs the seeds and jumps to one side. Scud frikkin zaps the hand-Irav twice. Heavy blasts. The hand-Irav is dust, and the swallowed head of Yampa is dissolved into ashes and radiation as well.

Scud stands there in the wake of the explosions, unsteady on his feet, staring into the air. "The pictures," he mutters. "Yampa's pictures. They were still in her head. And now—" He gestures as if he's touching invisible things. "I see them all. They came to me. Thank you, Yampa."

This is when Pickpeck glides down and petitions the boys for her promised allotment of caraway seeds. At first they don't even understand what she's saying. Scud is dizzy from the images in his head. And Villy wants only to get to Zoe. Once he picks up the thread of the importunate bird's requests, he hands the jar of seeds to Scud.

Scud angrily accuses the big robin of setting them up for the ambush. Pickpeck huffily denies it, and who knows, maybe she's not lying. She is, after all, a birdbrain. Just to be rid of her, Scud gives her some seeds and she flaps away. And then he flops down onto the ground, lying on his back, as if staring up at an inner holographic slide show of their trip.

Meanwhile Villy has taken over Pinchley's task of helping Zoe breathe. Rather than pushing on her chest, Villy presses his open mouth against hers and breathes in and out. Zoe is glad for Villy's touch. But she's cold, cold, cold—right down to her core. This is how it feels to die.

And then she's gone.

Dead? She's in—a room. Like the guidance counselor's office at Los Perros High, with shelves of books. An oriental rug on the floor. Battered wood furniture. Sitting behind the desk is a—presence. Flat-nosed, solemn, with intent eyes. She resembles a Latina woman with her hair pulled into a topknot. She has extravagantly curved lips, and her nostrils are like scrolls. She glows a warm shade of white, diamond bright, but the light doesn't dazzle Zoe, and why should it, given that Zoe's—dead?

"I'm Goob-goob," says the woman. Her motions sweep out sheets of light. Her voice is as rich and layered as choral song. "You're Zoe. I sent Pinchley and Yampa to enlist you."

"Yes," says Zoe. Her pain is gone, but she can't move her tongue. She's speaking with her mind. Teep. She feels horribly sorry for herself. She and Villy were at the dawn of a lifelong love story. And now she's facing some bullshit interview in an afterworld office.

"You're not gone yet," says Goob-goob. "You can go back and save your planet. You and Villy and the despised Scud."

"Despised?" says Zoe, slightly cheered by the spot-on word.

"You'll lead them," Goob-goob tells Zoe. "On to Szep City and Sky Castle. You'll ride a jet stream to New Eden, and cross the ridge to Van Cott. And there you'll find a mighty unspace tunnel to Earth. The saucer-master Groon will seek to pass through. Your crew will knot Groon within the tunnel like garbage in a bag. And thus will end an evil age." The glowing shape laughs. Not exactly a laugh.

"How—" begins Zoe, but she doesn't know where to begin. Instead, she's obsessively flashing on a mental image of her body lying motionless on the seat of the purple whale. Maybe she's teeping the sensations of Villy watching her die? Maybe her seeming conversation with Goob-goob is a death-spasm brain-glitch.

"And if you're *not* returning to life, I have some forms for you to fill in," says Goob-goob, suddenly turning all gray and middle-aged. She conjures up a meter-high stack of papers on her desk. Her manicured hand tap-taps the stack. Her topknot inclines. "Your application, Zoe. It's still not done."

Zoe cries out, and the office disappears. She's lying on a cloud, surrounded by music. Not exactly a cloud. It's slimy and alive, with a faint smell of honeysuckle. And, wow, she's breathing again. Something is nursing on her chest—an eel. Sucking out the poison where the dart hit her. Thank you.

Villy is sitting beside her, his hand on her brow. Scud and Pinchley aren't around.

"You're back," whispers Villy.

She smiles at him. How wonderful. Her lips can move. "We beat the Iravs?"

Villy nods. "But they killed Yampa. And your horn is gone."

Three translucent, pocked, wobbly cubes are near them, making music. One is a rich lavender, one's pale red, and

the other is acid green. Their sides pulse deep notes, and
their little holes sing high ones. Threads crisscross their
insides. They rest amid the drifts of white slime.

"Harmons," says Villy, gesturing at the waist-high
cubes. "You'll like them. Can you stand?"

"Let's try."

Villy helps her to her feet. Dizzy. The healer eel drops
from her chest and wriggles off. Zoe leans against darling
Villy, alive alive alive. His warmth, his touch, his scent, his
outsider face.

"We made love last night," says Zoe, savoring the
memory. Although now she wonders how long she's been
unconscious. While having a wack near-death vision of
Goob-goob in a high school office. Goob-goob offering
her a choice. Fill out a gigundo application form—or
come back to life and do—something. Save Earth?

"It was *two* nights ago," corrects Villy. "But we also made
love yesterday morning, remember? And then the Iravs
ambushed us, and you got hurt, and you slept straight
through, all afternoon and all night. Pinchley had a healer
eel in his tool belt, and it worked. Dear Zoe." Villy pauses,
caresses Zoe's cheek, continues. "Pinchley's acting weird.
More weird. He keeps imitating Yampa. I guess because
she died. Hard to imagine how bad that would be. Scud's
trying to cool him down."

"The despised Scud," murmurs Zoe absently. "So where
are they?"

"Working on the cars," says Villy. "The purple whale,
plus Pinchley's old yellow convertible that the Iravs were
driving."

Zoe doesn't want to talk about the Iravs. "What's this white stuff on the ground?" she asks. "I like it. Did it help me get well?" Actually, she's not a hundred percent well. Her knees feel like they could bend in any direction at all.

Villy wraps his arms around her. "Want to sit down?"

"Not yet. Tell me about the white stuff."

"Smeel foam," says Villy. "It links the Harmons together. A basin-wide overmind. The Harmons are like living musical instruments. Try playing them!"

Zoe is so tired that it feels like she has wet bags of sand sewed inside her chest. But for sure she wants to play the Harmons. Villy helps her over to the red cube. She pats it on the side, and it goes *oom-woom-oom*. The other two Harmons echo the sound, riffing on it. Zoe prods and thumps them as well. *Oom-woom-ga-honk-squonk-boomy-bomp-oom.*

"Jam session," she whispers, briefly happy. But her body is a wobbly stack of dishes. She slumps to the ground in a snowdrift of smeel foam, and she's out again.

This time Zoe dreams of Maisie, wearing yellow tights and a pale blue jersey. Maisie's saucer disk sticks out around her waist. She's decorated the disk with symbols for musical notes. Maisie's got her floppy hair in a pony-tail and she's carrying her trombone. Even though Zoe's asleep, she realizes this isn't a dream. It's Maisie teeping her again.

"Sistah!" goes Maisie. She raises her trombone and sounds a wet bleat. "Welcome to the music world."

In her odd, half-waking state, Zoe can feel the tingly smeel foam on her skin. She's picking up the vibes of a hundred thousand Harmon cubes, all of them teep-linked together. Like she's in a stadium full of musicians tuning up. The biggest jam band ever.

Maisie leans over Zoe and does a soft *wah-wah* with her slobbery trombone. Maisie's tomboy features are intent. "Reveille, sis."

"You should let me sleep," says Zoe. "Instead of pushing into my mind."

"News flash," goes Maisie. "You've barely driven twenty thousand miles. You've got nine hundred and eighty thousand miles to go before Szep City. You're too slow."

"What am I supposed to do about it?" says Zoe. "We're driving a car. Also—I might be dying right now. In case you didn't notice."

"*Such* the thespian," goes Maisie. She leans way back and blats a *haw-haw-haw* with her horn. She lowers the instrument and studies Zoe. "Listen to me. You and Villy need to get musical instruments from the Harmons. The music will help you go faster. So that it doesn't take you, like, six months to hit Szep City."

"I'm confused, Maisie. I almost died. Make it simple for me. Tell me what to do."

"Beg me," says Maisie, flipping her saucer-skirt. "Say: *Please mighty Maisie.*"

Zoe doesn't like this. "I thought you said I was nice to you in school and that you don't bear a grudge."

"Maybe I've changed my mind. *Please mighty Maisie.*"

"You're a geek and a loser."

"There's the real Zoe," goes Maisie, enjoying herself. "Maybe I should leave? And then the leech saucers will eat everyone's soul. All because Zoe Snapp is a snooty pig. Unless—"

Maisie breaks off and razzes a slow, wavering crescendo on her trombone, as if to indicate rising tension—a sound like on a quiz show when the audience is waiting for a contestant to answer.

Zoe isn't fully focused on Maisie's teep. She's adrift in a psychic sea, vast and planetary, with the Harmon cubes like plankton, and the smeel foam like currents. By way of focusing Zoe's attention, Maisie starts bumping her with her stupid trombone.

"All *right*," teep-yells Zoe. "*Please mighty Maisie*. Help me go faster. Okay?"

Maisie does an Egyptian-style dance step, profiling her face, holding her arms at angles like in a hieroglyph, waggling her trombone, and printing the word "YAY" all over her saucer rim. *So* corny.

"Do you have something to tell me or not?" goes Zoe. This conversation is way too long. She wants to nod off in the foam.

"Stratocasting," says Maisie. "You'll be able to crank the car's speed to a hundred thousand miles an hour. Not just *one* thousand miles an hour. You'll reach Szep City in a day." Maisie strikes a fresh pose, holding her trombone sideways at her waist like a guitar. "*Deedle deedle deedle*. You and Villy. You play lead guitar and he does rhythm. Get the guitars from the Harmons."

"Guitars are lesser," scoffs Zoe. "Villy—okay, fine—he plays surf guitar. But horn is what I play. Can't I use a trumpet?"

"*Deedle deedle deedle*," repeats half sister Maisie. "Your horn's gone. Now you use a gee-tar, baby." Her expression is intent. "Stratocasting."

"God you're a pain in the ass."

To make it worse, Maisie starts shoving Zoe with her feet, rolling her out of the big, comfy smeel-foam drift. Zoe snaps fully awake. She's lying on the bare ground. There's no Maisie in sight. Just Villy. But Zoe is hearing the stratocasting sound in her head. A soaring pair of guitars.

"What up?" goes Villy. "You passed out again, but just for half an hour. You were arguing with someone and then you rolled out of the foam."

"Maisie," mutters Zoe. "Guitars." She rubs her face and looks around. It strikes her that she's now completely well. Here with the Harmons and dear Villy. It's the start of a new phase. Yeah.

"You and I are supposed to play guitars," she tells Villy. "So that our car goes fast. A hundred thousand miles per hour."

"We don't have guitars," says Villy, totally doubting her. "And you don't know how to play one."

"Stratocasting," says Zoe.

"*Stratocaster* is a model of Fender guitar," says Villy, talking slow like Zoe's out to lunch. "As it happens, my brah Znork in our surf trio plays a Fender *Telecaster*. Me, I have a cheap-ass git-box from N-Mart."

"I'm not talking about models," says Zoe, rising to her feet and meaning to stay there. "Stratocasting is a sound, Villy. A screaming double line that probes to the edge of the universe. *Deedle deedle deedle*, understand? A ladder of notes, climbing the frets to heaven. Like Kiki Krush and the Kazakhstan Guitar Army? I'm way better on the guitar than you realize. But meanwhile, is there anything I can eat?"

"Glad you're hungry," says Villy. "Avid Zoe." He produces a linty, sticky food mint from his pocket. "Here's the turkey one. Healthier than living on smeel foam."

"Got it," says Zoe, popping the turkey mint in her mouth. "That smeel foam—already I like it too much."

"It feels really good when it soaks through your skin," says Villy. "You could say the Harmon cubes are hooked on it."

"Like jazz musicians," says Zoe. "Can we talk to the cubes? Maisie said we could get our guitars from them."

"Try."

Zoe touches the red Harmon cube with her hands, and he responds with spacy warbles, but Zoe's also talking to him in words, and—to the extent that she knows how—she's teeping an image of what she wants. Two electric guitars: one maroon and one a sparkling black. One is a classic Flying Vee, the other is like Frank Zappa's Gibson SG.

"I'll ask Goob-goob for them," says the Harmon. "And you give me—what?" He sqwonks his question from a hole in his side.

Not having much else to offer, Zoe spits her turkey-flavored food mint onto the cube and—whoa—he likes it. But it's not enough. He wants more.

"You can have Pinchley's old car," says Villy out of the blue. Zoe seriously doubts that Villy has Pinchley's permission to make this offer. "You can drive all around Harmony in it," says Villy, kind of laughing.

The red cube makes a tuneful zooming sound, wobbles his sides, and—this is weird—unfolds his six sides, letting them flop onto the ground, making a shape like a flat red cross, with an extra square on one of the arms. Almost immediately something moves in the air above the flattened Harmon. It's a filigree of light, a three-dimensional moiré mesh, faint purple, glowing. Maybe it's the incarnate presence of the great god Goob-goob.

The mesh tendrils mass together and form a twisty pair of vines. Two buds dangle from the vine and fatten like ripening fruit. It's a pair of little guitars, about two-thirds of normal size, and they match Zoe's mental image specs, yah mon, it's a red Flying Vee and a black scrolly Gibson SG. The guitar necks glow and flex as they dangle from the vine. Their bodies gleam with dark and kandy-kolor paint. They pinch free of the vines and settle onto the unfolded red Harmon. The vines and the moiré mesh are gone.

Zoe picks up the black Gibson SG and strums it. Strums *him*. He's warm to the touch. He flexes beneath Zoe's hands as if reading her mind. He has a dark-energy amp built in, or something like an amp, and he wails just the way Zoe wants, a tight feedbacky sound that gets gooder when Villy picks up his red Flying Vee and lays cosmic reverb across Zoe's filigrees.

"I call these god chords," goes Villy.

"We fit," says Zoe, playing on. "We'll stratocast together. A hundred thousand miles an hour. I love you."

"I love you back," says Villy. "Rocker girl. You're well."

"Ready for the roll," says Zoe, fingering the strings and savoring the chiming of the notes.

Done with being flat, the red Harmon cube has folded himself back up. He studies Zoe and Villy with their new instruments. "Don't forget my car," he says.

"Let's find Pinchley and Scud," says Villy.

The guys have the Szep's old car parked beside the purple whale. They sit behind the two steering wheels, gunning the engines like gearheads.

"Those are cool midget guitars," says Scud, leaning out of the purple whale's window.

"They're not exactly guitars," says Zoe. "They're, well, Goob-goob made them. And this red Harmon here, he helped."

"Is that my car?" says the Harmon, bouncing over to where Pinchley sits at the wheel of his big-wheeled yellow convertible. The boys have dusted it off and have applied a nice shine. On its hood it still bears a large red P&Y monogram.

"What you talkin' there—*my car*,'" goes Pinchley. "This is Pinchley and Yampa's P&Y." For whatever reason Pinchley is doing a perfect imitation of Yampa's voice, and he's moving his arms like his dead wife.

"Pinchley is wack," Scud tells Zoe.

"I, uh, told this Harmon here that he could have your car in exchange for the two guitars," says Villy, looking abashed.

Pinchley glares in outrage.

Zoe strikes some notes on her Gibson. *Deedle-dee-dle-deedle*. "It's a good deal," she says. "With these guitars we'll be stratocasting at a hundred thousand miles per hour. And, um, when our trip's done, you can keep Villy's purple whale, Pinchley."

"What are you saying?" cries Villy. Now *he's* the one getting screwed.

"Can we just *go?*" says Zoe.

Somehow, with much grumbling, they get things smoothed out. The four of them stand by the purple whale. The red Harmon cube takes the wheel of Pinchley's powerful yellow convertible—and drives off, careening through the white foam, blasting big band jazz.

Fortunately for Villy, Pinchley is too far into his Yampa-imitation routine to keep yelling about the deal. "The lovers' limousine leaves," is all he says, using Yampa's voice, his tone wistful. "Bereft Pinchley yearns for Yampa. Funky, flash Pinchley with his stinky, slippery *grabb*." Pinchley reaches towards his crotch.

"No!" yells Scud. "Don't show us your *grabb*!" By way of changing the subject, Scud quickly tells the others, "Pinchley says it's his turn to drive. Even if he doesn't have his car."

"Pinchley will drive us home to Szep City," says Pinchley. "For Yampa's woeful wake."

"We'll be going really fast," Zoe reminds Pinchley. "A hundred thousand miles an hour. The whale's steering is gonna be very twitchy."

"Which is why rip-roaring, road-wise Pinchley will wield the wheel," says Pinchley "He reacts far faster than bucolic, bush-league ballyworlders."

"I don't get how we'll go that fast," puts in Scud.

"Thanks to our Goob-goob guitars it'll be like we're in a really high gear," says Zoe. "For ten or eleven hours. It'll be rad."

"But we'll slam into things," says Scud.

"I'll levitate us the whole time," says Villy. "As if we're flying low."

"Wow," says Scud, fully onboard. And then he starts with the demands. "Let me be the one to levitate the car. Let me hold the saucer pearl. I know I can fly us if you let me try again."

"Fine," says Villy. "You sit in front with Pinchley. Zoe and me will be in back. Playing our guitars."

Scud grins. "Let's do it, bro!"

TWENTY-TWO

stratocast

villy

Villy's two-thirds-size Flying Vee guitar is alive. Basically she's an alien. A type of Harmon. She stretches her neck so she can nuzzle Zoe's black guitar, who is male. The instruments chime softly to each other. Villy thinks of them as a pair of race horses that he and Zoe are about to ride.

"Or magic broomsticks," says Zoe inside Villy's head. The guitars seem to be giving them teep.

Crazy Pinchley's at the wheel, his head cocked at an odd, coquettish angle. Still doing his Yampa routine. Crazy or not, he's just now used his fractal ant to make the car a little more like an airplane, that is, he's placed a vertical stabilizer fin on the roof, complete with a rudder. And he's added an elevator fin across the back of the roof. The elevator has a pair of flaps to adjust the flying whale's pitch. With these aeronautic enhancements in place, along with suitable cockpit controls, Pinchley is pretty stoked about the upcoming trip, and he's stopped bitching about his forfeited yellow convertible.

Scud's in front, next to Pinchley, holding the saucer pearl. But there's a snag. Scud's still not able to levitate the car.

"Just think of a fin all around the pearl," Villy tells his brother. "And the fin is part of you? Don't hold back. You have to merge into the whatever."

"Merging isn't my thing," grumbles Scud. A full minute of silence. And then, finally, Scud gets it. "You do this all the time, Villy?"

"It's how I surf."

The purple whale rises high into the air, revealing a vista of Harmon cubes amid streaks of smeel foam. Mintgreen critters scamper about. They have T-shaped bodies, with big eyes on the sides of their hammer heads. They thump the cubes like gongs.

"Gear we go-go!" says Pinchley, still talking like Yampa. He guns the engine—and nothing whatsoever happens. Oh, right, Scud's levitated the whale, and therefore the gigundo tires are spinning in empty air.

"You'll do stratocast now?" says Scud. "Is that the word?"

"Gear we go-go," says Villy, kind of mocking Scud and Pinchley.

Zoe stares into Villy's eyes. She looks zonky and vamp. Like a goth rocker. They poise fingers on their frets. Each of them holds a triangle of seashell for a pick. Zoe nods her head once and: *Zam deedle squee.*

Zoe's leading the way, sailing the sonic sea, and Villy's close behind. The two of them do a virtual dance in music-space, orbiting each other like strands of DNA, growing a heaven-tree of sound. Sweet. Villy didn't know

Zoe could play guitar like this. But, um, the car's still not moving. It's just floating there.

Zoe breaks off, embarrassed, and begins tuning her guitar, or trying to, except that it doesn't actually have tuning pegs. The car hangs in the air like a ripe fruit, very slowly drifting forward under the influence of the unaided saucer pearl. Pinchley and Scud turn around to glare at the would-be stratocasters.

"Looks like we'll do the damn drive in the dumb dirt," says Pinchley. "Set us down, Scuddy."

"Wait," says Scud. "I'll give Villy and Zoe caraway seeds." He produces the jar. "Everyone in mappyworld loves caraways, right? Maybe there's a reason. They have a special effect here?" Scud pauses, takes a couple of seeds from the jar, and nibbles them with his front teeth like a rat. "Curved," he says. "Rye bread aroma. And I feel maybe even smarter now. If that's possible. Go for it, Vill and Zee."

So Villy and Zoe eat some caraway seeds, pretty much a whole teaspoon of them apiece, crunching the seeds with their back molars. Villy definitely feels a lift. He sees colored shapes from the corners of his eyes. Like virtual pastel caraways. When he turns his head, the quick bright crescents scoot out of sight. They're hella shy.

"I see the colored things too," says Zoe. "Smeel boomerangs. We'll chase them with our notes. Stratocast a goblin march."

"That's not science," says Scud.

"Shut your crack," snaps Villy.

Zoe strikes a fresh chord. She goes for a bluesy beat, a cycling rhythm beneath jai-alai scribbles of smeely grace notes. Villy gets into it as well, gazing towards the horizon as he plays. In his peripheral vision the smeel crescents creep forward. They're like frail, lace-winged insects edging the cones of his eyebeam headlights. He gooses them with pecks of his pick.

So, *yaaar*, Villy and Zoe are playing at a new level now, into the flow, elaborating riffs like logical syllogisms, and where the hell is Villy getting words like this—oh, he's siphoning vocab from Scud and Pinchley and Zoe. All four of them part of the pudding, with the ghost of Yampa in the mix as well.

The purple whale begins moving. Slow, then fast, borne upon the stratocast of sound. They rush across the Jell-O-salad expanse of the Harmony basin, swifter than a strafing jet. At the wheel, pilot Pinchley tweaks their path, trimming the flaps, sloping a route that crosses the basin's far border much sooner than seems possible. Scud levitates for all he's worth, barely making it above the ridge between Harmony and the next basin.

"Close shave," goes Scud. "Those mountains came up fast."

"Hundred thousand miles per," gloats Pinchley. He's abandoned his Yampa imitation and sounds like his old self. "Make some noise, Zoe-Villy. This new basin is called Wristwatch, I do recall."

Villy peers down, putting his guitar fingers into a reptile-brain ostinato mode. The Wristwatch basin is cogs and gears, a vast array of them, slowly turning, with levers and springy coils and, weirdly, big patches of honey here and there, clogging up the works. Ants in the soft honey, timekeeper ants. How can Villy be seeing such tiny details with them careening past so fast?

"Frog tongue eyebeam," goes Zoe. She looks very cryp and glam, with glowons highlighting the outlines of her far-gone face. She's playing Coptic seven-tone crescendos, accompanied by teep images of, like, jackal-headed gods marching into a pharaoh's tomb, and semi-unwrapped mummy-girls shaking their booties beside the curly purling of the river Nile.

Villy harmonizes, making a sound like the argle-bargle of man-eating crocs. As he plays, he comes to understand what Zoe's remark meant. That is, even though they're topping a thousand miles a minute, it's possible, what with their caraway-seed-enhanced mental powers, to shoot out an eyebeam quick as a frog's bug-catching tongue, and to leave your eyebeam in place for a few secs, and thereby to vacuum up a mini video of what is/was happening there. Frog tongue eyebeam, yes.

Goofing on the Wristwatch basin, Villy notices independent little batches of cogs and worm-gears bustling around on their own, rooting at the planetary timepiece and prying off toothsome wheels to take unto themselves. For its part, the basin-wide master-clock is of course eating as many of the ticking freebooter assemblages as it can—sometimes trapping them in the ants' honey-ponds.

Lots of time down there. And then the time's up. They squeak over another ridge.

"Cuttle Scuttle Swamp," intones Pinchley.

A flying cuttlefish thuds against the grill of the car, sending them into a wrenching 3D tumble. They're in danger of blacking out from the centrifugal gees. Zoe bears down on her guitar and gets into feedback mode. The internal amp drives the strings that drive the amp that drives the strings—a jitter of *skronks* and *wheenks*. Dark energy on parade. Somehow the way-sick bleat sets their yawing vessel aright. Thank you, primordial chaos.

Scud in the front seat has become wary. Looking far ahead, he zaps the next incoming cuttlefish before it arrives. Not that the cuttlefish are attacking them, per se. They're into some intramural scene of their own. A civil war?

Two populations of cuttlefish inhabit Cuttle Scuttle Swamp: red ones and green ones. The red ones fly, beating their skirt-fins, and the green ones disport themselves in the shallow, smeely waters. The air cuttles dive down at the water cuttles, and the water cuttles power themselves into the air like breaching manatees. When two cuttles collide, they tangle their tentacles and—are they biting each other?

"Making love," says Zoe, and she segues her solo into a steamy, insinuating beat. "Gettin' down. Like you and me, Villy."

Villy crafts a squalid bass line to match Zoe's mood. He's never played this well. Basins flit past. For half an hour, he and Zoe are fully zoned into the stratocast. And then they happen to notice the landscape again.

"Gold Bug basin," goes Pinchley. The dude has the whole sector mapped inside his head.

Shiny black beetles are excavating galleries and crafting lacy mounds. Beetles like the living cars of the Van Cott streets, but less citified. More tribal. Their antennae bear rows of sideways branches. The beetles fart explosive gas to help with their excavations. *Ftoom*. They're digging for lumps of gold. A midnight-blue beetle displays a large nugget in triumphant mandibles. Villy's focus twitches forward from the prize nugget to the next highlight—a crater filled with dome-backed beetles waving their fringed June-bug antennae and worshipping a golden beetle-god the size of a blimp. Glowons add to the graven idol's luster.

The appreciative Villy and Zoe glide into a shimmering musical fantasia of lush flourishes. Scud torques the car up over the beetle basin's onrushing ridge. Pinchley trims their onward course. The four travelers take a feral pleasure in their phantasmagoric speed. More basins and more.

"How do you know which direction to go?" Scud asks Pinchley.

"Two ways," says Pinchley. "First of all, there's Groon's jet stream." The Szep points towards a faint line along the horizon. "Runs between New Eden and Groon's lair—what we call the Pit. The jet stream's full of saucers going back and forth. And our Szep City is in the next basin over from the Pit."

"Bad neighborhood, huh," says Scud. "What's the second way to find Szep City?"

"Thar she blows," goes the Szep. "The plume out yonder? Near the far end of the jet stream?"

Villy slits his eyes in order to do a mental zoom—and he's able to see a downy upright feather on the far horizon, a thunderhead of clouds that must tower a thousand miles high.

"The cloud over Szep City," says Pinchley. "That's the one we call Sky Castle. You'll go there later. But for now, here comes the li'l ole basin that we call Funky Broadway."

Zoe chimes a downward arpeggio, and Villy stays in teepful sync. Funky Broadway is a world of living cities, blocky hives trundling across a fruited plain. The cities are inhabited by races of monkeys. Here and there pairs of cities batten onto each other. Their primate passengers clamber from one metropolis to the other. Ape-men brandish exquisite works of art in offer for trade—only to be taken prisoner by brutal lower orders who feed the unfortunate captives into meat-grinder gear-trains embedded in the lowest foundations of the towns.

Zoe plays the sounds of stabbing cries, and Villy styles moony evocations of wasted lives. A heart-searing duet. And that's just a start. Zoe and Villy lose themselves in ever-richer stratocast harmonies, sailing across more basins and more.

"Paramecium Pond."

It's a five-thousand-mile puddle that is a luminous shade of yellow-green, vibrant with algae, shiny with microorgasmic tides. Paramecia, amoeba, volvoxes, rotifers—teeming, breeding, and consuming their fellows when they can.

"An octillion in all," says science-boy Scud. There's quite the teepy vibe inside the car by now, what with the living Harmon guitars, the saucer pearl, the kids' mental acrobatics, and Pinchley's off-kilter state.

As they fly above Paramecium Pond, Zoe and Villy spin a sludgy mat of notes—a recursive musical fugue. Right about now the microorganisms' population count seems to be dropping at a logarithmic rate. The individual cells are eating each other and getting bigger—like rivals climbing up through the brackets of a tournament tree. A mere billion of them remain. A thousand. A hundred. And then—but one. A paramecium the size of a continent.

The slimy titan lolls in the planetary pond. A plutocrat in a bathtub. Suddenly the glowing waters slosh. Something's wrong? A dark spot has appeared upon the tyrant's ciliated pellicle hide. A raging infection, a rogue colony of his erstwhile lower companions. The master paramecium springs a leak and—*pop*—he's back to square one. An octillion rivals in a planetary pool of goo.

Inspired by the scene, Zoe and Villy craft a bombastic rock anthem. More and more worlds strobe past.

Trumpeting the thousand names of Goob-goob, elephants carry smaller elephants to and fro, building elephantine mounds that stretch into the sky. Pinchley steers among the wobbly columns, and, where necessary, Scud zaps a grabby trunk.

Milk-spurting udders flop in high green grass. Towering flowers chide the udders in snobby British accents. Vines sprout floating cucumbers like miniature zeppelins. Tiny uniformed airmen gather on the taut hulls to dance hornpipe jigs.

Mermen and sirens loll beside a glassy black sea. Loch Ness monsters ply the inky waters, their heads like prows of Viking ships.

A sky full of barking dogs, with a suburban grid of doghouses below. Sinister rabbits slink from doghouse to doghouse eating puppies, quite heedless of the fruitful carrot patches in the doghouse yards.

Wee gnomes juggle bristly ogres in the air. Steaming cauldrons of porridge await. The ogres dwindle to raisins in the mush.

Flying jellyfish carry shrimp-people. The treacherous shrimps set the jellies to lashing each other with stinging strands. Beneath the fray, striped sea snails cheer and toss bouquets to the shrimp.

Hopeful pigs join snouts in pairs, disk to disk. They spin upwards like helicopters, shedding rashers of bacon that settle onto slippery, overcrowded streets.

Hippos in a basin of braided rivers that cascade from the cliffs along the basin's edge. Flying bales of alfalfa appear. The hippos roar in joy, showing stubby peg-like teeth.

A herd of sinister eyeballs rolls across a plain, forever watching a commanding central figure who feeds upon attention.

All along they've been moving in parallel to Groon's jet stream. If Villy squints his eyes, he can make out the steady flow of saucers within. The Szep City cloud called Sky Castle is no longer so impossibly far. Onward.

Zoe and Villy stratocast the purple whale across a watery basin rife with whirlpools that split and merge. Above the sea, tornadoes fill the misty air, as if mirroring the maelstroms below. Small, isolated thunderheads scud among the tornadoes, exchanging lightning bolts like phrases in a ceaseless conversation.

In the next basin, crystals sprout like hoarfrost ferns, then snap loose and tumble, transforming themselves like shards in a kaleidoscope. Arpeggios ring from the crystals, rising towards an elusive climax. Zoe's and Villy's rhythms push the swelling harmony over the edge. The crystals shatter into specks that spring into the sky.

And now comes a basin that's entirely filled by a single, planet-sized human corpse. Pygmies and homunculi feast upon it, like fiddler crabs on a dead dolphin.

Gray light, a drizzle of steady rain. Fish walk on pairs of legs. Chickens in mortarboards declaim from ladders.

Crawling naked brains play cards and promenade in patterns. A supernal book of wisdom takes shape amid the brains. Living pairs of scissors dart forward and snip the book's pages to confetti.

"One last basin before Szep City," says Pinchley. "The Pit. It's like a deep well with Groon at the bottom." The dark Pit's walls are vertical, like the vent of a volcano. The jet stream they've been tracking—it makes a turn here and dives into the Pit. A wailing drone sounds from the abyss.

Pinchley pumps his arms as if he's dancing a jig. "Groon's music," he says. "He's a giant bagpipe. He's the one who controls the leech saucers. This jet stream runs from the Pit all the way to New Eden at the other end. It's like a two-way river in the sky. Groon pumps new saucers out towards New Eden, and he sucks in fat old saucers from there. Levitate your ass off, Scud. No way we want to be sucked to the bottom of the Pit or, worse than that, end up inside Groon's sack."

Naturally, life being the way it is, the purple whale ends up in a downward death spiral around the saucer-filled jet stream that runs into the Pit. It's like they're moths around a flame, or kids around an ice cream stand, or hayseeds around a county fair burlesque show.

It's because of Groon's hideous bagpipe music. It worms its way into Villy's head, and he begins playing his guitar in harmony with it—dippy jigs and manful marches and cornball choruses—it's total crap, but Villy's playing his ass off. And meanwhile Zoe's playing a soaring soprano descant to accompany Villy's bagpipe tunes, even though she's rolling her eyes in frustration and disgust.

Whenever one of Zoe's hands is free for a second, she whacks it against the body of her little guitar. Like she's trying to wake herself up. "Stop it!" she yells to herself as much as to Villy. "These songs stink!"

Meanwhile Pinchley's getting nowhere with the purple whale's controls. "Groon's slurping us towards his gullet," yells the Szep. "He'll eat us, and blast out our remains like turd scraps along the middle of his goddamn jet stream geyser."

This deep in the Pit, they're hella close to the jet stream. It's narrowed down to a couple of miles wide. A cascade of downward-bound saucers fills the outer surface of the stream—and a faintly seen plume of saucers flows up along the axis of the core.

What makes the present situation truly hopeless is that Scud is in thrall to the ghastly bagpipe as well. Not only are Villy and Zoe helplessly circling the plume, Scud is allowing them to descend. And Pinchley's best efforts with the rudder and the flaps are hopeless against the folly of the three kids. Nose first, the purple whale spirals ever deeper into the screeching clamor and the fetid gloom.

"We're doomed," says Zoe. But she's high enough from her music that she manages a laugh. "Doomed yet again, that is."

"We'll make it past this frikkin bagpipe," says Villy. "We're cosmic mythic heroes, right? Isn't that what you said?"

Peering through the windshield of the purple whale, Villy sees a vast, ungainly sack at the bottom of the pit—a heaving, floppy bag the size of a mountain. Groon. He bears two great horns or chanters: one is wide and one is thin. The horns are nested within each other, the thin within the wide. The jet stream's flows are nested as well—saucers spew forth from Groon along the jet stream's core, and they drift inward along the outer circumference of the stream. The wide outer horn gathers up the incoming saucers, and the narrow inner horn one spouts them out.

Entranced, Villy gazes at the monumental alien bagpipe, wondering at its odd design while obsessively humming the cheesy tunes that he and Zoe feel compelled to play.

For a wonder, Groon doesn't seem to notice them at all. He has a variety of feelers on his surface, but it's not clear if any of them are eyes in the usual sense of the word. And even if the cosmic bagpipe *can* sense their presence, he may be oblivious to them, so deeply steeped is he in the ecstasy of his ceaseless piping. Or it may also be that, by their involuntary act of echoing the alien's tunes, Zoe and Villy have made their purple whale seem like an ally. They reach the bottom of the Pit and circle the great sack quite undisturbed.

"No Szep nor human has ever been this close to Groon before," whispers Pinchley. "His hide's kind of transparent, ain't it? Like thin greasy leather. Look towards the bottom, where he stashes the saucers he's sucking in. See those fleshy things like laundry wringers next to them? And the big pan underneath? Groon milks smeel from the new arrivals. And over there, see them long fingers massaging the milked saucers? Groon's squeezing out their eggs. For growin' a fresh crop."

"So—biological," says Zoe, clearly repelled.

"And look where the saucers go back out," says Scud, getting into Pinchley's spirit of zoological investigation. "He sends back the saucers that he's milked and egged— and he launches baby saucers from his egg hatchery as well. The newbies and the retreads go shooting out through the thin horn that's inside the wide one."

"Groon sucks *and* he blows," blurts Zoe, and breaks into shrill laughter.

Somehow, Zoe's rude, despairing gaiety is enough to break the two musicians' trance. Gathering the full force of her quirky personality, Zoe segues from her hideous bagpipe tune into a low-down hoochie-coochie vamp. And Villy's only too glad to build a bed beneath Zoe's rolling and tumbling line.

Groon twitches, not liking these sounds. Sensing the evil bagpipe's discomfort, Villy and Zoe play the harder. And now, energized by the musical rhythms of physical love, Scud regains his saucer pearl mojo. With a massive effort of will, he levitates the whale back to the mouth of the Pit. With Scud and the stratocasters back in control of themselves, Pinchley's free to pilot the purple whale away from the jet stream saucer plume, over the Pit basin's ridge—and into the overcast basin next door.

Szep City. It's a single metropolis five thousand miles wide, but sparsely populated, from what Villy can see. Some sections are in ruins, and other districts are burned out. Red-eyed leech saucers cruise above the empty streets.

Villy and Zoe's stratocast has them moving too fast to land right away. The whale flashes across the planetary city like a flaming jet liner with insane terrorists at the controls. Zoe and Villy slow their tune, and Pinchley bends their path into a circling loop. They're homing in on a sweet spot.

Overhead, the Sky Castle cloud is a low, dark thunderhead, ruffled by an endless gale and flickering with lightning. A mile-high smokestack stretches towards the sky. It has indecipherable lettering on its side. Squalls of rain spatter against the whale's windshield.

Villy and Zoe go ever lighter on their guitar strings, and Scud reduces their altitude. The smells of the city drift in the purple whale's open windows. The dusty scent of a summer storm. Deep-fried food. Tobacco smoke, gasoline, roast meat, magnolia blossoms, coffee grounds, sour curry, sewer gas.

Carefully Pinchley guides them down. And now, the long journey over, they're beaching the whale, touching down a million miles from home. Thump and bounce. Szep City.

TWENTY-THREE

wand

scud

The buildings of Szep City are pink, gray, and tan—smooth and rounded, like porcelain baked into retro-future shapes. Towers with raygun-style fins. Egg-shaped halls with domes on domes. Walls banded with deco tiles bearing alien glyphs. Apartment blocks like Archimedean solids, jazzy with polygonal facets.

The streets are full. Crowded sidewalks, faces in windows, transport tubes of heavy green glass. Aerial roadways swoop from tower to tower, teeming with cars.

The purple whale rests in a public square, a social space alive with voices. Rain-wet benches, flowers, cafes, pancake trees, oily communal tubs—and old-school metal and plastic cars around the plaza's edges. Three red-eyed leech saucers loaf overhead. Patrolling the square. Their upper surfaces are mirrored, as if to fend off zap-rays from the sky.

The thronging Szep have warm-colored skins, ranging from creamy lemon to baked terra-cotta, with occasional shades of blue. They're a spindly race, with thin limbs, puppet-like jaws, and big lips and eyes. Some of them have such short legs they resemble freestanding hat racks.

"Do you think this place looks like San Francisco?" unworldly Scud asks his older brother. They're still inside the car.

"A little, maybe," says Villy. "Or LA."

"The roast reds are Rubtans," says Pinchley. Again, he seems overcome by grief. "The lovely lemons are Trubans. Poor Pinchley and yesterday's Yampa are Trubans." It's like landing here has flipped him back into his nutso Yampa imitation.

"Stop that!" says Scud, his voice tense and low. He grabs Pinchley's skinny shoulders and shakes him. "*You're* Pinchley." The Szep's big jaw wobbles and clacks. His arms are like a disjointed doll's. Scud keeps at him. "You, Pinchley, you made us come a million miles. And now we're here. Help us finish. Don't act crazy."

"Small boy, big dream," mutters Pinchley, turning his head back and forth, taking in the scene. Like he's waking up. Some of the Szep seem to be moving in on them, a mixed gang of Trubans and Rubtans. They're grim and glassy-eyed.

"*Hey!*" Scud yells at Pinchley, giving him another shake. "I said we need help!"

"I'm Pinchley, yaar," the Szep finally says, slow and mournful. "They killed my wife."

"We'll avenge her," says Scud. "You'll get us a wand at Lady Filippa's place, right? We'll make friends with the wand, and we'll find our way home to save Earth. And along the way, I want to visit Nunu and my saucerbabies in New Eden."

"Meanwhile it looks like we're facing a lynch mob," puts in Villy. "And three hostile saucers."

A Szep bungees up onto the hood of the car. She's thin and has a baked-red skin. A Rubtan. She has stubby legs. She peers in at them through the windshield. She moves her arms in exaggeratedly feminine gestures, greeting them. She's not an enemy. She wears a small crown, a gold coronet whose projecting spikes are tipped with pearls.

"Behold the intrepid Pinchley," she flutes, her voice very upper crust. "Returned with his recruits."

"Flipsydaisy!" Pinchley calls out through the driver's side window. "Did you know I was coming?"

"Yes, and I know you're single again," replies Flipsydaisy. "My sympathy, dear friend. I'll come aboard?"

Pinchley nods. Flipsydaisy slides in through Scud's window, nimble and knobby. She lands on Scud's lap, with her tidy crown still atop her head. The Szep has a smell of onions and fresh-cut grass. She studies Scud, then plants a thin-lipped kiss upon his cheek—possibly just to bug him. Scud wipes the kiss away.

"No doubt Flipsydaisy's here to collect the gifts for our Lady," says Pinchley. "Understood. But I don't like all them others milling around."

"Goob-goob, Lady Filippa, and I are the ones who engaged Yampa and Pinchley to fetch you heroic humans," Flipsydaisy tells Scud. "Yours truly being the field agent. There was talk of you arriving with a stash?"

"You mean those freaking caraway seeds?" says Zoe. "For Lady Filippa?"

"*Hsst*," goes Flipsydaisy. "Ixnay on her amenay. There's been another coup. This crowd around us—most of them are saucer zombies. Drained of their smeel by the flying leeches, and destined to be meat for the Tollah dogs."

"Oh hell," says Pinchley. "But our Lady is alive?"

"Lying low, don't you know," says Flipsydaisy.

The crowded Szep are rhythmically tugging the door cords, rocking the car as if wanting to turn it over. One of the three leech saucers hovers directly overhead, glaring down with its red eye, in control of the zombies. Pinchley frowns, produces one of his tool-belt critters, sets it on the dash, and hollers a warning out the window, using the Szep tongue.

"*Nincs itt skorkers!*"

The tool critter on the dash is a tiny man made of lightning bolts. He reminds Scud of the old-school power company cartoon character named Reddy Kilowatt. Little Reddy flicks his fingers, shedding dark energies. The outer surfaces of the car begin to buzz and crackle. One of their attackers catches a jolt and unleashes a lurid scream. The other saucer stooges edge back.

The saucer overhead makes as if to attack the purple whale herself. With a certain sense of entitlement, she lowers towards them, like a duchess preparing to feed. The leech saucers have been in power for a long time here.

Almost without even thinking about it, Scud shoots a really juicy dark-energy bolt from the saucer pearl. It arrows out the window and into the flabby belly of the leech saucer, who at this point is only ten feet above the roof of the car.

Bingo! The saucer's flesh explodes into red scraps that patter down onto the heads and shoulders of the crowd. Neither of the other two patrol saucers seems interested in getting involved.

"I *say*," exclaims Flipsydaisy, coming on all British. "Well done, Scud. That's showing the rabble some grit."

Villy congratulates Scud too. And, better than that, Zoe hugs him. A first. "Can you give us some context?" Zoe asks Flipsydaisy. "The darker Szep are Rubtans, and the lighter ones are Trubans, and therefore—?"

"Most Trubans work for Rubtans like me," says Flipsydaisy. "We're wealthy and we run things. Our Truban friend Pinchley was Lady F's chauffeur, and Yampa made image-clouds that the Lady used for, well, for curtains and slipcovers and scarves. I was the Lady's interior decorator. Still am. Wait till you see how I've outfitted her new hidey-hole. Chic and lavish." Flipsydaisy pauses. "Chic if viewed a certain way."

"How will we get there?" asks Scud, keenly aware of the jar of caraway seeds in his pants pocket. "We need to meet the Lady in person."

"I've hatched a strategy," says Flipsydaisy. "My methodologies are famously baroque. I'm really much more than a decorator, you see."

"Tell us about Groon," interrupts Scud.

"A parasitic bagpipe thing who slithers from world to world," says Flipsydaisy. "Currently he lives in our neighboring basin, the Pit, worse luck. He sneezes out saucers like a puffball sprays spores."

"We saw him just now," says Scud. "We were all the way down in his hole."

"Truly you and your companions may be our long-awaited saviors," Flipsydaisy tells Scud with a grave nod. "Did you bring chocolate for me?"

"I'm holding the caraways," says Scud. "Not sure where the chocolate is."

"Here you go," says Pinchley, extracting the battered cocoa tin from a pile of rags and handing it to Flipsydaisy with a bow. "Maybe—maybe you and I can get together for a session after this hoo-rah damps down," he tells her.

"I am pleased by this prospect," says Flipsydaisy, dipping her hand into the tin and a savoring a taste of the powder. She smiles beatifically, and the tin disappears into her purse. "And now?" she says.

"Don't ask me," says Scud. "We have no idea what we're doing."

"I say we disperse the rabble," goes Flipsydaisy. She makes a contemptuous gesture towards the crowd of Szep around the car. Something flashes on her wrist.

"You've got a new Aristo wand?" says Pinchley, noticing the twinkle. "And there's an extra wand at Lady Filippa's—all set to meet the kids?"

"*Shhh!*" goes Flipsydaisy. "I already warned you. Don't say her name in full."

"Nobody's listening," snaps Pinchley, quite incorrectly, as events will very soon reveal. Perversely he makes his voice louder. "Here's the story, kids. The Aristos produce these special wands. And you guys will get a chance to adopt one. Up at Lady Filippa's."

Pinchley has now said Lady Filippa's name once too often. It's like he's triggered an alert. A ululating howl blasts from a nearby tower, which is attached to a vast domed arena-like building. The saucer-zombie Trubans and Rubtans around the car hold their arms high as if in prayer. But they're not praying. They're preparing a mass attack. As for the pair of leech saucers still on patrol—they're hanging back, expecting their zombie slaves to do the dirty work.

"Had to run your mouth, eh, Pinchley?" says Flipsy-daisy, kind of enjoying herself.

One of the saucer stooges tosses a grubworm into the car. The thing humps along the dashboard at about ninety miles per hour, pounces on the Reddy Kilowatt zapper, and eats him whole. The saucer-zombie Trubans and Rubtans are all over the car by now, preparing to assault the passengers. The shrilling from the tower goes on and on.

Flipsydaisy makes a regal gesture with two fingers of her left hand—the hand with the twinkle at its wrist. Immediately there's an explosion on the other side of the square: a concussive crack followed by screams and a prolonged sound of concrete chunks thudding onto the ground. A stone waterfall of rubble is streaming down the side of the tower where the evil voice wails. A raised roadway up there is collapsing, a section at a time.

"Our local Saucer Hall," says Flipsydaisy. "I'm teaching them some manners."

"There's lots of saucers inside, aren't there?" says Scud. "Are they coming out?"

"Unless they're wearing mirror-shields on top, they tend to lie doggo in the daytime," says Flipsydaisy. "The Aristos up in Sky Castle shoot them on sight."

Meanwhile a platoon of armed Szep soldiers rushes out from a low arcade. A loyalist anti-saucer counterforce.

They beam tightly focused energy rays at the rabble of saucer zombies surrounding the purple whale. The victims scream as the beams cut them into pieces. A smell of ammonia and burnt flesh.

The yowling from the tower above Saucer Hall has continued all this time, and now it redoubles. It's more like the sound of an animal than the voice of a Szep. The saucers are loath to emerge, but in their place a squad of saucer-controlled Szep troops streams out of the great dome. The zombies wear mirrored armor, and each of them wears a helmet formed into the traditional flying saucer shape.

The zombies set upon the loyalist Szep troops, using sabers and electrified morning stars, that is, spiky balls tethered to sticks. A loyalist hurls a grenade into a crowd of saucer zombies. They toss back a grenade that sets a recreational oil-bath vat alight. Greasy flames gutter to the sky, wreathed in plumes of sooty smoke. It's total anarchy. Scud looks up, following the smoke. He'd like to see some of those high-flying, saucer-killing Aristo snipers that Flipsydaisy was talking about.

Meanwhile a Rubtan saucer zombie wielding a long-handled battle axe is chopping at one of the purple whale's tires. Scud flattens the assailant with a spark of dark energy from his pearl. A zombie soldier with a spark-buzzing morning star makes it onto the hood. He positions himself to shatter the windshield. Just in time, a pulsed energy beam stitches a row of holes across his chest, laying him low, but also puncturing the purple whale's windshield. The voice in the high tower shrills on, a threnody of empty menace. A grenade explodes about twenty feet away, and shrapnel thuds into the panels of their car.

And then a raygun beam drills a hole into Scud's saucer pearl, extinguishing its inner light. By some stroke of luck, the ray fails to damage Scud's hand. But there will be no more levitating or zapping from the pearl. Its surface is crazed into an intricate maze of cracks. The pieces drop to the car's floor. It's time to bail.

Flipsydaisy, Pinchley, Scud, Zoe, and Villy clamber down from the purple whale. Villy and Zoe have their guitars, but there's no time to bring anything else. And by the time they've gone thirty feet, their battered, hard-working, heavily modified whale is totally on fire— lit off a grenade and an intense saucer zap. The awesome wagon that carried them a million miles from Earth is gone. Tragic. And how will they get home?

Pinchley's as upset about the whale as Villy, maybe even more so. He and Villy stand there staring at the car's collapsing frame, the greasy flames folding over themselves, and the disintegrating quantum shocks doing strange things to the perspective. It takes Scud, Flipsydaisy, and Zoe a minute to get the two gearheads moving again.

With Flipsydaisy and Pinchley leading them, the kids wend their way through the carnage. Flipsydaisy's gold coronet grants them some measure of high-class Rubtan status. And perhaps it helps that Flipsydaisy has a wand. The shiny patch on her left wrist seems to be the hilt or the handle of the wand, although Scud's none too clear on where the rest of the wand is.

It also helps that Villy's looted a saber from a saucer zombie's corpse. The blade is thin, as if only a few molecules thick. Flipsydaisy says it can slice anything whatsoever in half. Even so, Scud is deeply afraid. And then he hits on the idea of wreathing them in a Flatsie cloud of unknowing. After all, he still has his teep slug. Scud does the deed, and now their party moves on unseen.

By the time they reach the edge of the square, they're clear of the melee. And the two patrol saucers seem to have lost track of them. Short-legged Flipsydaisy walks with her head high, coronet in place, her left hand extended in a fashion-model pose—leading them along a stone arcade lined with deluxe shops. She signals an abrupt right turn into an alley off the arcade, and they proceed through a mazy series of ever-smaller lanes, ending at the entrance to a courtyard the size of a handball court.

It's calm here, far from the thuds of the grenades, the beeping of the ambulance pods, and the sinister baying from the tower. Scud tilts back his head and gazes upward. No saucers in sight. Windowless walls stretch towards the low sky. Swirls and spits of rain drift down, sprinkling his face. Thanks to the shared cloud of unknowing, Scud's companions can only be seen as holes in the mist.

"You can turn off that crude Flatsie invisibility charm now," says the citified Flipsydaisy. "More fun if we see each other. Lady F. has her lair beneath a trapdoor at the center of this yard. Don't you adore how I've decorated it?"

Decorated? At first glance the little square resembles a flea-market, crowded with bric-a-brac. Single shoes, twisted forks, Szep headrests, portrait gourds, arcane technokipple. Standing amid the debris are five Trubans—pale, thin fellows. They chatter to each other in a twangy sliding dialect of the Szep tongue. They're keenly aware of Scud and the others.

"Merchants?" Scud asks Flipsydaisy.

"Guards," she says, saluting them.

Right about now Scud notices the really odd thing. The stuff in the courtyard isn't, well, it isn't lying on the ground. All the goods are floating at waist level. Suspended by a levitation field. So when you wade on in, as Flipsydaisy now makes them do, you're surrounded by random junk that bobbles against your butt and thighs and crotch. It feels creepy.

Yellow Pinchley and adobe-red Flipsydaisy are in front, heading towards the center of the pool. They're erect and solemn, as if approaching a throne room. Scud walks behind them, with Zoe and Villy in the rear, doing their lovey-dovey thing, holding hands and gesturing with their guitars as they gloat about the great riffs they played during their stratocast.

Scud is nervous about tripping and falling down. So nasty to have all this flea-market-type crap touching him, none of it new, most of it dirty. Tiny items like fasteners and machine parts fill in the spaces between the bigger things. He can't even see his feet. Filthy, semi-transparent alien cockroaches are down there, no doubt. And—*ew*—did he just now step on a turd?

It's too much. Scud feels like he might puke. He stops walking and breathes through his mouth. Flipsydaisy pauses, waiting, all the while holding forth about the elegance of this floating pool of crud. Supposedly she hand-curated the choice of each individual item, and there are deeply significant links between them, and their cumulative impact is, in some sense, a dynamic mandala representing the ancient and noble lineage of Lady Filippa's Aristo race.

"Look out!" yells Zoe right about then. "A snake!" Off to the side, something bright is slithering amid the levitated sheet of debris.

"Is that what I think it is?" Pinchley asks Flipsydaisy.

"Our Lady's gift to the humans, yes," says Flipsydaisy with a nod. "Who gets it?"

"Scud," says Pinchley, waggling his lumpy jaw. "He's the one."

Flipsydaisy raises a dark, elegant finger and points at—

"Don't!" cries Scud. "Not me!"

The bright shape wriggles closer. She's a living female being with a flat crystal for a head. Her supple body glows gold. And she's heading for Scud, yes indeed. The pale guards show no interest.

"That's your Aristo wand," goes Pinchley. "You gonna like it, son."

"Help me, Villy!" yells Scud.

So Villy rallies to his little brother's defense and begins taking wild swings with his super-sharp saber. Effortlessly the wand evades the blade—it moves with preternatural speed and guile, weaving loops and knots, crooning all the while in a high, thin voice. Villy's manful but futile swings intersect, in turn, a hovering anvil, a red glove, a really big vacuum tube, a large dead rat wearing a cloth jacket, a triangular book, a gemmed crab shell, a meaty orchid, a porcelain soup tureen, and very nearly the neck of one of those pale, thin guards, who ducks just in time.

Repeatedly, in between dodging Villy's saber strokes, the singing wand jabs Scud's butt with her sharp tail, as if tasting him, or teasing him, or savoring his cries. For the finale, the wand writhes around Scud's left arm like a stripe on a barber pole and sinks into his flesh, completely disappearing—save for a flat, crystal-like head, which now rests upon the back of Scud's wrist like the face of a watch.

"Rad," goes the unsympathetic Zoe.

The crystal on Scud's wrist bears an iridescent pattern like the spot on a peacock's tail. Oh, it's an eye. So—the wand can see.

"My name is Skzx," the wand's voice whispers inside Scud's ear. She's using teep. "I like your feel, Scud. Kinkier than I expected. I thought you'd be dull. Maybe I really will help you stop Groon and his saucers." Her voice is husky and intimate. "I wasn't sure if I'd do it or not."

"Get out of me," yells Scud, waving his left arm, longing to eject the parasite.

"We're only starting," murmurs the wand. "But I have a feeling this partnership is going to work. I'm savoring your panic. So jagged, your mind. Later you'll come to love me. Have a taste of candy." A warm glow runs up Scud's arm and into his chest. For the first time in hours— or maybe it's days—Scud's all-consuming fear retreats.

"You can open the door to Lady Filippa's lair now," Flipsydaisy tells Scud. "It seems that you are worthy." She's smiling at him as if he's handsome. And Villy is looking at Scud with new respect. For, yea, Scud Antwerpen is destined to be a man of the wand.

Scud makes what he supposes to be a commanding gesture, and the floating garbage moves to the sides, exposing the center of the courtyard. No cockroaches, no dog turds. Blank stone, set with a sturdy trapdoor a full fathom wide, chased in bronze, and bearing a mighty handle in the likeness of a Szep. The door swings open at Scud's first touch. He can see a spiral staircase below.

The four others gather round, with the five pale guards at their perimeter.

"If you permit," says Flipsydaisy stepping first onto the stair. "Rank hath its privileges. Scud, you come last. Protect our rear. Come now, Zoe and Villy." Flipsydaisy makes a curious gesture with her wand hand—like she's laying a spell on the lovers.

Meanwhile Scud's wand continues diluting his fear, giving him a confidence that is not well founded. For not only is that creature from the tower still wailing, its yowls are growing closer. Might it be hunting them down?

One by one, and all too slowly, Scud's companions go down the staircase. The slender guards shift uneasily; they watch the alley and jabber to each other. Flipsydaisy, Pinchley, and Villy have descended out of sight. Zoe is starting down the stairs, and Scud is next. But then the self-dramatizing Zoe pauses on the stairs to cock her head and stare dreamily at the sky. *Oh, the wonder of it all.*

"Hurry up, goddamn you!" screams Scud, losing control of his voice.

Too late. Just as the now-frowning Zoe disappears down the stairs, a gray, ravening, wild-eyed, six-foot-tall dog-thing comes loping down the alleyway into the courtyard, loudly baying, closing in on his quarry. The spindly sentries fire some weak-ass beams at the beast, but the monstrous dog is completely unfazed. The guards might as well be white asparagus stalks. No way is Scud is going to have enough time to get down those stairs and slam the hatch.

But he's got his wand. Before he even knows what he's doing, he's holding out his left arm with his fingers spread—just like he's a videogame sword-and-sorcery wizard casting a spell. *Whump*. He feels a full-body pleasure wave as Skzx the wand pumps out the baddest-ass zap-ray ever. It's like firing a bazooka, man. Way better than a saucer pearl zap. And, check it out, the giant dog is gray ashes.

Scud grins, savoring the glory of the moment. He's a superhero. But wait. The ashes sift and spiral. They're spinning themselves into dust devils, taking on shape, undead and implacable. *Eeeek*! The five guards take off work for the day, running out that alley to the town. For his part, Scud hurries down the spiral staircase after turning the handle that locks the hatch shut.

Meanwhile Pinchley and Flipsydaisy are engrossed in a conversation with Lady Filippa. And Villy and Zoe are gaping at the Lady's hideaway like hicks dropped into the lap of inconceivable luxury. They've wandered over to a table with food and drink.

To Scud's eyes, the Lady's room is a low, littered den—and his companions are literally eating garbage. The room is lit by some glowing knobs of fungus on the walls. Thanks to his wand, Scud sees the true nature of these quarters. And he sees Lady Filippa for what she is: a meaty, yam-like form on a heap of rags. She's wide in the middle and pointed at both ends, with about three dozen eyes set into her surface. She has a slit mouth at one end. Just now she's slurping at a cracked bowl of water. Presumably this what an Aristo looks like. In no way does she resemble a Szep.

Flipsydaisy sashays over and makes a languid, knowing gesture. She favors Scud with an arch smile. "Can you find it in your heart to see our Lady Filippa as she wishes to be seen?"

"Never mind that," hisses Scud. His heart is pounding from his near escape. "There's a monster outside, the thing that was wailing in the high tower. It's like a giant dog."

"Groon grows those things," says Flipsydaisy, speaking too quietly for Zoe and Villy to hear. "We call them Tollah dogs. Tollahs are worse than saucers—they eat Szep alive, and I suppose humans as well."

"I zapped the one outside into dust," says Scud. "But— "

"But he's not dead," confirms Flipsydaisy. "He'll soon regain his vigor and his vim. The Lady and I mean to open the hatch and let him come in. You epic heroes are to be the bait. Handling the Tollah will be one of your tests, hmm? To ensure that you are worthy of your mission. But meanwhile, Scud, can you be a gentleman as I asked? Do us the favor of honoring our Lady's artifice." With another of her odd smiles, Flipsydaisy raises her left hand, as if proposing a toast.

Not fully sure what Flipsydaisy is playing at, Scud echoes her gesture. A quick flash passes between the wand crystals the two of them wear on their wrists. A spell. And now Scud's seeing this room the way he's meant to.

"Quite stimulating, all this to and fro," says a woman's plummy voice. "I welcome you, Sir Scud. I think the wand likes you."

It's Lady Filippa. To Scud's now-ensorcelled eyes, she looks like a distinguished Szep lady, at ease on a low, elegantly curved velvet lounge-chair, with a fizzy drink at her side. She's more filled out than Yampa was, and redder. Like a high-ranking Rubtan.

Seen as the Lady wills it, this cellar resembles an old-school British club, with oriental carpeting, burnished walnut wainscoting, plump chairs, stained glass windows, and walls of books. Triangular books.

"Why are you so uptight?" Zoe asks Scud. "This place is great."

"Great," echoes Scud. In the courtyard above, the Tollah dog whines and scratches at the trapdoor. Zoe doesn't seem to hear him.

"Might the three of you perform something as a trio?" asks Lady Filippa. "Scud might test his proposed partnership with Skzx the wand. And Zoe and Villy might use their guitars."

"Ah—what kind of song?" asks Villy. He's munching on what he thinks is a cookie, and sipping what appears to be a cup of tea.

"Song?" replies Lady Filippa. "Well, an improvisation. Your clever brother Scud can lead." She glances over at the staircase.

Flipsydaisy stands beside the stairs, one foot on a step. "Shall we begin?" Flipsydaisy calls.

"I'm not ready," blurts Scud. "The caraway seeds—I have to give Lady Filippa the seeds. As a way to impress her and the Aristo wand, right?"

"Ah, the seeds," says Lady Filippa. In Scud's eyes, her image jitters between Rubtan lady and many-eyed yam. "I relish those seeds when sprinkled upon a very particular food," continues Lady Filippa with a self-effacing laugh. "I'm the greedy one, aren't I. I'm expecting you to provide me the special food as well as the seeds. But first I'll fully execute my part of our deal. I'll teach you how to work with your proposed wand. Skzx is a close relative of mine." And with that, Lady Filippa locks every one of her eyes on Scud's—and they enter a moment of deep teep.

With the silent singing of the wand mixed in with the teep voice of Lady Filippa, the experience is heavenly. Scud doesn't want it to end.

TWENTY-FOUR

lady filippa

zoe

Zoe and Scud are compulsively feeding at a table of canapes in Lady Filippa's fancy underground apartment. The cookies, petit fours, and crustless sandwiches are toothsome in the extreme. But Zoe's starting to feel sick to her stomach. Maybe she should be drinking tea like Villy, instead of champagne? For sure she feels gross. Is the food maybe spoiled? But it smells and tastes so good.

Zoe and Villy have barely spoken to Lady Filippa, even though meeting her was supposed to be the big reason why they drove a million miles to get here. Instead they've been pigging out on the free food. Meanwhile, the drop-dead-elegant Lady has been talking to Flipsydaisy and Scud. But just now she looked over at Zoe and Villy and said that the three kids should play some music for her. As a trio. Not that Zoe feels all that much like playing—not right after that marathon stratocast session. Not while she feels like puking. And not with Scud.

Thanks to the glowing wand inside his arm, Scud's weirder than ever. He was screaming at Zoe like a crazy person right before she went down through the trapdoor. And why? Just because some dog was barking, and Zoe wanted to take a thoughtful look at the romantic, otherworldly sky? And then when they all got down here, Scud began frantically whispering to Flipsydaisy. And now he's staring at Lady Filippa like he's in a trance.

Speaking of trances, why *do* Zoe and Villy keep eating the snacks on this table? Not only does she feel sick to her stomach, the snacks don't really look normal. They change when she looks away from them. And when she looks back, there's more of them, or they're shaped differently. And whenever she thinks of something she'd like— such as a square of lox on a slice of peeled cucumber on a tiny round of rye with a squirt of lemon juice—well then, *bam*, it's right there. Something's wrong. Come to think of it, right before they came down the stairs, Flipsydaisy flashed Zoe and Villy with her wand crystal, and—

"Bogosity," Villy mutters to her. "Fake. Hold tight to your guitar and get some sanity. This is a basement and we're eating rotten meat and rancid fat and I think maybe we're drinking, uh, urine? But we're, like, under a spell, and that's why we don't want to stop."

It helps to clear Zoe's head to hear this out loud. She drops her glass to the floor and bends forward, wanting to vomit, but she can't bring anything up. She clutches her curly black guitar, hoping for strength. He moves in her hands like a sturdy, reassuring pet, and she feels reality return.

Scud is still fixated on Lady Filippa—they're doing teep. And Flipsydaisy's heading back up the corkscrew stairs. Is she planning to leave? Zoe hears some kind of faint sound, a tiny scratching and mewing, like from way, way out on the edge of the world. Or no, wait, the sound's not far away at all. It's right outside the hatch at the top of the stairs. And that's why Scud's been so uptight. Flipsydaisy's not going to open the hatch is she? Is she? *Is she?*

Zoe clutches her soft strong guitar, clarifying her focus. By the gloomy light of the fungus on the grungy walls, she truly sees the manky burrow, and the saggy thing on the pile of rags, and the nauseating crap on the table beside her, and the two pitchers of—is it really pee? She sniffs. No, it's stagnant water. With a trillion insane alien microbes in every sip. Champagne, right? Or does milady prefer English Breakfast tea?

Scud is still obliv. "*Look at us!*" Villy yells at him. "Pay attention."

Dire though the situation is, Zoe's glad to have Villy in it with her. Ah, the stories they'll tell when they're safe back in Los Perros, married, living in a basement or a trailer, with Zoe giving music lessons, and Villy a car mechanic—and that'll be enough, because success doesn't matter, and love conquers all, and—

Now Scud is back. He flips his hand, and his wand slides out. The wand's not acting snaky now. It looks like a gold baton with a flat crystal on the top. Scud points the wand at Zoe like a band leader about to signal the downbeat. He pauses to share some words of inspiration.

"That thing outside the hatch," goes Scud, weirdly calm. "It's a Tollah dog. Frikkin Flipsydaisy is going to let him in. And we three are supposed to tie him up. How? I have a plan. I'm going to make your music into threads. Follow my lead and we can do it." He gives Zoe a know-it-all nerd look.

"Go to hell," she says, not even pausing to think. "You're an immature idiot with a brain like a soft-boiled egg."

There, she's done it again. But it so annoys Zoe that Scud has the wand that was supposed to be hers. She's way more sensitive. Scud is, face it, subhuman. And *hello?* It's only thanks to Zoe that they made it to mappyworld at all.

Meanwhile Flipsydaisy is busy with the hatch at the top of the stairs. Zoe sets aside her hissy fit. And remembers what's actually happening. And flies into panic mode. She yells, "*Oh god no don't do it, Flipsydaisy, don't don't don't.*"

So of course—*clang*—Flipsydaisy flings open the hatch. Zoe hears a sound like a tornado, like a cartoon Tasmanian devil, and it's the Tollah dog coming in. She can see him, he's an alien wolf bigger than a person, gray with red eyes and mongo claws and teeth. He's swarming down the stairs –

Scud flicks his baton and, *oh* yeah, Zoe is very definitely playing guitar if it's gonna help. She amps from zero to eleven in, like, one nanosecond, and Villy's with her, in sync, as before, now and forever, amen. Weird as it seems, the music lines are visible, like Scud said they would be—scrawny, colored threads that fade out after a second or two. Thanks to Skzx the wand.

Scud's got something else going on. The tip of his wand spouts a sheet of gold ectoplasm that forms a dome around the three kids. A living sheet like the smooth water of a waterfall. A magic gold igloo that the frikkin Tollah dog can't get through.

Across the room, Flipsydaisy does a similar move. She has herself and Pinchley and the yam-shaped Lady Filippa inside a transparent pod of gold, wide in the middle and pointed at both ends, with the two Szep nestled tight against the nasty Lady.

The Tollah flings himself at the Lady Filippa pod with his slavering jaws wide open. As soon as he touches the pod, it goes *doink*, like an error-sound in a videogame but with a heavy sting attached, and the Tollah yelps like a hyena and runs all around the room breaking things, as if that matters, given what a total shithole the Lady's lair is.

Scud waves his baton-wand in rapid figure eights—and gestures with his free hand for more volume. Zoe follows his lead. She gets into a riff that circles back on itself, seeming a little higher and louder each time. It's the old Escher staircase routine, a tower of Babel. Villy adds accents to the riff, like spikes sticking out of the stairs, or like a rain of razorblades. And—here's the wand coming into full effect—their music forms thicker threads than before. The threads spill from Villy's Flying Vee guitar like glowing spaghetti. Zoe's chords grow like festive twine.

At first it seems like the sound-threads might stay trapped inside the gold igloo with them. The spaghetti and the twine are feeling around like worms looking for an exit from the igloo, and they're not finding a way out.

"Get Lady Filippa to help," yells Villy over the guitars.

"She won't," shouts Scud. "She and Flipsydaisy and Pinchley just want to watch how we do."

"Like this is a test?" says Zoe.

"Your neglected admission application," says Villy, weirdly amused. "Time to kick up our game, Z-bomb."

"*Yah mon*," she goes, heartened by his tone. "I'll bring it."

Zoe adds funk to her riffs, bending the notes and smearing them like you do with a Delta blues. Villy's with her again. The spaghetti strands and the twine get that much hairier, and they crawl up the walls of the sheltering igloo and, *thank you*, they sprout through all over, and the strings of sound are radiating out from the igloo like the spines of a sea urchin, or like glow-lines from a sun.

And this pisses off the Tollah dog, or scares him, and he charges towards them and leaps—like he's going to pop the igloo and tear the humans to bits. It's like a scene in a horror movie, with the giant tweaked-out wolf coming at Zoe in slow motion, trailing rabid slobber from his mouth.

Zoe and Villy bear down on their music, stratocast style, Scud sends some extra energy through his wand, and—the strands wrap all around the Tollah dog, layer after layer, tighter and tighter, until he's lying motionless on the ground, like a fly that a spider has cocooned for a later meal.

Moment of silence. The gold igloo and the yam's pod fade away, and here's the seven of them. The captive Tollah. The three humans. The two Szep. Plus Lady Filippa, the Aristo.

Lady F. has about thirty eyes on her body and she's dragging herself across the filthy floor. No arms or legs, but she's very dynamic. She gets right up on top of the shrouded Tollah dog, half covering him, and she looks over at Zoe with happy twinkles in her eyes. Pinchley and Flipsydaisy throw their arms across each other's shoulders, watching the show with big grins. Like they know what's next.

"Be so good as to sprinkle on the caraway seeds," says Lady Filippa. Her voice flutes out of the little slit mouth she has at one end. "A nice fresh Tollah is the special food I crave."

Scud hesitates. "Go on," says Villy. "This is what we came for, seems like. Give her all your seeds."

Zoe can tell Scud's got some reservations about this, and she can intuit why. That Goob-goob god who's been behind the scenes all along—no doubt Goob-goob is going to be wanting some caraway seeds as well. Playing it cool for once in his life, Scud pours a teaspoon of seeds into his palm, stashes the rest of the jar in his pocket, and makes a big hoo-rah about what he's actually doling out.

"Here we are!" he goes. "Knock yourself out, Lady F!" He scatters the seeds across the exposed parts of the music-thread-wrapped Tollah. Zoe can hear the pretty colored threads a little bit, humming and reverberating. The caraway seeds stick to the threads like sprinkles on a frosted cake.

And then Lady Filippa digs in. She worms around so her mouth is at one end of the laid-out Tollah. She opens her slit mouth very wide, and Zoe can see a nasty translucent squid beak inside. And then Lady F. is munching on her prey. She starts at the one end of the Tollah and eats him up entirely, working her way to the other end. Kind

of like how the hand-Irav did with Yampa, not that Zoe
wants to think about that.

When Lady Filippa begins chowing down, the tight-
wrapped Tollah is still alive. So there's anguished muffled
dog howls, plus a puddle of sick juice like yellow blood,
but Lady F. chokes down the whole entire meal. And then
she flops over to one side and lets out this huge fart. Then
closes all her eyes and falls asleep.

"Lifestyles of the Szep City Aristos," goes Villy, and
Scud cracks up, with all the crazy tension of the last hour
jittering into his shrill laugh.

Zoe laughs a little with the boys, but really she's too
far beyond disgusted to see the humor. Meanwhile
Flipsydaisy and Pinchley are gathering any extra caraway seeds that ended up on the floor and eating them as
fast as they can.

"How do we get out of here?" Zoe asks Pinchley. "How
do we get home?"

"Wal, Villy gave my car to a Harmon," says Pinchley.
"And your car is terminally trashed." Not that he sounds
worried about this. At this moment he's happy to eat a few
caraway seeds, and he's enjoying Flipsydaisy's attention.

"You'll fly back, my dear," languid Flipsydaisy tells Zoe.
"Goob-goob will help you. Take the tunnel to the smokestack and float up. I think you three can levitate?"

"Our saucer pearl got shattered," says Scud. "Someone
shot it with a ray."

"Never mind," says Flipsydaisy. "Your wand will help.
She's teeping me that she's definitely willing to partner
with you, all the way back to Van Cott. She likes the cut

of your jib, Scud. And I agree. That was a remarkably fine show you three put on for Lady Filippa. She was pleased."

"Such lovely manners she has," says Zoe, glancing over at the snoring Aristo. "Such a gracious way of thanking us."

"Snippy, are you now?" says Flipsydaisy, studying Zoe. "I suppose you're miffed you didn't get the wand? I don't blame you. I hate it when the men grab things that the women are supposed to have." Flipsydaisy glances at Lady Filippa. "Did I explain that Lady Filippa is a pupa? An alert, active pupa who's preparing for her next stage. Now that she's had her special meal, she's likely to split open, disgorge her adult body, and float away. But not until she wakes."

"Where are the Aristos from?" asks Villy. "What are they?"

"They're from the big cloud," says Flipsydaisy, pointing upwards. "Sky Castle? They have a life-cycle like an insect. The adult Aristos are fabulous glowing zeppelins. Very friendly with Goob-goob. Before the zeppelin stage comes the pupa stage where an Aristo looks like Lady Filippa. And before that comes a larval form. Can you guess what an Aristo larva looks like?" Flipsydaisy stares at Scud and titters.

"No!" yells Scud, thunderstruck. "This wand in my arm—it's an Aristo larva? Oh no! She'll eat my flesh and morph into a pupa. Like—Villy will go to wake me up, and the only thing in my bed will be a pointed yam with eyes."

Flipsydaisy throws back her head with in a delighted cackle. "Quick on the uptake, this boy. Too droll for words. It's as you say, Scud. Eventually a wand morphs into pupa resembling Lady Filippa. And, yes, the wand draws sustenance from her host. But she won't consume you entirely. She'll crawl free as a rather small pupa. Not to worry. As a courtier to the Aristos, I've hosted several wands myself. And I'm the better for it." Losing interest in Scud's predicament, she turns to Pinchley. "Shall we go to my digs for our chocolate party, dear?"

As for Zoe—now she doesn't want a wand after all. Truth be told, she feels a little sorry for Scud. But he's standing tall.

"Alright then," says Scud. "I can deal. Just so Skzx stays in place long enough for us to get home and stop the saucers. Or stop Groon? I'm still not clear on what we're supposed to do."

"You'll improvise magnificently," says Flipsydaisy. "Like the wily Odysseus of human myth!" The elegant Szep does her sophisto laugh.

"Oh, shove it," says Scud. "We need some hard facts. Pinchley? What was that about a tunnel to a smokestack? And how do we get home from Sky Castle?"

"We flew past that old smokestack," says Pinchley. "You saw it on the way in. It has Szep writing on the side? Says HAIL GROON. And like Flipsydaisy says, there's a tunnel runs from here to the bottom of the smokestack." Pinchley gestures to a low arch on the other side of the cluttered cellar, which is fitfully lit by the fungus and by the gleam of Scud's and Flipsydaisy's wands. "Right through there. Ain't far. Then you float up the stack. And once you make it to that big cloud, you find Goob-goob. And she'll hook you into the jet stream. And you ride the jet stream home. It's that same one that Groon runs. Plenty fast."

"What about us being mixed in with all those saucers in the jet stream?" asks Zoe.

"O ye cosmic heroes of little faith!" intones Flipsydaisy, treating her worries as a joke. "The mighty Goob-goob shall provide."

None of this is at all like what Zoe expected. Lady Filippa was supposed to be a fancy noble, not a creepy yam. The wand was supposed to be elegant, like in a fairy tale—and it's a sly parasitic larva. At least Villy is still like Villy. Zoe leans against him.

"Now I've got a boyfriend too," says Flipsydaisy, crinkling her eyes and twining both her arms around Pinchley's waist. "I've wanted this Truban for years. He's moving in with me. Or else!"

Pinchley looks both pleased and abashed. "I'll stay with you for a while, Flipsydaisy. But you have to throw a memorial bash for Yampa."

"*Mais oui,*" says Flipsydaisy. "I love parties. We'll serve turg, and flub, and burt, and gub."

"Szep foods," says Pinchley, glancing over Zoe. "I'm gonna say yes to Flipsydaisy. Gonna send you three off on your own." Saying this, he looks a little lost.

"Can't you come as far as the smokestack?" Zoe pleads. "How do we know it's safe?"

"It's been unused for years," says Flipsydaisy. "Ever since we switched to dark energy. You don't need more help." Flipsydaisy plants a proprietary kiss on Pinchley's cheek. "Let's be on our way, weary wanderer mine. By now the fracas in the central square is done."

Pinchley pauses for a time, looking at Zoe, Villy, and Scud. He seems misty and woebegone. "Hard to say this particular goodbye," he finally gets out. "Losing Yampa has me wobbly on my pins. We had a good run, didn't we, gang? Now go and save the frikkin world." He lays his hand on each of them, one at a time. Zoe shivers to feel the Szep's rangy, outsider vibes. It may well be the last time she sees him.

"Can I have your tool belt?" Villy asks Pinchley.

"Not hardly," says the skinny Szep. "You twisty enough on your own, Vill. You'll do fine."

"And what about the saucers patrolling Szep City?" worries Scud. "They'll nab us when we come out of the stack."

"It'll work out," says Pinchley. "Like we been sayin'— you're natural-born heroes. Boogie on."

And then Pinchley and Flipsydaisy are up the spiral stairs and out the hatch, leaving Zoe, Villy, and Scud alone with the sleeping Lady Filippa.

zeppelin

villy

So here's the three kids in the Lady's cellar. Villy feels jangled and afraid, though he doesn't like to admit it. He embraces Zoe for comfort. Meanwhile Scud's poking around, hoping to find something valuable in the junk, using his wand's crystal like a flashlight, augmenting the walls' patchy glow.

Villy likes having Zoe in his arms, even down here, even a million miles from home. His ragged breathing slows and falls into its familiar rhythm. Thanks to their guitars, they've still got a certain amount of teep. But talking matters.

"You okay?" Zoe murmurs.

"I feel like it's too much," says Villy. "And we can't do it."

"We have to," says Zoe. "But right now, yeah, I miss Mom and my safe room at home."

"And if we ever get back to Los Perros, we'll be sick of it right away," says Villy.

"I know," says Zoe, with the hint of a smile in her voice. "We're terrible."

"Our big adventure," says Villy, his spirits slowly rising. "It's not over yet. And right now, I'd like to find some real food. And a safe place to sleep. So tired."

"Me too," says Zoe. "We haven't stopped since the stratocast. But I'm never eating again, not after Lady Filippa's canapes. Why did she and Flipsydaisy mess with us like that?"

"For laughs?" says Villy. "We could get even. We could, like, *pop* Lady Filippa. While she's asleep. Jump up and down on her."

"Don't even," says Zoe. "So awful." She straightens up, does a theatrical groan, and raises a loosely clenched fist. "Onward."

"Yes," says Villy.

"The mission," says Zoe, still trying to crank herself up. "The quest." She plays a tiny *deedle-deedle* on her guitar.

"Look what I found," says Scud, walking over. He shines the tip of his wand on something like a dark walnut shell. The shell has a membranous hinge on one side, and when Scud opens it, the light reveals a half-teaspoon of minute, glittering polyhedra within, no two of them the same color.

"Like teensy gems," exclaims Zoe. "The nutshell is a treasure chest. I'd love to make those little things into jewelry."

"I'm keeping the nutshell," says Scud. "I'm bringing it home."

"How did you find it?" asks Villy. "On your own?"

"Sure, on my own," says Scud. "Nobody else is here. What do you mean?"

"Maybe Skzx the wand guided you to the shell," says Villy. "Skzx is an intelligent Aristo larva who lives inside you. And all the time she's teeping to you, even when you don't notice. Maybe there's some kinky Aristo motive for wanting you to bring that nutshell back to Earth."

"How about it, Skzx?" goes Scud, listening into himself. His eyes go blank and his lips twitch. And then he's back. He sighs. "You're right, Villy. Skzx didn't want to tell me, but she did in fact steer me towards the walnut. Seems the little gems are Aristo eggs. She wanted them to be a surprise, later on in Los Perros."

"Some surprise," says Villy. "Hundreds of aliens hatching in our hometown."

Zoe leans over, stares directly into Scud's eyes and speaks very slowly. "Don't. Bring. Them. Home."

Scud sighs and sets the nutshell on the floor. His wand throws an angry wriggle into Scud's arm, but the nutshell stays on the ground.

"While we're at it," continues Zoe, "What's going to happen to your friendly Aristo larva wand after the cosmic beatdown?"

Again, Scud looks into himself. "Skzx says she'll emerge—either as a larva or maybe as a pupa, depending how far along she is—and then she'll tunnel from Earth to Van Cott and then fly a million miles back to Szep City. She wants to reach adulthood here. Like her dad and mom."

"Hold on," says Villy. "Assuming Skzx is so eager to help us, why didn't she just fly to us in the first place? Then we wouldn't have had to drive a million miles."

"I already thought of that of that myself," says Scud, an odd expression on his face. A mixture of pride and shyness. "But I wasn't going to say anything. Too much like bragging. Thing is, Skzx didn't want to work with just anyone. She wanted to partner with someone special. Someone who could handle a million mile road trip. Someone like me."

"Good for you," Villy tells his kid brother, refraining from taking any credit for himself. "And I mean that, Scud. You've been outstanding. It's very cool if Skzx flies home when she's done. We're good to go." Villy pauses. "Um —where was it that Flipsydaisy told us to go next?"

"Tunnel, anyone?" says Zoe, brightly holding up her forefinger like she's proposing a parlor game.

"Tunnel to the stack," echoes Villy. "Right. Mile-high stack to the sky."

"I'll lead," says Scud, proudly bustling around. "Me and my wand." He heads towards the low arch.

"Do it, bro," says Villy. He takes Zoe's hand. She's his woman, he's her man. They belong together. Romance for real.

The tunnel is a connected series of cellars mixed with arched culverts and cobblestone passageways. The walls are mostly dark, with occasional streaks of glowing fungus. Side alleys lead into alternate underbellies, but Scud never wavers from his route.

Along the way, they encounter some really big rats— knee-high, Szep City rats that walk on their hind legs. They wear little tassled caps and embroidered jackets, and they even carry walking-sticks, some of them. Zoe and Villy are fascinated by the rat people and want to meet them, but Scud hurries their party on.

"I think some of the rats are following us," Zoe says to Villy after a while. "Hear them squeaking?"

"I bet they're friendly," says Villy. "They smell kind of good. A tingly musk. It makes me feel lively. Remember when Yampa sprayed that smell in the car?"

"We'll win the rats over," says Zoe, patting her guitar. It sheds a few notes, and the unseen rats mimic the sound with chirps. "Music charms the savage beasts."

"If the rats come after us in a bad way, we'll run like hell," says Villy. "That's Plan B." Villy always likes to talk about having a Plan B. It makes him feel competent and organized.

Soon he notices a growing draft, a breeze blowing at his back and towards their as yet unseen destination. And then they step through a final arch and space opens up. It's night, so there's no light, but Villy can sense vastness. The stillness, the reverberant echoes, and the upward flow of air.

Scud sets his wand to beaming like a flashlight, and yes, they're inside a titanic abandoned smokestack, with sandy ground underfoot. The stack is several hundred yards across down here, tapering to a smaller diameter as it rises—how far? At least a mile. Here at the bottom, the walls curve very strongly out, bracing themselves against the soil.

Looking back at the arch they came through, Villy sees glints of yellow in the tunnel darkness. The eyes of the rat people. Scud sees the glints too and he's scared.

"I say we float up the stack right away," goes Scud. "Goob-goob will take care of us up there. Like we're going to heaven."

"You sound like a brainwashed religious nut," says Zoe. "And even if you're right, I don't feature floating around in the sky just now. What if there's saucers? I'm so tired and hungry I can hardly think."

"And how would we float up the stack anyway?" asks Villy. "Can your wand levitate?"

Scud's quiet for a minute. "Skzx says she can levitate herself," he finally reports. "But she's not strong enough to lift us. It would be too much trouble. Also, she's hungry."

"I thought she'd be siphoning nourishment off you," says Zoe. "Like a baby inside her mother. I thought she didn't have to eat."

"Not much in me to siphon," says Scud. "I'm starving, same as you." He shrugs. "So fine, we spend the night down here. We can lie on the sand over by the slanting wall where it's low. We can take turns standing guard against the rats. I can use the wand to zap them if they come close."

"Those cute rats don't *have* to be our enemies," says Zoe. "And I bet we can ask for food! I'll be a Pied Piper with my guitar, Villy. I'll charm the rats in their darling little coats—and they'll bring us a feast."

"Oh *right*," says doubting Scud.

"Shut your crack," goes Villy. It's something he says to his younger brother a lot. Probably too often. Scud looks hurt. "Sorry," adds Villy. "It's just that I'm starving to death. Dim your light so the rat people aren't scared. Make it yellow and cozy."

So Scud does that, and Zoe leans over her guitar, lightly fingering a tune like a nursery rhyme, very thin and sweet. Villy joins in, adding frills and trills. And here come the rats, ten, twenty, fifty of them, skittish and ready to run away, but drawn by the delicate music.

Two rats hold hands—or paws—and begin dancing to the tune's beat. A boy rat in an embroidered shirt, and a girl rat in a dirndl. Their furry little legs rise and fall in the figures of their dance. Another pair joins, and another, and soon there's a whole circle of rat people disporting themselves, their feet light on the soft sand. Scud is softly beating time with his wand.

Villy stops playing and lets Zoe carry the tune alone. "*Nyum nyum*," he calls to the rats. He pats his stomach and makes chewing motions. Mimes putting things in his mouth. Ten rats lean their heads together, squeaking away, and they scamper off. By the time Zoe segues to the next tune, the ten rats are back, along with some new recruits. They're carrying bundles. The air fills with the rats' pleasantly musky smell.

Gaily squeaking, the rats lay out cloths and bedeck them with nuts, berries, tiny loaves of bread, and even some little wheels of yellow cheese. And this isn't just a tasting sample—the rats are really getting into it, with swarms of them coming forth with more food. A banquet. When the three kids sit down and tuck in, there's more than they can eat.

Zoe has stopped playing for now, but to maintain the convivial mood, Villy continues fingering notes on his Flying Vee—even while he's gobbling handfuls of those tasty little breads and cheeses, and wetting his whistle with bunches of berries like red currants. One music-loving rat takes a perch on the neck of Villy's guitar and scoots across the frets. Undaunted, Villy works the slide-guitar sound into his tune.

Villy, Zoe, and Scud try to get some teep going with the rat people, but that's not happening. And it's no use trying to winnow meaning from their squeaks. They're simple folk, these Szep City rats. Eating and dancing and tail-waving—that's as far as it goes, although at the end of the party, the little people manage to sing thirty-seven choruses of Villy and Zoe's final tune, which is, naturally, "Three Blind Mice."

"So now we quit while we're ahead," says Villy, laying down his guitar. Zoe thanks the rat people with effusive curtsies and bows. The rats gather up their possessions, and Scud urges them on their way by firing off a few airbursts from his wand. Looks like balls from a Roman candle, almost.

Villy and Zoe make themselves a comfortable hollow in the sand next to the slanting wall where the gigantic smokestack meets the ground. Scud politely beds down some hundred feet away from them, and it's lights out.

Tired though they are, Villy and Zoe have some energy from breathing the attar of the Szep City rats, and from all that cute doll-sized food. Zoe's teep is in fact torrid.

"Honeymoon," she whispers in Villy's ear.

Villy doesn't mind the wedding reference. If it came right down to it, he'd be glad to marry Zoe. Not that there's any immediate social pressure. They're a million miles from home. Also, Villy has that pocketful of condoms, so no worries about pregnancy. With his guitar to hand, he teeps all this to Zoe.

She purrs and closes in. They have glorious sex and conk out—naked and nestled tight together. They're tired enough that they sleep straight through the night. When Villy wakes, it's light. He raises his head to make sure his and Zoe's guitars are still there. Zoe, still in his arms, smells like nectar. Hooray for love.

Scud is standing out in the big patch of sand, a hundred yards off. He's holding his hand in the air with his wand Skzx sticking out—he's like a teen wizard summoning a dragon. Villy turns his head to the side so he can see up. High, high, high above them, the pale disk of the smokestack's vent glows with light of the sky. Something's up there—far and wee.

"Hi, lover boy." Zoe smiles at Villy. She's so cute—no, more than cute. Voluptuous. Gorgeous. He hugs and kisses her for a while. Eventually they sit up and start assembling their clothes.

At this point Scud starts jumping up and down, whooping at the sky. Something's landing.

"Is that a blimp?" Zoe asks Villy. "A zeppelin?"

"Gotta be an adult Aristo," says Villy. "Look, it's got tiny wings. And a bunch of tentacles at the back end. It figures Scud's wand would attract an adult Aristo. What with the wand being an Aristo larva."

"Totes," is Zoe's brief response. Like she's reluctant to get back into the heroic-quest routine. Playing it cool for another minute. Villy likes it when Zoe acts like that. Not letting herself be stampeded. "Check *this*," she goes, and produces a handful of about a hundred rat-baked bread-loaves that she'd stashed in her pocket. Each loaf is the size of a vitamin pill. They're fresh and delicious. Yeasty and crunchy.

The great Aristo zeppelin-creature lands next to Scud, fluttering his comically small bat wings and gesturing with his tentacles. He's teeping with Scud. He has half a dozen eyes scattered across his body like polka dots—not unlike Lady Filippa. The Aristo's eyes are big, with black pupils and yellow irises. For sure he sees Villy and Zoe too.

"Come on!" Scud screams to Villy, his voice shrill and cracking with excitement. Weird receding echoes off the high, cylindrical walls. *Come on, come on, come on!*

"Can yew understand what that thar boy is a-sayin?" drawls Zoe.

"Blub blub," goes Villy.

Cheerful and moving slow, the lovers finish dressing, then amble over to Scud and the Aristo, carrying their guitars.

"His name is Stolo," calls Scud as they draw near. "Stolo, this is my brother Villy and his friend Zoe."

"Uneasy," Zoe murmurs to Villy as she assesses the size of the Aristo. It's about 150 feet long, a miniature version of the classic *Hindenburg*, pointed on one end and blunt on the other. With tentacles on the blunt end.

The creature's body is translucent, ribbed, and filled with gas. Villy can see twisty intestines within, and feathery gills, plus all the usual kinds of shaped and rounded organs, everything bobbling around inside Stolo's taut hide.

Strange and powerful teep emanates from Stolo—an alien collage of color, scent, and sound. Basically, Stolo is urging them to ride on him.

"I don't like the tentacles," Zoe tells Villy. "You just know there's a nasty-ass killer beak in the midst of that squid-bunch bouquet."

"We won't go near that particular spot," says Villy. "We'll be sitting on top. Like on the back of an elephant."

"Sitting in a howdah," says Zoe.

"You're losing me there, Zee."

"The little benches they used to put on Indian elephants?" says Zoe. "Those were howdahs."

By now they're close enough to smell Stolo. A fishy odor, mixed with lavender and wax and latex rubber. The giant Aristo makes a wet blatting noise.

"That's his voice," says Scud. "He says he's glad to meet you. He'll fold a special wrinkle for us on to sit in. He says we should hurry. He doesn't want them to catch us on the ground."

"*Them?*" goes Zoe.

"Just hurry," says Scud.

"Where's he gonna take us?" she asks.

"To Goob-goob," says Scud.

Villy hears a sharp crack and a bullet tears past, ripping at the air. Shit. It's a party of the local Szep City zombies. Boiling out of the tunnel entrance at the base of the stack—twenty or thirty glassy-eyed slaves, armed with rifles and rayguns.

Stolo says something—that is, he makes another fartlike noise—and then, quick as a flash, he wraps three tentacles around the kids, one tentacle for each, and tucks them into a crease on his back. They rise like a helium balloon.

The belligerent saucer followers keep shooting at them, but Stolo's leathery underside is impervious to their bullets and rays. And then Stolo and his riders are a third of the way up the mile-high stack. Stolo isn't exactly using his little wings to fly—it's more like he's levitating, and he braces his wings against the air to steer. They're rising so fast that Villy has to yawn and waggle his jaw to equalize the pressure in his ears. Scud's exultant, and Zoe's laughing with relief.

The air cools as they continue to climb. An odd, wavering tone sounds from the top of the stack. As if a giant were blowing across a bottle. When they actually drift out the top, they encounter a howling, gale-force wind. The rushing storm separates them from that vast, intricate cloud the locals call Sky Castle. The great cloud's bottom is another thousand feet above them, with its underside ruffled and torn by the frigid blast. The gale is a thousand-mile-wide sheet, an interface zone.

Stolo is flying with his pointed end in front and his tentacles in the rear. His body vibrates in the wind—he bucks and shudders—and it feels like he might begin a wild tumble any time. Yet Stolo's teep indicates that he's not alarmed by that prospect. His body is designed to weather the tumultuous ascent through the gale to the Sky Castle.

Borne by the fierce wind, they're rushing along at several hundred miles per hour. Stolo plies his tiny bat wings, tweaking their pitch, roll, and yaw. All the while he's flexing the airfoil of his bulky body, steadily working his way closer to the Sky Castle cloud above.

Villy, Zoe, and Scud keep their legs tucked under the crease in Stolo's skin. Since they're moving with the wind, they don't even feel it that much. They're as safe and secure as if they're sitting in a bed. Or maybe not. A particularly strong gust flips Stolo to a vertical position, with his pointy front end down. If he was a boat you'd say he was pitchpoling, that is, about to do a flip.

The Aristo seems unconcerned. Perhaps he's even doing this on purpose. Villy picks up an odd image from the living zeppelin's mind. A man in a boat on a lake—fishing? In what way does this image apply?

Zoe doesn't like that Stolo's about to pitchpole. She's screaming they're about to die. Scud is catatonic with fear. Stolo doesn't care. He gives his wings a reckless twitch that sends them into full tumble mode. They flip, roll, and spin. The air currents have turned vicious. Scud and Zoe are hanging on for dear life.

But Villy—Mr. Surf King, Mr. Wise Man of Los Perros, Mr. Debonair—Villy loses his grip and—oh no, this can't be—he jolts out of his seat, bumps along Stolo's ridged hide, skids across the bulging cornea of one of the leviathan's eyes, fails to catch hold of Stolo's ragged wing—and goes into frikkin freefall, leaving his guitar with Zoe and Scud.

He's over a mile above Szep City, which stretches out beneath him as far as he can see. His one bit of luck: the wind is so insanely strong that, rather than falling, he's skimming along horizontally, bowling along like wind-blown trash, still at the same level as Stolo. And Stolo is in teep contact with him.

Gathering his meager wits, Villy surfs the wind instead of fighting it, yes, he's riding the gale, stabilizing himself with leaping-salmon-type bends of his body, keeping his arms at his sides, controlling his motion with subtle, fin-like movements of his hands. This is working, kind of, but the air is so brutally cold that Villy's going to be dead pretty soon.

That's when three flying saucers launch an attack. Weirdly calm about this, Stolo calls Villy's attention to the spot far below where the evil trio are rising from the Szep City Saucer Hall far. They're moving quite fast.

Villy remembers Flipsydaisy saying that the Aristos are good at killing saucers. But evidently their three approaching foes are willing to take a risk. Perhaps they're frantically excited by the chance to kill the freefalling Villy. They fire pale-yellow zap beams as they come, aiming some of the rays at Stolo and his riders, but most of them at Villy.

Via Stolo's teep, Villy can overhear that Zoe and Scud are imploring Stolo to pick Villy up before it's too late. But Stolo doesn't want to. Not yet. And then Villy picks up another of those odd fisherman thoughts from the alien zeppelin. It's an image of an angler tossing bait off his boat to attract large fish from the deeps. What do they call that again? *Chumming the water*. Villy is chum. A saucer ray sizzles past his feet, close enough that he feels the heat.

And now Stolo finally prepares to makes his move. With crafty gestures of his wings, the Aristo stabilizes his careening progress. Deeply focused and in a state of Zen-like calm, Stolo aims his tentacles. A sweeping grim-reaper saucer ray is about to put the quietus on Villy. With thoughtful aplomb, Stolo projects a fusillade of quick, efficient blasts from his tentacle tips and—*thip thip thip*—the three importunate saucers are dead, charred meat, and their grim-reaper rays are no more.

Moving with alacrity, Stolo swoops down to gather the dead saucers before they can drop from the sky. He seizes the corpses with his tentacles and—typical behavior for mappyworld—he devours them with his great, curved beak. Just like Lady Filippa with the Tollah dog. One, two, three.

Sated and pleased, Stolo spreads his tentacles with a flourish. Scud and Zoe cheer, their voices tiny in the roaring wind. Villy's teeth are chattering very hard. He's feeling bitter. Stolo pitched him loose on purpose, just to attract those tasty saucers. A stiff price to pay for a ride to Cloud Castle.

The now-genial zeppelin angles over to intersect Villy's path. Zoe reaches out and catches hold of Villy's ankle. She pulls him aboard and nestles him into the skin fold with her and Scud. She showers kisses on his face. His heart pumps warmth once again.

By way of celebrating Villy's rescue, Scud beams his wand's light through Solo's translucent skin and into the Aristo's great, airy body—illuminating the creature like a lantern. Perhaps there's some goading flow of dark energy from Scud's wand, or perhaps the meal of three saucers has strengthened the Aristo, or perhaps it's just that he's through fishing for saucers, but now at last Stolo rises the rest of the way through the layer of racing winds.

And so they enter the interior of Sky Castle, the thundercloud that's more than a thousand miles tall.

flat cow

Sky Castle isn't a regular cloud—it's neither haze nor fog nor mist. It's like a swarm of fireflies or a nest of grids or, more strictly speaking, like a 3D moiré. Not that anyone but Zoe Snapp would say that. Zoe is most excellent at seeing patterns.

All her life she's been fascinated by moiré patterns, the visual effects you get when, say, two window screens or two chain-link fences overlap each other. A fluid series of lobed interference-fringes emerges, light-show lop-lops that change as you move. What you'd call a 2D moiré. Old-school op-artists made moiré canvases from sets of bold stripes. Getting physical, textile designers can mash grooves into a fabric, not quite parallel to the cloth's ridges, and a flowing 2D moiré effect emerges—quite the high-end craze during Zoe's junior year. Too expensive to buy moiré dresses new, but Zoe made her own bitchin moiré ensemble by taking a pair of scissors to an upscale cocktail frock she bagged in a thrift shop. DIY forever.

Zoe has found that, once in a while, her mind creates moirés on its own. And sometimes when she's zoning out in her bedroom—deeply meditative or musical or bored or even high—she can see *three-dimensional* moirés. They're pale purple or even ultraviolet patterns, lucid and improbable as air. A bit like the presence of Goob-goob.

As Zoe sees it, the underlying ingredient for a 3D moiré is a pair of 3D grids that fill a whole room. These imagined grids might be, like, 3D graph paper, or miniaturized wire-frame models of cities, or glass honeycombs, or fine-meshed jungle-gyms for ants.

The two overlapping structures are ever so slightly out of phase with each other—and the interference patterns form the glorious, yummy 3D moirés. When Zoe gets her freak on, the melting, merging 3D moirés caper in her room like the luminous blub-fish of the Mariana Trench.

And when the visions get the best, Zoe starts to believe that she *herself* is a 3D moiré. Jiggly layers of Hilbert space yes-no quantum fields, right? Whatevsky. If you want fuller details—hey, go talk to a physics teacher or, if all else fails, Scud Antwerpen.

Anyway, up here in her big adventure with Villy, mounted atop a living zeppelin, Zoe sees that the Sky Castle is filled with—*ta-daah!*—3D moirés. Big ones, and wilder than what she used to see in her goth girl bedroom. She sees a striped tiger whose furry back is a mountain range. A marble statue of—how'd that happen?—Pinchley and Yampa. And, wow, a giant pencil wearing glasses on her perky sharp nose, and her pink eraser down low. And here comes a San Jose-sized locomotive, mutating out from the other moirés. The locomotive has dials on valves on tubes feeding into carburetors that power gears and cams pumping the pushy phallic connecting rods that drive the moiré juggernaut's adamantine wheels.

All these intricate apparitions are woven from the interplay between two cosmic meshes within the Sky Castle cloud. Black/white, one/many, male/female, plus/minus, raw/cooked, rough/smooth—the *names* of the two sides are illusion. The interplay is what matters.

"*Vive la différence*," Zoe gaily says to Villy. "Hither the yin, yonder the yang."

"And listen to the sounds," goes Villy, cocking his head. The space of Sky Castle is reverberating like a cosmic cathedral with two competing pipe organs, ever so slightly out of tune with each other. The dissonance produces what acousticians call *beats*, meaning that the two dense lines of melody are enhancing or cancelling each other, making chaotic blips and gaps that are a—

"Sonic moiré," goes Zoe, right on cue. Of *course* she knows what Villy's thinking. It's a teep-heavy zone. *And* they're still holding their magic guitars.

A polychrome kite drifts past, or no, it's a verdigris bronze Buddha with a million arms, or no, it's a brittle deep-sea starfish. The moiré shapes are dark, or flashy, or matte, or iridescent, with every attribute eternally subject to change.

"Where's Goob-goob?" asks Scud, peering around like a hick tourist.

By way of response, Stolo blats one of his wet blubs, then tweaks his ballast by laying a monstrous turd.

Oh, come on guys, isn't that a little too . . .

Wait, whose thought is that?

They rise through the Sky Castle matrix at an ominously increasing rate of speed. The meshes and their attendant moirés grow yellower, brighter, and then—

"That's her now," says Zoe. "Ready, boys?"

It's the same figure Zoe saw in the Harmony basin, when she was nearly dying, and she had that vision of a high school guidance counselor. Well, it's not *obviously* the same figure. But Zoe knows.

This manifestation of Goob-goob is a 3D moiré shaped like a stairstep-sided Mexican ziggurat-pyramid, a stone jungle ruin. The pyramidal bulk has the look of a sculptured Mayan head, with features etched across the steps by thick vines and weathered grooves. Some eyes, a nose, and a few mouths. One mouth is a fancy arch in Goob-goob's base.

The nearest side of the ziggurat wears a multi-angular Mayan headdress. Thick, snaky locks of graven hair merge into a stone topknot hair bun with a peculiar glow.

The ziggurat moiré wobbles in welcome, a gesture like a full-body wink. Tropical feathers sprout from the plinths. A truckload of merry skeletons cascades down Goob-goob's side, leaving bones in the steps. Zoe braces herself. *Be strong*.

"Zoe, Villy, Scud," intones the goddess. A smell of musk and jasmine and roast meat. The voice emanates from her topknot—but it's not a sound, it's teep. "I sent Pinchley and Yampa to enlist you. You'll trap and destroy Groon," says Goob-goob. "You'll end the plague of leech saucers."

"Yes, fine," says Zoe evenly "Anything if we can go home." She feels a visceral longing for her simple old life. She wouldn't have expected that. This trip has been strange and wonderful beyond imagining, but—she's due for some chillax.

"Are you ready for battle?" presses Goob-goob.

"I'd say we're done with basic training, right?" says Zoe. "Scud has his Aristo wand. Villy and I have our magic guitars. We trapped and killed a Tollah dog."

"Yes, yes, the guitars and Skzx the wand," says Goob-goob. "You should thank me. Be like Stolo."

The three kids are still perched on Stolo, by the way. He's turned himself around so his blunt end faces the ziggurat. He's got his tentacles spread in worshipful ecstasy, and his curved beak is wide upon—like he's swallowing the light from Goob-goob's topknot. Zoe thinks also of a weathered man in a hot shower—his first shower in many moons.

"I'm thankful, sure," says Zoe. "But I'm not feeling the let's-worship-Goob-goob thing. You've been gaming us pretty hard." Somehow, even here, Zoe finds finding the courage to say what she thinks.

Villy chimes in. "I think you're an alien from another dimension," he tells Goob-goob. "Not really a god. And the Aristos are alien parasites who rode in on you. Divine lice." Villy raises his voice. "No way we have to be your lice, too, Goob-goob. Fine, we'll run your scam or revenge or power-grab on Groon, whatever it is. Und, ja boss, ve'll be wery grateful if ve get rid of zaucers. But don't expect us to hymn your name."

"Won't be raising our cracked, humble voices in praise," adds Zoe.

"Not how we are," concludes Villy.

Scud starts laughing. He likes it when his big brother is rude to the authorities. And then, as usual, Scud goes too far. He yells a curse and gives Goob-goob the finger.

"Don't be angry with the boy," Zoe quickly says to Goob-goob.

"I accept you three as you are," says Goob-goob. "No aspect of this, my world, is odious to me."

"Odious," parrots Scud, probably on the point of cracking a vulgar joke.

"*You*," says Goob-goob, suddenly turning all her attention on the boy. A fierce eye-beam of light beams onto Scud's face. "Aren't you forgetting something?"

"Huh?" goes Scud, his voice turning to cracking squeak.

"My present?" says Goob-goob. "Your offering to me?"

"Oh, right, yeah, the rest of the caraway seeds, you bet," says Scud, hastily fumbling the jar out of his pants pocket.

Goob-goob's eye-beam twitches. The caraway seeds rise from the jar to the top of the ziggurat and go into orbit around Goob-goob's topknot.

"Servant, well done," intones Goob-goob. "Your provident benison will amplify the efficacy of my flat cow, Yulia. She's four-dimensional, and she's a part of me."

"Flat cow?" goes Scud, who has no idea what's going on. "Yulia?"

Scud looks over at Zoe, who favors him with a calming gesture and a smile. She's filled with a sense of peace because Goob-goob has just now teeped a secret message into her head. An infusion of wisdom from the stone topknot. It's a detailed plan for defeating Groon and the saucers. At least that's what Zoe *thinks* the message is. But it immediately percolates down into her subconscious before she can fully examine it. To be read later. Okay, fine. Transmission received and archived.

Meanwhile Goob-goob is on to her next topic. "Walk through the door now," she says. "All three of you."

"Okay," says Zoe. At this point, she's got no better option than to trust this god or super-alien or whatever she is. And thanks to that heavy teep message, whatever it was actually about, she kind of likes Goob-goob now. She takes Scud and Villy by the hands. "Okay to get off the blimp?" she asks the brothers.

"I'm ready," says Villy.

The three of them slide down the side of the living zeppelin, landing on a gentle slope of moiré cloud that feels reasonably solid—even though Zoe was half-worried they might fall right through it and tumble wildly screaming for miles, going *splat* onto a Szep City street.

Not, at this point, that dying would matter all that much. But wait, that's not a newly-energized-Zoe thought, it's a secretly-depressive-Villy thought that's been teep-moiréd atop Zoe's stream of consciousness. Scud thoughts are in her head as well—for instance, she's picking up a lustful image of Nunu the sexy flying saucer with her rim cocked at a randy let's-do-it angle. Ick. Goob-goob is a mirror that's absorbing and shuffling and reflecting all of their thoughts. Way teepy.

At this point Zoe hears the sound of some heavy farm-type animal munching food atop the Goog-goob ziggurat. Yulia the flat cow is eating the caraways? Zoe can't see that high because she's down near the arched door or mouth at the bottom of the pyramid.

The door is bordered by bas-reliefs of Mayan scenes—women grinding corn, men stabbing each other, children playing with bones, and gods accepting obeisances from squid-zeppelins. The images flicker with a moiré shimmer, creating a lightweight animation effect so the glyphs seem to bop back and forth. As for the freaky shadows and bright flickers visible through the door in the base of the pyramid—

"I feel an air current flowing into that door," observes Villy.

"I'm hoping the door is a teleportation gate," says Scud.

"For some reason I'm thinking of a Bible story," says Zoe.

"You?" goes Villy. "*Bible?*"

"Well, this is that type of setting," goes Zoe. "What with Goob-goob being like a god. In this one Bible story, Shadrach, Meshach, and Abednego are pious youths who refuse to worship King Nebuchadnezzar. And he throws them into a fiery furnace. So maybe this scene is like that. Us three about to enter an annihilating blast of dark energy."

"We shouldn't go through that door," says Scud very quickly.

"Ah, but Shadrach, Meshach, and Abednego weren't harmed by the furnace," says Zoe. Where is she getting this stuff? She sounds like a prize pupil Sunday-schooler. "Shadrach, Meshach, and Abednego walked freely among the flames, accompanied by a mysterious fourth figure."

Maybe Goob-goob has teep-triggered this latent memory as a subtle message?

Right about then a heavy, meaty shape slams into Scud's back, knocking him off his feet. Rebounding, the hairy form strikes Villy in the stomach, then flops against Zoe's side, sending her reeling. The boneless disk of muscle seems conscious, in a rudimentary way. Like an over-friendly pet.

"It's the flat cow!" cries Scud. "Yulia!"

Indeed, the creature smells like a cow, and she's mooing, and her hide has short cream-colored hair with three large brown spots. A brindle flat cow. Not that she's *shaped* like a cow. She's a big, flattish disk, thicker in the middle. Like, um, a flying saucer. No horns, no udder, no mouth. She does have a pair of dark brown eyes, and a cow-like tail. The tail is long and sturdy. Rather than having a tassel at the end, it just kind of stops, as if disappearing into another dimension.

"What do you want with us?" Zoe asks the flat cow.

Yulia flips herself off the ground and continues flexing her body against the kids, urgently mooing. Zoe quickly realizes the flat cow is *herding* them through that door they're scared of. And it's hard for Zoe to form any plan of resistance because everything in her head is so—muddled. It's that same thing she had a minute ago, with Villy's and Scud's thoughts blending into hers. What *is* Yulia?

"The fourth figure from the fiery furnace," says Scud, maybe out loud, or maybe in Zoe's head. Or maybe it's Goob-goob that says it.

And by now Zoe's been noodged through that frikkin door. The first one to go. "Not a furnace," she calls to the others, trying to sound upbeat. "More like a big closet."

Scud and Villy come staggering after her, off-balance, against their will. Instantly a trapdoor opens beneath their feet. The flat cow's done a number on them.

Next thing Zoe knows, the kids are in freefall, well clear of Goob-goob, tumbling pell-mell through the misty moiré of Sky Castle. Somehow Villy and Zoe still have their guitars—it's almost like the living instruments are clinging to them. And Yulia the flat cow is with them too, still mooing, although not in an agitated way. And just when Zoe feels she might relax for a second and catch her breath—*whoops*, they've reached the savagely speedy ocean of air that forms the lower boundary to Sky Castle.

"It's that same gale we were in before!" yells Zoe, even though she doubts the boys can hear her. The vagaries of the winds have positioned them at some distance behind her.

But Yulia is close by Zoe's side, eyes bright, and with her tail in motion, sometimes short, sometimes long, and with its tip never in view. Zoe gets atop the flat brindle cow and rides her, banking the disk, surfing the sky. And then, without too much trouble, she picks up the cheerful Villy.

"I like it when the worst thing possible happens," he says. "Then I can relax."

"Lie still on Yulia's back and grab two tufts of her hair," orders Zoe.

Then they get Scud, and they settle in with Zoe on the right, Villy in the middle, and Scud on the left. The visible section of Yulia's tail is outstretched like a pennant, although there's no telling about the invisible tip of the tail.

"I don't get it," says Scud. "Why a flat cow?" He's grasping for the logic of their situation.

"Moo spelled backwards is Om," goes Villy.

Zoe doesn't waste time on that. "I'm thinking this storm doesn't go far. It's wide and diffuse. It's not a focused jet stream like Groon blows. We'll need to get into Groon's stream if we want to ride to New Eden."

"We'll hit it soon," declares Villy. "As soon as we drift over to the Pit basin."

"But I'm worried about the saucers in the jet stream," says Zoe.

"Uh-oh, I see them now," goes Villy, still obscurely amused, as if jolly over the cascade of disasters. "There's the ridge between Szep City and the Pit, right? And the little things in the air after the ridge? Shiny specks, no two of them the same?"

"The saucers in Groon's double jet stream," says Scud. "This is bad. The saucers didn't notice us in the Pit because we were inside the whale and you guys were playing that crappy Groon bagpipe music. But if we go and get in tight with the saucers, riding down their private flyway—they'll slaughter us. I wish Nunu was here."

"As if she would help us," says Villy.

"I'm the father of her children," goes Scud.

"Oh please," says Zoe. "Can we not talk about that? So vile."

"Right now, this flat cow is the only friend we've got,"

Villy tells Scud. "Yulia. Think about *her*, okay? Think hard." He pats the flat cow's back.

Scud switches to his tedious logic mode. "Suppose Goob-goob did mean for Yulia to be like the fourth figure in the fiery furnace. If so, she's here to save us. How? First of all, she can blend in with the saucers. The way she looks, she'll be lost in the crowd. So therefore—" Scud breaks off, like he's repelled by his impending conclusion.

"So therefore we hide inside Yulia!" cries Zoe.

"*Muur*," goes Yulia. It's a rich, warm, friendly moo. As Zoe has already noticed, the tail is odd— it doesn't actually have a fixed tip. It just kind of disappears at the end. In any case, the flat cow now lengthens the visible section of her tail, as if reeling more of it in from hyperspace. A loop of the tail slaps against Zoe's right hand. Zoe takes the hint and pulls. And, ah yes, it seems Yulia's body can open up along its right side. The near end of the cow tail acts like a zipper-pull on the edge of a change purse you might get as a souvenir of a visit to, say, El Zigurat Fabuloso de la Goob-goob. And Yulia is the purse.

Taking care not to be swept away by the wind, Zoe folds Yulia's unzipped upper flap to the left. Yulia's cavity is lined with smooth red skin like fine Morocco leather. Zoe scoots inside. Villy does the same.

"I'm not going in there," says Scud, all tense and ready to throw a fit.

"So die," snaps Villy. He starts pulling the flap over himself and Zoe, as if he's totally ready to sacrifice his brother. This could be bluff, like a tough love thing— but it comes across as stone harsh. For all Zoe knows,

Villy might not be kidding. She still doesn't quite get the brothers' relationship.

Like, with all their shared history, why can't Villy and Scud can't be nice to each other? Not that Villy's exactly *wrong* to pressure Scud. The Sky Castle gale has brought them to the slopes of the ridge between the two basins. And they'll be plowing into that jet stream of saucers in less than a minute. But they can't just *abandon* Scud.

So it's up to Zoe to be kind and noble, sigh. How deeply uncool. But someone's gotta do it. She grabs the unhappy Scud and tugs him into the leather pita pocket with her and Villy.

"Thanks," says Scud very softly. He's sniffling, nearly in tears. Zoe pats him on the shoulder and gives Villy a hard poke with her other hand. Why are men such dicks?

Zoe turns her thoughts away from the psychodrama between the Antwerpen brothers—and makes an effort to understand what's going on Yulia's mind. The flat cow is acting like a psychic mirror, a little like Goob-goob had been doing. At any given moment Yulia's mind seems like a blend of the minds of whoever she's with. Maybe it's a defensive tactic, a trick for disorienting anyone near her. If you teep into Yulia's shuffled mimicry, it's hard to maintain your own train of thought. But Yulia's deeper inner self remains opaque.

Be that as it may, Zoe manages to formulate and transmit a request to the flat cow. The kids have to be able to *see*, or they'll go crazy in here. Obligingly Yulia forms transparent patches on her upper and lower surfaces. So now Zoe and the boys can press their faces against the skin and gaze out at, wow, so many saucers, they're on every side.

Yes, they're already at the core of the jet stream. The saucers in here are riding the air current to New Eden. At some distance from them, the jet stream's outer layer flows the opposite way—back towards Groon.

The saucers around them are, variously, like sombreros, donuts, serpents, soup tureens, battleship turrets, and lemon meringue pies. Their tints include, to name only a few, crimson, chartreuse, magenta, gold, and ultramarine. Their color designs are solid, spotted, blended, striped, or zigzag. Their skin textures are metallic, slimy, leathery, scaly, warty, bristly, and more.

In their protean variability, the saucers remind Zoe of the 3D moirés in Sky Castle. But they're solid and they're alive. Some of them are newly spawned slave saucers from Groon, and others are larger slaves—veterans of numerous cycles through Groon's smeel-wringer. The slaves all have red eyes. But there's an occasional dark-eyed saucer in the mix as well. Jet stream freeloaders. Like footloose hoboes on a freight train. And the others don't much care.

So okay. Zoe and her friends are riding towards New Eden inside a flat cow that resembles a flying saucer, a flat cow with little windows in her skin. The kids do their best to settle in. Zoe and Villy still have their guitars, who nestle against them. It's a pleasant temperature inside Yulia, with a steady supply of air, and the smell's not bad, once you get used to it. Those peepholes make a huge difference. The three can entertain themselves by watching the saucers, and looking at the many basins slipping by.

Scud estimates their speed by counting how many of his pulse beats it takes for them cross a basin. Assuming that the basins are five thousand miles across and that his pulse rate is, say, a hundred, Scud comes up with a rough speed of a hundred thousand miles an hour. Same as they'd been doing on the way out, thanks to Zoe's and Villy's stratocasting. With any luck, they'll be in New Eden before dark.

At some point Villy starts caressing Zoe. They're squeezed in as close as it's possible to be, and Zoe has to admit it's rather yummy to be making out in the dark like this. After an hour of kissing, Villy wants to go all the way—but, so sorry, darling, that's a *little* out of the question—what with brother Scud so attentively silent nearby. Supposedly asleep. I bet.

Zoe's not expecting this long ride to go completely smoothly, not with the way their adventure's been running—and she's right. The attack comes five hours into the trip.

A large gray saucer begins nudging Yulia. He's a male, reminiscent of Nunu's Uncle Boldog, but he's not a slave saucer. His dark black eye betokens the fact that he's acting on his own. He nips at the flat cow's long tail with big, stony teeth. He bumps her from below and from above. And then, how horrible, a waggling tube emerges from the blocky, square-jawed saucer's underside.

A reproductive organ? A feeding siphon? Whatever function the unwelcome tube is meant to serve, the brutish monster thrusts it against Yulia's body, feeling around with the tip until—oh hell—he locates the coin-purse slit along Yulia's edge and manages to pry it open.

So now here's the throbbing tip of the gray saucer's grisly appendage—right inside the secret, cozy pouch where the three kids are riding out the trip. The chilly air of the jet stream is trickling in, and with it comes the eerie sound of Groon's incessant bagpipe music, part and parcel of the million mile flow.

There's no way of knowing what the cryptic Yulia thinks of the attack, nor can Zoe judge what retaliation Yulia might be capable of. For the moment the flat cow is simply running her mirror mind routine: reflecting a mixture of the aggro saucer's greed and lust, plus Zoe and Villy's passion curdling to horror, plus Scud's powerful rage over the intrusion.

Scud is the one who takes action. With a deft snap of his wrist, he extrudes his Aristo wand—and sends a jolt into their abusive attacker's probing tube. This is no mere warning tickle, no. Scud delivers a powerful burst of dark energy that reduces the intrusive organ to ashes. The rogue saucer flounders wildly in the air, loses control, and, trailing smoke from his charred flesh, spirals through the two-way saucer traffic and down to an ocean basin populated by sea monsters. A spiky kraken launches himself high into the air, swallows the gray saucer in mid-flight, and splashes hugely down. That'll teach him.

"You're an animal," Villy admiringly tells Scud.

"I saved us, and I get to pick where we land," says Scud, very smug. "It'll be Berky in New Eden. We'll check out the human colony there. And Nunu. And my saucerbabies. And maybe Maisie will be there too."

Villy's ready to argue about all this, but Zoe shuts him down. "Scud's right," she says. "It fits with the plan."

"What plan?"

"Goob-goob teeped me details at the Sky Castle," says Zoe. "The plans are deep in my head. I can feel them, but I can't reveal them. You should think of the plan as an egg that's not yet hatched."

"Lady Filippa teeped me the plans too," goes Scud.

"Oh, what bullshit," says Villy. "If you two know something, tell me."

"Everyone already knows the general idea," says Zoe. "There's good saucers and bad saucers. Groon is the master of the bad saucers. They're gearing up for an assault on Earth. We're going to stop them."

"Yeah yeah, but what else?" says Villy. "Drop the self-important secrecy routine, will you?"

"No, I'm not telling you," says Zoe. "Not with so many of Groon's slave saucers around. They might be teeping us."

"If they were teeping us, we'd be dead," says Villy. "These dumb-ass saucers, they didn't notice us at all when we were inside Groon. And I seriously doubt their teep can reach us inside this flat cow who might in fact be a saucer herself."

"I've decided Yulia isn't a saucer at all," puts in Scud. "None of the saucers are this weird."

"I can feel a big round thing inside her meat with my feet," says Villy. "I'm thinking that could be a saucer pearl. But maybe it's too soft. An internal organ. Tell us, Yulia, are you a saucer?" As usual, no answer.

"Main thing is that Yulia's our friend," says Scud. "And Goob-goob sent her to help us in the cosmic beatdown. Our final battle."

"There you go with the know-it-all routine again," says Villy. "Come on, guys. Stop holding out on me. Tell me what the frikkin beatdown will be like."

"Oh, all *right*," says Zoe. "The idea is to imprison Groon inside the unspace tunnel from mappyworld to ballyworld. Someone will pinch off the two ends while he's in there, and that way Groon is like a pig in a poke. Love that expression. It means a pig in a sack? And the sack will shrink. Or something."

"Oh," says Villy with mock calm. "I get it. *Someone* is going to pinch off the two ends of an unspace tunnel while there's a hostile bagpipe the size of Half Dome in there. Let me take a wild guess who the someone's gonna be."

"Villy, you should trust the judgment of your intellectual superiors," says Scud. "Let the brains lead the brawn." Zoe can't stop herself from laughing.

Villy gets mad. "Go to hell," he snaps. "Both of you."

The second half of the ride isn't as mellow as the first. Weary and anxious, the three kids don't talk. And Yulia makes no sound as she glides along the jet stream's current. In the prolonged silence, Zoe can hear the faint, ongoing strains of Groon's piping.

TWENTY-SEVEN

new eden

scud

Just like Scud hoped, Yulia lands in New Eden. It's where the Groon jet stream leads anyway, so it's just a matter of Yulia going with the flow. Scud stares down through Yulia's peepholes at the checkered farmland of New Eden. Much of it seems to be inhabited by the honest non-leeching faction of the saucer race. Scud sees hay fields and apple orchards, pig pens and cattle herds. His guess is that the saucers use the crops to fatten up the livestock—who provide meat and smeel.

The jet stream angles down towards New Eden. On all sides, fat slave saucers are being swept up into the into the outer, Groon-bound layer, whizzing upward past the descending flat cow. The inner, Eden-bound core of the current—including the flat cow—is directed straight at the ground—they're going to crash!—*ooof.*

Fortunately, the flat cow contains a supply of Truban inertia gel, and the high-speed collision does no harm to Scud's party, nor to the flat cow herself. Yulia bounces across the plain of New Eden on her bottom, slows, rolls on her edge for a bit, wobbles, and comes to rest. With an annunciatory moo, she unzips her edge. Scud and his fellows sit up straight like royals in a convertible limo.

The faint sound of Groon's music can still be heard. It's like a delicate ringing in Scud's ears, and he can't even be quite sure that he's hearing it. But yeah, it's there. Presumably the music tells the slave saucers what to do. All around them stunned, newly arrived saucers come to rest, gather their wits, pick up on Groon's tune, and head for a nearby ridge that presumably separates New Eden from Van Cott. Scud supposes they're massing for the intended invasion of his hometown Los Perros via the giant unspace tunnel that's being built near Van Cott's Saucer Hall.

Yulia cruises over to an oak-shaded oasis near the base of the basin's steep red clay ridge. The flat cow settles down by an overflowing fountain beside a stream under a tree. Scud, Villy, and Zoe step to the ground and prepare to have a look around. All this time, Yulia never actually said anything to them—all she ever did was moo. Nor has it been possible to teep what lies in her mind. Hard to know exactly what she's up to.

Be that as it may, here they are in the hamlet of Berky with its tidy shacks and its expat Earthling colony. As they walk, Scud looks around, hoping to spot Nunu. It's a mixed crowd here beneath Berky's swaying trees. Along with friendly saucers and saucer-human mixes, Scud sees a fair number of expat Earthlings hanging out. They look like hippies and unkempt hermits, although some of them may have been professors, writers, artists, or techs before they moved to Berky.

Nobody bothers to keep up appearances here. Life is easy. It's a community of brooks and ponds, shady trees, cottages with soft beds. Scud notices a public picnic table laden with peaches, apples, pitchers of milk, loaves of bread, steaming tortillas, a grilled salmon, and a roast pig. New Eden indeed. But with the ever-present danger of the leech saucers catching hold of you and draining you dry.

And then Scud spots what he's been looking for. It's a simple wooden bungalow at the edge of Berky, with Nunu's car-sized father Pa Saucer sunning himself in the yard. He has a green dome and a yellow rim like Nunu. By way of being roomy enough for Pa Saucer, the house's ceilings look to be twenty feet high, and the front door is like a garage door. Cute little Nunu is on the wide wooden porch, resting in the shade, possibly asleep. A few little creatures buzz above her. Can those be—

Before rushing to Nunu's side, Scud checks in with Pa Saucer. Scud is a bit nervous, not entirely sure he'll be welcome.

"The eggs hatched out fine," booms Pa Saucer as soon as he recognizes Scud. "Thirty-six! Half boys and half girls. We set a tiny saucer pearl into each one. The pearls took hold, and all of my Nunu's kids can fly!" The old saucer is very much the proud granddad.

"Scud!" flutes Nunu from the porch. She alerts her children. "Father here!"

Many of the saucerbabies were resting on Nunu's rim. The full swarm heads for Scud. They look like tiny naked humans with saucer rims around their waists. And they have reddish hair like Scud's. And yes indeed, they fly.

"Daddy!" they shrill in their tiny voices. "Paw, Pops, Dada, Vovo, Scud Antwerpen!"

Scud's thrilled, and Villy likes the saucerbabies, and Zoe waves them off. Scud and Villy play with the little ones for a while. They vary in size from paper matches to the joint of a thumb. The very smallest ones buzz at the boys' nostrils and ears, the larger ones crawl about in their hair as if in two haystacks, and one of them dares to catch hold of Scud's upper front teeth with his hands and swing to a perch on Scud's lower lip, hollering into the cavern of Scud's mouth like a mountaineer—until Scud gently brushes him off. And now the saucerbabies begin a spirited game of tag, using Scud's shoulder as home base. Reluctantly amused by the frolic, Zoe picks out a tiny nursery tune on her Gibson SG.

Scud is flooded with unexpected affection for his offspring. He makes faces at them, widening his eyes, bobbing his head, and wagging his tongue. Villy gets one of the larger saucerboys to land on his finger, and he's coaxing the little fellow to call him Uncle Villy.

Meanwhile Nunu is everywhere, riding herd on the saucerbabies and planting kisses on Scud's cheeks. But somehow Scud has started feeling awkward about kissing a flying saucer. What was he thinking when he got himself into his affair with Nunu? Easy answer: reptile brain.

For Nunu's part, her flirtations also seem artificial—a bit too sunny and bright. Slowly it dawns on Scud that he has a rival. A dark male saucer of Nunu's size is resting on the porch as well. A young saucer named Krampus.

"Hope you don't mahnd I'm seein' Nunu," Krampus says to Scud, speaking in something like a farmboy accent. His dome is the dark green shade of an alligator, with shiny bumps. His rim is a paler green. He's got the dark eye of an honest, non-leech saucer, but he has two rows of fangs snaggling out from his rim. The rim is seemingly capable of opening up like a set of jaws.

"Oh, it's fine if you spend time with Nunu," Scud responds.

He's maybe a little surprised at himself. But, yes, he is in fact relieved to have Krampus in the picture. Krampus offers a way out. Scud doesn't really want to spend the rest of his life in New Eden married to a flying saucer. I mean, dude! Get a grip!

Fact is, Scud's been obsessing over Maisie ever since Surf World. Ever since he heard that Maisie likes him. He'd much rather have Maisie as a girlfriend than Nunu. Maisie will be a senior and Scud will be a junior. That could work. According to Zoe, Maisie is half flying saucer. And Scud does likes saucers. But a girlfriend who's only *half* saucer is enough.

Nunu interrupts his musings. "Krampus my boyfriend now, but you Scud always father of first batch my kiddies." Another kiss from Nunu, right on his mouth, a deep one, like when they were together in the back of the whale, a kiss to remember her by. She giggles as she breaks away.

And then Nunu and Krampus drift off with the thirty-six saucerbabies in tow. Well, no, just thirty-*five*. One of them, a saucerboy, is perched on Villy's shoulder like he means to stay. Villy looks glad to have the little guy.

"Maisie's right over there," Zoe tells Scud right around then. Scud reacts with a relieved grin.

Yes, Maisie is standing by a sparkling fountain some sixty yards away, chatting with Yulia the flat cow, still resting right where they left her. Evidently the brindle-spotted alien can in fact speak English when she feels it. Scud has a feeling that Maisie is watching him out of the corner of her eye. He waves to her, but she acts like she doesn't see him. In his chagrin, it occurs him that he's facing an entire lifetime of not understanding women.

Meanwhile, at Scud's side, Zoe is talking earnestly to an old man with a deep tan—oh, wow, that's Zoe's father from Los Perros, Kirkland Snapp, founder of the New Eden Space Friends. Kirkland is in a tall state of excitement, and his elbows bounce in and out, lanky old coot that he is.

Floating at Kirkland's side is a curvaceous female saucer who resembles a slightly larger version of Nunu. Soft pink skin, a large attentive eye, and full red lips. Zoe introduces Scud and Villy to her father and to his saucer consort, who is of course Meemaw and, let's keep this straight, both Nunu's mother and Maisie's mother. So effin' weird. Pa Saucer seems a little embarrassed by the introductions, and he goes inside his house. Meemaw makes much of the saucerbaby on Villy's shoulder. Her grandson.

Kirkland has an old-sounding voice, with a reverberation to it—as if there's a soap-film-like membrane of mucus stretching across the back of his throat. Scud remembers Kirkland from a few years back. The old man and his human wife or girlfriend Sunny Weaver came to the

Antwerpen home for dinner and Kirkland talked all evening, not letting anyone else get in a word edgewise. As Scud recalls, no matter what idea anyone proposes to Kirkland, his response always begins with "No," followed by an extensive exposition of Kirkland's opinions on these affairs. And the only time Kirkland smiles or laughs is when he's marveling at the magnificence of his own self. A total jerk.

As for Sunny Weaver, she seemed desperate. Even with his ignorance of the ways of the world, Scud could tell that Sunny was clinging to Kirkland like a drowning woman grasping a floating log. She'd laugh really hard at Kirkland's unfunny witticisms about how wonderful he was, and she'd keep her mouth open in a rictus of good humor for way too long, with her anxious eyes darting around to make sure some of the others were laughing too. Also Scud could tell that Sunny Weaver hated Zoe Snapp. As if Zoe were competition for Kirkland's attention.

Not only is Kirkland Zoe's father, he's Maisie's father too. Those fine young women have grown like roses in a garden bed of decomposing manure. And now Kirkland lives with the saucer Meemaw. In a way, Kirkland is Nunu's stepfather, and Nunu is Maisie's half sister. The tangled family tree is like a logic puzzle that Scud has trouble keeping straight.

Scud now notices that Meemaw has scars on her skin, and that she hangs a little crooked in the air, poor old thing. He excuses himself and makes his way across the field to Maisie. She regards him with the demeanor of the most wholesome girl next door imaginable. She's holding a purse.

"So, what's your part in our plan?" Scud asks her.

"You just come up to me and talk as if you know me?" says Maisie, a smile playing across her lips. She cocks her chin to indicate haughtiness.

"I see you at school all the time," says Scud.

"But you've never even said hi. Do you think I'm such a weirdo?"

"Not weird," says Scud. "Exotic."

"Feel this," says Maisie, and puts Scud's hand on the bulge at her waist. It's a fleshy little rim circling her body. A saucer disk.

"Zoe told me," says Scud. "It's cool." His face is glowing and his breath is coming fast. "I think you're great."

"I'm glad," says Maisie. She gives him a really nice smile and squeezes his hand. "I've thought you were cute all along."

By way of responding to that, awkward Scud can't manage much more than a grin. But that seems to be enough. At least for now.

Villy comes walking over to them, even though old Kirkland Snapp is bawling after him. "No, Villy!" comes Kirkland's voice. "You need to sit down and hear me out. You don't understand the plan."

"Senile dementia," Villy says to Scud, not even looking back. "The heartbreak of Alzheimer's."

"Mucus voice," goes Scud, knowing Villy understands that this refers to the hypothetical membrane of spit that blocks the back of Kirkland Snapp's throat. The phrase is part of the brothers' shared lexicon.

"Imagine him being my father-in-law," says Villy. "May Goob-goob have mercy on my soul. You could end up like

Kirkland yourself, Scud. If you stay here in Berky boning saucers for the rest of your life."

"I'm *not* staying with Nunu," cries Scud. "And I never *did* bone her. All we did was kiss—and she sampled some of my DNA."

"Vhatever vorks," says Villy in an accent, infuriatingly insouciant.

"Maisie's the one for me now," blurts Scud. "Not Nunu."

"With me in the Kirkland zone just the same," says Villy, smiling and shaking his head. "We'll stick together, you and me." He uses the tip of his forefinger to pet the head of the inch-high saucerboy who's resting on his wrist. "I like my little nephew. I'm calling him Duckworth. Your son. You mind if I keep him?"

"How do you mean keep him? You want to take him back to Earth?"

"If I ever get there," says Villy. "Near term, I'd like to have Duckworth with me for my big commando foray. Like my mascot, for good luck. And who knows—Duckworth might be some help against Groon."

"Can he talk?" Scud asks.

"Some father *you* are," goes Villy, shaking his head. "Not knowing a thing like that about his son. This saucerboy is lucky he has a kindly Uncle Villy. Right, Duckworth?"

Duckworth makes a high-pitched twittering noise—which Villy insists is comprehensible human speech. But maybe Villy's teasing Scud. Often Scud has trouble telling if people are joking. He tries to turn the conversation serious again.

"What kind of commando foray?" he asks Villy.

"What you and Zoe were talking about. It's gonna be

me pinching off the two ends of that big unny tunnel with Groon inside it. Remember?"

"Of course I remember," says Scud. "I'm not an idiot."

"You're always *claiming* that," says Villy, that old teasing smile at the corners of his mouth.

"Look, wiseass," goes Scud. "Do you have any idea *how* to close off the ends of a four-dimensional tunnel?"

"Villy will use the two super-strong, stretchable Neptune's tablecloths that I brought from Surf World," says Maisie. "Each of them is a big disk with an edge that shrinks to make a pouch. I've already stashed them inside Yulia. Villy will wrap the tablecloths around two spherical cross-sections of the tunnel, one on either side of Groon, and the tablecloth edges will shrink way down, pinching off the tunnel, and Groon will be isolated in a hell-world island universe on his own. Ta-da!"

"I still don't get why we can't just tie off the damn tunnel with two ropes," protests Villy.

"Everything's a dimension higher," says Maisie. "A regular tunnel is a stack of disks, but an unny tunnel is a stack of spheres. And it takes a sheet to wrap up a sphere and squash it. And thus to cut off the unny tunnel."

"You're so right," says Scud. He appreciates the fact that Maisie understands these things. More proof that he and she are meant for each other.

Villy throws up his hands, as if admitting defeat. "Okay, Scud, so I'm the idiot, and you're the savant. Help me."

"I need to draw pictures," says Scud, looking around. "The fourth dimension is too gnarly for words. What can I draw on?"

"Use my rim," says Maisie, cutely flopping her disk out from under her shirt. "I draw on it all the time. Or sometimes I project patterns. I'm like a cuttlefish or an octopus that way. Polka dots, checkerboards, paisley, lace, whatever. Draw with your finger, Scud."

Scud sets the tip of his forefinger onto Maisie's bared rim. A creamy black dot appears, and when he moves his finger, the dot extends into a curved line. Maisie makes a purring sound.

"Awesome," says Scud. "Can I draw, like five or six pictures? A science comic?"

"Decorate me," purrs Maisie, a trace of excitement in her voice. "All around my rim."

Zoe joins their group. She's left old Kirkland Snapp alone with Meemaw, and now the old couple are drifting back to their cottage. Zoe is strumming a nervous little tune on her Gibson SG guitar.

"My father is sulking," Zoe tells Villy. "At least his precious Meemaw always tells him he's wonderful. I can't believe that man. Abandons his family to have a completely disgusting affair with a flying saucer, covers it up by marrying that floozy Sunny Weaver, and then gets miffed when we don't want to listen to his self-aggrandizing drone."

"Does your father disapprove of me?" asks Villy. His tone is light, but Scud can tell his brother cares about the answer.

"Not particularly," says Zoe. "Disapproving of people means focusing on someone other than himself."

"I myself focus on you all the time," Villy tells Zoe.

Zoe smiles at him. "You make me glad."

"Well, check out what we're doing here," says Villy.

"Scud's giving us an illustrated lecture about how we'll kill Groon."

Scud smiles at Zoe. He's glad to have her here too. She's Maisie's half-sister! Which kind of puts her in a better light. Overhead the jet stream of saucers arcs across the sky like a confetti rainbow. And even now, if Scud makes an effort, he can hear the faint, meandering bagpipe bleat from the stream—Groon calling to his slaves. How strange a trip this is. His brother and the two young women are looking at him.

"For my illos, I'll draw Van Cott and Los Perros as if they're planes," Scud begins. "So you can see them as being parallel."

Scud makes a first drawing on Maisie's flap. "So we've got two universes drawn like planes," he says. "And we've got creatures in both worlds, and I'm drawing them flat too. Here's my Figure 1. A saucer and a boy in mappyworld, and a girl with a trumpet in ballyworld. Zoe and her horn. Normally these characters can't travel from one world to the other."

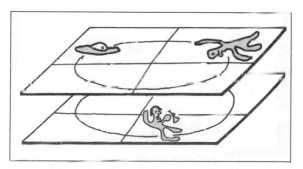

FIGURE 1: TWO PARALLEL WORLDS

"And you want to show how they *do* sometimes go back and forth," says Maisie.

"Exactly, says Scud. "They use what we've been calling an unny tunnel. Scientists call it a wormhole or, ahem, an Einstein-Rosen bridge."

"Don't do that," warns Villy.

"Okay, it's an unny tunnel," says Scud. "The idea is that you bulge down the space of one world, and bulge up the space of the other, and they meet and join together like soap films, and then there's, like, a throat connecting the two worlds. Unny tunnel, yes! There it is. With Zoe sliding up. And that saucer or that guy might slide down."

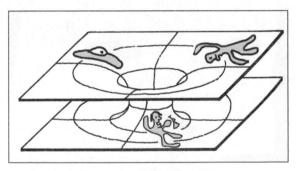

FIGURE 2: UNNY TUNNEL

"They float through the hole in the middle of the wormhole?" says Villy.

"No," says Scud. "They need to stay inside the surface of their world's smooth soap film. So they creep up and down the *sides* of the wormhole. Like living tattoos in your skin."

"Show me the part about trapping him in the unny tunnel," goes Villy.

Scud's finger moves caressingly on Maisie's rim. "A three-panel drawing for this, Maisie. If you don't mind."

"Do it. I like the attention."

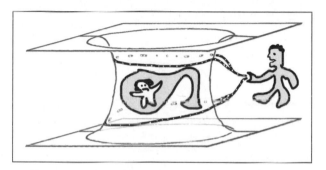

FIGURE 3: LASSOING THE TUNNEL WITH GROON

Scud draws his next image and explains. "In my Figure 3, Groon has slid down along the side of the wormhole from mappyworld on top. And the girl slid up from the world on the bottom and Groon happened to swallow her. And meanwhile Villy has torn himself out of ordinary space, and he's free-floating off the surface of space."

"And that stands for unspace," puts in Maisie. "Hyperspace."

"Notice also that Villy has lassoed the two ends of the tunnel," says Scud.

"I don't like seeing that woman being inside Groon!" breaks in Zoe, an edge in her voice. "That's supposed to be me? Go to hell, Scud."

"The pictures are hypothetical," says Scud. "Consider them a cautionary warning. Let's continue." His finger moves rapidly. "Now look at Figure 4. This is where Villy tightens up on two cross-sections of the tunnel. Pinches them down to points."

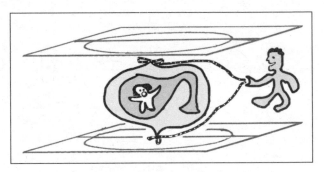

FIGURE 4: PINCHING OFF THE TUNNEL SECTION WITH GROON

"But instead of lassos, Villy will be using disk-like Neptune's tablecloths," says Maisie. "And tightening up their edges to pinch off spheres."

"Because of the fourth dimension," says Villy, kind of weakly. Like he's parroting a phase in a language he doesn't understand. Or like he's beaten-down political prisoner reciting an official pledge of allegiance.

Scud nods. He's enjoying this. "The Neptune's tablecloths are like higher-dimensional lassos, you might say."

"Might say," echoes Villy. "Might not."

Scud draws another image.

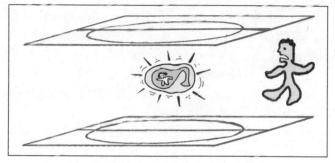

FIGURE 5: GROON'S ISLAND UNIVERSE SHRINKS!

"And here's the happy ending in Figure 5!" he says. "Villy tightens up the tablecloths so much that the tunnel pinches off in two spots and the universe flattens back out, and Groon is a pig in a poke. Trapped on the hypersurface of a pocket universe. No more Groon!"

"Eff you for drawing me in there at the end," Zoe says to Scud.

"Oh, probably you'll find a way out," says Scud. "The thing is to make sure you're not inside Groon and make sure to scoot out of the tunnel before Villy completely ties it off. I'm just drawing this way so you understand the risk. I'm your friend, Zoe."

"I wonder," she goes.

"I have a problem too," says Villy. "If I'm going to wrap Neptune's tablecloths around two cross-sections of the tunnel, I have to be floating in—4D unspace? How would I get there?"

"I'll carry yoooou!" says Yulia, very loud. "I'm ready to goooo."

This is the first time that any of them have heard the flat cow talk. And now that Scud hears Yulia's voice—well, naturally it's like a cartoon cow's. And a little like Goob-goob's voice, too. With an eerie buzz of transcendent power.

"So, great, the flat cow is finally talking!" Scud exclaims. "What are you, anyway, Yulia?"

She's not ready to give a straight answer. "A hyperspace coooow? But you can call me flat cow toooo. I'm ready for the cosmic beatdown on Groooon. You'll kill the bagpipe for Goob-goooob."

"Yulia and Villy's commando raid," says Villy, not showing much enthusiasm. "This hyperdimensional rump steak tosses me into the fourth dimension so I can pinch off a section of the tunnel ends with two monster disks from Surf World. And meanwhile I'm hoping my innards don't fall out."

"I'll keep you whoooole," says Yulia. "Get inside me and let's goooo." She waggles the visible section of her cow tail in an intricate pattern. The tail-section oscillates between short and long, like it's dipping in and out of four-dimensional space. Little Duckworth buzzes after the tail's motions. As always, no actual tip of the tail is ever visible. No telling how long it really is.

"I don't think we need to leave right this minute," says Villy.

Right about then the arcing jet stream shudders and— stops. Stray saucers scatter all about. Groon's stopped pumping them in and out of New Eden. A deep silence fills the air. The subtly irritating thread of Groon's faint music is gone.

"Uh-oh," says Zoe. "I bet that means the giant bagpipe

is on his way now. Flying a million miles from the Pit. How long will it take him, Maisie?"

"Not as long as you think," says Maisie. "Maybe three hours. He moves even faster than stratocasting. But finishing that giant unny tunnel in Van Cott could take till tomorrow afternoon."

"Villy, we should goooo," moos Yulia. "We'll hover in unspace beside the big hoooole. Go nooow. Get in place before Grooooon." The flat cow is being very pushy.

"Do you think you'll be all right?" Scud asks Villy, suddenly worried about his brother. "I mean—me drawing pictures is one thing, but you'll be putting your body on the line."

Villy studies Scud for a minute. "I'm glad you care," he says, fingering his guitar strings. "And I'm sorry I always teased you. Maybe I was just jealous of how smart you are at math."

"Me, I was jealous of how brave and coordinated you were," Scud tells Villy.

"We made a good team," says Villy. "When we weren't fighting. Brothers."

"We need to stop talking like we're about to die," says Scud. "We'll win."

"I like our odds," says Villy. "We've got Goob-goob, the wand larva, the flat cow, two idiots (you and me), plus Maisie and Zoe, to whom no insults apply."

Villy tells the flat cow to hold on for a goddamn minute, and he takes Zoe by the hand. The two of them walk off a little ways from the others and stand together, hugging and kissing and whispering promises. Watching them, Scud wonders how it is to be that way with a girl. Will he ever get there?

Villy and Zoe's farewell is over. Villy unzips the side of the Yulia the four-dimensional-and-not-so-flat-after-all cow. Or whatever she is. Little thumb-tip-sized Duckworth perches on Villy's shoulder, going with him on the trip. Villy settles inside Yulia and pushes his face against the eyegoggles in her skin. Zoe watches in silence, her eyes brimming with tears.

Working the drama of the moment, Yulia rotates herself ninety degrees sideways in the fourth dimension—and don't ask what that means. The effect is that Villy, Maisie, and Scud see a two-dimensional *cross-section* of Yulia, with her third dimension out there in hyperspace. Yulia looks like a slice of flat-cow salami with a Villy filling—they see a rind of hide, a layer of beef, a little air-gap, and then an inner rind of Villy-skin containing a way gnarly cross-section of Villy's head, as caricatured in Figure 6, although of course the real Villy is more handsome than that.

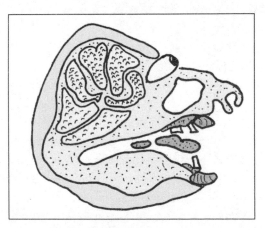

FIGURE 6: CROSS-SECTION OF VILLY'S HEAD

"Ugh," goes Zoe and plays a dissonant chord on her guitar. "So *wrong*."

"It's perfect," says Scud. "Science on parade! Dig the slice of skull. Don't worry, Yulia will keep my brother's innards in place. He won't spill. This is wonderful."

"It's a nightmare," says Zoe, her voice breaking. "It's horrible."

"Higher geometry," goes Scud. "You gotta love it."

As Yulia moves off into the fourth dimension, the effect is that her visible cross-section tracks down through the flat cow's body, and through the two folded-up Neptune's tablecloths, and through Villy's body, the cross-section wobbling and diminishing, reaching a zone where they see the two round slices of Villy's legs for a while, and then cross-sections of Villy's feet, and then no more Villy but still a little bit of cow-meat, and then nothing but the wobbly circular cross-sections of the cow's long tail. The tail part seems to go on for a very long time. Finally it morphs into a long sausage and twitches out of sight. Yulia and Villy are in unspace.

"What now?" Scud says to Zoe.

"I hang myself," says Zoe, consoling herself with sarcasm. "The love of my life is gone." She begins playing a schmaltzy, tear-jerker-type tune on her guitar, barely touching the strings with the tips of her fingers. It sounds like "Lara's Theme" on the short strings of a harp.

"Oh, stop it," says Scud, who by now knows Zoe's penchant for drama.

"Okay, right," goes Zoe, abandoning her plaintive tune. "What now? We go back to Los Perros. And then we get ready to stall Groon while he's inside the tunnel. Get in his way. So Villy and the flat cow will have plenty of time to pinch off the tunnel's ends."

"How will we know when the bagpipe's in the tunnel?"

"I have a distinct feeling it's gonna be a huge deal and very readily apparent to all," says Zoe. "Like the gigundo finale of a lumbering, overblown, high-budget SF movie."

"Yeah," goes Scud, nodding. "This movie I wanna see." He makes his voice as deep and portentous as he can. "*Teen Outcasts vs. Saucer Bagpipe: The Cosmic Beatdown.* Can you tunnel us to Los Perros from here, Zoe?"

"My puny little saucer pearl probably can't reach Earth from this basin," says Zoe. "And the bigger saucer pearls that we might find in New Eden—there's no knowing where they'd tunnel to. We'll walk over the ridge to Van Cott, take a look at the big unny tunnel they're working on, then use my trusty saucer pearl to tunnel home from there."

"You don't have to walk," puts in Maisie. "I'll drive you over the ridge. With my dune buggy."

"You have a car here?" says Zoe. "Awesome."

"I keep it in Dad's garage," says Maisie.

"*Ew,*" goes Zoe. "I have to see him again?"

"You should talk to our father a little more," says Maisie. "He's not completely brain dead. He just acts that way. We've got a little time before Groon lands. And like I was telling Yulia, making that giant unny tunnel is going to take them until tomorrow."

So Scud, Maisie, and Zoe walk over to Kirkland Snapp's cottage, a shaggy, leafy cottage with a porch and a garage.

Kirkland's in a rocking chair on the low porch drinking a glass of tea. Meemaw the saucer isn't around.

"'Sup, Dad," goes Zoe.

Kirkland kicks right into a monologue. Maisie and Zoe pretend to listen, but Scud zones out on most of it. The one interesting part is when Kirkland talks about how he seeded the mud behind the high school with saucer pearl spore culture that he obtained from—well, this is wild. It happened when Zoe was one year old.

Supposedly Meemaw the saucer appeared to Kirkland for the very first time one night, and she was flirting with him, and he was becoming obsessed with her, and suddenly she engulfed his right hand and pumped a couple of ounces of liquid spore culture into it. Kirkland's hand swelled up like he had an allergic reaction to a bunch of bee stings—with milky liquid oozing out. Meemaw then told Kirkland to help the saucers by fertilizing the likeliest fungal-growth-type spot he might know of. So Kirkland ran and dribbled the yucky juice from his hand onto a muddy patch behind Los Perros High.

"If it really *was* his hand," Scud thinks to himself. "And not—" Well, never mind.

Soon after that Kirkland became Meemaw's lover, and she gave birth to Maisie in New Eden, and she brought the saucerbaby to Kirkland to raise in Los Perros like a human. Now at this point, Kirkland already had Sunny Weaver as his human girlfriend, so he got Sunny to pretend that she was Maisie's natural mother. Then Zoe's mom threw Kirkland out. Kirkland married Sunny and the two of them devoted much energy to their club, the

New Eden Space Friends, living together for some fifteen years. But all along, Kirkland was seeing Meemaw on the side.

At this part Scud drops off to sleep, lying on his back on the porch, snoring with his mouth wide open. When he wakes—after who knows how long a time—Kirkland is still talking. He's up to the part where, a year or two ago, he turned against Sunny because she had thrown her allegiance to the leech saucers. The courageous Kirkland moved to New Eden to live with Meemaw, in hopes of finding a way to destroy Groon and to wipe out Groon's legions of leech saucers.

And then Kirkland gets around to Pinchley and Yampa. "They were looking for help," he says. "I told them my daughters could pitch in! Maisie and Zoe! So if you kids bring down grim old Groon, it'll be thanks to me!" Kirkland pauses, glowing with self-esteem. Before he can start again, the girls hop off the porch.

Maisie chugs her dune buggy out of the garage. It's a refitted VW bug with sparkly pink paint, glowon headlights, quantum shocks, and fat graphene tires, just like they had on the purple whale.

By now Kirkland is holding forth again, not wanting to stop talking to his two daughters. Two hours wasn't enough. And now, before they can finally get in the car and leave, Kirkland implores them to wait another moment. He strides long-legged into his cottage and returns with two large saucer pearls. Prize specimens, faintly luminous.

"One for you, Zoe, and one for your sleepyhead friend—was it Spin? He's Villy's brother?"

"Scud."

"Exceedingly valuable items," says Kirkland, handing each of them a navel-orange-sized pearl. "If you have a big one, you can use it to fly, or to send out bolts of lightning. They'll come in handy for the cosmic beatdown."

"They know about the pearls, Dad," says Maisie. "But thanks. That's great."

"Do you want one, too, dear?"

"Duh?" says Maisie. "I've had a saucer pearl like that since last year. I carry it in my purse."

"Ah, yes," goes her dad. "Of course."

TWENTY-EIGHT

going home

zoe

At this point Zoe figures they're done, but even now Kirkland isn't through. He begs her for one last word, in private.

"About *what*?" goes Zoe, feeling totally impatient.

"I still didn't explain the main thing," says Dad, leading her away from the car to his rickety porch. "I always talk all around what I mean to say, and I never get to the point."

"You know that about yourself?" says Zoe, a little surprised.

Kirkland makes a dismissive gesture. "It's a habit. All these years of cheating on my wives. And scheming against Groon. I need to tell you plain and clear that I've missed you, Zoe. And I'm proud of you. And I'm completely on your side."

"Why don't you come home?" bursts out Zoe. "Maybe Mom would take you back. She's lonely."

Slowly Kirk shakes his big head. "Too much water under the bridge. I'm used to life in New Eden. I belong with Meemaw."

"Okay then," says Zoe, her voice turning tight. "I gotta go."

"One more thing," calls Kirkland as she walks away. "Look out for that Sunny Weaver. She's flipped to the leech saucers' side."

"Got it."

And then Zoe's in the dune buggy sitting in front next to sister Maisie with Scud in back. On the road again. What a relief. Two million miles and counting.

Seventeen-year-old Maisie turns out to be a reckless driver, throwing up gravel with her bulbous tires and laughing gaily whenever she makes too tight a turn and the car spins out. Scud cheers her on, and pretty soon Zoe's laughing too. What the hell.

Even in the dark, the drive up the ridge isn't bad. They have headlights, and the road is a well-worn track that's been driven by a thousand expat Earthlings. High in the sky, saucers stream towards Van Cott. There isn't much action on the road, although at one point a chubby gray leech saucer darts out from a bend in the road where it's disguised itself as a boulder. Scud and Zoe give the hostile saucer a pair of zaps from their fat new pearls, and when the alien still shows signs of life, Scud turns him to dust with a crackling bolt from his wand.

At the top of the ridge they pause for a break. Unlike the other passes that Zoe's driven through, this isn't a three-way intersection. It's just a straight ridge with New Eden on one side and Van Cott on the other. The lights of downtown Van Cott beckon. And then Zoe notices she's hearing bagpipe music in the sky again. Loud and getting louder.

"Duck," yells Maisie. "Under the car."

The three kids scramble under the dune buggy. Zoe manages to lie on her back with her head sticking out. She wants to see their enemy fly by.

So, yeah, it's Groon the bagpipe, cruising past like a flying mountain, blatting a march-type song, already slowing for his landing glide, seemingly oblivious to the three humans atop the ridge. He's got his size tightened down to about a mile across. He glows from within, his vast hide lit in shades of ocher, beige, and umber. His nested doubled chanter horn bobs like a cheerful snout, and his feelers are combed back by the force of his passage through the air.

Zoe crawls out from under the car to watch the monster land. On the way down, he circles over the city of Van Cott, his song rising to a festive jig. Glowing leech saucers rise up and swarm around him like bees around their queen. The great pink and blue saucers they saw in Thuddland have arrived as well, wobbly behemoths as wide as the bagpipe who spawned them. What were their names? Something silly, Zoe can't remember.

The giants hover while Groon and his slave saucers converge upon Van Cott's core. A dust cloud rises when the mountainous bagpipe crushes the greater part of the night market. Straining her eyes, Zoe can see he's settled beside Saucer Hall.

Driving even more recklessly than before, Maisie careens down the slope into the basin, roars along a feeder highway, and slaloms into Van Cott via its grid of city blocks. She passes the remains of the night market and comes to rest by a freshly grown thorn barricade around Saucer Hall. Beyond the fence, Groon's mile-high bulk hulks against the night sky. His vile, exultant piping fills the air. The three kids get out of Maisie's car and work their way closer.

For some reason there's no other gawkers here—although there are some of those horsefly-sized saucers that want to bite you. By now Zoe and Scud know how to swat them as fast as they land, and Maisie has some kind of half-saucer vibe that keeps the mini saucers away from her.

Meanwhile Groon's leech slave saucers are crowding into Saucer Hall, flying in through the 120-foot-tall front doors. Zoe can't make out what's happening inside. One thing for sure—none of those saucers is coming back out.

"They're building the gate inside Saucer Hall," says Maisie. "The gate of the unny tunnel they're working on. The gate will be a sphere. They'll trundle it out through those big front doors when it's ready for Groon. Like rolling a giant ball out of an airplane hangar."

"If the tunnel's gate fits inside Saucer Hall, how can it be big enough for Groon?" asks Zoe.

"You must have noticed by now that you seem to shrink when you move into an unny tunnel," says Maisie. "Or you can say the space around the gate is stretched. From what I know, if the new gate is a hundred feet across, the space warp effects will be enough for Groon to fit. Even though he's a mile wide. The same size as those two giant saucers. Poppo and Bombo? They'll send those two big saucers through the tunnel first—to make sure it's wide enough for Groon."

Zoe glances upward. Somehow she hadn't yet grasped that the smooth, even lighting near Saucer Hall was emanating from fleshy pink Poppo and aquamarine Bombo. As before, with their hundreds or even thousands of dangling tentacles, they remind Zoe of flying jellyfish. Rather than devastating Van Cott on the spot, they're waiting to visit Los Perros. What a bad scene that will be. Does this really have to happen?

"How exactly are the slave saucers making the big tunnel?" demands Zoe.

"I bet I know!" exclaims Scud, wanting to impress his potential new girlfriend Maisie. "The leech saucers flying into Saucer Hall—each of them uses his or her internal saucer pearl to make a thin unny tunnel. And the tunnels merge together, one by one. Like stalks making a sheaf. Like whirlpools joining to become a maelstrom. Like tiny bubbles merging into a fat wobbler."

"Don't get it," says Zoe wearily. "And don't feel like you have to tell me. Not now." Today feels like it's lasted forever. Riding Stolo up the smokestack, visiting with Goob-goob, surfing the jet stream inside the flat cow, doing the scene with her father in New Eden, driving over the basin ridge, and finding their way to Saucer Hall.

"Can I draw on you again?" Scud asks Maisie, quite undeterred. "I want to show Zoe how the tunnels merge."

"Feel free," says Maisie, unlimbering her flap of skin.

Scud gets right to work. "My Figure 7 will be a pair," says he. "To show how the tunnels merge." The little threads smush together to make a thicker one.

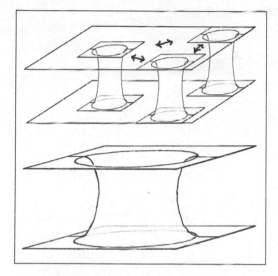

FIGURE 7: UNNY TUNNELS MERGE

"Yeah," says Maisie. "But there's a kicker. It kills those little leech saucers when they use their pearls to grow those thin tunnel threads. Even before the merge. That's why it's so horrible. They're sacrificing their lives for Groon. If you have a saucer pearl inside your body, and you grow it into an unny tunnel, then space's surface tension sends you sliding into the tunnel, and momentum carries you all the way through. And when you come out on the other side you're inside out. And that kills you."

"Stop it," says Zoe. "I've had enough."

"Wait, wait!" cries Scud. "I've got to visualize this." He falls silent for a full minute and then, in a burst of activity, he rapidly draws a series of six frames on Zoe's skin. "Behold Scud Antwerpen's mighty Figure 8!"

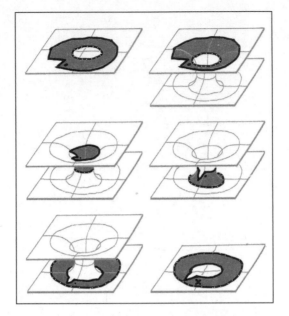

**FIGURE 8: TURNED INSIDE OUT BY SLIDING
ALONG A WORMHOLE INSIDE YOU**

"Those drawings make no sense whatsoever," says Zoe. "And did I mention that I'm tired?"

"Look harder," insists Scud. "The visual logic is quite compelling. Read across the rows and work your way down. It's what happens when a saucer goes through an unny tunnel that starts inside its body. I've drawn the saucer as a Pac-Man-style profile, with a wedge mouth and a hole in his middle to stand for the saucer pearl that turns into a tunnel. If you watch the mouth, you can tell when he's inside out."

"Go to hell," says Zoe.

Maisie cuts to the chase. "Zoe, the basic fact is there's going to be a hella pile of dead saucer meat over on the Los Perros side."

"Bizarre," says Zoe, finally intrigued. "What are people going to think?"

"They'll be saying it's the rankest senior-class prank ever," says Scud, geekishly smiling at the idea. "The dead saucer meat's gonna look like, I don't know, like the garbage pile at some cowschwitz feedlot slaughterhouse? As if some kid ordered up a truckload of that stuff. Intestines and cartilage and veins and gross organs nobody wants."

"I can almost imagine one of Tawna Garvey's boyfriends doing that," says Zoe.

"And it would totally impress her," goes Maisie.

"For sure," goes Zoe. "Tawna would be like, '*Ew*! You're so *crazy*!' And then she'd laugh with her mouth open really wide, kind of wiggling her tongue, like a deep-sea blub-fish luring prey."

"Tawna Blub-fish, yes!" echoes Maisie, and the two girls do a high five.

Their moment of cozy gossip is abruptly ended. A hostile leech saucer is bellowing at them from the thorn fence.

"Hey! You! Get outta here!"

The bullying saucer is a misshapen, red-eyed wedge with a crooked rim. By way of backing up his words, he fires off a zap jolt that barely misses them. They jump back into Maisie's dune buggy and retreat a block or two.

"I can use my teep slug to make us invisible," suggests Scud. "If we want to get back close to Saucer Hall and spy."

"Don't bother," says Zoe. "It's time to hop to Los Perros. That way we'll be on the scene when Groon tries to come through."

"I keep telling you people that won't be till tomorrow afternoon," says Maisie. "That tunnel's got a lot of growing to do. And those poor slave saucers don't add all that much apiece."

"I'm ready to go home anyway," says Zoe. "Are you coming or not, Maisie?"

"I'll be there," says Maisie. "There's a few underground rebels here in Van Cott I ought to get in touch with first. Eekra the dancer and that farm kid called Meno? If Villy really kills Groon, the humans will have a chance to wipe out the leech saucers for good. A sudden strike could do it. The good saucers will be on the humans' side. I have to tell Eekra and Meno to get ready. And then I'll jump to Los Perros. I'll be there sooner than you think."

"Meanwhile Scud and I need to rest," says Zoe. "Because tomorrow we fly into the tunnel from the Los Perros end—to slow down Groon. We'll hinder him with my music and with Scud's wand."

"We will?" goes Scud.

"*Yes*," says Zoe like a strict big sister. "If we distract Groon, Villy has more time to pinch off the ends of the tunnel."

"I hope you come to Los Perros soon," Scud tells Maisie. "I want to be sure I see you some more."

"That's nice," says Maisie, shooting Scud what's meant to be a smoldering look.

"Can—can I kiss you before we go?" says Scud, totally going for it. "Even though I'm sixteen, I've never kissed a girl before at all. Yes, I know that means I'm a loser. But if I end up getting killed by Groon, it'd be shame never to have—"

"Don't try and push your argument too far," says Zoe with a laugh. But Maisie and Scud aren't listening. They're locked in an embrace. In the background, Groon's music plays.

Zoe has the big new pearl that Kirkland gave her for zapping—she's tied it into the tail of her shirt. But for the hop home, she feels safer using the trusty little saucer pearl she's got in her jeans pocket. She gets it out and breathes on it, waking it up. For sure this pearl knows the way home. If she can activate it.

She does still have her guitar, and maybe she could use it to play the riff that transforms the saucer pearl into a tunnel. But it makes her impatient to think of fingering strings. She'd so much rather blow her horn. She holds up her black Gibson SG and talks to him.

"You've been an amazing guitar for me," Zoe says. "But—can you be a trumpet?"

No sooner said than done. The living guitar flexes, wads himself up, and unfurls into , yes, a shiny, brassy, honkable horn. Zoe holds him in her hands and grins. The horn is nothing less than a B-flat Martin Committee trumpet, just like Miles himself used. And *Zoe's* horn is alive.

"Ready now," says Scud, flushed and rumpled from kissing Maisie. "Done with the goodbye."

Zoe toots her stutter-step riff while holding her little saucer pearl. Great tone and awesome valves on this new trumpet. The pearl turns translucent, twitches, and gets a little larger. It's a gate to Los Perros. It's almost open, but not quite.

"I'll set it on the ground and play the whole riff," Zoe tells Scud. "Then we back off, and we run into the tunnel. Don't spaz out and fall. Go in there full-tilt, and run out even faster.

"Why?" says Scud, turning balky.

"Oh, stop trying to be smart all the time," says Zoe. "Just frikkin do what I tell you, or you'll die. I don't have time for a big science-nerd discussion about—"

"Go now!" shrieks Maisie. "Saucer!" A vampire saucer shaped like a flat pig is floating their way. Maisie is already in the seat of her dune buggy and she's got her dark-energy motor running. A quick wave of her hand and she peels out, spraying gravel. Zoe and Scud retreat around the corner of a building, with Zoe holding her trumpet and her pearl—whose frikkin tunnel still isn't fully open.

Dzeeeent!

An unbearably bright zap of light strikes the ground where Zoe was just now standing. Charred dirt puffs into the air. Staying out of the pig-saucer's line of sight, Zoe tosses her saucer pearl onto the ground and plays her full riff, plays it fast. And now, just like that, the gate is clear.

Zoe and Scud charge towards the gate, only the size of a golf ball—but it seems to get bigger as they approach. And by the time they hit the entrance it's the size of a closet door. They're in, and the leech saucer can't touch them.

As before, Zoe sees weird mirror-like images of herself while within the tunnel—she's seeing clear around the circumference of the wormhole. Meanwhile the dim,

warped shape of nighttime Los Perros lies ahead of her,
complete with the glaring headlights of Mom's SUV.
Hoping that Scud grasps the program, she storms out
of the unny tunnel's Earth-side gate—and runs like hell
across the wet pavement of Los Perros to the safety of
the sidewalk. Scud's at her heels, yes. From the corner of
her eye, Zoe sees the flickering passage of her two earlier
selves. And the SUV skids to a stop, its horn blaring.

"Zoe!" It's Mom, of course, yelling out of the side
window of her car. "Are you crazy? The show's about to
start! And what did you do to your clothes? You're a *mess*!
Quick, quick, get in the car."

Wow. It's back to square one. Zoe isn't missing the
talent show after all. Even though by now she'd all but
forgotten about it. Good thing she's got her new horn.

"Okay," she tells Mom, kind of laughing to herself. "I'm
ready."

Scud begs off from accompanying them to the show.
He's going to sleep at his father's house. He and Zoe
agree to meet tomorrow morning at the graduation. And
for now, Scud will keep both the new saucer pearls.

Then Zoe's in the car with Mom. She rolls down her
window and listens. She feels like she can even hear
Groon's music over here. It must be filtering through that
big unny tunnel that Groon's crew is working on. Not
that Mom notices it.

"Are you high or something?" Mom asks Zoe. "Why
didn't you wear the clothes I laid out?"

"I can't do this conversation," says Zoe, waving Mom
off. "Can't even."

"So secretive you are," says Mom, bulling her car into the high school parking lot and claiming a handicapped space. She scored a blue sticker when she sprained—or *nearly* sprained—her ankle three months ago. "A musician's helter-skelter life," says Mom sententiously. "Promise me to at least wash your face before you go onstage."

"I guess I *am* dirty. I've been—" Zoe stops herself from trying to tell the whole hairball story.

"You're going to be wonderful," says Mom, patting her on the knee. "My amazing daughter."

"Thanks," says Zoe, caught off guard by the maternal support. So much happening at once. She feels like her head could explode. And when Mom kisses her cheek, Zoe damn near bursts into tears.

Guided solely by muscle memory, Zoe runs into the school through a side door and finds a little-used ladies' room. It's empty right now, which makes things easier. She steps to the sink. Hate to admit it, but Mom had a point. Zoe looks like a street person. She literally hasn't seen a mirror in—would you call it a week? The last mirror was at the Borderslam Inn. A long time ago. So, okay, wash face. Dab mud, saucer smeel, and bodily fluids off blouse. The jeans—never mind. Wash arms up to elbows. Use wet paper towels to dab pits, butt, and crotch. Comb out hair with spread fingers. Too bad she can't borrow a—

"Comb?" goes a girl, coming into the bathroom to join her.

Zoe looks over. Oh my god, it's Maisie. Carrying her purse and her trombone. And somehow she's all tidy, in a lacy white summer dress that's loose around her waist.

She's even wearing lipstick and blush. She looks excited, like she's about to burst.

"Where did *you* come from?" asks Zoe.

"I used the saucer pearl in my purse to tunnel back to the gym," says Maisie, very pleased with herself. "I started from the gym in the first place, you know. I did that original jump from the gym, ten minutes ago, Los Perros time. Because I'd seen that you weren't showing up for our concert, and I figured you'd gone off to mappyworld. So I followed you, and we've been over there chasing each other for, I don't know, a week of mappyworld time? And, you know how it works, when I jumped back, I came out at the same Los Perros place and time that I left from in the first place."

"I thought you said you have a lot of stuff to do in Van Cott."

"I did it!" says Maisie with a giggle. "Don't you understand yet? And all along I knew that when I jumped back I'd be in Los Perros tonight. Which is where I need to be."

"You're gonna play in the show?"

"Wouldn't miss for the world," trills Maisie. "My trombone and my frock were all set in my gym locker. Will Scud be at the show to see me?"

"I think he went home," says Zoe.

"Damn. I want to kiss that boy *again*. I'll get him tomorrow morning. Scud's another reason I want to be here, of course."

"Work it, girl," goes Zoe. "Are we still okay with time? You're sure Groon won't be coming through the giant unny tunnel until tomorrow afternoon?"

"No prob," says Maisie. "The big tunnel is still narrow. Not nearly wide enough for Groon. And not wide enough for those two monster saucers they want to send through before him."

"How do you know exactly how wide the tunnel is right now?" asks Zoe, suddenly suspicious.

"I saw the gate."

"But the gate's inside Saucer Hall with all those hostile leech saucers guarding it. Did they let you go in there? Are you friends with them? Are you on their side?"

Maisie smiles. "Only *one* gate is inside Saucer Hall, you paranoid freak. The other gate is, *ta-daaah*, inside the Los Perros High School gym. Where I just was. "

"Oh wow. And that stuff Scud said about the dead saucers? Is the gate—"

"You have no idea. Unbelievably foul and gnarly. Saucer meat piled twenty, thirty feet high, spread all around the gate like lava from a volcano. Pools of smeel. Every possible color of saucer skin. Eyes and fangs and innards and brains. Everything is completely dead and stock still. But then a minute later another slave saucer comes through, and it's inside out, and it's shrieking in terror and pain. But what you *hear* is just a faint whimper—because the saucer's inside out, right, so its mouth or speech organ is buried inside its meat. It whimpers a few seconds and then it dies. And its body comes apart. Ultra goth. You'd like it."

Zoe is half repelled, half intrigued. "So the dead saucers are already there during our talent show concert?"

"Unny tunnels," says Maisie. "They can connect anywhere to anywhen."

"If I go look, will I be late for our act?" Zoe wonders aloud. She has no precise concept of the show's schedule, nor, for that matter, does she know exactly what time it is.

But now the decision is taken out of her hands.

Here comes Ms. Boot, the vice-principal, doing a routine patrol of the off-the-beaten-track rest rooms, alert for drink and drugs.

"On stage, girls! It's Jazz Prowlers time! At least you've got your instruments. Zoe, you look like hell. You should learn from Maisie. Come on, come on, come on."

Ms. Boot herds them down the hall and through a secret door, and then they're with the other band members, finding their places on the high school auditorium stage. The act before them is filing off. Ten ballet dancers. Looking out at the crowd, Zoe sees that the talent show has drawn a full house. Does she remember her part?

TWENTY-NINE

cosmic beatdown, part 1

villy / zoe

The problem is that Villy can't see well through the goggles in the flat cow's skin. Depending which way he's facing, he might see Van Cott, or Los Perros, or the unny tunnel between them. But he doesn't see regular 3D objects. He sees oddly shaped 2D slices of the world, marbled and mottled with details, like very thin slabs of fruit cake, or slices of some quirky kind of salami you'd never want to buy.

He teeps with Yulia about it, and—*thank you*—she's much more talkative than before. She says Villy's effed-up vision has to do with them being in 4D space. She even shows him a Scud-Antwerpen-style Figure 9.

"On the left it's a Square in 3D trying to look at a 2D Triangle wooooooman," says Yulia. "And he sees a 1D stroooooke."

"Why is the Square's heart and flesh all covered up, and the Triangle has her guts showing?"

"A kindly magic cow gave the Square a smeel overcooooooat," says Yulia. "To keep his guts from falling oooout."

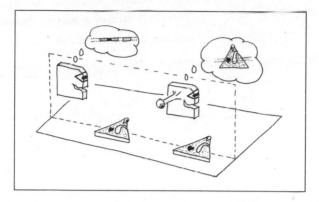

FIGURE 9: REGULAR EYE AND HIGHER-DIMENSIONAL EYE

"Nice of her," says Villy. "And why do you draw them thick?"

"Because it's truuuue," says the flat cow. "Beings of three dimensions have a slight thickness in the foooourth. But you should focus on their thooooughts."

"On the right, the hipster Square's grody 3D eye-stalk lets him see a fuller image?" says Villy, playing the good student. "He sees the Triangle's outside and insides all at once. A gods-eye view. Can I get a 4D eyestalk?"

"Noooo. You'll see through the 4D eye that I've goooot."

"Okay, then," says Villy, not entirely sure what they're talking about. "Start teeping me what you see."

"Will doooo!"

The flat-but-actually-4D cow begins feeding images into Villy's brain. The images aren't like photos, they're more like—like dreams. Or visions. Fully realized 3D scenarios. What you might call gods-eye views of mappy-world, ballyworld, and the unspace between them.

Villy sees the fields of the New Eden basin, and the inner mineral veins of the basin's ridge, and the insides of some rooms in Van Cott, and the gnarly inner architecture of the mile-wide body of Groon, who's still inside Saucer Hall.

The flat cow draws closer to Saucer Hall. Her 4D vision shows Villy a clear picture of the tunnel gate inside the hall. The ball is slowly growing, fed by a steady stream of slave saucers. Villy watches as a gray saucer pauses beside the big gate, says a prayer to Groon, and then disappears into a slender unny tunnel based on the saucer pearl within his own body. The little tunnel's glowing gate drifts a few feet across Saucer Hall to merge into the larger gate—which shows a nearly imperceptible augmentation in size. It's like building a haystack out of straws. Villy and Yulia watch for a while as this scene repeats.

"Do the slave saucers die?" Villy asks the flat cow.

Yulia bends towards a different direction of 4D unspace and now she's sending Villy images from the inside of the Los Perros High School gym. A pile of lifeless, inside-out, ripped-apart flying saucers litter the floor. Over a thousand of them by now. Enslaved by the bagpipe and killed on a whim.

"Mass suicide," murmurs Villy. "The cult of Groon."

Yulia flips her viewpoint back to the inside of Saucer Hall. Groon's slave saucers continue pouring in. So confident is the gross bagpipe of his eventual victory that he thinks nothing of sacrificing his troops. Villy is sickened by the heedless cruelty. How dreadful it would be if Groon were to control Earth.

"Show me Zoe," he implores the 4D flat cow. "Take me to her. We have time. Let me see Zoe Snapp. Has she done her concert yet?"

"Come see," goes Yulia.

After the extreme adventures that Zoe's recently been through, the Jazz Prowlers performance is a slight let-down. This said, there are some bitchin' moments where she's totally nailing her Miles Davis tune, "So What." And it's jolly to have younger sister Maisie right behind her with her slobbery old slide trombone at the ready for the next song. And sweet to see Mom's little face in the audience, smiling and nodding and glowing with pride. Maybe life doesn't totally suck after all.

Once the concert's over some of the kids are going to a party at Tawna Garvey's. Incredibly enough, Tawna herself asks Zoe to come.

"I never knew you could play like that," gushes Tawna. "You're deep."

Rich, rich praise. But Zoe bows out. She's gonna catch a ride home with Mom and go to bed. She's so tired that her knees are about to buckle. Mom herself is surprised that Zoe's coming home. Zoe's story for Mom is that she's worn out from studying so hard. Mom doesn't even pretend to believe this. She's always suspected that Zoe is a secret pot smoker. And Mom knows that pot makes you tired. She used to smoke a bit with Kirkland, back in the day.

"Can I sleep over at your place?" Maisie asks them just as they're going.

"Well . . ." says Mom, not sure what to say. Like, probably Maisie's a pot smoker too? And there's the whole history of Maisie's birth having sparked Mom and Dad's breakup sixteen years ago. That wasn't exactly the newborn baby's personal fault. But still . . .

"Sure you can," goes Zoe. "We can always fit you in, sistah."

"I can't face seeing Sunny," says Maisie. "My so-called mother. I didn't have a chance to mention this to you, but she's acting weird. More weird."

"How do you mean?" goes Zoe.

"It's like Sunny's been bitten by a vampire," says Maisie. "If you know what I mean."

"Got it," says Zoe, filling in the picture. And now she remembers Dad warning her that Sunny Weaver has gone over to the side of the leech saucers. But eff that shit.

Right now Zoe's feeling simple and happy, and she's thinking about how great she played, and how much everyone clapped. And that's the space she wants to be in. Stay in that glow and go to bed.

"I avoid Sunny Weaver like the plague," puts in Mom, with an odd, light laugh. "Despite her good deeds." At this point Zoe finally grasps that, at some level, Mom is *glad* that Sunny relieved her of Kirkland Snapp sixteen years ago. She doesn't want him back at all. Mom smiles at Maisie. "If you want to defect from Sunny's team to ours, that's fine. The more the hairier."

So Maisie beds down on the couch in Zoe's room. Maisie wants to have a sleepover gossip session, but Zoe can't even. In minutes Zoe and then Maisie are out for the night.

Yulia can't find Zoe's concert, but later the flat cow lets Villy peek at Zoe lying alone in her virginal teen-girl bed in her Mom's home, sound asleep. Zoe has a new trumpet next to her pillow—somehow Villy can tell the trumpet is the same living entity that was recently Zoe's guitar. Good for Zoe. Mentally Villy caresses her virtual form—as shown to him in holographic anatomical detail by Yulia's 4D eye. Being near Zoe feels soothing, good, and right. Villy realizes he needs some rest too. And then he's asleep. Little Duckworth nestles under his chin, sleeping as well.

She awakens to yet another perfect California day—bright sky with puffy clouds. An intense yottawatt sun. The air with a pleasant touch of coolness, somehow like clear water. Chickadees chirping, bees in the lemon tree, jasmine blossoms on the vine. Graduation Day. It's nearly ten a.m. The ceremony is in two hours. At noon. Everything's in place.

Except, *oh no*, today is also Groon Invasion Day. The sudden memory is like a horrible human-sized crab that races out from under Zoe's bed and seizes her wrists in its claws and shoves its churning mandibles into her face. She moans.

Maisie snaps awake, sits bolt upright, and starts talking a mile a minute. "I'm gonna go check out the gym right now. Gauge the size of the gate. And then, if there's time, I'll flirt with Scud. And then I wait till I see that you and Scud get into the tunnel without Sunny Weaver messing it up. And then I tunnel back to Van Cott. So I can be there in case

Groon tries to back out. And if you guys do kill Groon, I'll want to be in Van Cott for whatever happens next."

"Stop it," says Zoe, pressing her hands against her head.

"Good morning, sleepyheads!" calls Mom. "Zoe, you shower and get dressed, and we'll go right over to the school. You can hang with your friends and I'll grab a seat. Are you eating with us, Maisie, or do you have to go now?"

"I'm going," says Maisie, taking the hint. "Zoe said I could borrow her bike?"

Zoe hasn't actually said that, but whatev. She gives Maisie the key to the bike lock. Maisie snags a piece of cinnamon bread from their kitchen and peels an orange while she's at it. Gets Zoe's beater bike from the garage, and she's on her way.

"High school *romance*!" yells Maisie, as she cheerfully pedal-pumps off.

When Mom and Zoe get to the high school about an hour later, Scud comes up to Zoe right away. He looks inordinately happy.

"Saw Maisie?" says Zoe.

"Yeah," beams Scud. Zoe's never seen him so ebullient.

"Was your dad mad at you for leaving on the road trip with Villy?" Zoe asks.

"He hadn't noticed," says Scud, laughing. "It's not like we were actually gone for long. Not from his point of view. I told Dad about the trip, and for once he was interested in me. You remember about Yampa's pictures being in my head? Get this. Dad helped me use my teep slug to transfer Yampa's pictures from my brain into my internet image cloud. It was tricky, but we did it. So we've got a buttload of photos from ballyworld. Gotta be some fame and money in that, Zoe. If we survive."

"Sweet," says Zoe. But her thoughts on the upcoming battle. "Where's Maisie now?"

"She's talking to her mother. Sunny Weaver? Sunny started yelling at me when I said something about killing Groon. She says Groon is God. And that it would *behoove* me to welcome him. I've never heard anyone say that word before. I told her she's a psycho, and that she should stay the eff out of our way." Scud chuckles to himself. "I was like a mouthy skater kid. And then I walked off. Sunny was foaming at the mouth. So Maisie is trying to chill her out. Do you want your new saucer pearl now? We'll use them to zap and to fly."

"Gimme." Zoe's brought a loose cloth purse along, and she stashes her supersize saucer pearl in there. Scud's got his in his baggy pants pocket. She and Scud are amped on adrenaline, giddy with an insane undercurrent of tension. It's like they're climbing the steps of the highest diving tower ever.

"How soon?" Zoe asks Scud. "How soon do we go through?"

"Well, Maisie took me to look at the unny tunnel gate in the gym," says Scud. "Ten thousand dead saucers in there by now. So rank. The whole gym floor is covered with them. Piled thirty feet deep in the middle. And on top of them is the spherical gate. By now it's the size of an SUV. The smell in there—whoah. Like turds and turpentine."

"Why aren't there cops at the gym?" asks Zoe. "Or janitors or people just walking by? Isn't anyone going to notice a giant pile of dead saucers? They've been piling up since yesterday."

"Cloud of unknowing," goes Scud.

"Huh?"

"That teep invisibility spell?" says Scud. "Maisie and I were looking in through the gym door at the dead saucers, and a normal-looking security guard walks by—and I can tell that all he sees in there is the shiny wood floor he's expecting to see. An empty floor with the red and blue curving lines for the basketball courts. The gate and the saucers—they're hidden in a cloud of unknowing. You and Maisie and me, by now we're at a level where we can see through the cloud."

"Still seems like the cops would know," says Zoe. "From the smell."

"I think by now a lot of cops are saucer zombies," says Scud. "Getting their instructions from Groon and his saucers. And of course they're being told not to interfere at the high school today."

"Got it," says Zoe. "And—are we supposed to fly into that horrible, creepy death-tunnel right now? Or can I graduate first?"

"Might as well wait till something's actually happening," says Scud. "Don your cap and gown. Claim your diploma. That's what Villy would have wanted."

"Don't talk like he's dead!" cries Zoe. "He's not! He's in the fourth dimension!" Suddenly she's close to tears. She dreamed of Villy last night. Villy hovering near her bed, touching and kissing her.

Before long it's time for the ceremony to start. Zoe puts on her flimsy gown and the flat hat, and finds her assigned seat among the other graduating seniors. The grads and the onlookers are in folding chairs on the high school's huge, low lawn. The front end of the lawn slants up steeply to the 1920s neoclassical building. White stone steps run up the slope. Dignitaries are at the top, on a flat, grassy strip.

A speaker speaks, and then another. Zoe's not hearing a thing. She's scared to even think. And now someone's calling the graduates' names and they're trooping up there one by one. From the A's to the L's to the S's. Zoe Snapp's turn.

Villy awakens at—well, it's very hard to judge time out here in unspace. The 4D flat cow is floating near the tunnel between the worlds. Seen through Villy's own eyes, the tunnel looks like the surface of a sphere that changes as he moves his head. There are patches of pink and blue on some of the spheres. And squiggly stuff like guts. What's going on? Villy is energized enough that, just in his head, he's able to sketch a fresh line drawing to explain it, a Figure 10.

FIGURE 10: VILLY AND YULIA LOOKING AT THE UNNY TUNNEL

The Square sees the circumference of a disk. Villy sees the surface of a sphere. The Square Cow with the higher eye sees the two-dimensional surface of the tunnel. And Yulia with her wondrous 4D eye, she sees the 3D hypersurface of the tunnel. Which means what?

Well, Yulia's feeding Villy her image of the unny tunnel and it's like a 3D space that kind of wraps around. The analogies are breaking down. This is just weird. Studying Yulia's view of the hypertunnel, he sees it begin pulsing and flailing around. Like a snake that's swallowing a wild pig. And the tunnel space has a pink glob and a blue glob inside it. Big creatures sliding along the hypersurface of the tunnel.

"Is that already Groon?" Villy asks Yulia. His pulse is sky-high. "Shouldn't we hurry up and pinch off those two cross-sections? You do have the Neptune's tablecloths, right?"

"That's not the bagpipe in there, noooo," the flat cow says equably. "It's those mile-wide saucers, Poppo and Bomboooo. We'll let them go throooough. You and I keep waiting for Grooooon."

Villy is worried. "The giant saucers will trash my hometown!"

"Los Perros is defended by Scud's wand and Zoe's hoooorn. Powerful tooools."

Villy's guitar twitches at the mention of Zoe's horn, perhaps missing the stratocast duets.

"Let's at least keep an eye on what's happening in Los Perros," implores Villy. "And if things get bad, we pop out of unspace and help them. Okay?"

"We'll looook," says Yulia. "But our target is Grooooon."

So here's Zoe walking across the patch of lawn in front of the columned Los Perros High facade. She's wearing a white mortarboard and a white nylon rental robe. Her purse with the saucer pearl is under the gown, and her flexible living trumpet has twined himself around her leg.

Mr. Clark the principal hands Zoe a scrap of paper with a number on it. She'd been expecting a rolled-up parchment with a red ribbon around it, like in *Archie* comics. The numbered scrap merely *symbolizes* her hard-won diploma—which is to be picked up at the school office next week, assuming all her fees and documents are in order at that time.

Right in that moment of slight disappointment, the gym behind the high school explodes. Bursts like a steel, wood, and stucco bomb, scattering the unsavory remains of the leech saucers who died to make the tunnel. A mile-wide saucer slithers out of the rubble, expanding on the fly. Bombo. And here comes his mate, Poppo.

The two monsters jostle companionably, with the light aqua Bombo a bit higher in the air than pale red Poppo. He's half-resting on her back. They're like apocalyptic jellyfish, blotting out the heavens. Each of them has an evilly glowing red eye in their underside's center. They dangle a thousand oral arms—slimy, sticky, suckerless tentacles. Eager to feed upon the plentiful human prey, Bombo and Poppo set to work dragging their strands across the sidewalks, parks, and patios nearby. Poppo herself is combing the verdant front lawn of Los Perros High, which is dotted with imposing thick-trunked palms, arrayed with chairs, and crowded with the chic, well-off friends and families of this year's graduating class—who by now are stampeding in wild panic.

Oddly detached, Zoe gazes down from the hillock that serves as the graduation's stage. It's totally like a vintage

'50s sci-fi flick, she thinks. Like, *The Attack of the Giant Saucers*. Why do aliens always have to *attack*? Can't humans and saucers be friends? I mean, look at Scud and Nunu, or at Dad and—well, never mind.

Bombo is silent, but Poppo is singing—Zoe recognizes the icky, saccharine voice from hearing it in Thuddland. The tuneless wavering notes overlay the desperate shouts and screams of the crowd. Most of them can evade the slowly swaying oral arms, but Zoe can spot five or six victims on the ground, each with a dangling tentacle fastened to their flesh, siphoning away some portion of that person's smeel, or *élan vital*, or soul. This isn't a movie. This is real. This is the start of the cosmic beatdown.

"Scud!" hollers Zoe, and maybe she teeps her call as well. And here he comes, geekishly calm, hurrying up the high school's grand front steps to Zoe on the raised part of the lawn. He's carrying his navel-orange-sized saucer pearl, and Zoe's got hers out of her purse, and Scud's flourishing the cryptic wand that lives within his arm.

"Power up your pearl!" yells Scud. "And put your free hand on mine—we'll do like batteries in series. We need hella dark energy for this first jolt. Disintegrate Poppo before she sees us! Shock and awe, Zo-zo!"

Scud's voice is level and surprisingly strong. Maybe the boy does hold some promise, as Maisie seems to believe. But how can Zoe possibly thinking about Maisie's flirtations? Zoe and Scud are supposed to be saving the world. *Focus!*

Oh, oh, here comes Maisie with her weird stepmother Sunny Weaver on her heels, toiling up the steps to join them. Sunny's expression is truculent, but Zoe doesn't give her time to interfere.

Moving fast, Zoe unwraps her trumpet from her leg and tucks him under her arm, while holding her big new pearl in her hand. She lays her other hand on Scud's shoulder. Peeping into her pearl, Zoe powers it into zap mode. And then, heedless of the risk, she turns her body into a dark-energy amplifier—and funnels the zap-juice across her body and into Scud, who's feeding all of it into his wand.

Scud's normally callow face has taken on a hard and solemn look. He raises his wand. Glowing dots sparkle around its tip, and—

Ka-fooom!

It's like a skyrocket exploding above Zoe's head. The blast knocks her flat on her butt, and she damn near drops her pearl and trumpet. Her ears are ringing, but she can tell that Poppo's ooky song is gone. And what about the humongo pink saucer herself? She's dust, she's drifting down like pastel soot. Good one, Scud.

But Bombo's still here and, as Zoe can reasonably assume, he's upset about the loss of his mate. He's vibrating his body like a bass speaker, pulsing out dark notes and subsonic vibrations that Zoe senses as resonant vibrations in her gut. She feels like throwing up. Sparks are crackling from Bombo's edges towards the great red eye at the center of his mile-wide underside, like he's a wheel on a science-fair spark machine. His gaze sweeps back and forth across the lawn. His freaky throbbing rises to a crescendo.

"Here they are!" Sunny Weaver screams to the great saucer. Her voice is harsh and grainy. She's pointing at

Zoe and Scud, and staring up at Bombo. It's not yet clear if Bombo hears her. Sunny's jaw is jutting out at a weird angle. Every scrap of her plastic-surgery glamour is gone. She's acting like an evil toad. "Shoot here, master, shoot here! These two! They killed Poppo!"

Bombo falls ominously silent. His red eye's glow grows. Zoe and Scud sprint away from the stage and onto the flat part of the lawn.

Ka-raaack.

Again Zoe finds herself knocked off her feet and, oh my god, there's a fifty-foot-deep crater in the place of the Los Perros High front steps. The result of Bombo's zap. Surely it'll take the saucer some time to power up for his next shot, but now—*creak, creeak, creeeak*—oh shit, the school's elaborate, columned, pediment-topped facade is wavering, leaning, looming, and . . . falling forward in a slow-motion collapse.

Zoe uses her big saucer pearl to fly down to the lawn, with the tuned-in Scud at her side. The neoclassical facade comes down with an accelerating rumble and screech, ending with thudding chunks of masonry, a roiling cloud of dust, and sad, anguished cries.

At least a dozen people were on that strip of lawn up there. Prosaic, stoic Principal Clark, Ms. Boot the enforcer, Chau En Lai the valedictorian, handsome Coach Simmons, Amparo Quinonez from the Los Perros city council, and Zoltan Nemeth the photographer—all of them murdered by the giant saucer. Crushed to pulp. Tears spring to Zoe's eyes.

Bombo has lowered himself to a hundred feet above

them. His hateful ruby eye is directly overhead. His mile-wide body covers the entire sky. He's making that creepy booming noise, slowly rocking back and forth, feeling for the presence of Zoe and Scud. Preparing to fire again.

Zoe pulls herself together. She's standing at Scud's side with her pearl in her left hand, her trumpet under her left arm, and her right hand on Scud's shoulder. "Quick!" she says, "Take down Bombo!"

"If I can get my mojo back in time," whispers Scud. "I'm trying. But—oh shit—he's already running sparks across his bottom again. And his eye, it's flaring up—look out, Zoe!"

A second blast strikes the rubble and the lawn, making a crater that overlaps with the first one. The hit is blessedly wide of Zoe and Scud.

"Do it now!" Zoe screams. "Shoot!"

Okay, the dark energy is flowing through Zoe's body to Scud's, and he's raising his arm, and the evanescent fireflies of power are buzzing around his wand, and—

Eeek! It's that goddamn Sunny Weaver. She's got her hands around Scud's neck from behind and she's—are you kidding?—she's frikkin *choking* him.

"Leave the saucers alone!" Sunny yells. "It's the new dawn! Hail Groon!" Sunny cocks back her head. Her hair is sticking out on all sides, like from static electricity. She's locked into a master-slave teep loop with Bombo. "Here they are, Lord!" she yowls.

To make thing worse, saucer zombies are hurrying across the lawn towards Zoe and Scud. The latest zombies are people whom Poppo slimed. They're not dead, they're up and on their feet, twenty or thirty of them. And, oh god, it looks like there's a pair of zombie cops down by the street, getting out of their patrol car with pistols drawn. All of them following the mile-wide saucer's orders.

The immediate problem is to make Sunny Weaver stop choking Scud. Maisie is dithering, not quite able to take action against her stepmother of so many years. But Zoe has no such qualms. She raises her horn to her lips and sends a supercharged wake-up blast right into Sunny's spiteful marshmallow face—with the bell of the trumpet physically touching her. Sunny reels back with her hands over her ears. Scud is free.

By now, of course, Bombo knows exactly where they are. In fact he's beaming down a laser spotter beam that seems to be locked onto, um, the crown of Scud's head. Nowhere to run, no place to hide. Once again Bombo ramps up his beats, and his central eye lights in a deadly glow.

Zoe slips into panic mode. "Run!" she yells to Maisie. She's fully ready to abandon Scud. Who says Zoe has to be a hero? But Maisie grabs her arm, and Zoe can't get away, and Scud's expecting the help.

"Feed me your energy," yells Scud. "Do like with Poppo." The nerdy younger brother raises his wand. He's ready to face the mile-wide killer saucer in a final shoot-out. And Zoe has to go along.

"Okay," says Zoe after the briefest of pauses. "I'm in." Once again she channels the energies of her horn and of the saucer pearl to her friend. And Maisie's powering Scud too. Zoe wonders if Villy can see her from the fourth dimension. Oh darling, if only we'd had more time.

Scud and the saucer unleash their energy-bolts at the same moment. The beams collide in midair, sputtering into a painfully bright light. Like a welder's arc, like a miniature star. Scud doesn't let up; he stands there, silhouetted against the smoke and the sparks, urging his beam higher—up, up, and up towards floppy Bombo.

And then Zoe adds a touch that's all her own. She takes her trumpet in her right hand and blows a frantic solo, a clarion call that could tumble a castle wall. This tips the balance.

Fa-tooooom.

Bombo the mile-wide saucer is a fogbank of blue dust, softly settling onto the lawns and homes of Los Perros. Sirens wail—emergency vehicles, some on their way, some already here. Firemen dig for survivors in the rubble pits. Medics carry off the wounded and the dead.

Precious few others remain on the lawn. Empty, tumbled chairs—and fifty saucer zombies closing in on Zoe, Scud, and Maisie. Bombo had been urging the zombies to block the kids' attack. But now, with the saucer gone, his followers have fallen back on residual programming— which may or may not include orders to kill Zoe and Scud. At least they're being slow about it.

Sunny Weaver sits on the ground, dazed and confused. She looks dowdy, her years of flashy flirting long gone. An aging woman, sad and alone. For the first time ever, Zoe feels pity for her.

"You're my big hero," Maisie is saying to Scud. She's kissing him all over his face.

"Not done yet," says bashful Scud.

"We still have Groon," adds Zoe. "The main event." If they don't stop Groon, all this has been in vain.

With so much of the high school turned to rubble, Zoe can see through to where the gym was. The gate of the unny tunnel has grown to a hundred feet high. Zoe can see into it, a little bit. A dark, floppy shape is in there. Like a tadpole in a frog egg in a pond.

"You can do it," says Maisie, giving Zoe a kiss on the cheek. "I'll tunnel over to mappyworld and do what I can from over there."

"I'm terrified," confesses Zoe. "I'm sick with fear."

"Yeah, we're totally doomed," says Maisie, oddly cheerful. "Saying that out loud gets your energy up, hmm?"

"Wait," says Zoe. "In Surf World you told me that we're cosmic mythic heroes. So we can't lose, right?"

"That was just something I said," goes Maisie. "I said it to pump you up and keep you on the team. And that's why Pinchley and Flipsydaisy said it too. We could die any second. It's been that way all along. There's no guarantee. Goob-goob was running out of options. That's why she went ahead and enlisted us. A last-ditch kind of move."

"*Sir! Ma'am! We have to ask you to raise your hands.*" A voice through a bullhorn. Oh god, it's one of those zombie cops, still standing by the patrol car. He has a rifle.

"Don't stop now," Maisie tells Zoe and Scud. She fashions her saucer pearl into a one-person tunnel gate—and she's gone.

"*Raise your hands or we'll have to shoot.*"

Fat new saucer pearls in hand, Zoe and Scud swoop into the tunnel gate where the gym had been.

THIRTY

cosmic beatdown, part 2

Yulia streams images of Los Perros to Villy, and he witnesses much of Zoe's and Scud's battle against the giant saucers Poppo and Bombo, although it's confusing because Yulia sees everybody's insides as well as their outsides. The action scenes are intercut with immersive images of the great Groon slowly making his way into the tunnel. The warped space at the tunnel's mouth is making room for him, but even so, it takes a while because the bagpipe is so big. Villy thinks of a baby's head pushing out through a woman's birth canal. He's never quite understood how that's even possible.

"Like a camel passing through the eye of a needle, nooooo?" says Yulia, picking up on Villy's thoughts.

"Where are you from anyway?" Villy asks Yulia. "And what are you, if you're not a flying saucer? You still haven't told me."

"I'm a part of Goob-goooob," says the flat cow. "Like a lure dangling from a deep-sea fish's broooow."

"Goob-goob's a million miles away," protests Villy.

"Distances can be shorter in the higher woooorld," says the flat cow.

And now she shows Villy a 4D-rear-view-mirror-type image of her body. It turns out that her tail is a four-dimensional tendril or connector or umbilical cord that runs through unspace to the body of Goob-goob—who's ever so faintly visible as a Mayan ziggurat whose eye pokes into 4D unspace as well. The eye winks at Villy.

"Got it," Villy says and falls silent for a minute, absorbing the weirdness. Meanwhile, the little saucerbaby Duckworth is crawling around on his chest. Probably he wants to get out of the flat cow and fly around. Not yet.

Villy formulates another question for Yulia. "Why do you, or why does *Goob-goob*, if you're really part of her—I mean, why do you guys even need me to help? Why don't you trap Groon in the tunnel yourself?"

"You have a nimble boooody," says Yulia. "And it makes a better story to have a human do the joooob."

"Story?"

"The world is made of stooooories," says the flat cow, getting into a divine wisdom routine. "Not atooooms. Words weave the cosmoooos. A tangle of gossip, archetypes, and jooookes."

The moos echo in Villy's head. He's always imagined his thoughts to be images of the firm external world. But Yulia's saying it's the other way around. Villy tries to get to that state of mind. And for a few seconds he's there. Reality is a sea of sensations, feelings, and tales, intricately linked, with everything alluding to everything else. And the stodgy, solid, kick-a-brick, normative world—*that* part is the illusion. *That* part is the dream.

As for the split between ballyworld and mappyworld—there's really no difference between dreaming the world as a bunch of planets, or dreaming the world as an endless sheet of basins. Either way, it's the same gnarly thing underneath. Feet on a welcome mat. A tangle of talk. Yeah. Villy feels high as a kite.

"Time for woooork," says Yulia. She clenches her body, beginning to squeeze Villy out through the slit in her side.

"My brain will fall out!" cries Villy. "My organs and bones!"

"They woooon't," says the 4D flat cow. "I'll put a coat of 4D smeel slime on yoooou. Like in my picture of the Square."

"This year's fashion look for the unspace surf crew," says Villy, channeling his terror into a joke. "Why can't I stay inside you? Why do I have to go out there alone?"

"Because I'm scared of Grooooon," Yulia softly moos. "And of the unspace tuuuube. I'm just a coooow. I leave the tube to yooooou."

So here's Villy, adrift in hyperdimensional unspace, with the folded-up disks of the Neptune's tablecloths under his arm. He wears his guitar at his waist, and little Duckworth buzzes ineffectually near his head. There's not any regular air out (in? under? over?) here, but Villy feels no shortness of breath. The milky light of the higher world fills him with energy. And his 4D-smeel-glazed body is holding together fine. Like an assembled and plastic-laminated jigsaw puzzle. A Square in higher space.

Looking towards Los Perros, Villy sees slices of houses, cars, and dirt. Images that change when he turns his head or moves his eyes. Two-dimensional cross-sections. And that unny tunnel he's supposed to tie off, when he looks at that thing on his own, he sees something like a sphere with a big gnarly slices of mortadella salami on it. Presumably that's a cross-section of his archenemy Groon.

Once again the flat cow begins teeping Villy a stream of immersive, holographic images, which include Villy and his surroundings. He watches his body's fitful, four-dimensional motions as if watching a stranger have a seizure on a sidewalk. He feels fear and pity for that person.

Never mind. He keeps on twitching—bucking his bod like a frantic inchworm. In the process, he finds that his 4D-smeel coat contains—*score!*— higher-dimensional muscles that he can control. It's like he's inside a flexible 4D surfboard. And if he bucks and hyper-bucks in a particular kind of steady pulse—why, then he glides through unspace like an eel in a lambent tropical sea. Yah, mon.

Observing Villy's moves, the equally smeel-coated Duckworth learns to navigate in unspace as well. In this fashion our hero and his mascot approach the hypersolid unspace tunnel whose hypersurface contains Groon. With his bare eyes, Villy can't tell if Zoe and Scud are in there with Groon or not. What he sees is like a big ball with an intricate anatomy chart on it. Yulia's feed isn't all that much help because, Villy now realizes, she's editing the images that she sends him. He's liking this less all the time.

"Be ready to wrap those disks around two of the spots on the tunnel," orders the flat cow. "You'll want to have them in place by the time Groon's in the middle. And then I'll tell you when to tighten them."

"I dill ston't see why cou yan't do this instead of me," mumbles Villy, so disoriented that he's stumbling over his words. "I'm coo tlumsy."

The flat cow starts laughing at him, like *moo-hah, moo-hah*, but really it's Goob-goob laughing, given that the flat cow is Goob-goob's sock puppet. Eff Goob-goob and eff the 4D flat cow.

Clutching her big saucer pearl, Zoe sails towards the hundred-foot-tall mouth of the giant tunnel, with Scud close behind. The spherical gate rests upon the bombed-out rubble of the gym surrounded by the tens of thousands of dead inside-out saucers who gave their all. Meanwhile, the zombie cops on the lawn are firing their guns. Saucer stooges that they are. *Pop, pop, pop.*

Zoe does jiggly evasive swerves. Then they're safe in the tunnel, and the world of Los Perros dwindles to a luminous ball behind them. And ahead of them—

"Here we go," says Scud.

Groon is in there, as expected. A bagpipe who's the size of a mountain. He still has that giant saxophone-like horn bell with the narrow honky second horn in the middle of it. Thanks to the unny tunnel's curvature, Zoe sees ghostly duplicate images of Groon and, for that matter, of herself. Another effect of the tunnel's warp is that Groon's body seems to bend around to touch itself in back. Like a dachshund on a rug beside a fireplace.

The monster bagpipe wasn't expecting to meet anyone inside the tunnel. He greets Scud and Zoe with an angry squall of wheenks and squeals. Zoe pays close attention to the sounds. She purses her lips and fingers her trumpet's valves, thinking about how to imitate Groon.

Beyond Groon lies the exit to Van Cott—it resembles the exit to Los Perros. Both are airy balls with worlds inside them, each still looking about a hundred feet wide. Zoe reminds herself that when the exit balls begin to shrink, she and Scud need to get the hell out of here.

Groon may not have eyes, strictly speaking, but his teepy, wriggly feelers can sense the kids' every move. His squawking horn is homing in on them like a radar-aimed cannon. But Scud's already in battle mode. The boy raises his wand and—

Ka-fooom!

A blast from Skzx the Aristo wand. Zoe half-expects to see the big brown bagpipe dissolve into manure dust. But no such luck. For a few seconds, a reticulated network of sparks plays across the monster's hide—and then he shakes it off. Quite unfazed, the bagpipe finishes aiming his nested pair of horns and—

Squa-whonk!

The pulse of air is so narrowly focused that it hits only Scud. The supersonic stream propels the boy back out the Los Perros end of the tunnel—tumbling ass over teakettle. Quite unexpectedly, the blast's residual eddies have the effect of drawing Zoe *closer* to Groon. Making the best of it, Zoe flies directly at the bagpipe, meaning to park herself beside the base of his horns, there to find safety from his stormy blasts.

Deftly Groon counters her move. Rather than letting Zoe alight on his skin, he sucks a swirling maelstrom of air

into the bell of his large outer horn, thereby pulling Zoe—
oh no—into the cluttered inner recesses of his mile-wide
body. The turbulent currents ragdoll her limbs as she tumbles through funhouse passageways. She loses hold of her
big new pearl and it's gone. Round and round she swirls,
carried on by air currents and the spiteful jostling of Groon.
She lands on her feet—in a vat of congealed smeel, thick as
paste or quicksand. It reaches to her knees. This is insane.

Frantically Zoe looks around. She's in a vaulted chamber
amid the fleshy tubes and jaw-like wringers and squeezy-
hands that make up Groon's saucer-milking operation.
Nearby are the glowing bladders of his saucer-egg hatchery. And next to that is a loamy, fungal bed that grows
saucer pearls. The vat she landed in is a storage vessel for
Groon's smeel stash. Oh, why does this stuff have to be
so sticky? Fruitlessly she tries to extricate herself, but the
harder she struggles, the deeper she sinks.

To make things worse, several hundred baby saucers are
in here with Zoe. The great bagpipe isn't spewing them
out through his thin horn just now. So the babies are at
loose ends, buzzing around at random. And now the little
guys catch Zoe's scent. Being leeches, they flock around
her like mosquitoes in a swamp.

Thinking fast, Zoe puts her horn to her mouth and
begins imitating Groon. Enchanted by the tune, the baby
saucers fall into sync with each other and begin flying in
formation. Skillfully shaping her notes, Zoe sends them
out of Groon's narrow central horn.

The great bagpipe honks in irritation. But all the while
he continues moving forward through the tunnel. His

goal is, after all, to reach Los Perros. Zoe figures Villy should be tightening his Neptune's tablecloths around now. But that doesn't seem to be happening. The sizes of the Los Perros and Van Cott exits are holding steady, hanging there like house-sized Christmas tree balls, each with its own alternate world inside.

Weirdly weightless, Villy flounders and flaps in the 4D unspace as he and Duckworth prepare to wrap the first Neptune's tablecloth around what he sees as a blank spherical cross-section of the unny tunnel. Annoyingly, Yulia isn't showing Villy a full holographic picture anymore. And the jumble of spheres that Villy sees on his own isn't really worth jack shit. Some of them have the big salami slice on them, and some don't. Groon is indeed nearby. Villy can even hear the foul bagpipe's squeals.

Yulia has switched to feeding Villy images of mental *models* of the tunnel instead of straight-on holographic video. Like, she shows him a time-lapse movie of a weather balloon breathing in and out—with a capital letter G on its side for Groon. And then she switches to showing the tunnel as a cubist comic strip, featuring a cute high school teacher lady who's making love to conic sections. The woman, Villy is meant to understand, is his Los Perros High math teacher, and she represents the grisly Groon, and Villy has to be sure to trap her in between the two Neptune's tablecloths. Sigh. He gets on with his job.

As Villy unfolds the first tablecloth, he's waving his arms in four separate dimensions, which means his hands are flickering in and out of sight. Disturbing. He worries

his protective coating of 4D smeel might peel loose, and
that he'll see his forearm's bones go spinning away like
some crowd-pleasing drummer's tossed drumsticks.

Duckworth is a definite help. The basic move is that
Villy clamps onto a spot on the circumference of this
Neptune's tablecloth disk, and Duckworth latches onto
a spot on the opposite side of the disk, and then the saucerboy wriggles all the way around the unny tunnel, dragging the disk with him—and he brings his edge back to
Villy. And then Villy is holding two opposite points on the
edge, with the tunnel now partially wrapped in the tablecloth. You'd think the tablecloth wouldn't reach, given
that Groon is supposedly a mile wide, but as Yulia says,
in unspace, distances tend to be shorter than you expect.

Villy and Duckworth do their wrapping move six times
and end up with the first tablecloth fully wrapped around
one of the tunnel's cross-sections that doesn't seem to
have any Groon in it. Villy's got the tablecloth's entire
outer edge scrunched into his hand. So he effectively has
that particular section of the tunnel in a sack. When he's
ready to squash that part of the tunnel, he'll tighten the
sack by tugging out on the edge all the way around. But
first he has to move over a bit and wrap the second tablecloth. Again, you'd think he might have to move a whole
mile—the size of Groon—but, again, a relatively small
motion in unspace goes a long way.

To make Villy's task significantly more unpleasant than
it has to be, the tunnel keeps zapping him with hair-thin
sparks, as if from a buildup of static electricity, only it's
not electricity, it's dark energy, or perhaps it's some even

gnarlier unspace force. Each time a spark hits Villy, he experiences a jump-cut in his perception of so-called reality. That is, he loses about a second or two of his personal mental timeline. It's like the tapestry of his life is blemished with pocks of nothingness. A horrible sensation.

"I'm glad you're handling this so well," teeps Yulia, watching from a distance, all calm and fatuous.

"Can you tell that I'm having gaps?" asks Villy.

"You're like a stone skipping across a poooond," moos the flat cow.

"Which part is the water?" asks Villy, more than a little annoyed with Yulia by now.

"The water is the whoooole," says Yulia. "Life's floooow."

Another tiny spark zings Villy around then and he undergoes another jump-cut. When he comes back, Yulia has just finished mooing something else. But he didn't hear it.

"The air," says Villy. "If I'm a stone skipping over the water of life, what does the *air* stand for?"

"Nothing and noboooody," says Yulia. "I dread such a metaphysical zeroooo. That's why I make you do this joooob. I guide from aboooove. You're sturdy and looooow—"

"Kiss my ass," cries Villy. "I mean—you're *snobby* about me doing something too dangerous for you to try? I'm touching the unny tunnel because you can't? And you're saying I won't die because I'm, too—*stupid*?"

"Finish your woooork," says the pompous, controlling cow. "Wrap the second tablecloooooth."

"I want to know what's really going on inside the frikkin tunnel," cries Villy. "I can hear the bagpipe and I think I can hear Zoe's horn. I need to see what you see."

"Noooo."

Villy nods his head up and down, scanning through the cross-sectional layers of Groon. Every time he thinks he might see a slice of Zoe, a hair-thin spark leaps joyfully from the tunnel and digs a divot in his mind. Somehow the awfulness of this engages and even amuses the surfer side of Villy. Now *this*, this is a sick trip, my man.

Wearing a stark grin, Villy plows through the unceasing stutter of the insufferable jump-cuts, drawing heavily on little Duckworth's help all the while. And then the second Neptune's tablecloth is wrapped around a second Groon-free section of the tunnel. Villy now holds, in effect, the ends of the two sacks in his hands.

As it happens, the tablecloths are a little bigger than they needed to be, so some of the material overlaps above his hands. It's like when Uncle Scrooge grabs a money-bag and there's a floppy flounce of cloth above his ducky fist.

The plan? When Yulia gives the word, Villy will squeeze the sacks. He'll work more and more of the material past his hands, leaving smaller and smaller volumes for what's inside.

By now Villy is panting with exhaustion—not that panting matters much when there's no actual air. It's only the mysterioso light of unspace that's keeping him alive. But he's not letting himself think too deeply about this. And now that he's done with the wrapping, the sparks from the unny tunnel have stopped.

Yulia eases over to Villy's side, and—even though by now he hates her—he gets partly back inside her to be comfortable. He's still holding the necks of those bunched sacks in his hands.

"When?" he asks the flat cow.

"Soooon," says Yulia. "I want Groon to move just a bit moooore. And then Zoe and Scud fly to safety and—*boooonk*. You close the doooors."

Once again Villy twitches his head, unsuccessfully trying to catch a glimpse of Scud or Zoe amid the balloons-with-salami-slices that his eyes can see. He can hear Groon's squawks—and the clear tones of Zoe's trumpet. Meanwhile the frikkin flat cow is feeding him is a bullshit cartoon of a cowboy with two lassos.

"You'll truly make sure that Scud and Zoe escape?" begs Villy.

"No woooorries. Trust Goob-goooob."

Zoe's feet are still stuck in the vat of smeel. Wanting to distract Groon before he progresses much further through the tunnel, she puts her trumpet to her lips and plays very loud. Groon hesitates, not quite sure what's going on. And now Scud comes flying back from Los Perros with his wand extended.

Fa-tooom!

Another blast! Groon flinches, rocked by the hit. And Zoe's blatting solo is shaking the monster's belly like the worst stomachache ever. Seeking surcease, the noise-bag sprouts fleshy tendrils from the inner skin of his bag—he grows feelers to grope for his tormenter. As one of the tendrils approaches Zoe, she ducks and loses her balance and—*oh shit*—her left hand goes down into the vat's smeel and gets stuck as well. She's like a mouse in a glue-trap.

Desperate for Scud's aid, Zoe switches her trumpet-calls to plaintive bleats, wanting him to crawl inside the intricate bag and help her. But the boy holds back. Scud is leery of Groon. And he's worried about running out of time.

A fresh Groon tendril twines around Zoe's waist and starts towards her neck. She snaps it off with her free hand, only to have two more tentacles appear at the broken tip. *If only she could get loose*. Suddenly she has an idea.

She aims her trumpet downward, directly at the vat of smeel, and toots a machine-gun arpeggio of soprano notes. Almost immediately the staccato tune softens the sticky stuff into yielding gruel. *Yes!* Zoe pulls her left hand loose, rips all fleshy tendrils away from her body, and clambers free of the quicksand vat of smeel. Now to find her way out. *Hurry!*

Groon's forward motion continues unabated.

"Noooow!" the flat cow commands Villy. "Pull the sacks cloooosed."

"Are Zoe and my brother still in there?"

"Noooo! Don't worry soooo."

Manfully Villy hauls away on the edges of the two Neptune's tablecloths, constricting the exits on either side of Groon.

Peering out through Groon's translucent hide, Zoe notices something very bad.

The exit to Los Perros is shrinking. Fast. It's already too small for Groon. The bagpipe throws himself at the shimmering ball and—*bonk*—he can't fit through. He squeals in fury.

Scud flies close to Groon's translucent hide and gestures frantically to Zoe. Like—Come on! It's time to bail! Fly out of there!

Without her big saucer pearl Zoe can't fly. But she's doing her level best to hop and crawl and climb towards the hole where the horn leads out, scrambling through the tangles of Groon's innards, through slimy channels, along the inner surfaces of his sack, grabbing onto muscles and tendons and veins. But over and over, the vengeful Groon finds ways to stymie her progress—he yanks her ankles with his tendrils, he bucks his walls to shake her loose, he pumps blasts of air to toss her about. It's one step forward and two steps back—here in the mazy belly of the beast.

At the same time, Groon is lurching back and forth in the tunnel. He rushes towards the Van Cott exit. But that end of the tunnel is shrinking too. *Bonk*. He turns and speeds once more towards the Los Perros exit. *Bonk*.

Somewhere out there, Villy is tightening the Neptune's tablecloths. And that can only mean that Villy doesn't know that Zoe's stuck in here. How can that be?

Yet again, Zoe toots a wailing sob from her horn, hoping that somehow Villy will hear and understand. Not impossible. It's not, after all, an ordinary horn. Perhaps the horn's notes can travel through unspace?

Meanwhile Scud is doing his utmost to free Zoe. Wand in hand, he's blasting away at Groon's hide, wanting to make a hole for Zoe. But it's not working. Scud tries again, using the saucer pearl as well. He bears down, not wanting to stop. A minute passes. Groon's skin won't give way.

The gate to Los Perros has grown very small—it's not even three feet across. Scud's face is anguished. He gestures to Zoe that he's sorry. He can't wait any longer. He wriggles through the gate to Los Perros. By now the gate is a tiny bright spot, only a few inches across.

At this point it occurs to Zoe that she still has her tiny saucer pearl in her pocket, the one from before, the one she's already used for hopping four separate times, and she ought to be able to open this pearl up into a tunnel once again, right? And maybe the tunnel would lead back to that intricate intersectional moment on the Los Perros night street where Mom's SUV almost rammed them. Yes!

With trembling hands Zoe sets her little pearl afloat before her. And she plays the proper honks on her horn. But—nothing is happening. This isn't the right kind of space here, or Groon is spoiling the vibes, or the pearl's energy is down—whatever it is, the grubby little pearl is as lusterless and inert as a cheap plastic bead. Zoe plays her magic tune again, just in case, and one more time—no go. The pinpoint light of the exit gate is gone.

Groon thrashes, belches, howls, farts. The air is hot and foul. It's like being inside a garbage bag in the trunk of a car in the sun. Zoe is going to die.

Help me, Villy.

The flat cow now teeps Villy a clear view of how the tightening tablecloths have pinched through the narrowed necks of the tunnel. It's done. The spaces of mappyworld and ballyworld have healed with no scars. In between them is a small world, a pocket universe, sealed in on itself, gradually dwindling in size, presumably with Groon inside—but the perverse Yulia is hiding any images of Groon.

What bothers Villy is that he's still hearing Zoe's trumpet. High thin notes making their way through unspace. Like she's calling for him from inside that ball?

"Tell me Zoe's okay," Villy cries to Yulia.

"She's safe at hoooome."

Villy wants to believe this. But he doesn't. "Set me down in Los Perros so I can see her!"

"First I want to savor the death of Grooooon," says Yulia. "Victory is woooon. I speak as Goob-goooob."

"I can damage you," says Villy, goaded to fury. He feels around his leather-lined passenger compartment within Yulia's body and once again he finds the lump that he'd earlier thought was a saucer pearl. He puts a hand on either side of it and begins squeezing. It's quite flexible. Not a saucer pearl at all. An internal organ of some kind. Yulia flinches as he bears down on it.

"I'm going to pop this thing," Villy tells Yulia. "Unless I see Zoe."

"Low, hot-headed ruuuube," says Yulia. "You must goooo." With a quick twitch of her body, the flat cow sails down into the sunny reality of Los Perros and spits out Villy, Duckworth, and Villy's Flying Vee guitar.

The first thing Villy sees is his brother Scud. He's on the front lawn of the high school, which has very definitely been trashed. Scud is sobbing, terrified, and he holds up his hands as if to stave off a beating.

"Where's Zoe?" Villy hollers at his brother. "Did you leave her in the tunnel?"

"I tried to save her," cries Scud. "I couldn't. She got stuck inside Groon. My wand wasn't strong enough. There wasn't time. I'm sorry, Villy!"

"Yulia!" shrieks Villy, turning around. "Take me back so—"

The flat cow is gone. She doesn't care about his problems. She's lifted off into the fourth dimension and flown away. She's part of Goob-goob. And Goob-goob's war is won.

Zoe won't accept that she's going to die. Even though she's locked inside the stinky Groon ball. It's like being in a collapsing factory. Groon's ick innards are falling apart. The bagpipe's drone is but a hiss. Groon is giving up.

But Zoe believes in Villy. *He will save her.* She visualizes his face and his eyes. The abrupt motions of his legs. His long, sly smile. His shiny hair. His urgent embrace. She raises her horn, willing the notes out through unspace.

Is it a waste of time to be playing her horn? But—time—how can you waste time? You occupy, like, a cubic acre of it, or a kilowatt hour, or whatever. You have some given amount of time, and that's that. No spending, no wasting, no earning. You have time, and then you don't. End of story—or is it the start? Zoe's feels mentally vast, what with death so near and her life passing before her eyes. She's putting all of this into her song. Her bluest blues ever. For Villy.

"The sound of Groon," says the desperate Villy, cocking his head. Still standing by the ruined high school with Scud. "It's stopped. I don't hear anything."

Scud pauses, listens, thinks. "You're right. It was leaking through the tunnel, and now the tunnel's gone. And Groon's probably dead." He's rubbing at the shiny thing on his wrist, the head of the Aristo larva that's been living inside him. Skzx. She's crawling out. The wand floats in midair, contorting the bright rod of her body. She's getting a little plumper than before. More spindle-shaped. And she's popping out eyes on her side.

"She's turning into a pupa," says Scud.

"Tell her to go get Zoe," says Villy.

For a minute Scud silently teeps with the pupating wand. Then he shakes his head. "Skzx says she's done with us," he says. "She says she enjoyed me. And that's it. Bitch. Goob-goob and the Szep and the Aristos—they've all been using us. It was just about killing Groon."

Villy lunges forward, meaning to grab the slender pupa. Skzx giggles, bats her eyes, streaks away from them, and vanishes into a tiny, spherical gate in the sky. On her way to Szep City.

"Poor Zoe," Scud says and falls silent for a time. "At least we did kill Groon. Zoe didn't die for nothing." His voice catches. "She wasn't like anyone else, Villy. I loved her too."

"Stop that," says Villy, still cocking his head at odd angles. "Zoe's not dead. I can hear her horn! You can hear it too, can't you?"

"I—I'm sorry, but I don't," says Scud. He's backing off. Maybe he thinks Villy has flipped. Maybe he's wary of the beating that, in Villy's opinion, he so richly deserves. But Scud's still trying to ingratiate himself. "Villy, if you can hear sounds from unspace, maybe that means you can fly there?"

"I was wriggling all over the place in unspace, yeah," says Villy, continually twitching his head. "I was coated with 4D smeel that I could flex. Probably it's still on me. I was like an unspace eel. Maybe that's why I can hear what you can't. But—"

"Wriggle like an eel again," exclaims Scud, his tormented face brightening. "Do it! Peel out of our world and be in the fourth dimension. Go get Zoe, Villy! Save her!"

Villy flexes his body in that same weird way he'd been doing in unspace. He's holding his Flying Vee. One more twitch and the Los Perros landscape becomes a thin plane of dirt and cross-sections of houses. Villy's come unstuck. He's in 4D unspace.

The unspace void is dark. But when Villy strikes a chord on his guitar—it lightens. Zoe's horn calls out to him. Villy sees—a dim ball. A cross-section of the shrinking pocket universe with Zoe inside. Hard to keep his eye on it. The flat cow's not here to help. But Villy's got something else to guide him. Zoe's music. Again he twangs his guitar. Again she answers. Call and response. Ships in the night. They're going to meet.

Groon is weak now, past caring about Zoe, and there's no more grabby tendrils. Zoe is pointlessly dragging herself along the inner side of Groon's hide. She's a lizard on a wall in Nowheresville—which is getting smaller all the time.

And then she hears Villy's guitar. She sounds a response. She hears him again. He's coming for her. Wily Villy. Zoe visualizes her lover once again. She's drawing him closer with her music and her love.

A spot in front of her goes funny. It's a slice of Villy's head, floating there, it's like what she saw when he was inside the flat cow. The slice wobbles, rotates ninety degrees in the fourth dimension, and here's Villy's face, and then—*hooray*—the whole of him.

She floats into Villy's arms. He wriggles against her. They peel loose from Groon, loose from Groon's shrunken death world, and they swoop away. Well, not exactly *swoop*, it's more like spasmodic bucking, maybe even like sex. It gets the job done.

Looking back towards the horrible little Groon world, Zoe sees—is that a piece of Groon reaching out after them? Trying to follow them through unspace? Zoe hits the monster's tendril with an Armageddon-strength, Gabriel's-trumpet-type blast that flips Groon back into his tomb, his womb, his funeral coffin. And a moment later, *pffft*, Groon and his ball are gone.

Meanwhile Villy keeps writhing against her and then, *oh* yeah.

They're on the lawn in front of the collapsed high school building. Kissing. With Scud and Maisie cheering, and happy Duckworth buzzing around.

Here comes Sunny Weaver with two zombie cops who want to arrest them.

"Wake up," Zoe tells them. "It's over. No more Groon. No more leech saucers."

The blank, sullen faces lighten. As if a spell's been lifted. "Oh! Sorry to have bothered you!" Sunny and the cops walk away.

Zoe and Villy and Scud and Maisie hold hands and dance in a circle.

Celebrating.

afterword

I've always wanted to write an SF novel about a motley group of characters taking a long journey to visit a lot of planets, some of the travelers human, and some of them alien. To make it more fun, I wanted them to be riding in a car.

Why a car? Well, we already have plenty of SF novels about tourists in spaceliners, emigrants in generation starships, and troops in the space navy. In a *car*, there's no captain, and you can ride with the windows open, and you stop wherever you like.

Real-life road trips end before you want them to. You run into a coastline. The road stops. I wanted a road trip that goes on and on, with ever new adventures, and with opportunities to reach terrain never tread upon before. But how to do that in a car?

I peeled Earth like a grape, snipped out the oceans, shaped the flattened skin into a disk, and put a mountain range around it. Then I laid down a bunch more of these planetary rinds, arranging them like hexagonal tiles on a floor. Behold mappyworld! All set for a *Million Mile Road Trip*.

How did I decide on a *million* miles? Well, the edited-down Earth disk has a diameter of about ten thousand miles. And if we're generous and say our roadtrip will run across about a hundred similar planet-like disks—then we've got a million miles. $100 \times 10,000$ is 1,000,000. Nice and tidy.

By the time I was two-thirds done with my novel I realized I'd only traveled through six worlds. I needed to pick up the pace. The acceleration part was easy. I introduced an invented-on-the-spot SF technology I called stratocasting (for the Fender guitar). The hard part was actually *imagining* a whole lot of worlds. I figured describing thirty of them would be enough, and the rest could be a blur. But I was having trouble getting thirty unique worlds together.

At this point, in January, 2016, real life intervened. I had to go into the hospital for an especially traumatic hip operation. Here's an excerpt from my *Notes for Million Mile Road Trip*.

The third night the pain ramped up again. They gave me meds. I fell deeply asleep at 6:30 pm, and woke, soaked in sweat, in a state of delirium at half-past midnight. My bed seemed like the edge of an alleyway, and I was like a wet rag of clothing lying there, a wadded shirt. A nothing. Pathetic. Lost. Undone.

I was awake, but unable to remember who I was, or where, or what my significance was, or what ordeal I was undergoing, or what I was supposed to do. A wet crooked rag in an alleyway. I heard sounds from beyond a curved wall, which was the curtain across my door. I hoped someone would come in. They didn't. Eventually I found the ringer-button to call a nurse. I told her I couldn't remember who I was, and that the pain had gotten to me. She was sympathetic.

On the table by my bed, I found the paper scrap with my marked up draft of the "Stratocast" chapter for *Million Mile Road Trip*. I tell the nurse the scrap is from a science fiction novel I'm working on, and that I'm a writer, and that I'll now try to recover my personality by thinking about my book. She approves. I have all the time in the world here, anonymous in the middle of a hospital night.

After a few minutes I got the courage to call for a nurse again—a different one came, and she got me my laptop from my knapsack across the room. A few minutes later I called yet another nurse, and she fetched my reading glasses. And then I got to work, writing on till 3 am. The nurses didn't question what I was doing. I was happy to be writing in such an extreme situation, and I think the material came out pretty well. I ran twenty or thirty basins as a single block. A surreal mural.

By the way, you can read the complete *Notes for Million Mile Road Trip* online at the novel's webpage (see the URL at the end of the Afterword), and you can buy the *Notes* as an ebook or paperback. The *Notes* are a bit longer than the novel itself, which is typical for me.

That hospital experience reminds me of a sentence in a short story, "Miss Mouse and the Fourth Dimension," written by Robert Sheckley, the SF-writer-hero of my youth, and later my mentor. He was a wise, hip guy, and deeply funny to boot. Here's Sheckley's line:

> A genuine writer is a person who will descend voluntarily into the flaming pits of hell for all eternity, as long as they're allowed to record their impressions and send them back to Earth for publication.

I ended up rewriting my delirious draft five or six times over the following year. I always think a lot about what I'm writing. I'm a perfectionist. On the days when I can't get anywhere on my current novel, I work on my notes for it, thinking about my world and about the invented logical explanation behind it.

Speaking of which, there's a series of three moves that science fiction writers like me use. First, we cast off the surly bonds of fact and imagine a world we want to spend some time in. A place like mappyworld. Second, we use our finely honed bullshitting skills to craft an explanation for our world. A rubber physics, if you will. Third, as we're writing, we work back and forth between the vision and the explanation. On the one hand, the explanation prompts new ideas for the vision. On the other hand, the expanding vision adds fresh elements to the explanation.

If you happen to be Georg Wilhelm Frederich Hegel's great-great-great-grandson (like me), you might call this a dialectical process. The thesis is the fantastic vision, the antithesis is the pseudoscientific explanation, the synthesis is ramifying linkage between the two, and the process is the

the act of shuttling back and forth, repeatedly adding to the vision and the theory.

Of course *Million Mile Road Trip* is no ponderous work of phenomenology. It's light and playful. The heroes are three high-school kids with bad attitudes. And the aliens they encounter are, to say the least, flaky.

At one point I thought we might market my novel as YA book, but it seems better to call it literary SF. But, *psst*, if you *are* a YA-type person, this novel is *perfect* for you. Trust Professor Rucker.

Another element that influenced my composition is the style of Thomas Pynchon. I wanted to write a novel in the present tense like he does. Often readers don't consciously notice what tense a novel is written in—like, is it past or present? But for writers it's a fraught decision. I found that using the present tense gives a chatty feel, like someone recounting a tale. Another Pynchon move is to rotate the point of view from chapter to chapter. And he writes very close-up to the current point-of-view character, producing an effect like a real-time stream of consciousness. I did both these things, and I put the name of the current point of view character at the start of each chapter. I like to make things easy for the readers. In yet another nod to Pynchon, I often used very long sentences, with phrase after phrase being added on, like a carpenter working his way out on an increasingly rickety scaffolding that he's assembling as he goes along.

Regarding locale, I like to fold my real surroundings into my SF novels—it's what I call transrealism. SF that's set in the real world. This time around, my transreal world includes flying saucers—and they're not boring machines, no, they're live beings made of meat. The aliens don't *ride* in flying saucers, dude, they *are* flying saucers. I don't understand why more people don't realize this! Be that as it may, you can't really have flying saucers in a novel without a full-on "Attack of the Flying Saucers." And what better setting for such a scene than—the annual graduation at our local Los Gatos High School! I've been to quite a few graduations there.

I love the classic gimmicks of SF in the same way that a rock guitarist loves power chords. The trick is to bring fresh life to the fab old tropes. Given that we don't exactly see mappyworld floating around in our space, I needed to stash it in a *parallel world*. By way of revitalizing this very old notion, I brought in some little-known facts about the higher-dimensional geometry of tunnels between parallel worlds. Real math! And my deal about having some of the saucers turn inside out—that's an example of a detail I arrived at by thinking about my science explanation for what's going on. I did my best to explain the 4D stuff with words and scenes and line drawings, but if you want to go deeper, check out my non-fiction book, *The Fourth Dimension*, or my 4D novel, *Spaceland*.

In closing, I want to thank Marc Laidlaw for reading and discussing early sections of the novel. And Jeremy Lassen for acquiring the book for Night Shade Books—after a memorable conversation at the *Locus* magazine holiday party at Ysabeau Wilce's house in December, 2016. Hats off to my agent John Silbersack for closing the deal. Special thanks to Cory Allyn of Night Shade for his inspired and kindly job in shepherding my book through production. A shout out to Bill Carman for his terrific cover art. And I'm grateful to my Kickstarter backers for enhancing my advance—their names appear on the novel's webpage. Hugs to my dear wife Sylvia, and thanks for being amused by the unending flow of unseen fantastical critters that I bring into our life.

Most of all, I thank my readers, whether you've been with me for years, or whether you're just now joining the merry band. Welcome, friends!

For more info, see the novel's web page: www.rudyrucker.com/millionmileroadtrip.

Rudy Rucker
December 4, 2018
Los Gatos, California

turing & burroughs
a novel by
RUDY RUCKER

with an introduction by
EILEEN
GUNN

Rudy Rucker should be
declared a National Treasure
of American Science Fiction.
Someone simultaneously
channeling Kurt Gödel and Lenny
Bruce might come to approximate
such an Aumann-sensitive genius
but would be cheating by any
sane measure.
—William Gibson

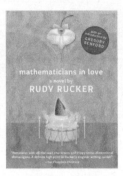

mathematicians in love
a novel by
RUDY RUCKER

with an
introduction by
GREGORY
BENFORD

"Percolates with off-the-wall characters and crazy extra-dimensional
demiurges. A definite high point in Rucker's singular writing career."
—San Francisco Chronicle

"A wild and exhilarating ride through the next 2,000 years
of human history, throwing up enough bizarre concepts
to sustain two or three careers of SF writing."
— Locus

saucer wisdom
a novel by
RUDY RUCKER

with an
introduction by
BRUCE
STERLING

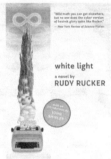

"Wild math you can get elsewhere,
but no one does the cyber version
of beatnik glory quite like Rucker."
— New York Review of Science Fiction

white light
a novel by
RUDY RUCKER

with an
introduction by
JOHN
SHIRLEY

with an
introduction by
PAUL
DI FILIPPO

the big aha
a novel by
RUDY RUCKER

"One of science fiction's wittiest writers.
A cult hero among discriminating cyberpunks."
— San Diego Union-Tribune

"Rucker stands alone in
the science fiction pantheon
as some kind of trickster god
of the computer science lab...
He is a peerless genius."
— SF Site

spacetime donuts
a novel by
RUDY RUCKER

with an
introduction by
RICHARD
KADREY

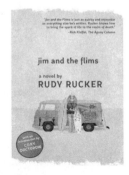

"Jim and the Flims is just as quirky and enjoyable
as everything else he's written. Rucker knows how
to bring the spark of life to the realm of death."
—Rick Kleffel, The Agony Column

jim and the flims

a novel by
RUDY RUCKER

with an
introduction by
CORY
DOCTOROW

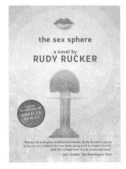

the sex sphere
a novel by
RUDY RUCKER

with an
introduction by
ANNALEE
NEWITZ

"Master of a playful, intellectual humor, Rudy Rucker's sense
of fun is rare indeed. He has been compared to Lewis Carroll,
and the comparison is not presumptuous."
— John Sladek, The Washington Post

with an
introduction by
KIM
STANLEY
ROBINSON

the secret of life
a novel by
RUDY RUCKER

"I love Rudy Rucker. The guy
is simply incomparable
when it comes to writing
science fiction, managing to
extremely blend highly
intellectual ideas with
extra-dimensional and
wholly whimsical and intensely
imaginative pleasures."
—Paul Di Filippo
HorrorWorld/Reviews

also from rudy rucker
and night shade books

Night Shade Books' ten-volume Rudy Rucker series reissues nine brilliantly off-beat novels from the mathematician-turned-author, as well as the brand-new *Million Mile Road Trip*. Conceived as a uniformly-designed collection, each release features new artwork from award-winning illustrator Bill Carman and an introduction from some of Rudy's most renowned science fiction contemporaries. We're proud to make trade editions available again (or for the first time!) of so much work from this influential writer, and to share Rucker's fascinating and unique ideas with a new generation of readers.

Turing & Burroughs	*White Light*	*Jim and the Flims*
$14.99 pb	$14.99 pb	$14.99 pb
978-1-59780-964-1	978-1-59780-984-9	978-1-59780-998-6
Mathematicians in Love	*The Big Aha*	*The Sex Sphere*
$14.99 pb	$14.99 pb	$14.99 pb
978-1-59780-963-4	978-1-59780-993-1	978-1-94910-201-7
Saucer Wisdom	*Spacetime Donuts*	*The Secret of Life*
$14.99 pb	$14.99 pb	$14.99 pb
978-1-59780-965-8	978-1-59780-997-9	978-1-94910-202-4

Rudy Rucker is a writer and a mathematician who worked for twenty years as a Silicon Valley computer science professor. He is regarded as a contemporary master of science fiction, and received the Philip K. Dick award twice. His forty published books include both novels and non-fiction books on the fourth dimension, infinity, and the meaning of computation. A founder of the cyberpunk school of science-fiction, Rucker also writes SF in a realistic style known as transrealism, often including himself as a character. He lives in the San Francisco Bay Area.